ONE-HUNDRED-AND-ONE
ASIAN READ-ALOUD MYTHS AND LEGENDS

One-Hundred-and-One
Asian Read-Aloud Myths and Legends

By Joan C. Verniero

BLACK DOG
& LEVENTHAL
PUBLISHERS
NEW YORK

Copyright ©2001 by Black Dog & Leventhal Publishers, Inc.

Published by
Black Dog & Leventhal Publishers, Inc.
151 West 19th Street
New York, NY 10011

Distributed by
Workman Publishing Company
708 Broadway
New York, NY 10003

Design by Liz Trovato

Manufactured in the United States of America

ISBN: 1–57912–164–0

h g f e d c b a

Library of Congress Cataloging-in-Publication Data

Verniero, Joan C.
101 read-aloud Asian myths and legends: 10 minute readings from
the world's best loved Asian literature / Joan C. Verniero.
          p.   cm.
          I S B N 1 - 5 7 9 1 2 - 1 6 4 - 0
1. Tales—Asia. [1. Folklore—Asia] I. Titles: One hundred and one read-aloud
Asian myths and legends. II. Title.
PZ8. 1. V478 Aac 2001
398. 2'095   2001025062

CONTENTS

INTRODUCTION

Cultures across the globe celebrate gods and goddesses, heroes and hero-ines, queens and kings, princesses and princes. The myths and legends of Asia distinguish themselves by their unique richness. Humans interact not only with immortals and magic, but with demons (good and evil), philos-ophy and religion (martial arts, shamanism, Confucianism, Buddhism, Taoism), intelligent animals, dragons and mountains. Even the animals engage in shape-shifting, and some even wear clothes.

Dragons and bears give birth to a people in Vietnam and Korea. Rocks and mountains split open, too, to create or provide release from prison. In the mythology of China, Yu's wife transforms into a boulder. She fears him as the bear he becomes when he tries to stop the flood with Magic Mould. But their son is born nonetheless from the boulder. Yu himself comes to life from his father's body. His first appearance is as a dragon.

Natural and concrete images are bridges from Heaven to earth. Shrines play large roles as the link between gods and humans. In the mythology of Japan, Izanagi and Izanami come from Heaven to earth upon a beautiful rainbow, the Floating Bridge of Heaven. It is not a problem that they are brother and sister. When they meet, they hold hands and are married. The Tibetan kings, too, descend to earth from Heaven from a rainbow ladder. It is called a dmu.

Deities, too, play their roles as liaisons between Heaven and earth. In the Tibetan myth about the monkey and the ogress, the Lord of Mercy gets involved in the monkey's quest to learn compassion. While mastering the lesson, the monkey is duped by a female ogre in the form of a woman. Their children are monkeys, and the evil ogress sets out to eat them. The monkey flees into the forest with his children and returns to his mountain sanctuary to continue to meditate on compassion. When he returns, he finds the children have given birth to many more children. Their tails have fallen off, and they look less like primates. They have tasted the food of the forest, so they must assume the form of humans.

Monkey, born, too, from a rock in the mythology of China, is the mischievous, immortal, shapeshifting hero. When on earth, he resides with the tribe of wild monkeys in the Curtain Cave behind the waterfall on the sacred mountain. At other times, he takes positions in Heaven under the watchful eye of the Jade Emperor, or he travels with a holy priest to bring the sacred scrolls to the people of China. His adventures involve not only Buddha, but Lao-tzu.

In many instances, the heroes of Asian mythology are aided by creatures of fantasy. The mythology of Japan brings us Yoshitsune. The warrior's captain is Benkei, who is a tengu, a Japanese mountain goblin. Benkei's mother, the daughter of a samurai warrior, falls in love with a tengu, Benkei's father. After thirteen months of pregnancy, Benkei is born, an unusually tall boy with long hair and all of his teeth.

Gods and goddesses in Asian mythology are extravagant. The King of Heaven plays cards while a toad and his companions, the bees, cock and tiger, wait for an answer to the drought on earth in the mythology of Vietnam. In Japan, Susano cannot get into enough trouble. In China, The gods of water and fire, Gonggong and Zhurong, have a god-sized battle. In the mythology of Korea, Hamosu becomes so intoxicated at his wedding to Willow Flower that he is trapped by her father inside a leather bag.

Welcome to the world of Asian myths and legends. It is rich and exciting. I hope you enjoy what these pages bring, again and again. I wish the same for the young people in your life.

CHINA

PANGU'S BODY

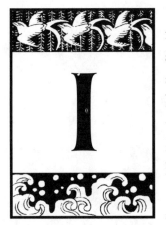n the beginning, everything was one murky substance. It swirled over and under and swirled around and around. Nothing had a form. Everything was confused. And everything was totally dark. The murky confusion existed for ages and ages. It was called Chaos. Neither the Heavens nor earth existed.

Chaos was like a big hen's egg. Then, after ages and ages passed, the first living creature appeared into the big hen's egg in the darkness. He escaped into the Chaos with a hammer in his right hand and a chisel in his left, and the shell of the egg shattered around him. His name was Pangu, which means that he hatched from Chaos.

When Pangu cracked the egg, pieces of it broke free in all directions. Slowly and without a sound, the lighter and purer material from the Chaos went up to form the sky. Gradually and quietly, the weightier, less pure substance of the Chaos rained downward to make the earth. It was the birth, too, of the forces of yin and yang. The female force yin was colder and darker. The not-yet-created moon and the earth are yin. The male force was yang, and it was warm and light. The not-yet-formed sun and the heavens are yang.

When Pangu was born, he was a fully-formed creature. At first, he was short in height. He had two horns on his head. Some say he bore the head of a dragon. Some say he had a serpent's body. Some say he was covered in a bearskin. Others say he wore leaves over his body. Pangu felt it necessary to prevent heaven and earth from coming together once more to again form Chaos. To accomplish this, he pressed his feet as hard as he could against the surface of the new earth. He raised his head high and pushed as forcefully as he could to support the new sky. Each day, he pressed and pushed with more effort. Each day, he grew an additional ten feet to accomplish the task. As Pangu got taller, the distance between heaven and earth increased by the same ten feet.

When he was happy with his labors, the weather was fine. When he grew tired or restless, his mood created storms. Day after day, he toiled. Sometimes he grew so tired, he used his hammer and chisel to help him hold up the heavens and push away the earth. Finally, Pangu no longer felt any resistance from the two forces. He slowly stopped holding the sky with as much power from his head, and the heavens stayed in place. He gradually eased the pressure of one foot against the earth, and it did not budge. He eased the force of his other foot, too, and nothing happened. A long time had passed since he began the work, 18,000 years in fact. Now a gap of 30,000 miles separated heaven and earth.

Pangu was very tired from his long labor. He felt he could now lie down to rest without any danger of a return to Chaos. Gently, he covered the earth with his body that now measured 30,000 miles in length. He closed his eyes, knowing his work was complete. A great storm erupted. Great noise sounded. The heavens quaked, and the earth rumbled. The exhausted Pangu, who had put heaven and earth in their places, died.

Parts of Pangu's body began to change into other living things. His head transformed into the Mountains of the East. The Mountain of the Center grew from his stomach. His left arm became the Mountain of the South. The Mountain of the North grew from his right arm. The Mountain of the West emerged from Pangu's feet.

The sun came into existence from his left eye, and the moon grew from his right eye. His beard made the constellations. His eyebrows and the hair on his head changed into the stars and planets. His breath transformed into the wind and clouds. Thunder and lightning emerged from his voice. The rain came from his perspiration. The rivers and seas began to fill from his blood. The fields and soil came into being upon the earth from his flesh. The herbs and trees created themselves from his skin. The layers of the earth grew from his nerves.

Pangu's teeth and bones changed into metals and stones. The marrow in his bones transformed into jade. Other fluids from his body changed into pearls.

NUWA AND FUXI: THE CREATION OF HUMANKIND

he goddess Nuwa had the head of a human and the body of a dragon. She was a shapeshifter, too. Each day, she entertained herself by changing into something else. Sometimes she was a bird, and she flew high into the heavens. The next day, she might become a river, and she flowed far until she came to the sea. But even changing shapes became tiresome after ages and ages of doing it.

"I wish I had the company of humans," Nuwa said outloud to herself one morning.

She had slithered to the edge of the river and already had transformed herself many times since sunrise. She imagined humans, but as yet none existed on earth. Bored with shapeshifting, Nuwa decided to create humans that day.

While she was thinking about how to accomplish making humans, she gazed at her reflection in the river. She often did this to keep herself company. Absently, she lowered her forefoot into the river and swirled it through the water. Wet clay from the riverbed accumulated under her claws, which gave Nuwa an idea. She deposited the clay from her wet forefoot into the forefoot that was dry. Dipping the first one into the river again, she withdrew a larger amount of clay.

Now she put the two forefeet together and sculpted a small figure. Instead of a tail like her own, she chose to give the figure two limbs with feet and toes upon which it might support its body upright. Rather than forefeet, she gave it arms with hands and fingers. Nuwa gently placed her creation upon the ground. The first human ever created immediately began to dance upon the feet she had made.

All that day and the night that followed, Nuwa entertained herself by sculpting humans. Just like the first one, they came into life dancing. Their laughter delighted the goddess, and she kept working. She was certainly not bored any longer. By dawn of the following day, however, Nuwa was very tired. The task ahead was great, for she desired to populate the whole earth with humans.

"What was I thinking?" she asked herself outloud.

Still, Nuwa did not relent from her wish to fill the earth with humans. From a nearby tree, she picked a vine. Now she had a tool to make her task easier. Putting the vine into the river, she swished it around until it stirred up clay from the riverbed. In circular motions, she twirled the vine with the clay that clung to it through the air.

Nuwa dipped and redipped the vine into clay. She twirled and twirled until a mass of humans danced before her on the riverbank. Still, she realized, she had not made nearly enough to populate the entire earth. So she changed some of them into female humans. She transformed the rest of them into male humans. Now they could give birth and populate the earth by themselves.

The goddess shared the idea with the new people, and they rejoiced. Then she told them that the small group of humans she sculpted herself would be rich and fortunate. The humans that came into life as drops of clay from the vine would be the humble, ordinary people. Together, the rich and humble humans danced and laughed.

Nuwa had a husband, a god who looked like she did, with the head of a human and the body of a dragon. His name was Fuxi, and he was the son of the Lord of the Thunderstorm. When Fuxi learned of Nuwa's creations, he appeared suddenly.

Fuxi taught the humans how to make fire. He showed them how to rub two stones against each other. The humans used the gift to keep themselves warm and to cook their food.

The humans that Nuwa created were able to speak their thoughts to one another from the beginning. Now Fuxi showed them how to record eight ideas in writing. Three solid lines, one above the other, meant Heaven. Three split strokes, one above the other, meant earth. Water was a solid stroke in the middle of two split ones. Fire had a split stroke in the center of two solid ones.

Fuxi taught that a solid stroke above two split lines meant mountain. Storm was two split strokes on top of a solid stroke. Wind had two solid strokes above a split one. And, last, marshland was a split stroke above two solid strokes.

The new humans thanked Nuwa and Fuxi. They took up residence upon the earth with the gifts of knowledge. They knew, too, how to give birth and how to record what they saw.

Fuxi was the First Sovereign of China. Some say he had four faces and that each face ruled over one of the four directions. Besides teaching people to write, he gave other valuable instructions. He taught them how to fish with nets. He also showed humans how to live peacefully with animals.

THE QUARREL BETWEEN GONGGONG AND ZHURONG

hurong was the Fire God, and he was the ruler of the universe. His governing was strict, yet fair. Everything was orderly and balanced in the heavens and earth. People and animals lived side-by-side in peace. The sun appeared each day in the sky. Crops were abundant, and the rivers and seas were full. Everyone had plenty of food and water. People danced and laughed as they had from the day Nuwa made them.

Gonggong, the Water God, was envious of the Fire God's power. He determined to oust Gonggong from power and to take his place as ruler of the universe. Gonggong had the body of a snake. His human head bore a patch of shockingly red hair. As though Gonggong's appearance was not awful enough, the looks of his top two officials were worse. The nine-headed, green, scaly body of the top official, Xiang Liu, was downright frightening. The image of the second official, Fu You, was so terrifying that no one could describe it. When he died, he turned into a huge red bear.

Gonggong summoned his two officials. "Let us attack Zhurong this day. Call my forces together," he ordered.

With no delay, he and his legions from the water kingdom were ready. Gonggong was seated at the lead upon his chariot driven by two fierce dragons. Xiang Liu and Fu You were next in line. Behind them were the sea nymphs and river spirits. Last came the underwater creatures and monsters. Gonggong and his legions caused the seas to grow turbulent and the rivers to spill over their banks in great waves. A terrible flood raged over the earth.

But Zhurong, Spirit of Fire, retaliated. He caused a great heat to cook the earth in order to stop Gonggong's flood. Flames shot up everywhere in the path of the attackers. Gonggong's eldest son was killed in battle and became a terrifying ghost. He began to wander the earth in fear of red beans. To this day, people leave cooked red beans in their homes to keep him from crossing their thresholds. Both of Gonggong's officials fled in fear of dying in the fierce battle. The sea nymphs, river spirits and underwater monsters hurried back to the safety of their homes.

Gonggong, Spirit of Water, remained alone in desperate defeat. His hopes to unseat Zhurong as ruler of the universe were destroyed. Seeking retaliation, he rushed to Mount Buzou. It was the pillar in the western corner that supported the sky. Butting it with his red head, he made it collapse into a mass of rubble. Great holes opened in the heavens, and the sky that Pangu had set in place fell once more. Again, there was Chaos. Off balance, the world suffered terrible fires on the higher grounds and major floods on the lowlands. The animal kingdoms screeched in terror and began to threaten the people. No one was safe. Gonggong vanished.

Nuwa saw that her children were in terrible danger. She rushed to the riverbed where she had made them. This time, she withdrew a collection of pebbles in every color available in the universe. She made a great fire and began to cook the stones until she could mold them into whatever shapes she needed. Flying up to heaven, she used them to fill every single crack that Gonggong made in the pillar. When she completed her repairs, she wanted to make certain nothing could destroy the heavens again.

She found a giant tortoise and killed it. Then she removed its four sturdy legs. Flying to the four corners of the heavens, she lay a leg under each one. Now the sky would remain where Pangu had set it forever.

But things would never be the way they were. When Gonggong knocked against the pillar, the earth shifted to the northwest. The rivers and lakes spilled their waters out to the southeast, which made a great ocean. Even now, China's rivers flow east and empty into this ocean.

Nuwa had to calm the flow of water so the flood would stop. The animals still cried wildly and flew or stormed across the earth. She had to tame the birds and beasts. She had to set the sun, moon and stars in their rightful places in the repaired sky.

After a time, the sun appeared regularly again. Crops grew plentifully once more. People and animals were at peace as they had been. Lastly, Nuwa gave her children the sheng huang. It was a flute carved from a half-gourd with thirteen bamboo pipes that fanned out like a bird's tail. The people rejoiced in its music and thanked Nuwa for restoring peace on earth.

Some Ugly Gods Who Rewarded Humans

L ei-kung was called My Lord Thunder. He was repulsively ugly! Not only was he shown with a blue body, but he had wings and claws, too. He dressed only in a loin cloth. At his side, he carried one or more drums. He carried a mallet and a chisel in his hands. He used the chisel to punish the guilty. Some say he used the mallet to create a drumroll of thunder. Others say he drove in the chisel with his mallet.

Lei-kung had orders from heaven to punish those humans who had committed a crime unpunishable by human laws. He often required the aid of humans to enact the punishment. Here is a myth about My Lord Thunder.

One day, a hunter was eagerly in pursuit of game. A violent storm took him by surprise in the thick of the forest. The storm was punctuated by lightning and thunder so fierce in intensity that the hunter was terrified. The outbursts seemed to be at their strongest directly over a tree with uplifted branches. The frightened man had never seen such a tree in his life. It resembled none that grew in the land. It certainly was not a mulberry, or fusang, tree, about which many stories of sunrise were told. No, the tree did not belong in the forest so familiar to the hunter. Worse still, the strange tree was not far from where he stood.

When the hunter lifted his eyes, he saw something even more unusual. In the tree was a child, holding a coarse flag. The flag was nothing more than a piece of filthy cloth tied to a splinter of wood.

My Lord Thunder also noticed the child. Just as the god was about to let loose a loud clap, the child waved the flag. Lei-kung suddenly stopped the outburst cold and retreated.

The hunter knew well that Lei-kung, like all gods, deplored things that were unclean. Usually, such things were the work of an evil spirit. The man loaded his gun, raised it and shot down the flag. Then, My Lord Thunder struck the tree at once. The hunter was very close to the tree when the thunder struck, and he fainted.

When the man revived, he found a small roll of paper in his grasp. The message on the paper read: "Life prolonged for twelve years for helping with the work of heaven." Next to the shattered tree, the hunter saw the grotesque corpse of an oversized lizard. He realized the dead demon to be the true form of the child he had seen with the filthy flag.

The god of Examinations, named K'uei-hsing, was also one of the ugliest divinities in existence! He wore a constant grimace on his face. Bending forward, he held his left leg raised in a running posture while he propped on the head of a turtle called Ao. The god of Examinations had as a usual companion, the god of Literature, called Wen Ch'ang.

K'uei-hsing carried a bushel basket in his left hand and a paintbrush in his right. With the paintbrush, K'uei-hsing put a mark next to the names of the humans lucky enough to be chosen by the August Personage of Jade, Father-Heaven. In his bushel, he measured the talents of all candidates.

When the Chinese Emperor gave an audience to scholars who passed their doctoral examinations, the Emperor said, "May you alone stand on the head of Ao, the turtle that supported the god of Examination. What follows is a story about the student who took an examination.

The young student had worked hard in his preparation for the examination. The student, however, was not satisfied with his performance when he returned to his home. He knew that Wen Ch'ang and K'uei-hsing rewarded the efforts of hard work.

The student begged the gods to help him obtain good results from the examination. When the student slept, Wen Ch'ang appeared to him. In his dreams, the student saw the god throw a bundle of examinations into a stove. In the bundle, the student saw his own test. When the god removed the tests, they were entirely changed. Wen Ch'ang handed the student his examination, and the student knew to study the changed material very carefully.

Upon waking, the student learned that a great fire had destroyed the examination building during the night, and all the tests were burned. Consequently, every examination candidate had to take the test again. With the new knowledge that the god had given him, the student passed with honors.

THE MAGIC MOULD

he Yellow Emperor, also known as Huangdi, was the Ruler of Heaven. He was very troubled over the behavior of the humans on earth. They argued more often than they got along with one another. Their wars caused the Yellow Emperor deep grief. To stop the aggression on earth, he ordered Gonggong, Spirit of Water, to punish the people with rain.

Happy to do the Yellow Emperor's bidding, the mischievous Gonggong's downpour flooded the earth. He brought water in such intensity that the rivers overflowed onto the land. Valleys that once gave humans pastureland and farms were hopelessly underwater now. People were forced to watch their homes float away, and they soon grew hungry. The fortunate escaped to the hills. Every cave in the land brimmed with humans who had sought refuge. They barely had enough air to breathe, however, because the caves were so crowded. And they had nothing to eat besides the morsels of rice that remained from what they had hurriedly taken with them before they fled.

The ruler Yao could not tolerate the deaths and suffering of his people any longer. He required the help of a god, yet he did not dare ask the

Yellow Emperor directly. No, Yao decided to ask for the mercy a different god, a god he hoped could influence the Yellow Emperor. He called upon Kun, Huangdi's grandson. The spirit answered Yao's request to speak with him. He appeared as a white horse.

"Please, help me and the people against the wrath of Huangdi, the Yellow Emperor," Yao pleaded.

Kun shook his mane, thoughtfully. He shifted his weight from hoof to hoof. His beautiful white tail responded to the arch of his broad back. "I've watched the suffering of earth from Heaven with a heavy heart. Yet I'm afraid I can't go against my grandfather," Kun answered, unconvincingly.

Yao repeated his request, for he knew Kun really wanted to help. The second time that Kun answered, he reluctantly agreed to intervene against the workings of Gonggong. But, rather than confront Huangdi directly, he determined to try to fix things himself.

Kun started to build dams. Throughout the land, he tried to block the water of the great rivers with rock and stones and to push them back to their banks. Dam by dam, Kun's barriers broke. He was unable to stop Gonggong's downpour from flooding the land. And still the rains continued, causing ever more water to appear on earth.

The spirit in the form of a white horse was disheartened. He realized that he would have to tell Yao he had failed to change anything. He began his gallop to deliver the news when he was stopped by a black tortoise and a horned owl. Helping each other travel upon the water, they asked to speak with Kun.

"What troubles you, Kun?" the owl inquired.

Kun confided that the dams he tried to build were too weak to stop the flood that Gonggong made for the Yellow Emperor. He told the tortoise and owl how badly he felt over the suffering of the humans. The black tortoise had an idea.

"Steal the Magic Mould from the Yellow Emperor. Surely, you can, because you are his grandson," the tortoise suggested.

Now that he was actually here, Kun wanted to help the people on earth even more than when he was in Heaven observing what was happening to them. He reluctantly agreed to steal some Magic Mould from Huangdi. He knew how badly his grandfather would punish him if he found out.

Kun returned to Heaven. He changed himself into a breeze to avoid the notice of the soldiers who guarded the Yellow Emperor's Magic Mould. It was also known as the Swelling Earth. Sweeping up a small handful the size of a bean of the enchanted soft, green earth, Kun the breeze reappeared on earth. He began to do his work on top of the highest mountain.

He blew a tiny piece of Magic Mould into the great river below him. With a great swooshing sound, the river started to retreat to its former banks. As it moved, great bubbles emerged from the bottom. When the bubbles evaporated, Kun could see brown earth not too far below the water. Shortly, the water was gone entirely. Left behind was a massive soggy marsh. But the Magic Mould grew until the marsh, too, was gone. It kept growing until what remained was dry, brown dirt. Even the rain grew lighter.

"Stop now," Kun commanded the Magic Mould. And the enchanted substance stopped its drying.

Humans ran out of every crowded cave in the land. Their cries of happiness filled Kun's soul with laughter. Now that their suffering was ended, they began to plant the seeds they had the wisdom to put in their pockets when they fled. Soon, when the new vegetation showed its face, they would no longer be hungry.

THE SWORD OF WU

fter Kun made the rain stop with the Magic Mould, he continued to work. He had to be sure that Gonggong, Spirit of Water, did not cause too much water to flood the earth. Gonggong was following the heavenly orders of the Yellow Emperor, Kun's grandfather, and Kun knew how strong those orders were. Who would be more powerful, Kun wondered, Gonggong or himself? So determined was the compassionate Kun to stop the suffering of the humans who had nearly starved to death during the early flood, that he did not pause to think of the punishment that awaited him from the Yellow Emperor.

Kun's task was great. But he had the Magic Mould on his side. The troublesome Gonggong only had water. For nine years, Kun labored in the battle against Gonggong's flood. Finally, with the aid of the Magic Mould, he thought he was winning against the water that still tried to take hold of the earth.

In the sixty-ninth year of the reign of Yao, the Yellow Emperor decided to take revenge. He had not forgiven his grandson for going against his wishes as Huangdi and for stealing the Magic Mould. The Yellow Emperor called Zhurong, Spirit of Fire, to his throne in Heaven.

"You must go to earth and punish my grandson. The sentence he has earned is death," said Huangdi.

This time, Kun had a greater adversary than Gonggong. Zhurong was a powerful god. He was the same spirit who once had beaten Gonggong and his followers in battle. When the black tortoise and horned owl heard of Zhurong's intention, they hurried to tell the news to Kun. He thanked them for their generosity.

The Yellow Emperor's grandson made haste for the far reaches of the earth. But no matter where he fled, Zhurong was in fast pursuit. The Spirit of Fire tracked Kun to Feather Mountain, located close to the North Pole where the only light to be found came from the Candle Dragon. A single candle in the mouth of the dragon that guarded the area provided the flicker. Nearby in this land of extreme cold and darkness was the City of Silence. The souls of humans who had died rested there. Upon Feather Mountain, Zhurong drew his sword. He pierced Kun's body and killed him. Returning to Heaven, Zhurong told Huangdi of his success.

But, instead of turning to the decay that came with death, Kun's body, though it was dead, did not rot. The compassion that inspired him when he was alive to stop the flood and to rescue the humans on earth seemed to continue living. Three years passed, and Kun's body looked as fresh as it had on the day that Zhurong killed him. It still held the strength of Kun's compassion.

In the meantime, there was no one to ward off the continuing rains of Gonggong. Gradually, rivers filled to their brims. Some of them were beyond filling. They had started flowing out onto the pastures that Kun had dried with the Magic Mould. More and more humans were forced once more to seek shelter in the caves. The caves were becoming increasingly crowded.

One day, in the flickering light of the Candle Dragon, Zhurong appeared again. This time, he wielded the sword of Wu against whose power no one could succeed. The Yellow Emperor had loaned the Spirit of Fire the invincible sword, with the instructions to cut open the still-strong body of Kun. Huangdi feared any further disobedience from his grandson. Already, he had seen how strong Kun's resolve was in the fight against Gonggong. The Yellow Emperor did not wish to wait for any further show of resolve to threaten his heavenly power.

Zhurong unsheathed the powerful sword of Wu. With it, he cut open the body of Kun. No, the dead body did not start to decay at that moment. On the contrary, a new life was born. The new life had grown inside Kun's dead body, feeding upon the strength of his compassion.

A mighty young dragon escaped from the slash that Zhurong made in Kun's body with the sword of Wu. Its horns were strong for its age. It opened its majestic wings, and their span was great. Its plated chest was noble and proud. Great spines covered the length of its backbone to the sculpted tip of its long tail. It was a male dragon.

The dragon was Yu the Great, son of Kun. Yu came into life to succeed in the task that his father Kun began. His mission was to stop the flood that was ordered by the Yellow Emperor, his great-grandfather.

YU THE GREAT AND GONGGONG

hen Yu the Great came into life from the body of his father Kun, he emerged as a great dragon. He flew immediately to the throne of the Yellow Emperor, Huangdi. Huangdi was his great-grandfather. Landing in the presence of the Yellow Emperor, Yu the Great changed into the form of a man.

"Greetings, noble great-grandfather. I have come to finish the work of my father," Yu the Great said.

"Your father? Hah! He stole the Magic Mould from me, then he disobeyed my plan to punish the earth with a flood," shouted the Yellow Emperor.

"Kun was wrong to steal. I have come instead to ask permission to use the Swelling Earth to stop the flood," responded Yu, humbly. He called the enchanted substance by its other name, hoping to receive a more favorable answer than if he spoke the words Magic Mould. Perhaps Huangdi would overlook for a moment his anger with Yu's father.

"Do not try to appease me by your words. The truth is that your father went against my wishes," corrected his great-grandfather.

"I am sorry for my father's dishonesty, yet he tried to help the pitiful humans escape Gonggong's flood. I am before you, Huangdi, to ask you to share your Swelling Earth. I humbly state that enough water has fallen already to punish the earth," responded Yu.

The Yellow Emperor was silent for several moments. Perhaps his great-grandson was correct to say that Gonggong had made enough rain fall to teach humans to stop arguing among themselves. Moreover, he liked the boy's honesty and straight-forwardness.

"I admire your manner, great-grandson. Like your father, you show compassion, a fine virtue. I have decided to give you what you ask. You may take as much Magic Mould as fits upon the back of the black tortoise," the Yellow Emperor said.

At Huangdi's call, the black tortoise appeared. When the Heavenly Ruler summoned again, a mighty winged dragon showed himself. Yu the Great greeted the tortoise and dragon, respectfully.

"The tortoise will carry what you have requested, and the dragon will help you in your labor. I have decided also to forgive your father, for his strength now lives in you. He has changed into a yellow dragon and now resides at peace in the Feather Grotto," said the Yellow Emperor.

Yu thanked his great-grandfather, who wished him well in his pursuits. The son of Kun returned to earth with the winged dragon and black tortoise. Upon the tortoise's back was a great pile of Magic Mould.

To Yu's dismay, the situation on earth was worse than when he departed. Gonggong was angry. How dare Yu the Great compromise his purpose? Even if Yu was Huangdi's great-grandson, hadn't the Yellow Emperor given him, Spirit of Water, a task to do? Now Huangdi was helping Yu to control Gonggong's flood. What an insult, Gonggong thought. He fumed and fussed over his diminished position. He decided to retaliate. He made things unbearable on earth.

Yu and his companions returned just in time. The rivers that had overflowed their banks like great, far-reaching blankets of water in the lifetime of Kun, Yu's father, were now wild with waves. The sound of water howling against everything in its path was deafening. Trees responded by crashing into the turbulent waves. The furious water rose to drench even the caves where so many humans were able to find safety in Kun's days. Water stretched to the sky. People screamed and cried in terror.

Poor Yu looked around himself at the amount of work he had to accomplish to quell the flood. Despite the magnitude of the task, he was clear that the first thing to do was to stop Gonggong. He summoned the spirits to attend a gathering on Mount K'uai-chi. All of them came immediately, except for Gonggong and one other, the Stormguard, whose name was Fang-feng. Fang-feng came late. Yu the Great called the Stormguard a traitor, and he killed him. Fang-feng was so large that, years later, when one joint of his skeleton was found, it took many people to lift it. When they did, the joint filled an entire cart.

The loyal spirits resolved to punish Gonggong, Spirit of Water, for his exaggerated displays. They formed a great army and set off in hot pursuit. Seeing them approach, the troublesome Gonggong panicked. He fled to a hiding place, where, to this day, no one has found him.

Now Yu the Great turned his anger upon Gonggong's chief official. His name was Xiang Liu. Xiang Liu had nine heads, each with human faces. They were like nine mountains. His snake body was green. His vomit erupted into foul springs and poisoned marshlands.

Yu tracked down Xiang Liu, and he killed Gonggong's top official for the role he played in the terrible flooding of earth. Stinking blood spilled out from his green body. When he fell, the blood continued to pour from him, and it would not stop. Now Yu the Great had to control a second flood. The putrid blood turned the raging rivers brackish and brown.

Yu the Great dug under the awful outpouring of blood until he was sure the hole was deep enough. Then he constructed a tall tower in the middle. Inside the tower, he locked up the awful body of Gonggong's top official. His foul blood no longer polluted the earth. Now Yu could begin the task of stopping the flood.

YU THE GREAT AND THE FLOOD

u the Great looked at the gigantic waves that crashed upon the earth. He heard the terrible cries of the humans who lost all hope of trying to escape the mountains of turbulent water. Even the crowded caves on the highest ground, which had provided people with refuge, were threatened by the rising waters.

Yu had one consolation. At least Gonggong, Spirit of Water, and Xiang Liu, his top official with nine terrible heads, were stopped. Gonggong was in hiding, and Yu knew he was too frightened of the thousands of other angry water spirits to show himself. The putrid dead body of Xiang Liu was closed up tight in a tower in the middle of a deep lake. His evil blood could no longer pollute the earth by mixing with the waters created by Gonggong.

The Yellow Emperor's Magic Mould was safe on the back of the black tortoise. It would swell and dry the water wherever Yu threw it. The Winged Dragon was ready to help, too, with the great task of stopping the flood.

"Let us begin by damming the springs," Yu said to his two companions. In this way, he was continuing the work of Kun, his father. Kun had first tried to control the waters by building dams of rock and stones to stop the flow of the rivers.

But when Kun built his dams, he did not yet have the use of the Magic Mould. Yu the Great had enough of the Swelling Earth, another name for Magic Mould, to accomplish what his father had begun. One by one, he visited the springs. Into each spring, he tossed some of the enchanted dirt that the Yellow Emperor, his great-granfather allowed him to take. In spring after spring, the enchanted dirt grew in size until it sopped up the water that rushed out.

Yu the Great went farther in his work than his father Kun had when he tried to build dams. Because Yu had the Magic Mould from Huangdi, the Yellow Emperor, he could construct dikes with handfuls of the enchanted dirt. The great ditches acted like banks and trapped the rivers inside of them.

All in all, Yu, the tortoise and the dragon visited 233,559 springs. With the Swelling Earth forming dikes in all of them, now the waters were still. Next, Yu the Great decided to build mountains at the corners of the earth. So, the three companions traveled to all four corners. At each corner, Yu put down small heaps of Swelling Earth. The small heaps grew and grew until they formed great mountains. If ever another flood happened, the mountains would stop its flow.

But what would Yu do with all of the water already on the earth? It is true that he had made many rivers with his dikes, but they were too numerous. He had to get rid of some of them. But how?

Now he put the Winged Dragon to work as his helper. The long tail of the dragon cut ditches into the earth. Yu the Great opened the dikes he had created just enough to allow the rivers to flow into the new ditches.

The water moved through the ditches into the river beds. From there, the extra water flowed out into the sea.

Sometimes, the mountains were in the path of the water as it tried to travel to the sea. Now Yu the Great had a new problem. How would he move the mountains? He realized this was impossible. The better solution was to dig through them. Once he made tunnels, the water would move through the mountains easily out to sea.

The Winged Dragon used his powerful claws, and Yu began to dig with his hands. But his hands were not strong enough to cut through the rock of the mountains. What could Yu the Great do now that he had come this far in his great task?

He changed himself into a bear. Now he, too, had claws. Yu the bear and the Winged Dragon dug and dug. If they found or made a crack too big in the mountain, one that would divide the flow of water to the sea, the dark tortoise came forward with his backload of Swelling Earth. Into the crack, Yu tossed some of the enchanted dirt, and the fissure closed. The water went on a smooth path now to the sea.

The bear and dragon dug until they made tunnels in all of the mountains. The black tortoise followed with his heavy load of Magic Mould. They labored and labored for thirty years. Because they did, the earth was once again dry. During all of this time, Gonggong never again showed his face.

YU'S WIFE DUSHAN AND SON QI

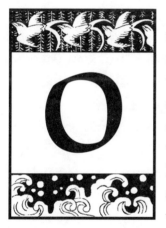

ne day, Yu realized that it was time for him to marry. He had been working without rest for thirty years to stop the flood on earth. Waters still spilled out in places, but Yu had made great progress. His companions, the black tortoise and winged dragon, were a blessing. The tortoise continued to carry the Magic Mould from the Yellow Emperor upon his strong back. The dragon made deep canals for the water with his great tail. The tortoise and dragon worked hard and were good company for Yu. But he yearned for human companionship as well.

Yu wondered how he might find a wife. True, he had covered the land in his travels, yet nowhere had he met a woman with whom he might enjoy spending his future days and nights in marriage. He knew he required a sign from Heaven to direct him to the right woman. Understanding this, he felt better and continued his work. He trusted in Huangdi, the Yellow Emperor in Heaven. After all, Huangdi was his great-grandfather. Surely, Heaven would provide a sign.

As it happened, Yu and his two companions were directing the flood-water through a small forest. A cluster of willow trees caught Yu's attention. He stopped to inspect the trees for a moment. Underneath them, he saw a small creature. It was a white fox with nine tails. Yu was certain that the white fox was the sign he desired. What did the fox tell him about his future though, he wondered.

Just then, Yu recalled a song from his childhood. The throne belongs to the one / to whom a white fox comes / A line of emperors belongs to the one / who weds the maiden from Du Shan. Here was his answer in two parts. The white fox told him he would be emperor. The woman he would marry and give him a son lived in Du Shan. Yu was grateful and thanked the Yellow Emperor.

Leading the black tortoise and winged dragon toward Du Shan, Yu sang the song from childhood. Soon, he arrived at Mount Du. A maiden sat upon the summit. She was fair, and her eyes were clear and intelligent. She told Yu her name was Dushan. Yu recognized the name as a good omen. When he asked for her hand in marriage, Dushan agreed. She told Yu she would be honored to marry him, for she knew him already from his labors to stop the flood on earth.

Yu and Dushan were happy together in marriage. But, after a short rest, Yu knew he had to return to work. Dushan willingly accompanied her husband in his travels across the land. Now Yu had three companions, and he saw he was truly blessed. Each day, while he labored with the tortoise and dragon, Dushan waited. She read, or sang, and prepared the food. She met Yu each day at lunchtime with his mid-day meal. Although he had traveled a distance with the tortoise and dragon since the morning, Dushan could always find him. He told her where he was by beating a drum.

One day, Yu and his two companions came upon a mountain. Yu saw that he would have to make a tunnel through the rock for the water to pass to the other side. He began to dig with his hands, and the winged dragon tried to help with his tail. But the mountain was strong. Yu recognized what he would have to do. He changed himself into a bear. Now that he had claws, the digging was much easier.

During the dig, Yu the bear knocked against the side of the mountain. It was close to lunchtime, and Dushan was listening for her husband's drum. She heard the sound the bear made against the rock wall, and she thought she heard the beat of Yu's drum. Dushan hurried toward the sound with her husband's food. She always looked forward to sharing the mid-day meal with him.

As she neared the spot where she thought she had heard the sound, Dushan began to call out her husband's name. "Yu, Yu," she shouted. Without changing back to his human form, Yu ran toward his wife. He was eager to see her. In the clearing, a great, shaggy bear greeted Dushan. His huge paws raised to clutch her, mud clinging to their sharp claws.

Poor Dushan was terribly frightened. She fled into the woods, running for her life. Yu called after her, trying to explain. "I am your husband," he shouted.

Dushan did not stop. She ran faster still. But no matter how fast she ran, the bear got closer. "I am your husband," Yu repeated over and over. Maybe this was what Yu really looked like, thought Dushan in horror. Fear overcame her now. A steep hill, called Lofty Peak, lay ahead. How could Dushan possibly outrun the bear up the hill? She threw herself to the ground, and she transformed into a boulder.

Heartsick, Yu the bear stood before the boulder. Not only had he lost his beloved Dushan, but he had lost the child that she was carrying in her womb. He reared onto his hind legs and shouted at the boulder. "Give me my son," he bellowed.

Immediately, the boulder split apart. A handsome boy emerged upon two dragons. Jade ornaments decorated the youth. "I will call you Qi," said Yu, for the name meant "split."

Qi grew to be a lover of music. As a descendant of Heaven, he often rode his dragons to hear the music played at the court of the Yellow Emperor. He made notes of what he heard for his return to earth. It is said that Qi gave music to the people of the world.

The people of the world were grateful to Yu the Great for his labor. They appointed him the first emperor of the Hsia dynasty. While Yu ruled for only eight years, the Hsia reigned for 439 years. When Yu died, his son Qi succeeded him. The words of the song that Yu remembered under the willow trees had come true.

YU AND THE JASPER LADY

 u the Great was trying to control the floods. But the waters that Gonggong rained on earth to please the Yellow Emperor kept falling. Yu's father Kun had begun the process of stopping the floods when he stole the Swelling Earth from the Yellow Emperor, or Huangdi. Yu changed the pattern. He wanted to gain Huangdi's approval in his effort to quell the damage from Gonggong's waters. Rather than use the stolen Swelling Earth like his father, Yu asked Huangdi to give him permission to use it. The Yellow Emperor liked Yu's nerve in asking, and he agreed.

Now Yu the Great was at work by the teeming waters of the river near Mount Wu. Suddenly, a fierce wind swelled near the spot. The mountain alongside the river shook, and the waters turned violent. The valley between Mount Wu and the neighboring mountains collapsed into the torrent as the flood overran it. No matter how hard Yu attempted to dry up the waters, and even with the Swelling Earth, he could not make any headway. The floodwater raged through what had been the valley only a short time ago.

So intent was he in his work that Yu did not feel the eyes of Lady Yun-hua watching him. The twenty-third daughter of the Queen Mother, Lady Yun-hua, was the younger sister of Princess Tai-chen. Yao-chi, or Jasper Lady, was her personal name. Let us call her Jasper Lady for this story.

Jasper Lady could visualize the valley as it had been before the howling wind began to do its damage. She saw the dark woods and sculpted rock cliffs like an altar in her mind's eye. Wanting to help Yu with his labor, she materialized beside him on the boulder where he stood. Yu was relieved to see the beautiful lady appear.

Suspecting her to be immortal like he was, he bowed. "Can you help me?" he asked.

She answered his bow with a respectful nod. Her hands suddenly held the Book of Rules and Orders for Demons and Spirits. "I will summon my spirits to assist you. Take your orders from this volume, and they will obey," said Jasper Lady.

Yu the Great happily accepted the book from her. Even as he began to read, Jasper Lady proved true to her word. She called her spirits, and they appeared immediately. Before her, they hovered, attentive. K'iang-chang, Yu-yu, Huang-mo, Ta-yi, Keng-ch'en and T'ung Lu waited for their orders. Yu the Great told the spirits to stop the waves with rock from Mount Wu. He had not noticed when Jasper Lady disappeared, but she was no longer alongside him on the boulder.

The book, too, disappeared as the spirits heeded Yu the Great's order. They set about hewing rocks, cutting them from the side of the mountain into smaller shapes. The spirits tossed the rocks into the river to deepen it. Then they made more rocks and built canals to move the water along a course to the sea. When Yu saw the water level decrease, he seized the opportunity to begin to dry the land. He threw down a clump of Swelling Earth. A speck of dry land showed its face. Another clump brought up a bit of soil. Clump after clump allowed the valley to spring forth once again.

Thanking the spirits for their assistance, Yu the Great wished to proclaim his gratitude to Jasper Lady, too. He climbed to the peak of Mount Wu before he saw any trace of her. But, when he found her, he was disheartened to see that Jasper Lady had turned into a stone statue at the top of the mountain. Yu the Great lamented that she was no longer the beautiful lady he had admired.

Suddenly, the stone statue of Jasper Lady was no more. Now she became a light, fluffy cloud, and then the cloud turned dark and heavy. Before the cloud grew heavy enough to cause a downpour, it let go of just enough water to make a late-day shower. The shower stopped, and a winged dragon flew across the sky. Then a crane soared in its place. Yu the Great saw it was impossible to communicate with Jasper Lady. He wondered in fact if she might be a demon instead of an immortal like himself.

One of Jasper Lady's spirits spoke. It seemed that T'ung Lu had read Yu's thoughts. "She is the Mother of Metal. When she is among humans, she changes to a human. She becomes an animal in the company of animals. You have seen only a token of her ten thousand appearances," said the spirit.

T'ung Lu brought Yu the Great to Jasper Lady's palace. Eight spirit guards were at the gates. The beautiful lady waited for her visitor on a terrace of jasper, which was a clear purplish-gray quartz. Yu the Great thanked Jasper Lady for lending him her spirits to stop the floodwater. They spent several days together, deep in conversation. Before Yu returned to the valley, Jasper Lady named him the True Man of the Purple Palace.

Yu the Great and the Nine Cauldrons

hile Yu the Great was stemming the floods of earth, he came upon a deep cave. He and his trusted companions, the black tortoise and winged dragon, entered the cavern. It was dark and wet inside. Taking handfuls of the Swelling Earth from Heaven off the back of the tortoise, Yu began to plug up the holes in the cave walls through which the water seeped.

Suddenly, he had the feeling they were not alone in the cave. He turned to find Fuxi, husband of Nuwa the mother of humans. Fuxi appeared with the face of a human and body of a serpent. As both Yu and Fuxi were immortals, they recognized each other immediately.

"How is your great-grandfather, Huangdi?" Fuxi asked, respectfully.

"He was splendid when we last met," responded Yu. "How is the great mother?" he inquired, paying his respects to Nuwa.

"She is ever watchful over her children," Fuxi answered.

Fuxi grew solemn. He handed Yu a slab of jade. "Use this to measure the Earth. It is a scale," Fuxi said.

Yu the Great realized the importance of the gift that the god gave him. He graciously thanked him. Acknowledging Yu's gratitude, Fuxi vanished. Now Yu had another task to do as he tried to stop the flood waters with the Swelling Earth.

He called upon two spirits for help with the measuring. They began to do what he asked immediately. One spirit traveled the earth from north to south. The other spirit traversed it from east to west. From time to time, the spirits visited Yu, usually on different days, to report their findings. Each time one of them gave him information, Yu took the jade slab from Fuxi in his hands. He interpreted the spirit's news about the earth into actual measurements by using the god's scale.

One day, both spirits arrived at the same time. The spirit who traveled the earth from north to south had finished and gave Yu the Great its final report. The spirit who traversed the world from east to west also gave its last bit of information, for it, too, had completed its travels. The two spirits waited while Yu used his scale to interpret the news they had brought.

"The earth is a perfect square. It measures 233,575 paces between each of the four cardinal poles," said Yu with great excitement. The spirits, too, were happy.

The spirits gave Yu other news, too, before they departed. They had counted the number of fissures and crevices on the earth through which water still leaked. Yu was surprised to learn that 233,559 water holes still remained. It is for this reason that, to this day, the earth still experiences floods. But, thanks to Yu the Great, the floods have never been as great as they once were.

Now that Yu had the measurements of earth, he saw that he had other tasks to do besides filling all of the holes that remained. He had to make a place on earth where the gods could visit when they came. Upon his winged dragon, he returned to Heaven. Digging up the Kunlun Mountains, Yu flew them down to earth. He planted the sacred mountains in the western region of China so their three peaks would be a ladder to Heaven. Humans grew interested in the appearance of the mountains. From that day, if a human reached the first peak, he or she would be immortal. A human who reached the second summit gained magical powers. The rare human who scaled the third mountain to its peak gained entry to Heaven and became a spirit.

Now Yu decided to show the people of earth some of the things he knew. He summoned the nine regional stewards to bring metal to him. The stewards were the heads of the mining clans. Yu had met them long ago in his work moving the waters of the flood through passes in the earth's mountains. The stewards heeded the call and arrived promptly, each with a different metal.

They helped Yu the Great to forge Nine Cauldrons. Upon the cauldrons, Yu cast images of the gods who were helpful to humans. He wanted to show to people the harmony between Heaven and earth. By so doing, he hoped to teach them to be careful of the harmful spirits and demons they might encounter in their lives. Yu also drew how the earth measured a perfect square. He depicted the products and people of the many regions on the cauldrons, too.

Since the day that Yu created the Nine Cauldrons, they have been honored by the people of China as divine. They first were the possession of the Hsia dynasty, because Yu the Great was its first emperor. Since the beginning, the Nine Cauldrons have had a special power. They have been able to judge the moral value of a ruler.

If a ruler was just, the Nine Cauldrons were very heavy, and no one could budge them. But, if a ruler was wicked, they became extremely light and were easily moved to a different ruler in a distinct land. For example, after the time of Yu the Great and his son Qi, there was a mean tyrant as ruler of the Hsia dynasty. His name was Chieh. The Female Tortoise of the North, whose head faced to the right always, transported the Nine Cauldrons to the house of Shang where they remained for six centuries. Chou, Shang's last ruler, was wicked, so the Female Tortoise of the North brought the cauldrons to a new dynasty.

Yu the Great's Nine Cauldrons have passed from dynasty to dynasty since their creation. They remain in a ruling house when the emperor is good. They depart when the ruler is unjust.

THE YELLOW EMPEROR

uangdi was the God of Heaven. He had four faces. When the goddess Nuwa grew tired of her work as the mother of all humans, she returned to Heaven with many stories about earth. Huangdi listened and asked many questions. An idea came to him.

"I must visit earth and become the Supreme Emperor there. For this, I need a palace. Other gods from Heaven will stay in the palace when they visit, too," said the God of Heaven and Supreme Emperor of earth.

The palace was at the top of Mount Kundun. The mountain was in the center of the earth, and it reached to Heaven. Rich gardens and rare animals surrounded the palace. Jade and pearls grew on trees. A clear spring flowed with the pure water of Heaven. A god with two heads, eight legs and the tail and hind quarters of a horse guarded the water. Living food in the form of an animal with thousands of legs and no skeleton grew on the mountain to feed the gods. The God of Heaven created the food so that every time a god became hungry and tore off one of its legs, another limb grew to take its place.

Now that he had the palace as his earthly home, Huangdi decided to choose a color to show his authority. He became Huangdi, the Yellow Emperor. He wanted the other powerful gods to have colors, too. First, he divided the earth into four territories to show the gods' greatness. He chose to give each of the four gods a different season to rule.

Tai Hou became the Green Emperor. His kingdom was in the east, and he ruled the spring. The god of the sun, who was called the Fiery Emperor, became the Red Emperor. He ruled over the kingdom in the south and the season of summer. Huangdi gave Shao Hao the name of White Emperor, whose kingdom was the west and season was autumn. He called Zhuan Xu the Black Emperor and gave him the kingdom of the north and the season of winter to govern.

The Yellow Emperor went back and forth from Heaven to earth to make certain that things went according to his plan in both locations. For entertainment, he enjoyed taking short trips from place to place on earth. He never traveled anywhere without his favorite possession. It was a precious black pearl.

One day, Huangdi, the Yellow Emperor, was on an earthly excursion north of Scarlet River. The black pearl was safe in the pocket of his tunic. He strolled along the bank of the river for most of the afternoon until he decided it was getting late and he was hungry. So he turned for home. As he was climbing Mount Kundun to get to his earthly palace, Huangdi reached to feel the black pearl in his pocket. He gasped to find it was no longer there.

He summoned the god of Knowledge, who was called Zhu. Surely, Zhu would easily find the pearl on the bank of the Scarlet River where Huangdi must have dropped it. But Zhu could not find the precious object.

Next, Huangdi called for Li Zhu, the god who guarded the trees of pearls and jades in the palace garden. Familiar with gems, he would know how to find one missing black pearl. But Li Zhu returned without it.

Huangdi asked Chi Gou, the god of Debate, to look for the gem. Chi Gou always found the words that he needed to speak. But the god of Debate was unable to find the Yellow Emperor's black pearl.

Next the Yellow Emperor called upon Xiang Wang, who was known as Shapeless, the most careless of gods. Huangdi had no hope that Shapeless would find the pearl. But his most trusted assistants had already failed. What did he have to lose?

Whistling idly as he walked along the river bank, Shapeless spotted something shiny in the reeds. He bent down and picked up the black pearl. Then he meandered in no particular hurry back to the palace on Mount Kundun to present Huangdi with his find. The Supreme Emperor of earth was ecstatic to see his pearl. In a gesture of gratitude and with a pang of guilt for having doubted Xiang Wang, he entrusted the careless god with the safekeeping of his gem.

Shapeless haphazardly stowed the pearl up his sleeve and departed. Word that he was the one guarding the object spread. It reached the ears of the daughter of the god Zhen Meng, who liked to cause mischief. She stole the black pearl from Xiang Wang's sleeve and hid. The Yellow Emperor's guards found her not far from the Wenchuan River. Frightened, the girl swallowed the pearl, dove into the water and swam downriver furiously. She changed into a water spirit with the body of a dragon and head of a horse. The Yellow Emperor never saw his prized black pearl again. As for the daughter of Zhen Meng, she helped Yu steer the waters of the Wenchuan River during the flood.

King Yao's Officials

In legendary China, King Yao was the peaceful ruler of a peaceful kingdom. The people loved him, because he lived like they did. In the summer, Yao wore a sackcloth as his robe. He donned deerskin in the winter. If his subjects were starving, King Yao blamed himself for their lack of food. When they were naked, he said it was his fault that made them so. When the disaster of the flood struck the land, King Yao was the ruler who called upon Kun, father of Yu the Great, to help dry the earth.

King Yao enjoyed it when the subjects showed him honestly how they felt. He was fond of sharing the story about the time he decided to name the successor to his throne. Yao was an old man, and he knew his rule would not be much longer. He preferred to name wise Xu You, who lived in Yangcheng, over the eldest and evil prince Dan Zhu. Having made the decision, Yao determined to go to Yangcheng himself to tell Xu You he had selected him to govern the nine provinces.

When the king arrived in the village, the people greeted him warmly. They directed him politely to the cottage of Xu You. Finding the house with no difficulty, the king knocked. Imagine his surprise when Xu You treated him with disinterest. Xu You was so fearful that Yao would ask him to do a service that he ran away. He did not stop running until he reached the Yinshui River that flowed through the Jishan Mountains.

But Yao did not take the man's behavior to heart. As soon as he returned to his humble hut, he sent one of his officials to the Jishan Mountains. Perhaps the official would be more successful than he in speaking with Xu You.

Word reached Xu You that an official of King Yao was interested in speaking with him and would arrive shortly. Xu You did not linger. Instead, he ran to the river and began to wash the information he received from his ears. A friend approached to give his cow a drink from the river. His name was Chao Fu.

"Whatever are you doing, washing your ears so vigorously?" Chao Fu asked.

"I do not wish to know about the post the king wishes me to accept," complained Xu You.

"How arrogant you are. If you wished to remain unknown to the king, you should have lived all of your years in Yangcheng. But you traveled around the provinces, and you made a good name for yourself. No wonder King Yao is looking to enlist your services," mocked Chao Fu. His cow finished drinking, and the friend departed, laughing heartily at his friend Xu You.

The official returned to the the king and told the story. Yao, too, laughed at the behavior of Xu You. Over the years since that time, many people have enjoyed the official's tale.

King Yao chose his officials very carefully. It was another reason that the people respected him. Mostly, they were fond of Gao Tao, the minister of justice.

While he had a reputation for being strict in his judgments, Gao Tao was admired for his fairness. He was loved, because he was peculiar. He had a green face that looked like the skin of a watermelon. When he spoke, his mouth was that of a horse. The people were always delighted to hear human speech from such a mouth.

Gao Tao used a quirky method to make his decisions. He called upon the help of Xie Zhi. Long, tangled wool, green like Gao Tao's face, hung from the back of the one-horned sheep. Its head was as big as the head of a bear. In the summer, Gao Tao had to make his rulings near the river. It was the home of his sheep during the hot weather. In the winter, Gao Tao decided his cases in the pine forest, for this was where Xie Zhi preferred to live in the cold months.

Because the single-horned sheep Xie Zhi had come from the gods, the animal never faltered from the truth. If a person committed a wrong, Xie Zhi struck the criminal with its horn. But the sheep stood as still as a statue when a person was innocent.

Another favorite official during the reign of King Yao was Kui. Born one-legged, he was minister of music. The people believed that Kui's ancestor was the Kui cow from Liuposhan in the east. They said that the cow taught him the tricks to make anyone who heard him play, even the birds and animals, begin to dance. Neither humans nor they could resist. Even the king danced.

So it was, that by choosing his officials wisely, King Yao kept his peaceful kingdom at peace.

THE FIRE DANCING OF THE TEN SUNS

he god of the east and the goddess of the sun were married. His name was Dijun. He was also known as the Supreme Ruler. The goddess was Xihe. The ten suns were their children. They lived in the enormous Fusang tree, a mulberry tree so gigantic that one thousand humans who were holding hands could not reach around its trunk.

Its roots were anchored in the depths of the distant and boiling Eastern sea. The nine branches reached through the clouds into the sky, so the family was protected from the intense heat of the sea below them. Nine young suns rested on the nine branches. At the treetop, the tenth waited. The suns took one turn each at the top. They rested there before they brought in the new day. Then they gave up the top for nine more days until it was their turn again. The top of the Fusang tree was called Chenming, and it meant early dawn.

Now one sun waited at Chenming. He was bathed and ready to take his turn. He heard the flapping of great wings. Dragons! The cart was coming. It was drawn by six dragons. His mother was seated upon its bench. The sun dropped down to Feiming, or beginning dawn. The dragons hovered for him to mount the cart. Now they flew to Danming, which was the place of complete dawn. The people on earth felt the sun's heat, and the land reflected the light of early morning.

Sometimes, the sun's mother accompanied him in the dragon-drawn cart to the western abyss, where they paused to give a display at sunset. Other times, Xihe ordered the dragons to stop at Beichuan. She waited for the sun to exit the cart. Bidding him farewell, she asked the dragons to fly her home. The sun was free for the day to dance across the sky. The only condition to the freedom was that he make his way to the Western abyss at day's end before coming home. Up until now, everything happened exactly according to plan. The suns enjoyed their turns. Xihe participated when she desired and had leisure time otherwise. The dragons were pleased with the arrangement. And the humans and animals on earth got warmth and light for themselves and the crops they ate.

One evening, however, everything changed. The suns were alone. The nine who had stayed behind waited to hear their brother relate his adventures. There was more excitement than usual, for Xihe had chosen to see to her own affairs that day. The sun who danced in the sky, all morning and afternoon, had everyone's attention.

He told of flying across the heavens in pursuit of a golden eagle. The sun heeded the eagle's reprimand when he got too close and burned its tail. After he apologized and put enough distance between himself and the bird, the sun and eagle swooped and soared and found new places neither of them had ever seen. "Ah!" replied the nine suns, who were listening to the tale.

The sun who related the tale sparkled brighter than usual. He was excited by the fun he had that day. "We can bring the dawn without the dragon cart, can we not?" he asked. One by one, the nine suns were excited enough to consider what their brother suggested.

Earlier than usual, Feiming, the place of beginning dawn on the Fusang tree, was active. No single sun waited to take his turn at Chenming, the uppermost place of early dawn. All ten suns were bathed and assembled at Feiming instead. They jumped free at the same time. It was too early for either the dragons or their mother Xihe to have any suspicion. The suns danced to Danming, the place of complete dawn. In unison, they approached the sky over earth.

The humans greeted the coming of light with the same cheerful attitude they felt every day. Not much time passed, however, in the new day before they realized this day was very different. The sky was so bright, the blue that usually lived there was washed away by a glaring silver-gold light that hurt their eyes. Plants that were still green yesterday were scorched to brown. Fields erupted in flames of a short duration, and white ash covered the ground afterward. Rocks and boulders melted, it was so hot. And the ten suns kept dancing. They laughed and shouted, gleefully, for they were having more fun than they could have imagined. Tomorrow and the next day and the day after that, forever, they would dance across the sky, they resolved.

Good King Yao saw the people suffer. Dijun, the Supreme Ruler, heard the emperor's pleas for help. He spoke with the ten suns when they returned to the Fusang tree, explaining the consequences of their merry-making. The suns answered that they were gods. They told their father they would not stop dancing, ever.

Dijun had no choice but to call his official, Yi the Archer. He gave Yi a new red bow and a quiver of ten white arrows. "Threaten the suns with these. They will see reason," Dijun said.

But, when Yi arrived on earth from heaven, he was most disturbed by the suffering he saw. Without trying to reason with the suns, he took aim and let an arrow fly. It hit one of the suns, and he fell to earth as a three-legged raven which began to walk about in confusion. Eight more times, Yi repeated the gesture. Now there were nine three-legged black birds clustered together in confusion.

King Yao anticipated a disaster after Yi's second shot. He sneaked one of the arrows from Yi's quiver. So, when Yi reached for the tenth arrow to shoot down the last sun, he found none. Thankfully, one sun remained to warm the earth.

CHANG E AND THE MOON

hang E and Yi the Archer lived in heaven. They were small gods when compared with the powerful gods like Xihe, goddess of the sun, and Dijun, god of the east. But though they were less powerful, they were immortal because they lived in heaven.

Yi was an official in the service of Dijun. He could shoot an arrow and hit his mark better than any god. Sometimes, the gods asked Yi to entertain them with his skill. He would shoot down a tiny, darting sparrow out of the distant sky or a trout in mid-jump from a faraway river. But Yi was as honest as he was brave, so he did not often engage in displays. He loved all living things and disliked seeing them suffer or needlessly die.

Chang E loved living in heaven. While Yi practiced his archery, she reveled in the beauty around her. The perfectly clear water, lush flowers and exotic foods charmed Chang E. She could not imagine being anywhere else. She saw herself enjoying heaven always.

Dijun sent Yi the Archer and Chang E to visit earth so Yi could assist

King Yao. The ten suns had to be stopped from their arrogant behavior. While they danced and played together in the sky, the people of earth and their crops were dying from the heat the suns caused. It was ten times hotter than it should be if one sun took his rightful turn. Yi shot nine suns out of the sky with his sharp aim so earth would suffer no longer. Then he and Chang E returned to heaven, expecting Dijun's gratitude. They did not anticipate what they would find.

"I cannot look at your face any longer. You have killed nine of my sons," proclaimed Dijun.

Yi the Archer began to protest that he was doing Dijun's bidding by stopping his disobedient suns. But the Supreme Ruler silenced him. "Why did you not try to negotiate with them first before murdering them?" he wanted to know. When Yi started to describe the suffering the suns caused on earth, Dijun would not listen.

"I banish you and Chang E to earth," said the Supreme Ruler.

Suddenly, everything was very different in the lives of Chang E and Yi the Archer. Finding herself on earth, Chang E complained bitterly to her husband about the injustice. She blamed Dijun for punishing her when Yi was the one who shot the suns out of the sky. As for Yi her husband, she blamed him for his foolish actions. Nothing he said did anything to soothe Chang E's frustrations.

Yi went hunting every day in the forests of earth to occupy himself. He took on an apprentice hunter, named Peng Meng, and began to teach him the skills of archery. While he missed the life of heaven, he was doing his best to adjust to his new circumstances.

But not Chang E. Every day, earth seemed more horrible to her than the day before it. One day, she had an inspiration. She blurted it out to Yi as soon as he returned home from the hunt.

"Our only hope is for you to visit the Queen Mother. Go to her in the west on Mount Kunlun and ask her to give us an immortality potion to allow us to live forever. If she gives it to you, at least we won't die even though we have this change of residence," said Chang E.

Yi the Archer set out at once for Mount Kunlun. He stated his request to the Queen Mother, whom he had met once in heaven. She was willing to honor what he asked. Disappearing for a few moments, she returned with a box which she gave to Yi.

"Inside you will find enough liquid for two potions. Care for it well, for it is the last of the immortality serum I have. Divide the liquid in half. Each of you will drink one-half. It will make you both immortal, but it is not powerful enough to transport the two of you back to heaven. While you will be immortal, you will live your lives forever on earth. The potion is only strong enough to transport one of you to heaven for eternity," explained the Queen Mother.

Yi the Archer thanked the goddess for the potion. Returning home, he presented the box and the Queen Mother's instructions to Chang E. He placed the box on the shelf, thinking they would take the potion on a day when they decided to celebrate. He went to the forest to hunt.

When Chang E could no longer hear her husband's footsteps, she hurried to the shelf and tore open the box. Cracking open the small flask inside, she drank the entire amount of immortality potion. She felt the sudden strength in her body.

Wanting to avoid for a while any disapproval from heaven over the fact that she did not share the serum with her husband, Chang E took a detour to the moon. What a surprise she found when she arrived. A lone cassia shrub and a straggly rabbit were the only life she saw in that barren, cold place. She resolved to go immediately to heaven and face whatever disapproval she might receive. But she could not transport herself.

The powers that brought her to the moon were gone now. The moon had taken them away from her.

When Yi came home and saw the cracked flask on the floor, he recognized what Chang E had done. If only she had waited for him, they would have had each other as companions forever. Now all that Yi had to occupy himself was his bow and quiver of arrows.

THE OX HERD AND THE WEAVING GODDESS

he Heavenly God summoned the Ox Star, because he needed a messenger. "Go and speak to the people on the earth. Tell them they must not eat as much food as they have been eating. Otherwise, the food they have will not be enough," said the Heavenly God.

"What exactly will I tell them to do when they ask me questions about how much and when they should eat?" the Ox Star asked. He was not a thinker. He was an obedient messenger.

The Heavenly God answered, "Tell them to eat one meal every three days plus an occasional snack."

The Ox Star nodded that he understood. A short time afterward, he arrived on earth with the message. The people gathered about him, eager to hear what the Heavenly God wanted them to know.

The Ox Star spoke to the gathering. "The Heavenly God has ordered that every day you must eat three meals, plus an occasional snack." The people of earth welcomed the good news. They invited the Ox Star to share in a banquet to celebrate. Afterwards, he returned to heaven, pleased with the outcome of his mission. He was most anxious to share his adventure with the Heavenly God.

Perhaps you guessed that the Heavenly God was angry. In fact, he was furious with the Ox Star for how wrong his message was that he punished him. He sent the messenger to earth to pay for what he had done. Since the Ox Star told the people to eat so much, for the rest of his life he had to help them as a work animal. From that day forward, the Ox Star has been a servant to humans in their fields.

Ox Star went to work for a young man whose parents recently had died. The young man, now an ox herd, had two older brothers. After their parents' death, the brothers divided the family wealth and property into three shares. They took all of the money and the best property for themselves. The ox herd was forced to live in a tiny hut and to work from sunup to sundown to grow enough food to survive. The Ox Star helped the honest, hard-working young man in the fields.

The ox herd began to wish that he had a wife and family. But he labored for so many hours each day that he never met any women. One day, the Ox Star confided in the ox herd that he had once lived in heaven. He offered a suggestion.

"If you want to meet a wife, go to the spring tomorrow. You will find the Heavenly Maidens, who bathe naked. Gather up one pile of clothes from the shore. The maiden to whom the clothes belong will be your wife," said the Ox Star.

The following day, the ox herd did as the Ox Star instructed. While the Heavenly Maidens bathed, he crept up to the shore and took one pile of glittering cloth into his arms. The Heavenly Maidens emerged from their bath. All but one dressed and departed for heaven. Gently, the ox herd approached the naked maiden who tried to hide behind a clump of nearby bushes. "Do not worry. Here are your clothes. I borrowed them only to meet you and to ask you to marry me," he said.

The Heavenly Maiden was moved by his sincerity, and she agreed to the marriage. She told the ox herd that she was the granddaughter of the Heavenly God and Queen Mother. In addition, she was the Weaving Goddess. The couple were married immediately. The Weaving Goddess spun beautiful cloth, which sold well in the market. The ox herd did not have to work such long hours anymore. Their days together were very happy. Several years later, they had children, first a boy, then a girl.

In the meantime in heaven, the Heavenly God and Queen Mother missed their granddaugher and her beautiful weaving. "I will send messengers to kidnap her and bring her back," determined the Heavenly God. And he did.

The ox herd and the two children grieved over the loss of the Weaving Goddess. The Ox Star heard their tears and could not bear them. He spoke again to the kind ox herd.

"I am old now and will soon die. When I do, remove my hide and put it on yourself. With it, you and the children can travel to heaven to find the Weaving Goddess," said the Ox Star. That day he died.

Again, the ox herd heeded his words. Wearing the hide, he put a carrying stick across his shoulders. At each end, he attached baskets for the children. Since the daughter was small, he placed a ladle in hers so the two baskets balanced. As the Ox Star said he would, he easily flew to heaven with his son and daughter. When he arrived, he caught a glimpse of his wife, the Weaving Goddess. She saw him, too. They ran toward each other.

But the Queen Mother intervened before they reunited. Removing her sheng, the ornament she wore in the knot of her hair, she drew a line in the heavens. It became the Starry River, also called the Milky Way. The ox herd could not cross the river to reach his wife.

"Father, take the ladle from my basket and scoop up the water quickly," cried the daughter. The ox herd and his son and daughter took turns scooping, but the river refilled itself no matter how hard they worked. They cried and cried. The Weaving Goddess matched them in tears from the other side of the Starry River.

The Heavenly God took pity on them. "On the seventh day of the seventh month every year, you may join one another. I will order the magpies to fly up to heaven and form a bridge for you," the Heavenly God decreed.

And that is what happened for a very long time. After ages and ages, the ox herd and the Weaving Goddess changed to stars in the heavens. He became Altair in the constellation Aquila; the Weaving Goddess became Vega in the Lyra constellation. The children, too, became stars.

THE STONE MONKEY

ver since Pangu created the world, an egg-shaped stone rested at the point on the top of Aolai Mountain in the middle of the Eastern Sea. It was also known as the Mountain of Flowers and Fruits. Its sides were steep, and the rocky point on top was thirty-six-and-a-half feet high and a circular shape. The circle measured twenty-four feet around.

The egg-shaped stone at the top of the point and in the middle of circle was powerful. Since the beginning of time, the breath of the wind had nourished it. One day, the egg cracked open. A stone monkey was born. The newborn stood and bowed to the four directions to give thanks. From his eyes, golden lightning shone all the way to the North Pole Star. The yellow rays filled the rooms of the northern palace. The monkey's eyes glowed with golden lightning until the day he was old enough to eat the flowers and fruits of Mount Aolai. Afterwards, his eyes shone with his own light.

The monkey grew to be an average-looking monkey. He did normal monkey things, too, like savoring the fruits he found on the mountain and slurping up the water from its springs. He jumped from branches, and made high-pitched sounds like monkeys do. He had an extraordinary disposition. He was always happy, because he was always well-fed. Even when the elements became disagreeable and caused nasty weather, he knew how to find shelter, too.

The monkey was not the only creature cavorting about the top of Mount Aolai. No, there were also cranes and deer and peacocks and many other types of animals, including a tribe of wild monkeys. Ever since the stone monkey was born, the wild monkeys had been watching his antics. They decided he was no ordinary monkey, basically because he was so happy and well-fed.

One day, the wild monkeys introduced themselves. They asked him to be their leader. The offer delighted the stone monkey who was interested in understanding what it was like to be a part of a group.

He suggested that they find a secure home where the tribe would be safe no matter what happened. "Where?" the tribe asked. The stone monkey led the others to a cave hidden behind a waterfall on Mount Aolai. As soon as they saw it, the tribe named their new home the Curtain Cave.

"You shall be our king," they proclaimed. The stone monkey accepted the honor, and he ruled the wild monkeys for 300 years. One day, he called a meeting.

"I am concerned about our future," he announced.

"Why worry? We have such a good life here," the tribe asked.

"At some point, we will face death," he responded.

The wild monkeys told their king about immortality. It was the gift of living forever without dying. The monkeys told him about the master who taught how to achieve immortality.

"I will find the master. When I have the gift, I will return to the Curtain Cave," he said. He left on his journey immediately.

For eighteen years, the monkey traveled in search of the master to teach him how to live forever. Over the course of these years, his appearance changed. While his face remained the face of a monkey, he took on the clothing of humans. Resembling the people he met along the way, he began to appear civilized.

One day, the monkey in human clothing came upon a woodcutter who lived on a mountain. He asked the kind woodcutter if he knew how he might find the master he sought. He explained that he wished to learn the way to eternal life.

"This path leads to a cave at the top of the mountain. There you will find the master," said the woodcutter.

The cave was at the end of the path as the woodcutter said it would be. But a wooden door barred the entrance. Deciding it would be rude to knock, the monkey climbed the nearby pine tree and began to munch on its nuts. Suddenly, the door opened, and the monkey jumped down from the tree. A page asked him why he had made so much noise.

"I did not make a sound. I only ate pine nuts while I waited," the monkey answered.

The page explained that the master had told him to admit the seeker who would come to learn the way to immortality. Realizing that the master was expecting the monkey, the page invited him into the cave. For when he asked his disciple-to-be where he lived, the monkey told him that his home was on Mount Aolai. Many seas lay between the master's cave and Mount Aolai. The master knew that no ordinary monkey could have crossed them. The holy man suspected the monkey of lying. But seeing from the monkey's eyes that he spoke the truth, the master accepted that this was no ordinary monkey.

He gave him the family name of Sun, which meant monkey in Chinese. He called him by a personal name, Discoverer of Secrets. For 20 years, the monkey studied under the master. He was a good disciple. He learned how to fly through the air, doing somersaults, and how to change into 72 different shapes. Finally, the master taught his disciple the way to immortality. Monkey thanked his teacher, and he set out to share what he learned with his tribe at the Curtain Cave.

MONKEY IN THE UNDERWORLD

onkey learned from the master teacher how to live forever. The master also taught him how to fly over wide distances. Now that Monkey knew the secret of immortality, he started out for home. Easily crossing the many seas between the master's cave and home, he arrived at Mount Aolai.

He hurried to the mountaintop, eager to share that he knew how to live forever with the tribe of wild monkeys. They had made him their king hundreds of years earlier. Together, they lived in the Curtain Cave behind the waterfall. Imagine Monkey's surprise to find the wild monkeys scattered over the mountainside like they had been when he first met them.

"Why are you not in the Curtain Cave?" he asked a group of them.

One wild monkey spoke. "The demon Hun-shih Mo-wang has taken over our home. He threw us out the day you began your journey to the master. He's been in the Curtain Cave ever since," she said.

Monkey knew what he had to do. He flew to the Curtain Cave and called to the demon to come outside. The large ugly creature lumbered his way out to the waterfall where Monkey stood. He had grown fat and lazy over the years when no one challenged his right to the cave. He jeered at Monkey, expecting him to be no competition.

The demon opened his big, sleep-crusted eyes wide when Monkey took to the air, however. In one sweeping somersault, Monkey kicked him right over and he landed with a thud into the waterfall. While the demon struggled to get to his feet, Monkey changed himself into a shark. Opening his jaws wide, he snapped the demon in two, and the monster died. The tribe had been watching the battle. Now they cheered and hurried to take possession of the Curtain Cave.

While the wild monkeys set about cleaning up the mess that the demon made in their home, Monkey knew what he had to do. He realized the day might come when he alone was unable to defend the tribe. A proper weapon was what he needed for future battles.

He paid a visit to Lung Wang, the Dragon King of the Eastern Sea. While he was in the dragon's kingdom, he saw the perfect weapon. Without the king's permission, Monkey stole it.

The weapon was an iron pillar planted in the Eastern Sea. Yu the Great planted it in the ocean bed to regulate the waters during the flood. Changing himself into a giant sea monster, Monkey pulled the pillar out of its foundation. With it safely in his grip, he returned to his true form. He put gold bands on each end. He engraved the pillar so it read, "Gold-tied Wand of My Desires." With more magic, he commanded it to change forms. He could make it grow as tiny as a needle or as large as a staff to use in battle.

Monkey fled the palace of Lung Wang, the Dragon King. While still in the Eastern Sea, he battled the Four Kings of the Sea with his new weapon. Beating them with very little effort, he won the loyalty of the other kings of the sea. They ordered a great banquet to prove their allegiance.

At the banquet, two uninvited guests appeared. They carried strong chains. One of the kings said they were messengers from the Underworld. Hearing his words, the strangers explained that they came for Monkey. The king of hell had received a complaint about him from Lung Wang, the Dragon King.

As hard as Monkey tried, he could do nothing to stop the messengers from the Underworld from tying their chains around him. Nor was he able to escape the chains during the trip to hell. He struggled so hard that he passed out. At the gates to the Underworld, Monkey awoke with renewed energy. Trying a variety of shapes, he finally slithered free. During the capture, he had transformed his magic pillar into a sewing needle and had hidden it in his shirt. Now he changed it into a fighting staff. With it, he killed the messengers from hell.

Monkey shouted for the ten judges from the courts of the Underworld to appear. They responded, holding their scrolls of names. One of the judges held open the book with the names of monkeys and showed Monkey his own name. It read, "Soul number 1735, Sun, the Enlightened One." Sun was the Chinese word for monkey.

"That is impossible. I know the secret to eternal life," Monkey shouted. He grabbed the book from the judge's grip and tore out all of the pages with the names of monkeys on them. With the pages and his magic pillar, he fled from the Underworld to the Curtain Cave .

MONKEY IN HEAVEN

he Dragon King of the Eastern Sea spoke with the Jade Emperor. "Monkey stole the iron pillar planted by Yu the Great from the floor of my sea," he complained.

The King of Hell, too, complained to the Jade Emperor. "Monkey interfered with the rules of the Underworld," he said, vehemently.

The Jade Emperor hated the disruption in Heaven caused by whining. If the Dragon King and the King of Hell were unhappy, who would be the next one whom Monkey would anger? He summoned the Deity of The Golden Star, whose domain was Venus. "Fetch Monkey and bring the troublesome creature to Heaven. I will give him a meaningless title and keep him under my supervision. This way, he can cause no further difficulty on earth," he said.

The Jade Emperor appointed Monkey to the position of Grand Master of the Heavenly Stables. He had to feed and water the Supreme Ruler's horses and keep the stables clean. Monkey enjoyed the work, and he particularly liked brushing and grooming the sleek, muscled horses.

One evening, another heavenly appointee invited him to a banquet. Monkey dressed in the fine garments he found in the wardrobe of his small palace and arrived in his finery at the banquet. During the meal, Monkey asked the holder of a heavenly post how much he might expect to be paid for his commission at the stables. Everyone at the banquet table began to laugh. Finally, one appointee answered the question. "Paid? It is foolish for you to expect to be paid for your lowly work. Even your title is imaginary, for you hold an office lower than the least office in Heaven," said the appointee.

Monkey was understandably furious. He had been duped into believing he held a worthy commission. Now he found out the title was worthless and he was not even to be paid. He knocked over the banquet table and returned to the Curtain Cave on Mount Aolai.

When the Jade Emperor heard of the matter, he again sent for the Deity of The Golden Star from Venus. "Fetch Monkey to Heaven once more. This time I will give him an important title, but with no responsibility attached to it. I will call him Grand Saint, Governor of Heaven. That should please him and keep him from mischief," he said.

Monkey was indeed pleased with the new title, and he liked the fact that he had no work to do. His second palace was larger and more luxurious than the first one, and the garments in his wardrobe, finer. To occupy himself since he was so important now, he made banners announcing his title. They flew from every window and door of his palace. Before long, the idle Grand Saint, Governor of Heaven decided he must raise an army and fly the banners into battle across the earth.

The Jade Emperor was losing patience with Monkey. He appointed him Grand Superintendent of the Heavenly Peach Garden, explaining that the post was of utmost significance. Monkey's new responsibility was to see that no harm came to the fruit of the trees in the garden. The peaches bloomed once every six thousand years, and they were now in blossom. Monkey did not understand the significance of the post until the Jade Emperor told him that the peaches were for the gods to eat to replenish their immortality. Even gods who lived forever had to nourish themselves every once in a while to stay immortal. The Jade Emperor forbid Monkey to eat any of the fruit. Monkey agreed. With the new post, he earned an even bigger palace and grander clothing.

But Monkey could not resist the temptation of the plump, sweet-smelling peaches when they appeared on the branches. One afternoon, he threw off his fine garments and climbed a tree. He took a bite of one of the peaches and admitted to himself that even on Mount Aolai he had not tasted fruit as sweet. Each day, Monkey ate more of the fruit.

Soon the maids to the Queen Mother appeared in the peach garden. They came to gather fruit for the Queen Mother's banquet, where she would serve the peaches to the gods who attended. Looking about the garden to pay their respects to the Grand Superintendent, they did not find Monkey. Shrugging, they decided to pick the fruit from the branches. But there were very few peaches on the branches. One of the maids shook a low branch to see if it held any fruit that was beyond her reach. Monkey was asleep on the branch, and he fell to the ground. He demanded to know what the maids were doing in his garden.

Imagine his surprise to learn that the Queen Mother was having a banquet and he was not invited! Monkey put the maids under a sleeping spell. He left his post in the peach garden. Since he was not invited to the Queen Mother's banquet, he flew back to earth to the Curtain Cave.

MONKEY AND TRIPITAKA

onkey was dissatisfied with his treatment in Heaven. He had not been given the respect he deserved. First, he was awarded a meaningless title and a small palace. Later, when his title was more worthwhile and his palace larger, he was told by the Jade Emperor not to eat the peaches of immortality. Why should he not have the same right to live forever as the other gods in Heaven? he thought. So he ate the peaches anyway to ensure that his immortality would not fade away.

The final insult as far as Monkey was concerned was when the Queen Mother did not invite him to her party. After that, Monkey did so much mischief in Heaven that Buddha himself put him in prison. Buddha locked Monkey deep inside a mountain and put a spell on the rock so it was impossible to escape. Hundreds of years passed, and Monkey was still in the mountain prison.

One day, Guanyin, Goddess of Mercy, and Buddha had a conversation in the Eastern Heaven. "I wish to send a priest and a companion to the Western Heaven for three scrolls that contain the teachings to help the people in China. But the road to the Western Heaven is 108,000 li, or about 36,000 miles," Buddha said.

"I will search for the right pilgrims. On their journey, I will protect them from harm," offered the Goddess of Mercy Guanyin.

"Perhaps after you locate the priest, you might go to the mountain cave and free Monkey, but on one condition. He must agree to behave himself and act as the priest's disciple," suggested Buddha. The goddess set out immediately.

Her travels brought her to a monastery. A kindly abbot recognized the Goddess Guanyin and welcomed her. After hearing the story of her search, the abbot told a tale. Long ago, he had seen an object upon a plank, floating in the river. When he drew the plank closer with his staff, he found a baby in a basket upon it. He raised the child and called him Shuanzhuang. Now Shuanzhuang was his best priest. Calling the priest, the abbot introduced Guanyin to him.

The goddess knew the young man to be the pilgrim she desired. The priest accepted the mission, and Guanyin named him Tripitaka. It was the word for the sacred teachings that the priest would bring back from the Western Heaven.

Tripitaka set out early the next morning upon the long road to the three scrolls. At the end of the day, he came upon a hunter in a very dark forest. The hunter invited Tripitaka to spend the night in his cottage.

The following morning, as the priest was thanking the hunter for his hospitality, the ground beneath them rumbled. Trees bent as though they were blown by a hurricane. A voice rang through the woods as loudly and violently as an earthquake.

They followed the voice, careful to keep a safe footing while the ground continued to shift from the force of the sound. Pursuing the rumble down into the valley, they came to the base of a great mountain. They saw a crack in the rock. Through the crack, they were amazed to find the out-stretched arms of Monkey in tattered sleeves.

"Oh, thank the Goddess Guanyin you have come. Please, release me at long last from this wretched mountain prison," he pleaded.

"How can we release you when Buddha himself has cast a spell upon the mountain to keep you inside?" asked Tripitaka.

Monkey answered that Guanyin had visited him and explained Buddha's condition for his freedom. She said he would be released when the priest Tripitaka arrived to break the spell. "Let me out, I beg you," he cried.

"But I don't have a saw nor an axe," protested Tripitaka.

"Do you see the sheet of paper over the crack in the rock? Remove it carefully, then step away from the mountain," said Monkey.

Tripitaka reached for the paper. His fingers barely touched it, and it flew from him. He and the hunter stepped away from the mountain, as Monkey instructed.

"Not far enough. Get as far away as you can. Quickly!" Monkey shouted.

A sound more powerful than Monkey's calls through the forest practically shattered their eardrums. Putting their hands over their ears to protect themselves, Tripitaka and the hunter sighed in amazement. The small crack in the rock burst open so that the very mountain was split in half. Monkey leaped forward, out of his imprisonment and into the freedom of the daylight. Bowing to Tripitaka, he promised his allegiance, which the priest accepted. They bid farewell to the astonished hunter.

MONKEY, THE PRIEST AND THEIR COMPANIONS

onkey and Tripitaka the priest set out upon their horses on the road of 108,000 li. On a mission from Buddha, they were in pursuit of three sacred scrolls. The scrolls would teach wisdom to the people of China. Their location was the Western Heaven.

The travelers came upon a rushing river and began to look for the best place to cross. Suddenly, the huge head of a dragon emerged out of the rapids directly in front of them. Its mouth was wide open and revealed two rows of enormous, pointed teeth. In seconds, the beast's great shoulders appeared, and it thrust itself forward in a gesture of attack. Monkey grabbed Tripitaka off his horse and sat the priest down behind himself on his stallion. The dragon seemed satisfied to devour Tripitaka's horse without its rider.

"You big worm. How dare you eat the horse of a priest?" challenged Monkey.

In that instant, Guanyin, Goddess of Mercy, appeared. She had promised Buddha to protect the pilgrims against harm during their long journey. "Calm down, Monkey. I placed the dragon in your path. No common horse will be good enough to carry Tripitaka to the Western Heaven," she explained.

Monkey was perturbed. How can the priest ride a dragon, he thought to himself. As he was trying to figure this out, he saw the goddess remove the pearl from beneath the dragon's chin. The dragon changed that instant into the exact form of the priest's white horse whom he had devoured.

Now the pilgrims set out to cross the rapids, each upon his own horse. They rode peacefully for the remainder of the day. That evening, they sought shelter in a dilapidated hut. But what should enter but a big, ugly hog demon?

Monkey took his magic staff into his hands. "Don't come one step closer, or I'll use this weapon. I must protect the holy priest Tripitaka," he said.

"Tripitaka? The Goddess of Mercy told me I could gain favor with the Jade Emperor if I protected Tripitaka on his journey. You see, I was banished from Heaven. My job was Guard of the Heavenly Moat. I tried to kidnap one of the gods who visited the Jade Emperor," explained the hog demon.

Monkey introduced the demon to Tripitaka. The priest named him Hog of the Eight Abstinences, and Hog promised to become a vegetarian. He vowed to give service to Tripitaka during the journey.

The next morning, the three companions set out at sunrise. Not long into their travels, they crossed a great beach. Out of the sand, there emerged a monster with red hair. It had a head and body of sand, two bulging eyes and a necklace made of nine skulls.

"Get back," shouted Monkey from his horse.

Again, he took his magic weapon into his hands. But Hog snorted and reared on his demon legs against the sand monster. Monkey grabbed the reins of Tripitaka's dragon-horse, and he led the priest to the outskirts of the nearby pine forest. They had a full view of the battle between Hog and the sand monster.

Each time Hog made ready to attack, the sand monster retreated to the safety of quicksand and disappeared. Monkey wished that Guanyin would come to help, for they needed to cross the beach to proceed. In an instant, the Goddess of Mercy stood before them and offered Monkey a gourd. She told him to blow through it to summon the sand monster. When the monster answered, she said to explain the priest's mission. Monkey was skeptical, but he did as she instructed.

The sand demon responded to the call, and it listened attentively. "I was once in Heaven. While I was a waiter at the Queen Mother's peach banquet, I broke a jade platter. I am here on earth as punishment. I will accompany you and protect Tripitaka," the demon said.

The priest named the demon Sandman Priest and welcomed his services. Now the four companions set off safely across the beach. Monkey had to swallow the anger that he began to feel over the Queen Mother's slight to himself. He had promised to behave without mischief.

Tripitaka and his disciples, with the help of the Goddess of Mercy, weathered eighty different mishaps and difficulties during their journey. Finally, they were at the gate to the Western Heaven. Because the people who lived there obeyed all of Buddha's teachings, the land was more beautiful than anything any of them had ever seen. Flowers in every color, even some that were new to them, bloomed in all corners. The ground beneath their feet was as rich and green as the sky was blue.

MONKEY, THE PRIEST AND THE SCROLLS

ripitaka the priest and his attendants Monkey, Hog and Sandman traveled for fourteen years on the road to the Western Heaven. The journey was a great distance. The distance was equivalent to 108,000 li, or 36,000 miles. Along the way, they had eighty adventures. The adventures were very dangerous. But Guanyin, Goddess of Mercy, protected them every time they asked for help. She was glad to give assistance, because their journey was of the utmost importance. They were going to the Western Heaven to bring back to China the three sacred scrolls. It was Buddha's idea. He recognized that some people in China needed more wisdom, and he knew that the scrolls would provide the way for them to learn.

One day, Tripitaka remarked, "We have reached the western land."

Monkey understood why he said what he did. None of them had ever seen such a lovely place. The grass beneath their feet was suddenly a plush carpet. Tiny flowers in every imaginable color dotted the rich green carpet.

Truly the people in this land obeyed the teachings of the sacred scrolls, for nowhere in China was any place as perfectly beautiful.

Ahead of them was the Mountain of the Soul. It was the home of Buddha and the three scrolls. Glistening in the sunlight, the mountain sat on the other side of a wide river. Across the river was a very narrow, wooden bridge.

"I am afraid to walk on such a narrow bridge," said Tripitaka the priest. Despite the numerous times that Monkey crossed from one side of the river to the other to prove how safe the bridge was, the priest remained fearful. He confessed to Monkey, Hog and Sandman that he never learned how to swim.

A man in a rowboat appeared and offered to ferry the party across the river. Hog and Sandman got into the boat. Monkey waited for Tripitaka before boarding. But the priest refused, saying that the boat did not appear sturdy enough to hold them. Acting swiftly, Monkey shoved Tripitaka into the rowboat.

The middle of the boat had no bottom, and Tripitaka plummeted through the hole into the river. The boatsman, who was a minor god, pulled him from the water, shivering and frightened. Then he started to row toward the Mountain of the Soul. Alongside the boat, a corpse floated. Though safely in the boat, Tripitaka shuddered when he recognized the corpse to belong to himself. Monkey explained to him that now he must be a deity, becaue he had no further need for his old body.

Entering the Mountain of the Soul, the four companions met Buddha. They bowed and waited for Buddha to speak. When they heard his command to rise, they saw that Buddha's attendant held the three sacred scrolls in his hands.

"What will you pay for these scrolls?" asked the attendant.

Monkey was indignant. "We have come a great distance for them. You see we have no money. Our coming here should be enough payment," he answered.But the priest held out his begging bowl. It was what he used to receive food from the kind people they met on their journey. The attendant took the bowl and placed the sacred scrolls in the Tripitaka's outstretched arms.

The four companions bid farewell to Buddha and set out for China to deliver the scrolls to the emperor so the people could learn wisdom. Guanyin, Goddess of Mercy, arranged with the Golden Guardian god to give the travelers an easy trip home within a large cloud. Outside the mountain, they found the cloud waiting, and they boarded it. The cloud floated high into the sky and moved quickly toward China.

Meanwhile, Buddha asked his attendant how many adventures Tripitaka had endured during his trip to the Western Heaven. "Eighty," the attendant answered. "The perfect number is nine times nine. He must have one more adventure for perfection," Buddha responded.

Suddenly, the cloud opened, and the four travelers fell from the sky. They landed upon the earth near a river. Monkey knew the spot. And he knew what to do. He called upon the White Turtle, who immediately raised its head from the water.

"Please, take us to the other side. We have valuable cargo from Buddha," he said. The White Turtle swam into shore and allowed them to sit upon its broad back.

It was a clear, windless day. However, the priests in the temples of China noticed that that the trees were leaning toward the west. "They are returning with the scrolls," said one priest after another. The word spread quickly. A large party awaited the homecoming of the pilgrims. The high priest gratefully accepted the three sacred scrolls from Tripitaka and, with solemn ceremony, placed them in a shrine. Soon the people of China would begin to learn the words of wisdom written on the scrolls.

In an instant, Tripitaka and his three attendants found themselves again at the Mountain of the Soul. Once more, they were in the presence of Buddha, and once more they bowed. Requesting that they stand, Buddha told Tripitaka he was to remain in the Western Heaven at his side. He had finished his time as a human. Buddha named Hog the Cleaner-in-Chief of his Altar. Sandman became one of Buddha's companions. Horse returned to the Western Ocean. Before he did, he transformed back into a dragon.

Lastly, Buddha forgave Monkey for all of his mischief. Making him a deity, he called Monkey "The Victorious One in Battle." The new deity flew home to the Curtain Cave to reunite with his wild monkey tribe.

PAN HU, THE DOG

he kingdom of the Yin people was often invaded by the Jung-wu clan. Kao Hsin was king of the Yin. He was tired of the invasions. One day his wife, the queen, got an earache that caused her great pain. No matter what remedies she took to make the pain stop, they never worked. For three years, Kao Hsin worried about the invasions. The queen suffered the pain of an earache. Something had to be done.

The queen's doctor tried and tried to help. Imagine his surprise one afternoon when the sun was at its brightest. He saw the reason for his patient's pain crawling around inside her ear! Without a word, the doctor gently inserted tweezers into the queen's ear canal to pluck out the culprit. Gaining hold of the invader, he pulled and tugged and pulled some more. The doctor's mouth opened wider and wider with each tug. Finally, out came a worm as big as a cocoon. It was two zhang, or about twenty feet long!

The queen's pain stopped that instant. "What happened?" she asked the flabbergasted doctor.

When he hesitated a moment, she urged him to explain. From behind his back, the doctor produced the giant worm. He was having difficulty keeping it within the grip of the tweezers.

"Let me have it," said the queen. She produced a gourd basket, and the doctor gladly released the worm into it. Quickly, the queen covered the top of the basket with a nearby plate.

Days passed, and the earache never returned. With each new sunrise, the queen checked and fed the worm, of which she had become quite fond. One sunrise, something extraordinary happened. The queen lifted the plate, and a dragon dog leaped from the basket. He had scales of five splendid colors. Peeking inside, the queen saw nothing and realized the worm had transformed into the dog. She named her new pet Pan Hu, which in Chinese meant "Plate Gourd."

King Kao Hsin, meanwhile, was still troubled by the Jung-wu invasions. They were more frequent than ever, and the enemy under their leader Fang Wang occupied a growing amount of the Yin kingdom. Kao Hsin called his ministers to a meeting. Pan Hu sat at his side. The dragon dog was now the king's favorite pet. Everyone in China knew of Kao Hsin's affection for the wondrous animal with the coat of a dog and scales of five colors.

"I offer a reward of caskets of gold, a palace and my own daughter the princess. Whoever brings me the head of Fang Wang wins the contest," said Kao Hsin.

Not one minister offered to try. As if their lack of bravery and loyalty were not bad enough, Pan Hu disappeared. He was gone for many days, and the king grew even more disheartened.

What Kao Hsin did not know was that the dragon dog understood his offer. After hearing it, Pan Hu went directly to Fang Wang's palace. When the enemy king saw the Yin king's pet dog in his palace, he took the event as a favorable omen.

"When even Kao Hsin's dog is disloyal, we are the victors," Fang Wang jeered. He ordered a banquet for that evening to celebrate his sure victory over the Yin.

The banquet was served in great finery. Nothing was spared, including succulent meats and tremendous quantities of wine. Fang Wang drank much of the wine. At his side throughout the meal, Pan Hu saw the enemy king become more and more intoxicated. Finally, Fang Wang passed out. Pan Hu jumped to his feet and bit off Fang Wang's head. He raced back to show the prize to his master.

Kao Hsin was very grateful to his dragon dog for accomplishing what none of his warriors attempted to do. He, too, ordered a banquet to celebrate. He commanded that Pan Hu receive the best cut of meat of anyone present. But, when the meat was served, Pan Hu did not budge from the floor. In fact, he looked away.

The princess approached her father. "How can you not keep the promise you spoke before Heaven and your kingdom? If you do not honor it, you do not deserve respect from either place," she scolded.

"But Pan Hu is a dog. How can a dog marry a woman?" he demanded.

Then Pan Hu cleared his throat as though getting ready to speak like a human. Everyone in the banquet hall was astonished. In a clear voice, he said, "Cover me with a large gold bell for seven days and seven nights. Do not disturb me during this time. At the end of seven days, I will emerge as a human man."

The king's attendants brought a bell into the hall and covered Pan Hu with it. Three days came and went, and no one heard a sound from the dragon dog underneath. The princess began to grow worried that Pan Hu would die without food or water. On the fourth night, she lifted the bell and peeked underneath. She saw the body of a man with the head of Pan

Hu. The spell was broken. Now Pan Hu would have to remain as she saw him.

Nonetheless, Kao Hsin arranged a wedding ceremony. The princess and Pan Hu were married. Upon her head, the princess wore a shaggy-haired hat to honor her husband with the head of a dog.

After the ceremony, Pan Hu renounced the other gifts that the king offered to the winner of the contest. The only gift he wanted was the princess. The couple moved to the land of the Southern Mountain, faraway from the day-to-day doings of humans. They lived happily in a small hut, where they survived from the rewards of Pan Hu's hunting. They had four children, who in turn had many offspring. In time, a large clan grew. Pan Hu and the princess were their ancestors.

WEI AND THE GIRL AT THE MARKET

ei's parents died when he was a boy, leaving him a sizable inheritance. But despite his wealth, he had a problem. Now that he was old enough to marry, Wei could not find a woman to agree to become his wife. Even on the few occasions when someone took an interest in him, her parents would not permit the match. The reason was that before their death, Wei's parents did not arrange a marriage for their son. People in old China believed that marriages were blessed in Heaven. First, the parents of the future bride and groom consulted the gods. Then they agreed to their children's match.

Poor Wei, who grew disheartened after so many refusals, decided to look elsewhere for a bride. His slave packed their belongings, and the two men set out on a quest for a wife for Wei. For ten years, they traveled without having any luck at all.

Late one day, they came to the city of Song. They stopped in a small inn for the evening. After dinner, Wei remained downstairs while his slave unpacked. A man from the city introduced himself to the traveler. He was friendly and kind, and Wei confided in him about his problem over finding a woman to marry.

"Meet me early tomorrow morning at the temple outside this inn. I will bring the city marshal with me. He has a daughter of marriageable age. Perhaps he will agree to her marriage with you," said the man.

Wei was excited about his prospects and slept very little that night. He rose well before dawn to meet the kind man and the city marshal. Telling his slave to wait at the inn, he went directly to the nearby temple.

An old man sat upon the stone floor outside the temple, leaning against a sack. He was reading a book by moonlight, for it was still not dawn. Standing a respectful distance from the man, Wei happened to glance at the writing in the book. He expected to find Chinese characters, but instead he could not read a single word. The writing was unknown to him and looked something like tiny crickets upon the page.

Wei cleared his throat to gain the old man's attention. "Excuse me, what manner of writing is in your book? I know many languages, yet I have never seen anything like it," he asked.

"You never would have seen such writing, for it is not of your world. I have brought this book from the Underworld. I am the Old Man in the Moon, the marriage god," replied the old man.

Wei could not believe his fortune. He explained how he intended to meet the father of his future wife. He asked the god if his marriage with the marshal's daughter would be successful.

"She is not the wife for you. Do you see this sack? Spools of red thread, invisible to the human eye, are inside of it. The thread ties the ankles of every baby who is born with the ankles of another baby. That is how marriages are made. You are tied at this moment with a three-year-old girl who lives in Song and who is destined to have many riches. You will marry her when she reaches seventeen years of age," said the Old Man in the Moon, the marriage god.

He invited Wei to accompany him to the market to get a look at the little girl for himself. When they arrived, Wei could not believe what he saw. A one-eyed woman was setting up a fruit and vegetable stall for the day. A little girl stood at her side. Both were dressed in filthy rags.

Wei rushed back to the inn, refusing to believe that the waif of a child could possibly be his future wife. After all, he had plenty of money. Despite what the marriage god predicted, the girl was too poor for him. Never would he marry her. When he found his slave, Wei handed him a knife. Promising a reward of money in addition to freedom, Wei told the slave to kill the little girl.

The servant went to the market and tried to do just that. But when his knife was poised to pierce her heart, the little girl moved. The knife stabbed her in the middle of her forehead instead. Nonetheless, for the attempt, the slave earned his freedom and the reward. The next day, Wei left the city of Song and forgot about the little girl from the market.

Fourteen years passed, and now Wei lived in the town of Shiangzhou. One day, the governor, who was Wei's grateful employer, offered to grant him his daughter's hand in marriage. Wei was very pleased, and the marriage took place with great ceremony.

The governor's daughter was extremely beautiful with one distinction. She always wore a patch in the middle of her forehead. Even when she slept or bathed, she kept it there. Some time passed, and Wei, who had forgotten entirely what took place in Song, asked his wife about the patch.

"I'm not really the governor's daughter. I'm his niece. My real father was the governor of Song. Shortly after his death, my mother and brother died, too. My loyal, one-eyed nurse took care of me. She worked in the market, selling fruits and vegetables. One day, an insane man stabbed me in the forehead," she said.

Wei recalled immediately what happened. He explained how he hired the slave to kill her. His wife forgave him and thanked him for telling the truth. They loved each other dearly for many years afterward.

THE CRANE MAIDEN

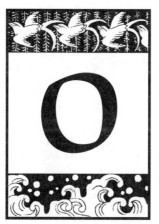

One morning long ago, three maidens were bathing in their favorite pond. They treasured the pond's pure, jade-colored water. There was a natural spring in the middle, and the maidens loved to swim through it to feel the cold on their limbs. The bathing experience was the next best thing to being in Heaven.

Just before noon, a peasant named Tian Kunlun happened to pass the pond. He saw the lovely maidens in the water, and he hid in the nearby brush to watch them splash one another and play. To his surprise, the maidens finished swimming and began to exit the pool. They were unaware of the peasant behind the bushes and made for the three piles of clothing on the sand. Quickly, Tian Kunlun came out of hiding and swept up one pile of the white silk garments into his arms. He clutched the clothing tightly.

Then another surprise opened the peasant's eyes wider. The maidens changed into three sleek cranes. Flapping their white wings, they dried the water from their bodies. Two cranes gathered their clothing and flew away with it in the grasp of their long beaks. To Tian Kunlun's wonder, they disappeared high in the sky. He never before saw a crane fly so quickly and so far.

The third crane interrupted his musing. "Give me back my garments," she demanded.

"Not until you tell me who you are," answered the peasant.

"I am the daughter of the Supreme God of Heaven. The cranes you scared away are my sisters. Our father gave us the garments to wear so we can leave Heaven for earth and then return. Now give them me back to me," she said.

"I won't do what you ask. If I give them to you, then you, too, will fly to Heaven. But you can have my clothes to wear, so you will stay," said Tian Kunlun.

Clutching the white silk garments tightly in one hand, he removed his outer clothing with the other and handed it to her. Without an alternative, the crane reached for the peasant's shirt and trousers with her wing. She flew behind a tree for privacy. The peasant was delighted to see her return as the lovely maiden he found in the pool, but wearing his clothes.

In a moment of rapture, he proposed that they get married. The daughter of Heaven reluctantly agreed, for she did not have a choice. How would she eat otherwise? Where would she live if she did not marry him?

Tian Kunlun brought his new love home to meet his mother. The old woman was overjoyed and welcomed the beautiful maiden into the household as her daughter-in-law-to-be. The following day, the daughter of Heaven and the peasant were married.

That evening, Tian Kunlun told his mother of the circumstances of his acquaintance with his bride. He showed her the silk garments and asked her to find a good hiding place for them. He made her promise never to reveal the secret of their location with the crane maiden.

Time passed, and one day the crane maiden gave birth to a son. They called him Tian Zhang, Zhang for short. When Zhang was three years old, his father was summoned to war. On the day he departed, the peasant reminded his mother of her promise over the clothing. The old woman told her son not to worry.

Every morning, the crane maiden approached her mother-in-law. She begged to be allowed to see her precious garments. Every morning, the old woman pretended that she did not hear the entreaties.

One morning the crane maiden cried more sorrowfully than her mother-in-law had heard anyone ever cry. "Please, I am so homesick for my family. I merely want to look at the garments," she asked.

The old woman lifted the secret plank in the floor under which she hid the white silk clothing. Seeing was not enough for the crane maiden after all. She grabbed the garments out of the old woman's hands and flew away to Heaven with them in her beak, just as her sisters had done so many years earlier. Poor Zhang wept when she did not return.

Tian Kunlun came home from the war, and he was furious with his mother. Leaving his son with her, he disappeared down the road and never returned. Zhang wandered the countryside, searching for the crane maiden. He wept and wept.

One day, he came upon an old man, who asked the reason for his tears. When Zhang related his story, the old man had a plan. He told the boy to go to the pond with the clear, jade-colored water and wait for the three maidens to appear.

"Two of them will notice you. The one who tries to ignore you is your mother," said the old man.

The next day, as luck had it, Zhang saw the maidens at the pond. Two approached, saying what a beautiful child he was. The third pretended not to see him. Zhang ran to her and embraced her around the middle. "Mother, it is you," he cried.

The crane maiden was filled with love for the son she missed dearly during her days in Heaven without him. Her sisters were touched by her emotion. Without stopping to swim, they departed for Heaven. The crane maiden held Zhang in her beak and brought him with her.

THE DRAGON AND THE SOLDIER

he Emperor of Ming wanted a new city for his capital; however, he chose an unwelcoming spot. The land was soft and wet. It was a great salt marsh, where cattails and tall grasses grew in abundance. Worse still, dragon lines crossed through in this area. The people of that time believed that no one should build over a dragon line. The lines were said to be the veins of the earth.

Dragons were friendly to people unless they were angry. In fact, they were very helpful creatures who dwelled in rivers, lakes, springs and the sea. They assisted humans during times of drought by breathing clouds so rain would follow.

The ministers were fearful to follow the emperor's orders to construct the new city. But the emperor paid no attention to their fear, because his favorite god told him not to worry about the dragon lines. The god was annoyed over how much power the people assigned to dragons. He wanted to show that dragons were second to gods in importance. He advised the emperor to have the foundation of his palace built directly over the lair of the dragon who governed the water of this area.

The ministers had no choice but to obey the emperor's orders. Construction of the palace began. That evening, the emperor had a dream. An old man and old woman appeared in it. They had two jars of water in their cart and asked permission to leave the city. The emperor gave his consent. When he awoke in the morning, he heard shouting and crying outside his royal tent. His chief minister threw open the flap.

"All of the water is gone from the new city. Not a drop remains in a single marsh or stream," he said.

While the emperor was dressing, the god who told him to build, spoke to him. "It was the dragon over whose home they began the digging. Ask your ministers to find out who left the city overnight and from what gate. Then you will know how to stop the dragon before he spills the water into the sea," the god said.

The emperor knew immediately that the old man in his dream was the dragon. It was the way of dragons to appear as humans when they communicated with humans. How could I have given permission, he admonished himself.

The chief minister reappeared. He said an old man and woman departed with a cart and two jugs during the night. They left through the west gate. Both the emperor and minister realized the sea was due west. The dragon must be stopped immediately.

The emperor assembled the army and asked for a volunteer to stop the dragon. While the other soldiers shifted their weight from foot to foot and lowered their eyes, a soldier named Gaoliang accepted the challenge. The chief minister gave Gaoliang his orders.

"Say nothing. With your lance, puncture the jars of water. Ride as fast as you can back to the city. Do not turn around to look until you are inside the city walls," he said. Gaoliang nodded and rode off to the west.

Shortly, he came upon the old man and woman with the jars of water in their cart. The soldier punctured the first jar with his lance without saying a word. When he tried to remove the weapon in order to pierce the second jar, it got stuck. The old man changed into a huge dragon with a scaly body, four clawed feet, a horned head and a spiny tail. Realizing that he could not fight the dragon, Gaoliang rode quickly toward the new city.

The sound of thunder crashed about him. The great, gushing noise of water pursued him. But Gaoliang did not turn to look. He did as the minister instructed and looked straight ahead toward the city. The thunder continued, and the gushing grew even louder. Finally, he saw the city in the near distance. He focused on the minister, whom he could now see, waving him forward. The walls of the city were very close. But the water behind him seemed closer. The west gate was just ahead of him. When his horse was a pace away, Gaoliang could not resist. He turned to look. The rushing water overcame him, and he drowned.

The emperor ordered a bridge to be built to honor the brave, young soldier who brought back half of the new city's water. He called it Gaoliang Bridge. The water that rushed from the first jar was enough for the people to survive. But it was bitter. All of the sweet water remained with the dragon's second jar in the hill above the city. The people called the spot where Gaoliang and the dragon met the Hill of Jade Springs. Even today, when they desire sweet water to make their tea, they travel to the hill and bring it back to the city.

WU AND THE YELLOW DRAGON

u was thirteen years old and did not say much. Like his grandmother, with whom he lived, Wu liked to observe what happened and to think about what he saw. He also lived with his father Yin, who was a farmer. His mother died when he was a baby.

One day as Wu was sitting just inside the gate to the garden, he saw five strangers approach on horseback. A young man who looked like a prince was dressed all in yellow and sat upon a white horse in the middle of the group. An attendant held an umbrella over his head as if to shield him from the sun.

"We wish to rest awhile in your cottage," the young man in yellow said.

"I agree," Wu answered. He led them down the dirt path and into the cottage.

Wu's father Yin served his guests food and tea, and the strangers were grateful. They spoke amicably with Yin, then stood to leave. Wu said nothing, but he watched everything. He walked out to the gate with the guests.

Seated upon his horse which had been tethered to the fence with the others, the young man in the yellow suit said he would come again tomorrow. "I agree," Wu answered. Then he went inside the cottage.

"What did you observe about the strangers?" Yin asked his son.

Wu explained how both times that the attendant passed through the gate with the umbrella, he held it upside down. He added that the strangers' clothing was made without any seams, that their feet and the horses' hooves did not touch the ground when they walked, and that the white horse had spots of five colors and scales instead of hair. Yin exclaimed that the visitors were demons. Wu was not afraid like his father. Yin led his son by the arm into his mother's bedroom. She was fast asleep and deaf.

Yin ordered Wu to tell the old woman about the visitors and their odd behavior. Shouting so she could hear him, Wu obeyed. Like her grandson, the old woman was unperturbed.

"You have been visited by the Yellow Dragon god and his four attendants. The horse is a dragon-horse. The upside-down umbrella is a good omen," she answered before going back to sleep.

Wu, who never said too much, decided to tell his father something else about the visitors when they were back in the kitchen. He told Yin that he watched the five men ride down the road until they were nearly out of his sight. Then they rose into the sky upon their horses and disappeared into the clouds. Yin grew worried, for dragons were known for bringing rain. He hoped the storm would not be too great.

As soon as the sun went down, it began to thunder. The thunder brought lightning that ripped open the sky. Rain followed in great quantities. Yin was very frightened, but not his son. Wu donned the yellow robe that his grandmother had given him. By the light of a yellow lantern, he began to read the spells she taught him from a yellow book.

All night long, great cracks of thunder sounded over the village. It rained so furiously that the animals moaned and cried horribly as they sought dry ground. Yin ran to the window in a panic. He told his son that he feared that they and their cottage would be washed away. Wu went to the window and looked up. It was sunrise.

"The dragon has spread his hood over our roof. It's not raining upon us," he said, calmly.

The rain stopped. Father and son strolled through the village. Only a few cottages remained. The others were washed away. The ground around their house, however, was bone dry. Not a drop had fallen upon their small piece of land.

When the sun came out, the five strangers appeared at the gate on horseback. Wu greeted them, but Yin shrank back in horror. The young man in the yellow suit reached down to the neck of his white horse and plucked out a scale. He handed it to Wu, saying he was unable to enter the cottage today. Then the five of them rode away, vanishing into the cloudless sky.

Wu woke his grandmother to show her the gift. "You must treasure it and keep it safe. When the emperor calls for you, go to him with the scale," she advised before going back to sleep. Wu put the scale into a wooden box.

Days passed, and he checked to make sure the Yellow Dragon's gift was safe each evening. One day, royal messengers arrived to invite him to the palace of the emperor. Wu and Yin left immediately with the messengers after bidding the old woman good-bye.

The emperor asked Wu to report the happenings of the visit and what he observed during and after the storm. Word had reached him of the strange event. Wu obeyed, then opened the wooden box. The scale shone brilliantly in the late afternoon gloom. The emperor's chamber brimmed with yellow light.

"You are to remain here as one of my sages, for the Yellow Dragon has given you power and wisdom," said the emperor.

Yin returned to the village to the home of his mother. Within a short amount of time, Wu had a reputation for his wisdom. He earned many riches, including a fine house where he brought his grandmother and father to live.

THE PUMPKIN GIRL

hile Shih Huang Ti was emperor of China, two families lived next door to each other. Their homes were on either side of a high wall. In the spring, both families planted a pumpkin seed. Neither family thought about what the other family might be planting. They looked forward only to the pumpkins that would grow from their seeds the following fall.

As spring turned to summer and the seeds began to grow, a tall stalk showed itself on either side of the fence. One stalk grew on the side that belonged to the Meng family. A second stalk hugged the side of the fence that belonged to the Chiang family. Both families were delighted that their seeds produced such fine strong stalks.

"Oh! We will have a tremendous crop of pumpkins soon," said the Meng's on their side of the fence.

"Any day now, a bountiful supply of pumpkins will appear," exclaimed the Chiang's from the other side of the fence.

But the most curious thing happened. The stalks on both sides of the fence grew and grew. Even as summer was waning into fall, not a single pumpkin appeared on either stalk. The Meng's scratched their heads at the anomaly. The oddity produced wrinkled eyebrows from the Chiang's.

One early morning, as both families had taken to doing, the Meng's and Chiang's cried out in unison from both sides of the fence. "Oh, my, what a pumpkin!" they both exclaimed.

Sure enough, upon the very top of the fence, right in the middle where the stalks had wound around one another, there sat a pumpkin. It was no ordinary pumpkin either. No, it was the largest, plumpest, most exquisite pumpkin either family could have imagined.

"Now what will we do?" the families wondered. The first thing they both did was run for a ladder. One of the Meng's propped a ladder against one side of the fence. One of the Chiang's leaned a ladder upon the other side of the fence. They reached for the pumpkin at the same instant! They looked at one another for the first time in a very long time. Then they both stared at the pumpkin.

"It belongs to both of us," said the person from the Meng family.

"Let's split it in half," said the representative of the Chiang's.

So they did. Imagine their surprise when they cut open the luscious pumpkin and found a baby girl inside with the pulp and seeds. Since they had been willing to share the amazing pumpkin, they decided to share the upbringing of the baby girl. They even gave her both their names. She was called Meng Chiang.

Meng Chiang enjoyed the love of the two families who raised her. This made the Meng's and Chiang's happy, too. Now they spoke to one another every day and realized that they liked it.

One evening when Meng Chiang was a young woman and the moon was full, she realized how romantic the night was. Bathing in a pool in the woods behind the houses of her foster parents, she began to sing. "If anyone sees me bathing here tonight, I will marry him without a question," she sang.

Little did Meng Chiang know, but a man was hiding in the branches of a tree in the same woods. "I see you, and I accept your proposal of marriage gladly," he replied. His name was Wan.

They were married at a splendid celebration given by the Meng's and Chiang's. While the happy couple were dancing, unexpected guests arrived. The emperor had sent his guards to arrest Meng for insubordination. Meng Chiang asked for an explanation. She learned that her husband Wan had gone into hiding to avoid being put to death by the emperor. The guards took him away despite her cries of protest.

The reason the emperor wanted to kill Wan was a bit complicated. The Emperor Shih Huang Ti had tried unsuccessfully to have a wall built along the northern frontier of China to protect the empire from invasion. But every time a new section was built, it collapsed. The empires' sages told him that the collapses were the work of demons. One sage said to bury a person along every foot of the 10,000-foot wall. But a second sage suggested that many lives could be saved if the emperor instead killed and buried Wan, whose name meant "ten thousand." For this reason, Wan had gone into hiding.

Poor Weng Chiang was heartbroken to lose her husband of only a few hours. She went immediately to the Great Wall and insisted that the emperor's guards show her where they buried Wan. When they did, she scooped his bones into a silk scarf and demanded to see the emperor. Reluctantly, the guards heeded her demand. When Shih Huang Ti saw the beautiful young woman, he asked her to marry him and become empress.

"On three conditions, I will marry you," she responded.

At a nod from the emperor to proceed, Meng Chiang spoke the conditions. "First, you must have a burial feast for Wan that lasts for fourty nine days. Second, you and your chief officials shall attend the ceremony. Third, you will have an altar of forty-nine feet built to honor my dead husband. There we will be married," she said.

The emperor agreed. At the end of the forty-nine days, they were married. During the marriage ceremony and before all of the invited guests, Meng Chiang climbed to the top of Wan's altar. She spoke out strongly against the emperor's cruelty, yet he said nothing. Then she threw herself into the river below and drowned. The astonished Shih Huang Ti shouted to his guards to grind her bones into fine dust. The guards obeyed the cruel words. The emperor then ordered them to throw the dust into the river. What a surprise for everyone when the guards obeyed the second command.

The water of the river changed the dust of Meng Chiang's bones into tiny, silver fish. Sparkling in the light, the fish swam to safety. The sages said that each fish was a small part of Meng Chiang's soul. Now she would be reborn every time another tiny, silver fish came to life.

THE STORY OF THE TWO DOVES

Part I

 ong ago when emperors ruled China, T'so Ling, a rich mandarin widower, lived with his only daughter, Koong-se. When he was an official for the emperor, T'so Ling had taken bribes. The money came from people who wanted T'so Ling to gain them favor in the eyes of the emperor. Now that he was retired, T'so Ling worried that someone would discover he had committed these crimes. So he hired a young clerk named Chang to destroy all of the records that showed his misdeeds.

Day after day for many days, Chang tore up evidence of the bribes in the house of T'so Ling. Young Koong-se found herself looking forward to Chang's arrival every morning. The two young people began to meet in T'so Ling's garden in the early evenings after Chang finished working. Surrounded by persimmon, peach and almond trees, they fell in love. Chang wrote love poems to Koong-se that were very beautiful. While she was as happy as she had ever been, however, Koong-se knew her father would never permit her to marry a clerk. After all, she was the daughter of a wealthy mandarin. One evening, she gave Chang a necklace of blue beads.

Seated near a plot of irises, she spoke of her love for Chang to her handmaid, the wife of her father's gardener. The handmaid was the only one who knew the secret. One dark evening when the air held the promise of spring, T'so Ling decided to saunter into his garden. What a surprise he found when he saw his daughter and the clerk Chang alone in the garden house. The furious T'so Ling banished Chang from the premises forever under penalty of death if he dared return.

The next morning, he fired Koong-se's handmaid and hired in her place an elderly woman with a sour face as puckered as a prune. T'so Ling ordered a tall, sturdy fence to be built around the house and confined his daughter to her quarters. Her only means of exit was through his salon. The window of T'so Ling's salon faced the river. The bridge under the weeping willow was the only possible means for Chang to reach the property.

Her father gave her some news one morning. "When the peach tree blossoms, you will marry a Ta-jin of high rank and great wealth. You should be grateful. He is as old as I am and very wise."

Poor Koong-se was miserable. No matter where she went, she suffered the scrutiny of her sour-faced handmaid. One day, she was unable to bear being inside the house another minute. With the handmaid a few paces behind her every step, she took a walk by the river. Half of a coconut shell floated upon the water. Eager for diversion of any kind, Koong-se fished it out with her parasol. Imagine her surprise to find one of the blue beads she gave Chang seated upon a folded poem in the shell. Before the handmaid took notice, Koong-se dropped the bead and poem into her parasol. Alone in her room, she read Chang's poem. It said: "When the peach tree blossoms, I will plunge into the river's depths." Koong-se realized that Chang was nearby and that he knew of her dreaded marriage to the Ta-jin.

Very soon afterward, peach blossoms showed their faces upon the tree in the garden. The Ta-jin arrived with his servants to dine with T'so Ling, as was custom before a marriage. T'so Ling came to his daughter's room with a lacquered box of precious gems as a gift from the Ta-jin to his future wife. All evening long, as Koong-se fretted about her fate alone in her room, she heard the merrymaking at her expense from the great hall. She could tell from the shouting and song that everyone was intoxicated on her father's wine.

Early the next morning, her suspicions were confirmed. As she tiptoed out of her quarters without waking the shrivel-faced handmaid, she found no guards to stop her from departing alone for the river. In her hand, she held the half-coconut shell into which she had placed a note for Chang. The note read: "Rescue me."

Within an hour, a stanger appeared on the bridge. But the guards and servants were still drunk, and no one stopped him from entering the house. Koong-se saw Chang approach, and she grabbed the box of gems from the Ta-jin. The two lovers fled in a boat that Chang rowed quickly downriver and away from T'so Ling's house.

A short distance away, the former gardener and his wife, Koong-se's first handmaid, welcomed the pair to their humble cottage. They hosted a marriage celebration for Koong-se and Chang. In the back of the house, they prepared quarters for the newlyweds. Peach blossoms littered the ground like a snowstorm had fallen. Koong-se and Chang were very happy.

THE STORY OF THE TWO DOVES

Part II

iscovering that Koong-se was missing, the angry T'so Ling, her father, awakened the drunk Ta-jin who was to have been her husband. The Ta-jin was even more furious than T'so Ling. How dare the ungrateful Koong-se insult him? After all, he was a wealthy, powerful mandarin. He and everyone at T'so Ling's house knew why and how Koong-se had disappeared. Chang, the lowly clerk, was responsible. It was unthinkable that the beautiful daughter of a mandarin would choose a clerk for a husband over the Ta-jin. To make matters worse for the Ta-jin, the sour-faced handmaid reported that the lacquered box of precious gems he had given Koong-se as a marriage gift was also missing.

"I order the death of Chang when they are discovered. He is a thief," shouted the Ta-jin.

The search for the young couple began in earnest. Both T'so Ling and the Ta-jin hired guards to scour the countryside for them. The only good thing about the situation was that T'so Ling exacted a promise from the Ta-jin that his daughter's life would be spared if she agreed to return home. Chang, on the other hand, would lose his life as punishment.

The gardener and his wife expected that a search party would be commissioned by Koong-se's father and husband-to-be as soon as they discovered the girl gone. They designed a plan as a sign between them if danger became imminent, meaning if the guards were close by. The wife would know to expect the guards to come if her husband did not return home at the end of the workday. One stormy day, the gardener was late in coming home. After a time when he had not appeared, his wife was unsurprised to hear a loud knock.

The woman decided to keep the guards in conversation so that Koong-se and Chang, in their room, could devise a strategy of how to escape. Chang told Koong-se he must flee through the window to the river. There was no other possible means of escape, as the guards were positioned at the door.

"But see how hard it rains. You will surely drown," protested Koong-se.

"Do not fear. I will swim until I find a boat. Then I will row back to get you," vowed Chang. With that, he quietly opened the window, and he was gone. Koong-se lingered and watched until she could no longer see his tiny head against the fierce, storm-blown current.

In the meantime, the guards were growing restless. They were annoyed that the woman was keeping them so long in conversation. "All right, I will tell you where Chang and Koong-se are. They like to walk in the rice fields on rainy days," said the woman. The guards heeded her words and departed for the rice fields.

When the woman looked in the back room, she found no one there. Wet footsteps were all she saw. She threw open the window and saw

Koong-se and Chang in a boat, rowing away. She knew she would never see them again.

A good amount of time passed, and still T'so Ling and the Ta-jin did not give up the search. They grew old, yet their anger did not subside. Koong-se and Chang found an island in the river and decided to settle there. With the box of jewels from the Ta-jin in hand, they rowed to the nearest village across the river and purchased the materials to build a house. They also bought the seeds and sprouts to grow flowers and food. Chang proved himself to be a skilled farmer. He also continued to write his beautiful poems. From time to time, he rowed to the village across the river to sell his produce, flowers and poetry. Soon, his reputation reached far.

Word of him found the ears of the Ta-jin, who was now quite old and still vengeful. One fateful day, the Ta-jin's guards stormed the island abode of Koong-se and Chang. The happy couple was startled at the intrusion. Before either could protest, a guard drew his sword and obeyed the Ta-jin's order of long ago. With a stab to the heart, he killed Chang. Unable to bear her husband's death, Koong-se threw herself into the river and drowned.

Honoring their tireless love and devotion, the gods responded. They changed Koong-se and Chang into two white doves. Now they could love each other without the intervention of anyone. Both T'so Ling and the Ta-jin, on the other hand, lived out the rest of their lives as lonely men. They died with no one to love them.

JAPAN

IZANAGI
AND IZANAMI

ong ago, there was no earth or sea or sky. There was
no place for the winds or rain. There was only a
thick substance like oily mud, floating everywhere.
There were no sounds, only silence.

This lasted, unchanging, for millions of years.
Finally, one day, the the mud that was less heavy
and thick began to rise. Some of it became the sky,
and some of it created the high plains of heaven
itself. The heavier part of the mud stayed where it
was. It kept floating. It did not change.

More time passed, and three gods were born in the plains of heaven.
These were the God of the Center of Heaven, the High God of Growth,
and the Divine God of Growth. One day they began looking at the earth
below.

"What is that?" one god asked. "I don't know," said the other. "I'd like
to clean it up, but I don't know the first thing about where to begin."

"I've always wanted a sea, with islands," said the third. "There would be
lovely gardens on the islands, with trees and beautiful rivers and even a

mountain or two," said the third. "Let's ask the August Lord of Heaven," they all exclaimed. Together they went to pay a visit.

The August Lord did not like the substance below any more than the three gods did. In answer, he sent a new race of younger gods to the high plain. Perhaps they will have some answers, he hoped. All sat down to talk together, but no one knew what to do. Everyone was afraid of failing at the task. They were just as afraid of going back to the August Lord of Heaven and telling him they could not succeed.

They decided to send the two youngest gods to try to solve the problem. "If they don't make it, no one will blame us! All the blame will fall on them!" said one to the rest.

Izanagi and Izanami were sent off to the August Lord of Heaven, who looked at them kindly. He knew why the other gods had given them this task. He was not the August Lord.

As a gift, the August Lord gave Izanagi a beautiful spear, covered with jewels. It was one of the treasures of Heaven.

Izanagi and Izanami needed a way to get down from Heaven to the place where they could begin to create the world. The August Lord of Heaven gave them a beautiful carriage of colorful clouds. As they were standing by the carriage, Izanagi was confused.

"What will the carriage ride on to get us to where we need to go," he asked the August Lord.

"Touch the tip of your spear to the ground," answered the lord.

A beautiful rainbow appeared. "This is the Floating Bridge of Heaven," said the August Lord.

Izanagi and Izanami floated off. Eventually, they drifted down to the end of the bridge. The bridge's end was just above the floating mud. The mud looked sticky and smelled awful. "This is it?" asked Izanagi. "What a beginning! There's not even a place to stand," Izanami said.

"Wait," said Izanagi. "I'll see if I can find one!" He thrust his spear into the mud. Feeling nothing, he pulled it back out into the air. A drop of mud clinging to the speartip fell back into the oily substance. Suddenly, there was a little spot of solid, dry land. Izanagi shook his spear again and more drops added to the solid land in front of them. They formed the first island. Once that was complete, the spear began to rain water around the island. The ocean was created.

With joy, Izanagi and Izanami stepped from the Floating Bridge of Heaven on to the island they had created. They walked on the beach, on the rocks, over the high hills and the mountain at its center.

Izanami looked at her partner. "Izanagi," she said, "this beautiful place is to be our home. We would not have had it without the urging and the help of the August Lord of Heaven. Let's build a shrine here, where we can serve the great gods and live peaceful lives," she said.

Izanagi and Izanami spent days building the shrine, which had a great pillar in the center that pointed to heaven. That way they always felt close to their former home.

Once the shrine was finished, Izanagi and Izanami made formal preparations to dedicate it. They chose names for the island, shrine, and column. They prayed that the shrine might be blessed by the August Lord of Heaven.

The island was called Onokoro. The shrine was called Yashirodoro, or the palace eight miles wide. They called the pillar the August Pillar of Heaven.

THE BIRTH OF THE ISLANDS OF JAPAN

zanagi and Izanami lived happily on the beautiful island of Onokoro. In time, though, they became bored with seeing the same things again and again.

"We have been happy here, but our island, Onokoro, is really very small. Perhaps we should try to create another island, so we can go and visit it, too?" said Izanagi.

"That's a wonderful idea, Izanagi," said Izanami. "Perhaps we should create more than just one. I would like to never run out of beautiful places to visit. Any maybe some creatures and some trees and plants to go with it? Don't you think that's what the August Lord of Heaven had in mind when he sent us here?"

"Let's go to the shrine and try to find out," Izanagi suggested.

Hand in hand, the two went to the shrine to look for guidance. They wanted to get divine blessings for the task they thought they should perform.

Quietly they sat in the shrine, hoping for inspiration from the August Lord of Heaven. Suddenly, an idea popped into Izanagi's head. "Izanami, I

think the August Lord has given me an inspiration. I know what we have
to do to create the other islands, and everything that should go on them.
We must become husband and wife!"

"Izanagi, is that all we have to do?" asked Izanami. "It sounds easy
enough. How do we go about it? Is there a ritual? I love rituals!"

"Yes, there is a ritual," he said. "We get dressed up. Then we circle the
Pillar of Heaven." Izanagi and Izanami had built the pillar in the shrine
when they first came to Onokoro.

"You go to the right of the pillar. I will go to the left of the pillar. We
will meet each other again on the other side. When we come together
again, we will be married. The gods told me that we will be able to have
children afterward. Our children will be the islands!"

Izanami was confused. She had no idea that creation of a thing involved
giving birth. She did not know how she would give birth to an island! But
she trusted in the gods. If they intended her to give birth to a whole ocean
of islands and everything that went on them, she would.

She went with Izanagi to the column. They met each other on the other
side. "Now we are married," they said to one another. Shortly afterwards,
Izanami began to feel different. "I must be with child — no, I must be with
an island," she corrected herself.

In time, Izanami became big, as future mothers do. When her time
came, she gave birth to a healthy, beautiful young island. That evening,
after walking all day around the new creation, the two talked eagerly about
the islands they wished to create. Both prayed for help to the August Lord
of Heaven.

The next morning, they returned to the Pillar of Heaven. They walked
around it once again. The sky grew golden and warm. Izanami became
pregnant again. This time, she gave birth to all the islands in what is now
Japan! The two went to the pillar again. This time she gave birth to a great

number of gods and goddesses. The gods of wind, of rain, of mountains, of trees, of mist on the mountain tops, of the creeks and streams and rivers and the seas were all her children.

They went to the pillar again. Izanami gave birth to the seasons, birds, plants and flowers! Look around you. Everything you see is a child of Izanami! Even the sun and moon!

Izanami was joyful that she was creating the world and everything in it. She never thought that she could get in trouble. But she did.

The last time Izanami and Izanagi walked around the pillar, she conceived the fire god, who was always in flames. When she gave birth to him, he burned her very badly. She became very sick. She was close to death.

Izanagi and Izanami had lived together for many years. He was extremely upset about losing her. He was angry, too, with the fire god.

"Wife, what will I do without you?" he asked, tenderly.

"Do not despair, husband," she answered. "We have had a long and beautiful life together. The world is alive with the sounds of our children. Some day we will meet in the underworld. I am sure of it."

Peacefully, Izanami died. Death came to the world for the first time. Izanagi was very sad.

IZANAGI'S
DESCENT TO YOMI

ithout his wife Izanami, Izanagi was filled with grief. Crying, he walked on the islands she had created. He visited beautiful Onokoro, the first place on earth they had lived. It had been long since the August Lord of Heaven had sent them to the unformed earth, asking them to make the world. The years had been full of joy for them, but now Izanami was dead.

He remembered her last words. "Some day we will meet in the underworld," she had said. Some day was too long a wait, he thought. If he died, they could both live in the underworld. But the underworld was dark and cold and miserable. It was better to live here. Suddenly Izanagi sat up. He had an idea. He would go to the place of the dead. He would bring Izanami back to the world of the living!

Izanagi searched, and he finally found the gateway to the bleak and sorrowful road that led to the underworld. As he climbed down onto it, he remembered the rainbow-bright floating bridge of heaven that had brought them to this world. He looked at the quite different, bitter-smelling darkness that surrounded him. He stepped into the muddy ooze that threatened to pull off his sandals. "The road to the underworld will be long," he thought.

He started to walk nonetheless. Now and then, strange sounds came out of the darkness. Some were faint and far away. Some roared at him right next to his ears. Sometimes he thought he heard Izanami, calling for his help. But he was sure it was only his imagination. After days on this road, he believed that the creatures who lived there could imitate anything to attract their prey.

The mud slowly turned to pavement, and Izanagi realized he had reached the end of the road. He was in the underworld. Immediately, he started to look for his wife, but he couldn't find her. He searched for days. Finally, in despair, he sat down to rest. Suddenly he saw Izanami. With a cry of joy he rushed to greet her.

"Have you died so soon, husband?" she asked.

"No, I have not. But I cannot live without you. I have come here, even though I am alive. I want to bring you back with me to our beautiful home!" he said.

"Oh, husband, I wish with all my heart I could come back. But I have eaten the food and drunk the wine of this terrible place. Because of this I have changed. I must remain here, and I can never return to you. If only I had known you were going to come so soon!" She started to weep.

Izanagi's heart was cold with fear. No one who ate in the underworld could ever leave. But he had more courage than anyone alive. "Nothing will force me to return without you!" he vowed.

"Oh, my husband. For love of you, I will go to the Lord of the Dead. I will plead with him to allow us to return together. But you must make a promise to me. Once I have left you, do not enter my room. It is very important that you keep this promise to me! Do not enter my room!" She departed and he was alone.

For hours, Izanagi waited. Around him, it grew colder and darker. He began to shiver. "Where can she be?" he wondered. Growing more and more anxious, he began to think something had happened. Perhaps the Lord of the Dead was keeping Izanami. Izanagi would go and fight! Nothing would stop him!

Jumping up, he ran to the door. Forgetting his promise, he pushed it open and entered the next room. Before him, lying on a bed, was Izanami. Surrounding her, he saw ere eight foul demons of thunder.

They were eight feet tall, and their red skin was hard and scaly. They had big horns, bulging eyes and long fangs, and there were thick claws on both their hands and feet. The air flickered like fire as they breathed in and out.

Izanami opened her eyes and sat up. "Husband! Could you not have been more patient? Our bargain was sealed. The Lord of the Dead agreed that I could go, if only I could live through a night surrounded by these demons," she cried. She wrung her hands and sobbed. If only he had kept his promise! Now she could never go. And they would have to kill Izanagi for breaking the vow.

Izanagi ran. Pursued by the demons, he tore back up the road. The demons were very fast, and he could not get away from them. They surrounded him. They lunged at him, snapping at his neck with their fangs, snatching with their great claws. One kept jumping up and down, taking deep breaths and blowing fire at him. But Izanagi fought back.

He drew his sword. He hit them with it, but he was compassionate, and did not try to kill them. Even horrible demons had a right to live, he thought. Once he had hit them hard enough to make them dizzy, he pushed his way through them and ran on.

At the gate to the underworld, Izanagi found a giant boulder. He rolled it to the gate, and was about to seal it off. Suddenly, he heard the voice of Izanami.

"Husband, wait. I am still very angry with you. Why did you ruin our chance of return? I am now shamed before the Lord of the Dead," she said.

"I was foolish, Izanami. But perhaps we were taught a lesson by the Lord of Heaven. Those who remain in the world of light can never regain those who go into the dark," Izanagi answered. He sealed the gate of the underworld and walked away. Some day, perhaps he would meet Izanami again in the land of the dead.

AMATERASU AND SUSANO

zanagi's experience with the dark land of Yomi had left him feeling unclean in body and in spirit. To purify himself, he went to a small stream on Kyushu, the biggest island in Japan. There he took off his clothes, and slowly entered the stream.

The cool, fresh water flowing over him helped Izanagi wash away the horrors of his trip to the underworld. He had gone there to try to bring back to earth his beloved wife Inazami. But he had failed.

As Izanagi took his bath, wondrous events happened. Many gods and goddesses were born. Some came into being from the clothing he wore. Others received life when the water touched his body. The Sun Goddess, Amaterasu, appeared when he washed his left eye. Tsukiyomi, the moon, came out of his left eye. And Susano, the Raging Male who was God of Storms, came from his nose.

While in the bath, Izanagi thought deeply about the years that were to come. He decided that it was time to leave the responsibilities of ruling the earth and heavens to the younger gods. He himself would retire to heaven.

He divided his kingdom among the first three children. Amaterasu would rule the high plains of heaven. Tsukiyomi would govern the night. And Susano would rule the ocean.

All but Susano accepted their gifts gladly. "The ocean? It is not worthy of me," he cried.

"Your mother and I were sent to the ocean by the August Lord of Heaven! How can it not be worthy?" Izanagi replied.

"There is no land there except for a few islands," Susano responded. "It is not worthy of me."

Susano's disobedience made Izanagi furious. He decided to banish his son to the earth. Then Izanagi ascended into heaven.

Before he departed for the earth, Susano decided to visit his sister Amaterasu. She did not trust Susano. She believed that he was coming to visit her only to try to cast her out and take over the Plains of Heaven.

Quickly, Amateraus prepared for battle. Like all warriors, she arranged her long hair in bunches. She armed herself with a bow, two quivers of arrows, two swords, and glittering armor. She also had to prepare her mind for battle. She shook her bow angrily. She stomped the earth beneath her feet as she waited for him. She was ready.

Arriving, Susano bowed gracefully to his sister. He recited a poem.

"You are always so polite, brother," she said. Susano was never polite. Amaterasu was hinting that he had other motives for being there.

"Be at peace, sister. I intend no evil to you or anyone," Susano said.

"Father believes otherwise. Or he would not have exiled you," she answered.

"Father feared my strength," Susano said.

"That could never be. For I am stronger than you!" said Amaterasu.

"That is not possible!" Susano challenged.

To test who was stronger, Amaterasu and Susano decided upon a contest. They would see which of them could produce more gods. Whoever did would be the winner.

Amaterasu asked for her brother's sword. She broke it into five pieces. Chewing the metal, she spat out three graceful goddesses.

"Can you do no better than this? You were supposed to create gods," Susano sneered.

He asked for the long strings of beads which Amaterasu wore in her hair and around her arms. He held them in his hands a moment. From the beads, he created five male gods.

"The victory is mine!" he said.

"Not at all, brother. Your creations came from my possessions. I have won!" replied Amaterasu.

"What nonsense is this?" asked Susano.

"It's quite logical," Amaterasu said.

"Only you would think so," said Susano.

He rushed past her, breaking down the ridges of the divine rice paddies. Water flowed everywhere. He covered up the irrigation ditches until everything was dry. He threw dirt into the hall where the first fruits of the harvest were tasted, defiling a sacred place.

"See what strength I have," he shouted to Amaterasu.

"All that you have done is break great things that others have worked hard to build," she answered.

Furious, Susano tore a dappled pony from the sky where it had made its home. He hurled it through the roof of Amaterasu's sacred weaving hall. The flying pony killed one of the maidens who served Amaterasu. The hall collapsed.

Amaterasu fled in fear. Susano remained behind, boasting over the ruins he had created. Amaterasu sought refuge in a rock cave in the mountains. She had to think about what could be done to answer Susano's crimes.

AMATERASU AND THE SUN

fter her fight with Susano, the god of storms, Amaterasu desired to speak with no one. She sat angrily in a cave. Hour after hour, she thought about what Susano had done. The rice paddies were broken, the irrigation ditches were filled! How would they have any food now? She would never forgive him either for the dirt he flung and the horse he hurled through her roof! Amaterasu wondered where all of the other gods and goddesses were when her brother destroyed everything. Why were they not there to help? "Well, if they need me now," she resolved, "they will have to wait on my pleasure."

All of earth and all of the heavens waited for Amaterasu the next day. She would not come out. She shut the door of the cave tightly and barred it. But Amaterasu was the goddess of the sun! When she did not come out, the sun did not rise. Earth and the heavens stayed completely dark.

Week after week, and month after month, everything was in blackness. It grew very cold. Snow fell, and there was ice and very cold winds.

Amaterasu stayed in the cave, angry and alone. Finally, the gods became worried. They began to talk among themselves.

"The rice will not grow! The flowers will wither! The humans, the animals, the birds, even the insects — all will shiver and grow faint with hunger! The bitter winter and the darkness may kill all that lives! What must be done to get Amaterasu to reappear?" the gods and goddesses cried.

One goddess suggested that the sounds of roosters might move Amaterasu to shine the light of morning. They tried, but to no avail. Then Omori-kane came up with another idea. It was complicated, they all agreed, but it might work.

They started by building a magic mirror. They hung the mirror from the branches of a sacred tree. The tree stood in front of the cave in which Amaterasu was hiding.

Then they built a stage. While the other gods and goddesses formed a chorus, the Goddess of Dawn began to dance. She pretended she was not a good dancer. She would often slip, or slide, or fall down.

Many of the gods thought that Dawn's dance was the most humorous thing they had seen in their lifetimes. They laughed. They stamped their feet, they clapped their hands so much that the plains of Heaven shook.

Amaterasu heard the laughing. She unlocked the door of her cave, and opened it a crack. "What is going on out there?" she shouted.

"Is that you, Amaterasu? It's about time!" said Dawn.

"Why are you laughing?" Amaterasu demanded.

"We are laughing, because we are happy. We are happy, because we finally found a god that is better than you at bringing light to the earth. We do not need you any more!" Dawn answered.

While Dawn spoke to Amaterasu, two gods aimed the mirror. They pointed it in the direction of the door of her cave. Another very strong god hid by the door.

Growing angry at the idea that heaven and earth could do without her, Amaterasu opened the cave door. As she stepped out, she looked right into the mirror. She was amazed. She thought she was looking at another god when she was actually looking at herself.

The strong god jumped from behind her and held on to Amaterasu. A goddess shut the door to the cave and stretched a magic rope across it. "This is as far as you can go," they said to her.

At first, Amaterasu was angry that the other gods had played a trick on her. She decided to calm down. Then she realized that she had been acting as badly as her brother Susano.

"If I fail to shine in the heavens and on the earth every day, nothing will grow, I could do more evil than Susano did," she realized.

All of the gods and goddesses were very happy that Amaterasu was back among them. But they realized that it was unfair to let Susano go unpunished. They brought him before a heavenly court.

"Are you guilty or not guilty?" they asked.

"Not guilty," Susano lied.

"You caused this crisis!" said the gods and goddesses.

They gave Susano the greatest punishment that the law of heaven allowed. He had to pay a fine. He had to load a thousand tables high with gifts. These were presents for those he had hurt. Susano's beard and hair and the nails of his hands and his feet were also cut off.

Finally, he received the worst punishment of all. He was forced out of heaven. He had to live on the earth. It would be a long time before any god would ever think of letting him come back. He never returned.

SUSANO'S DESCENT TO EARTH

usano had been exiled from Heaven for his crimes against his sister Amaterasu. Amaterasu was the Sun Goddess. First he had disagreed with their father Izanagi over which part of his father's kingdom they would inherit. Then, after losing a contest with his sister to see who was stronger, he had let his temper run wild. He destroyed works in heaven which took years to build, defiled sacred places, and killed one of Amaterasu's servants. For this, the gods exiled him to earth. Susano was depressed and angry.

"You won't get back to the heavens for years, if you ever do. You may as well make the best of what you have here," he said, blaming himself.

He looked around and sighed. It was rocky. And it was cold. There was no grass. No trees. There were no people to be seen. "How could I have been so foolish? What have I done?" he asked himself.

For days, he walked through the wilderness. Slowly the area improved. Here and there he saw a tree. Then he spotted a few plants. Finally, he came to the banks of a stream. He sat on the shore, and looked at his reflection in the water. He sighed again.

Suddenly, a pair of wooden chopsticks approached in the water. Susano became excited. "There must be people living upstream. I must go and find them," he said to himself.

For half a day, he walked upstream. Finally he came to a small hut. Outside were three people, an old couple and a beautiful young woman. All were crying bitterly.

"Excuse me, please, I don't mean to interrupt. Is there anything I can do to help?" asked Susano.

"Thank you, young man, but I'm afraid there's nothing you can do," the old man answered.

"The young woman before you is named Rice Paddy Princess," he continued. "She is the last of our eight daughters. All of the others have been eaten by a monster, whose name is Yamato-no-Orochi. It has eight heads and eight tails. Each of the heads is big enough to eat you with one bite. Each of the tails is big enough to crush you with one swat. It's breath is harsh enough to make your skin shrivel and fall off. Tomorrow it is coming to eat her. No human can stand up against it."

"I can," said Susano, boldly.

"That's very brave, young man, but I do not think you realize just how ...," began the princess's father.

"Excuse me, sir," Susano replied. "Please, do not be alarmed, but I am the god Susano."

At once, the three humans dropped to their knees. They touched their heads to the ground. Susano stopped them. He explained that he was going to be staying on earth for a while. He did not like the idea that monsters could walk the earth, eating beautiful young women. He smiled at the princess, and she smiled back. The old parents promised to give him their daughter's hand in marriage if Susano saved her life.

Susano went to work. Inside himself, he was not at all sure that he could kill Yamato-no-Orochi one-on-one in a fight. Yamato was very big. He knew that, to beat Yamato, he would have to use his wits. To protect the princess, Susano turned her into a comb, which he inserted into his hair. Then he told the couple to fill eight large tubs with the rice wine called sake. Susano put the tubs on eight platforms. He surrounded them by a fence with eight openings. Yamato-no-Orochi would find the sake impossible to resist.

The next morning, the monster took its time in approaching the trap. As Susano waited, he suddenly smelled a foul reeking in the air. Then the earth began to shake. Over the horizon came the monster, making great crashes as each of its tails hit the ground. The earth shook under Susano's feet.

Yamato-no-Orochi sniffed the air with its eight noses. For two hours, the monster drank sake. Susano began to wonder what would happen if the wine ran out. But his fear was unnecessary. Finally, one after the other, the eight heads nodded off in a drunken sleep.

Susano approached the first head, which had its eyes shut. He drew his sword, and he crept closer. The eyelids of one of the other heads popped open. Susano froze. The eyes closed, and the head went back to sleep.

Quickly, Susano cut off the eight heads. Then off he cut the first, second, and third tails. As he pierced the fourth tail, his sword got stuck! Slowly and carefully he cut out the obstacle. It was a sword! He named the sword "Grass Mower," and he later gave it to his sister Amaterasu.

Quickly, he finished the rest of the tails. The monster was dead. The Princess was saved!

Susano changed the Rice Paddy Princess back into her human form. Her love for him and gratitude knew no bounds, for he had saved her life. They married happily, and went to live at a large palace that Susano built in Suga in Izumo Province. From there, he accomplished many famous deeds.

SUSANO AND THE FOOD GODDESS

usano was the god of storms. He was passionate about conflict. Everyone who came across his path had to fight with him, even the gods and goddesses.

Susano fought as often as he was able. He was big. He was burly. He had long, dark hair which he shook from side to side, and a thick, long beard. Early on in life, Susano even fought with the food goddess Ogetsu.

She was one of the older goddesses, and she looked like a little bird. She was very polite and refined. But underneath, she was very strong. Ogetsu could also be very sensitive. All of the gods and goddesses and all of the people on earth knew she had to be treated very politely and with great respect. She had to be entreated constantly to provide good harvests, so people and the gods would have enough to eat. But Susano did not believe he had to be polite to anyone, much less an older goddess like Ogetsu.

One day, he even shouted at her across the room. "I'm hungry! Get me something to eat!" Susano liked to be disrespectful. A few of the younger gods laughed.

The other gods and goddesses looked around nervously. Ogetsu politely ignored Susano. She pretended she had heard nothing.

"What's the matter?" Susano bellowed. "Can't you hear me?" His young friends laughed and laughed. "I said, GET ME SOMETHING TO EAT!!!!!"

Most of the gods now became angry. Some left the room. Ogetsu again ignored Susano. "Some of our companions are speaking a little too loudly today," she said to a friend. The friend smiled back.

Susano walked over to where Ogetsu sat. He stood right in front of her. He stamped his feet on the floor, hard enough to make the chairs and tables shake. Ogetsu looked away, and pretended to read a scroll. Susano pulled the paper out of her hands, and threw it on the floor. He yelled as loudly as he could. "I'M HUNGRY!!!!!!!!!!"

Ogetsu stood up. Her face was red with rage. "I have listened to this long enough. You are a disgrace to yourself and to the memory of your father Izanagi. You are an embarrassment to all the gods. Most humans act better than you. The humble farmer behaves better than you. You listen to me! If you wish to eat any of my food for the rest of your life, be quiet!" she shouted.

The gods and goddesses lived for a long time. None of them had ever heard Ogetsu speak like this. One by one, even the youngest among them nodded approval of her words.

One of the gods turned to Susano. "We think you should leave now," he said. Humiliated, Susano stalked from the room.

Back at his house, he was furious. Never would he forget the humiliation of being spoken to the way Ogetsu had spoken to him. He had forgotten about the manner in which he had insulted her. Susano was always good at paying no attention to what he had done to cause something to happen.

"I cannot stand how she spoke to me! She insulted and embarrassed me before all the gods and goddesses! I cannot appear in public again! Every one will smile when I come into a room! I cannot live with this!" he said to one of his comrades.

"You cannot mean you are going to kill yourself?" the other young god asked.

"No, never," Susano answered. "But I will kill Ogetsu."

"That you cannot do," said his friend. "Killing her will mean no more food for all of us."

"That's ridiculous. Food will come from elsewhere! The world will be better off without the approval of those other gods!" said Susano.

He drew his sword and rushed off. His comrade hurried to warn the other gods and goddesses. When they rushed to Ogetsu's house to protect her, it was too late. Susano had broken in and killed her. He was nowhere in sight.

Sadly, the gods and goddesses gathered up Ogetsu's remains. They buried them in different parts of the earth. All wondered how they would survive without food.

It was Ogetsu who was the victor in the end, though. A few weeks after they had buried her, the gods noticed that crops were beginning to sprout from the ground, in the places where her body had been buried. In one place they found rice. In another, millet. In yet others, red beans and soy-beans.

Food would keep coming back year after year, even without Ogetsu there to make it happen. The goddess had won a victory. Once again, Susano had lost.

OKUNINUSHI AND THE WHITE RABBIT

usano, the God of Storms, and his wife, the Rice Paddy Princess, lived together happily for many years at Suga. Susano had married her after he defeated an eight-headed monster and saved her life. At long last, Susano died and became a lord of the underworld.

Susano and the Rice Paddy Princess had more than one hundred children. The most famous of them was Okuninushi. He was called the Great Land Master. Okuninushi was not always famous.

When they were young, there was a lot of conflict between Okuninushi and his eighty brothers. One day, for example, all of them decided at once that they wanted to marry the beautiful princess Yagamihime of Inaba. In a great flurry, they rushed off to see her at the same time, having decided they would offer to marry her all at the same time. She would have to decide instantly whom she wanted.

Okuninushi said that this was not a practical way to pay court to a great princess. But his brothers ignored him. They rode off in a pack, pushing and shoving to be first. By choice, Okuninushi stayed far behind them.

On their way to see the princess, they came upon a rabbit who was lying by the side of the road. Its fur had been pulled out. It was red and sore all over and in great pain.

"Please, sirs, might you tell me how to heal my wounds?" asked the gentle rabbit, quietly.

Many of Okuninushi's brothers were very cruel. They decided to tell the poor rabbit things to do that would hurt him. "Go bathe in that salt water over the hill," suggested one. Salt water on a wound is very painful, but the rabbit didn't know that. Once he had bathed, he hurt twice as badly. The brothers rode on, laughing.

Eventually, Okuninushi rode by, and he stopped. "Hello, Mr. Rabbit. Why are you crying?" he asked. The rabbit told him what had happened, and Okuninushi became very angry with his brothers. He looked down the road where they had gone, and then back at the rabbit. "I will stay with you until you are healed. But I need to know how this happened to you. Then I can learn what the right cure will be," Okuninushi offered.

"Oh, thank you, sir," the polite rabbit said. "I feel a little better already. My story is really very simple. I had sailed over to the island of Oki on a little boat to go and eat some sweet greens. When I got out, I tied the boat to a tree. When I came back, something had chewed through the rope. The boat was gone. There was a family of crocodiles living close by.

"If there's one thing Mother Rabbit taught her children, it's 'don't trust a crocodile'! But I truly needed help. I had no other way to get back. I convinced the crocodiles that they should lie end-to-end and form a bridge. Then I could walk across the crocodile bridge and get across the water. They said they would do it if I counted how many of them there were. They said they did not know how to count. Off I hopped, crocodile to crocodile! I was up to one hundred and fifty-seven. I was just about to hop to the next, when I saw he was the last. Worst, he was facing me. His mouth was wide open. I prayed to the Great Rabbit, and hopped as high as I could! Even then, he almost caught me with his teeth. He tore out all of my fur. But I made it past him. I got back on to the land."

"What a terrible story, Mr. Rabbit," said Okuninushi. "I know just the thing to make you better." He took the rabbit to wash in some soothing, fresh water. Then he had him roll in the pollen of sweet flowers. "Everything will be fine," said Okuninushi. "Your fur will grow back almost immediately!"

Okuninushi stood by as the rabbit was cured. His fur grew back into a beautiful white coat. The rabbit looked at his image in the fresh water. "

"Thank you, Mr. Okuninushi. I have never looked or felt as good as this!" said the rabbit.

He asked Okuninushi why he was traveling. Okuninushi told him. The rabbit smiled.

"So your brothers are riding all that way to pay court to the princess?" he asked. "You should know that I am the princess' favorite rabbit! She'll be yours if I have anything to do with it!" he boasted.

Before Okuninushi and the white rabbit arrived at court, the princess had grown very bored. She had listened to all eighty suitors. So far none of them had said anything that would make her want to marry a single one of them. "There is only one thing any one of you can do to change my mind. My favorite rabbit is lost! Find him, and I might reconsider," said the princess.

Every one of the eighty brothers remembered the rabbit they had made suffer. They cursed themselves for having been so mean. Then Okuninushi and the rabbit arrived. The rabbit recommended that the princess marry Okuninushi, and she accepted the proposal in delight. The rabbit was an honored guest at the wedding!

OKUNINUSHI AND HIS BROTHERS

want to kill him," said one of Okuninushi's 80 brothers. "We all want to kill Okuninushi," said another brother. "LET'S KILL HIM," said all of them but one brother. "Wait, wait, wait," said the lone voice of the brother who knew that killing was wrong. "We can't kill our brother." "Oh, NO?" said the rest. "Just watch us."

"Brother dear," said one of his hateful seventy-nine siblings to Okuninushi. "There's a very large boar causing a ruckus over on the mountainside two hills from here. Since you're so good with animals, maybe you could go over there? Perhaps you could help the people protect themselves against the boar?"

His brother's request made Okuninushi nervous. He had plenty of reasons not to trust his brothers. There was not one good reason to trust any of his brothers. There was definitely no reason why any of them should tell him about a problem, or wish him to solve it. On the other hand, he thought, what if there was a boar? How many people could the boar hurt if it wasn't stopped.

Nonetheless, he decided to go and take a look. Okuninushi hated to see needless suffering. Boars were mighty fierce animals.

On the top of the mountain, his brothers were heating a large rock. It was so hot that it was changing colors. "It's red. That's not hot enough. Blue! Still not hot enough. White! Can't get any hotter than white!" said the scientific brother.

The scheming brothers saw Okuninushi, walking around the mountainside. He was looking for the boar. They pushed the rock over the side. It fell so quickly that Okuninushi couldn't tell what it was. He thought it might be the fearful animal! He tried to catch it, but it crushed him. Where he wasn't crushed, he was burned. He died shortly afterward.

Only one of the brothers felt wrong about what had happened to Okuninushi, the same one who had tried to discourage the others earlier in the day. He went to visit Okuninushi's mother, the Rice Paddy Princess, with the story of what had happened. She hurried to the gods. They agreed to bring Okuninushi back to life.

Returning from the land of the dead did nothing to make Okuninushi more popular with his brothers. "Can you believe it?" one asked. "If this ever happened to one of us, our mother would not take the trouble to bring us back to life," said a second. "It cannot happen more than once, can it, bringing someone back from death?" asked a third. "LET'S KILL HIM AGAIN!" said all of the brothers but one.

This time, one of the evil brothers pretended to write a letter to Okuninushi from his wife, the Princess Yagamihime. "Okuninushi, my dear love," it said. "My favorite rabbit and yours has hopped to the top of the very tallest tree in the valley. Can you please climb the tree and get him down? Love, your adoring wife."

That's odd, thought Okuninushi. Why would Yagamihime write him a letter when she could come and talk to him any time she wanted in person? This very well could be a trick, he resolved. But concern for his friend the rabbit overruled his caution. He set out at once to do what his wife had asked.

Standing before the tallest tree in the valley, Okuninushi looked up toward the top. It was odd that he did not see the rabbit, yet he convinced himself that he must check nonetheless to see if the rabbit was stuck. So he climbed and climbed. Nearly at the top, he thought, "There's no rabbit here that I can see." Suddenly, he felt the tree tremble. He looked down. There were his seventy-nine brothers, chopping down the tallest tree in the valley, with him in the top branches. He tried to climb down fast, but the tree fell faster. It crushed him and he died, once more.

Once again, the one brother who liked Okuninushi ran to his mother, the Rice Paddy Princess. She ran to the gods. Once again, they agreed to bring him back to life. "You know we like you," the gods said to the Princess, "but we won't be able to do this again if you come to us again."

When Okuninushi was fully revived, his mother and he had a little talk. "My darling son," she said. "You are compassionate and you are brave! But you need to be far more tricky! You need to look out for the people who are trying to do harm to you! Be cautious around the likes of your seventy-nine brothers."

She continued. "I think it is time that you had a talk with your father Susano. He lives in the underworld now. You can learn from him what it is to be clever. There's no one more clever at this sort of thing than he is. And while you are there, you can learn why people who are alive do not like the underworld! For that is where you will be if your brothers kill you one more time! If they try again and succeed, I won't be able to bring you back the third time!"

Okuninushi listened to his mother very carefully. He vowed to be more clever. The Rice Paddy Princess called for a servant to give him directions to the underworld and a box of food to eat on the way. Okuninushi set off to visit his father.

OKUNINUSHI AND SUSANO

rom the moment that Okuninushi walked through the gates to the underworld, he was afraid. The underworld was where the dead live. The road there was dark. It had a rotten smell. It was very still, yet he could hear things whispering, or breathing quietly.

Okuninushi could see nothing but the road. Sometimes, he thought something was following him. Sometimes he thought it was right behind him, breathing on his neck, or on the side of the road watching. He could never tell what it was.

To calm himself, Okuninushi considered his situation. He was going to visit his father Susano, the god of storms. Susano had angered the other gods, so they had exiled him to earth. When Susano died, he went to the underworld, like the other humans. But since he was a god, he became a powerful lord in the underworld.

Because his father was powerful, Okuninushi realized nothing would stop him on the road. He did not have to be afraid. He was powerful, too.

He had faced danger back on earth, he thought. His brothers had tried to kill him twice. The first time was for saving a rabbit to whom they had been cruel. The second time was for falling in love with a princess whom they wanted to marry.

Finally, Okuninushi arrived. Whatever he thought had been following him never caught him. He was glad to find his father. "Is it always so dark and damp and cold?" Okuninushi asked Susano.

"It is the underworld. You notice it far less once you have died," Susano answered. A beautiful young woman stood in the shadows nearby.

"Who is she?" Okuninushi asked. "This is one of my stepdaughters. Her name is Suserihime," Susano answered.

"She is very beautiful," said Okuninushi. He thought he saw Suserihime notice his attention.

At first, Okuninushi and Suserihime barely spoke to each other. But, little by little, they fell in love. "Suserihime, will you marry me?" Okunihushi asked one day. She agreed to his proposal, and they were married in secret.

Susano was very angry when he found out. "I think I am going to put an end to the life of that young man," he vowed to himself. One day Susano noticed that Okuninushi had a cold. "It is too cold in your room at night," Susano said to his son. "Why don't you sleep in another?"

Okuninushi was suspicious. He discussed his suspicions with Suserihime. "He wants you to sleep in the Snake Room. The room fills up with poisonous snakes at night. You will die!" she sighed.

To protect her husband, Suserihime gave him a magic scarf. If he needed help, Okuninushi should wave it three times. The snakes would disappear.

That night, he went to the Snake Room as Susano had requested. Suddenly, he heard a slithering and hissing in the dark. The hissing sound seemed to grow and grow. He lit a candle. There were too many snakes to count!

Okuninushi waved his scarf, but the snakes moved closer. He shook it again, and they came closer still! The third time he waved it, the snakes rushed out.

The next day, Okuninushi went to Susano. Susano was very surprised he had survived. "The room where you sent me already had creatures living in it. Can you possibly give me another for tonight?" he asked.

Suserihime laughed when Okuninushi told her the story of his meeting with Susano. "No one has spoken to father like that before! Maybe he will come to like you for it," she said.

The room the following night was again dark, cold and quiet. Suddenly, Okuninushi heard a buzzing noise sweep into the room. He lit a candle. There were bees, wasps, hornets, all circling closer and closer to him! Quickly he waved the scarf, once, twice, but still they moved closer and closer. When he waved the scarf for the third time, the insects flew around his head in a circle, then they left the room.

The next morning, Susano was furious when he saw Okuninushi still lived. "I need to take some archery practice. Fetch the arrows that I shoot," he said. Okuninushi was doubtful, but he accompanied Susano.

They went to a large field, and Susano shot an arrow. Okuninushi went to fetch it. Once he was far away, Susano set fire to the plain. Okuninushi watched nervously as the fire came closer.

"Excuse me, please," said a little voice from near his feet. Okuninushi looked down at a very small mouse. "Aren't you a friend of the white rabbit?" asked the mouse.

"Why, yes," answered Okuninushi.

"I am also, and I have heard how you rescued him," the mouse replied. "I can help you escape."

The mouse told Okuninushi to stamp his feet. Instantly, a large hole opened up. Both of them took refuge there and the fire burned over it.

Their hair frizzled and ashes fell around them, but they were safe.

Susano was amazed to see Okuninushi alive after his latest attempt to kill him. "You survived. You are smarter and stronger than I thought!" he said.

One day, Okuninushi was washing Susano's long hair, and Susano fell asleep. Okuninushi tied the wet hair to the rafters of the palace. Then, taking Susano's bow and sword, he and Suserihime ran away.

When he awoke, Susano was furious. He untied his hair, and, running as fast as he could through the underworld, he chased after Okuninushi and Suserihime. As he ran, he started to think about how clever Okuninushi and Suserihime had been. When he caught up with the couple at the border of the underworld, he left them alone.

"You will not have much trouble with your brothers," he said to Okuninushi. "To defeat them, use the sword and bow you stole from me!"

Okuninushi went on to rule the province of Izuma. He and Suserihime were happy. They lived long lives together.

SUKUNABIKO, THE DWARF GOD

Ruling the province of Izumo was not simple for Okuninushi. It had been difficult enough learning how to use his wits to outsmart his father-in-law Susano. Then he had to defeat his eighty brothers in battle. Getting his subjects to do what he wished was far more difficult than anything he had tried to do so far.

When he issued a command, they pretended to obey him. But they would do something else instead. To be a good ruler, he had to get his subjects to agree to his desires and act on them. In turn, he had to listen to their desires, and act on them. Combat with swords is much easier, thought Okuninushi!

People needed help in many other ways from their ruler, too. They needed forts and soldiers, to protect them from war. They needed medicine, to keep them from being sick. They needed food, always.

A ruler has to deal with too many things, thought Okuninushi. Right now, in Izumo, the people were suffering from a sickness. It gave them high fevers, and made them very weak for months. So many were sick that the plants were not being cultivated. As a result, there would be little food at the harvest.

How could he help the people get well, so there would be enough to eat?

When Okuninushi had to consider these things, he often went for a walk on the seaside. The ocean breezes, the sounds of the waves and of the seabirds, the patterns of the clouds all helped him to clear his mind. One day, while walking in the sand, he saw a small raft drifting in with the tide. He waited until it landed.

"Welcome to Izumo," he shouted to the man in the boat. "What brings you to our province?"

A dwarf jumped off the raft into the surf and approached the shore. Okuninushi had seen dwarves before, but this man was dressed very strangely. His clothing was made of little feathers and moth wings. Yet he carried himself with great dignity.

"They say you have trouble here. I have come to help! I am Sukunabiko, the Small Renowned Man, son of the Divine-Producing-Goddess. I am a doctor, and I know how to cure sickness. I know how to grow crops, too," he said.

Okuninushi was very happy. The two companions began to travel back and forth across Izumo province. With Sukunabiko's medicines, they cured the sick. With Sukunabiko's other skills, they helped the crops to grow. Not a day went by when they were not blessed by someone for their good deeds.

"People are happy when our ruler and Sukunabiko come to visit," said one farmer to another. "Any why not?" his friend answered. "Those who have been ill feel healthy and strong again. We have enough to eat. Our ruler pays attention to our needs and Sukunabiko is always kind and helpful," responded a third farmer.. "Okuninushi is what a ruler should be!" everyone agreed.

When there was a possibility of war, Okuninushi and Sukunabiko taught the villagers how to fortify their villages and protect their homes. They showed them how to build walls, how to dig moats around the walls, and how to fight off attackers. All of them learned how to use spears, arrows and swords. One time Toshiro, the worst bandit in Japan, came over the border with a thousand men. They rode past a few of Izumo's villages quickly, and just as quickly left! They knew that trying to conquer the villages would be too difficult! All of this was due to the efforts of Okuninushi and Sukunabiko.

Another day, Sukunabiko looked around him and realized that he had done all he could in Izumo. The province was strong and healthy once more. He told Okuninushi he had to leave.

Okuninushi was very distressed. "Please, my friend, I do not know how I can get along without you. I will make you co-ruler if you stay," he offered. But nothing he said could persuade Sukunabiko to remain.

The dwarf sailed off the following morning on his raft. As Okuninushi watched the raft grow smaller and smaller on the horizon, he was sad. "Now I am alone. How can I keep order in the land? Can anyone else help me?" he asked himself.

Suddenly, the sea lit up with a divine light. Okuninushi heard a voice. He bowed in awe. "You could not rule this country if I were not always by your side," the voice said.

"Who are you?" asked Okuninushi.

"I am your protecting deity, and my name is Omiwa," said the voice. "If you worship me on Mount Mimoro, I will always help you."

Sukunabiko lived a long life. He was always helping people. He was always kind. When he was getting near death, the gods told him to climb to the top of a millet plant when the crop was ripe.

As he was climbing to the top of the plant, his weight and the weight of the ears of the grain made the plant start to bend. The higher he climbed, the more it drooped. Sukunabiko began to worry.

Finally, when he was at the top, the plant was stretched down as far as it could. It started to shake, and then suddenly it snapped up. The plant flung Sukunabiko all the way to heaven.

Even today Sukunabiko sometimes appears on earth to help people in their search for better health.

THE LUCK OF THE SEA AND THE LUCK OF THE MOUNTAIN

osusori and Hikohohodeni were the two sons of Prince Ninigi. The younger son Hikohohodeni had the luck of the mountains in his hands. He was very skilled in hunting. Hosusori the elder son held the luck of the sea in his hands. He was equally good at fishing.

One day, the brothers met after they returned from the mountains and sea. "I'm bored with wandering the mountainsides. Let us just for one day exchange our luck," said the younger brother.

"Never!" said the elder. "I cannot agree to such a thing."

"What harm can it possibly do? Try it once!" pleaded the younger brother. With some doubt, the elder brother agreed.

Hikohohodemi handed his bow and arrows to his brother. He received a fish hook in return. Down at the sea, he did not catch a thing all day. Finally, he decided to fling the line out for the last time. There was a mighty bite. He pulled back as hard as he could, but the line snapped. His brother's hook was gone. On the mountainside, Hosusori's luck was just as bad, although he did not lose his brother's bow and arrows.

They met again at the end of the day. "The luck of the seas is not my luck," said the younger.

"And the luck of the mountain is not my luck," said the elder. "Here are your arrows. Now give me my hook!"

When the older brother learned his hook was gone, his fury knew no bounds. His younger brother was deeply ashamed. All night long he looked for the hook, but he could not find it. He decided to sacrifice his sword to make 500 replacement hooks for his brother.

"That's not good enough," said Hosusori.

Hurt by his brother's harshness, Hikohohodemi wandered up and down the seashore. No matter how hard he searched, he could not find the hook. After many tries, he sat down and wept. When he looked up, he saw a kindly old man.

"Aren't you one of the sons of Prince Ninigi? Why do you weep so bitterly?" he asked.

"I am the prince's son, sir. Please tell me who you are," answered the younger brother.

"My name is Shihotsuchi, and I am Lord of the Tide. Can I help you?" the old man asked. Hikohohodemi poured out the cause of his woe. "I can help you," the old man said.

Shihotsuchi gave him a basket, in which he could sail to the bottom of the sea. There he would find the palace of the God of the Sea. "If you hide in the top of a tree by the gate of his palace," Shihotsuchi said, "the Sea God himself will give you advice. Now go!"

Down sailed the basket to the gate at the palace of the Sea God. Out got the younger brother. He climbed up into the tree and waited.

An hour later, the Princess of the Sea appeared. She was going for her daily walk by the reef. Feeling that someone was watching her from the tree, she went up to it and looked around. The sight of the handsome Hikohohodemi made her shy. She ran back into the palace to tell her father.

When the God of the Sea came outside to investigate, he recognized the son of Prince Ninigi. "Why are you sitting like a bird in the tree?" he asked. "Please come inside."

The Sea God and his family were delighted with the younger brother, and he with them. Hikohohodemi fell in love with the god's daughter, and they married. They lived together happily for three years. One day, however, the younger brother remembered why he had come to the bottom of the sea.

The Sea God noticed Hikohohodemi's change of mood. He asked what the matter was. Hikohohodemi told the god and the princess the story of the lost fish hook.

"Don't worry. That's an easy problem to fix," the Sea God said.

All the fish of the sea, large and small, arrived at the Sea God's gate. "Have any of you seen or taken a fish hook?" he asked. None had seen it.

"Bream's not here," offered one fish. "She's had a sore throat for a while. Perhaps it's been caused by a hook." The Sea God summoned Bream, and he gently extracted the hook from her throat. He handed it to his son-in-law.

Hikohohodemi was sad to leave his wife, for they knew she was going to have a child. When he returned the hook to his elder brother, Hosusori was very pleased. He promised to serve his younger brother faithfully for the rest of his life.

Settling affairs with his brother took Hikohohodemi a long time. His wife became more and more impatient. Finally she, too, set out for the upper land. Husband and wife were very happy to be with each other again.

One day, the princess knew she was going to have the baby. "I must shut myself away for a while, my husband," she said. "I beg you, do not come and look at me."

Hikohohodemi waited and waited. Finally, he could not wait any longer. He opened the door to the room and peered inside. There was an eight-fathom-long crocodile on his wife's bed! His wife was a crocodile. Hikohohodemi became very angry.

The Sea God's daughter was very angry, too. "I asked you not to look, but you could not keep your promise," she said. "We could have had a lovely life together. But, because you broke your word, we must part.

Writing a song for her husband, she told of her sadness at how things had worked out. Then the princess and her child went down to the sea and remained there forever. All that Hikohohodemi had was her song, his brother's love and the luck of the mountain.

THE KAPPA
AND THE RIDER

oranaga-san was known by everyone as the best surgeon in Edo. No one with a broken bone who came to him ever went away unhealed. This was not as easy as one might think. In the days in which Toranaga-san lived, it was difficult to set a broken bone. Many bones that broke healed crooked, and some did not heal at all. Doctors who could heal every broken bone were rare.

One day, one of Toranaga-san's sons worked up the courage to ask him a question about his skill. "Father, may I please ask you a question about your skill?" he said.

"Certainly, my son."

"When did you first begin to know you had a gift as a bone-setter?" the son asked.

Toranaga-san looked carefully at his child. Although the boy was young, he was already one of his best students. Should he respect his desire and answer his question? The answer was not one he would expect to hear. Toranaga-san thought deeply. Yes, he would answer.

"It is not the answer you expect, my son. You could not even guess what it is," replied Toranaga-san.

"When I was young, I was not a doctor. I was a warrior, a horseman. I traveled to and from the capital, on my lord's business. I would always complete his business quickly, for that was my duty. Now let me ask you a question. Do you know what a kappa is?" asked the father.

"I think so, though I have never seen one," replied the boy. "That is one of the things the people in our village talk about. People there say the kappa is a descendant of the monkey that carries messages up and down the river for the river god. Sometimes they run in the trees, and sometimes they swim. That's why people say they look like monkeys, but they have fish scales or turtle shell instead of fur. There's something else. They are supposed to be small. Sometimes they look like children. Their color is yellow or green. They live in water. You're never supposed to go near one. They drink blood, human blood, but they also like cucumbers."

"Cucumbers?" said Toranaga-san, laughing. "Do they like cucumbers fresh or pickled?"

"Father, really, I am serious," said Toranaga-san's son. "One of the women from our village thought a kappa was after her daughter. She threw a cucumber into the river with her daughter's name on it. That made the kappa leave her daughter alone. This is what I've heard."

Toranaga-san was very happy with how much his son knew. "Well, son, you really know a great deal about kappas. But there is one more thing you should remember. A kappa has a hollow in the top of its head, with water in it. If that water is ever spilled, the kappa loses its magic powers. I know, for I saw one. In fact, I defeated it," he said.

Toranaga-san's son was amazed. His father had defeated a kappa! "Father," he asked in an amazed voice. "May I inquire how?"

Toranaga-san was very proud to tell the story. "Certainly, my son. I had just come back from a mission. I heard there was a kappa in a pond near my barracks. The pond was eerie. Birds and other animals avoided drinking there. I rode over and looked into the gray water. Suddenly, the kappa was there. As you said before, it did look like a small child. It was thrashing in the water, pretending it was drowning. 'Help me, Toranaga-san,' it cried."

"It knew your name?" asked the son.

"Yes," said Toranaga-san, "and I was so caught up in what was happening I did not even notice until it was over I was still up on my horse, and I reached down and offered the kappa my hand. As quick as anything that lives, it grabbed my hand. It tried to pull me into the water. I was afraid, but I knew what I had to do. I shouted to my horse to run. It was a good war horse, and it did. It galloped so fast it pulled the kappa right out of the water. It spilled all the water out from the top of its head.

"'Mercy, Toranaga-san,' it cried. 'As much mercy as you have showed your victims,' I told it. 'Please, Toranaga-san, please,' said the kappa. ' Let me go and I'll teach you something special.' ' What?' I asked. 'I'll teach you how to heal broken bones,' the kappa answered.

"I was amazed, but I was not going to let it know that. 'That's not good enough,' I said. 'Promise never again to kill another human. Promise to move to another pond,' I said. The kappa stopped to think, and I thought I was in for a fight. 'Yes, I promise,' it answered." Father and son were silent for a moment.

"You should know that kappas never break their promises," said Toranaga-san. "I spent a year with the kappa, and it taught me everything it knew about broken bones. I even healed a few kappa bones. But I will tell you about that another time. The kappa also promised me that among my descendants, in each generation, there would be at least one skilled bone setter, worthy enough to learn what the kappas teach.

"You and your children will pass the kappa knowledge on to future generations," said Toranaga-san. His son bowed with pride.

How Wo-usu Became Yamato-Takeru

The Emperor Keiko had 80 children. The oldest son was called Opo-usu. His brother Wo-usu was the second oldest. One day, the emperor called Opo-usu to him.

"Today I command you to bring back to me the two beautiful maidens we spoke about yesterday. I wish to make them my wives," said the emperor.

Opo-usu departed immediately. But when he saw the maidens, he was stupefied by their loveliness. Instead of obeying his father, he married them himself and did not return home.

Emperor Keiko summoned his second son, Wo-usu. "Go to the home of the two beautiful maidens and tell your brother I wish to dine with him tonight," he said. Like his brother had done, Wo-usu left the palace immediately.

For five days, the emperor hoped to see his eldest son at dinner. Yet he never appeared. On the evening of the fifth day, Emperor Keiko questioned the second son, Wo-usu.

"Why has Opo-usu not come to dine with me?" the emperor asked.

"I captured him, cut off his limbs, wrapped them in straw matting and tossed them in all directions," replied Wo-usu.

Emperor Keiko was troubled by his son's action, so he decided to send him away from Yamato. But while he was distressed over the murder of his eldest son, the emperor recognized the usefulness of Wo-usu's rage and strength. At the time, Wo-usu was still a boy.

"In the west at Kumaso on Kyushu, there live two powerful brothers. They do not pay me taxes, nor do they recognize my authority. Go to the west and punish them," said Emperor Keiko.

Wo-usu obediently accepted his father's order. Before he set out, however, he paid a visit to his aunt, Yamato-himeo. He asked her to help him protect himself against the powerful brothers he must punish. Yamato-himeo gave young Wo-usu one of her spare robes. Gratefully, Wo-usu accepted the feminine garment and put it into his pouch. He also brought with him his trusted saber, a sword with a curved blade.

When the boy arrived in the west, he found something unexpected at the home of the two powerful brothers. They were in the midst of preparing for a day of rejoicing. Guarding the house, Wo-usu saw three battalions of soldiers. It was impossible for him to gain entrance as the prince from Yamato, for the brothers would certainly distrust his intentions.

Wo-usu found a secluded spot in the woods. There, he donned his aunt's robe and stashed his own clothes in his pouch. Using a nearby pond as a mirror, he unbound his hair and combed it down in the fashion of young women of the time. Inside the robe, he hid his saber.

Presenting himself as an attractive maiden, Wo-usu easily gained entrance to the brothers' house. The brothers were very taken with the guest's lovely appearance. At the feast on the day of rejoicing, they sat the maiden between them at the head banquet table. When the guests were at the height of merrymaking, Wo-usu drew his saber from his aunt's robe. Before anyone realized what was about to happen, he grabbed one brother by his neck of his garment. Then he thrust the saber into the brother's chest and killed him.

The other brother fled the banquet hall. Wo-usu tackled him on the stairs. Piercing his behind with the saber, Wo-usu stopped the brother cold.

"Do not kill me before you say who are you, stranger," the brother cried.

"The boy prince of Yamato, son of Emperor Keiko who rules the Great Eight Islands. My father has sent me to punish you and your brother for not paying your respects nor surrendering to his greatness," responded Wo-usu.

"I see that Yamato has a man braver than my brother and myself, and that he is you. I call you Prince Yamato-takeru, Japan's warrior-hero," said the second brother.

Hearing the man's words, Yamato-takeru dug in his saber more deeply. Upon hearing the story, people told of how the boy warrior split the second powerful brother apart like a ripe melon. From that day forward, Wo-usu became known as Yamato-takeru throughout all of Japan.

On his return trip to his father's capital, Yamato-takeru engaged in numerous other battles. He decided the gods of the mountains were disrepectful. He fought against them and taught them respect. Next, he determined the gods of the rivers did not show the emperor honor. He battled them until he judged them honorable. The gods of the sea also did not revere his father properly. So, Yamato-takeru waged warfare against them until he deemed them to show proper reverence. Satisfied that the land to the west respected Emperor Keiko, the prince went home to tell his father of his adventures.

YAMATO-TAKERU AND THE BANDIT

 ven before his son's arrival from the West, the emperor proudly heard the news that Wo-usu was now called Yamato-takeru, Japan's warrior-hero. The second of the two brothers that the emperor ordered his son to kill had renamed the boy before Prince Yamato-takeru took his life. After departing from the home of the dead brothers, young Yamato-takeru taught respect for his father to the various savage deities that he encountered along the road to Yamato. Messengers also brought word of how Yamato-takeru tamed the spirits of the mountains, rivers and sea to the attention of Emperor Keiko.

With the capital at Yamato as his destination, the boy warrior-hero crossed into the Izumo Province.

"Who passes there?" demanded an argumentative voice.

Yamato-takeru did not see anyone in the nearby woods. "Who asks the question?" he answered.

"You are trespassing on my land," said the hidden owner of the unpleasant voice.

"This land is under the rulership of His Augustness the Heavenly Sovereign Emperor Keiko," responded Yamato-takeru, proudly. He did not wish to reveal that he was the emperor's son, the prince, however, until he knew the identity of the man who challenged him .

"This land belongs to the Izumo Province. I am the leader here." Menacingly, a rough-looking bandit stepped forward from behind a large-trunked oak tree.

Now Yamato-takeru was glad that he had not identified himself. Honor to his father and Yamato made it necessary to punish this bandit. He decided to pretend to gain the man's friendship. If he took a warring attitude, he would be outnumbered when the bandit called for help from his fellow bandits of Izumo.

"I beg forgiveness for insulting you on your land. Yet it was proper for me to pledge loyalty to the emperor, for you could have been one of his spies. Now that I know your importance, I ask for friendship," feigned Yamato-takeru.

"I must see to some business. When I return, we'll go fishing," said the bandit. He appeared pleased to make friends with a mere boy.

As soon as the bandit departed, the boy warrior-hero took his knife from his belt. He began to carve a sword from the wood of the oak tree. Then he hid the wooden weapon inside his garment. When the bandit returned, Yamato-takeru was waiting on the banks of the River Hi.

"Good. Let's catch some fish," the bandit said.

He removed his sword and laid it on the riverbank. He handed the young stranger a fishing pole and cast a line from his own pole into the water. The afternoon passed, and Yamato-takeru convinced the bandit by his camaraderie that he was a friendly stranger.

"Let's go swimming. I'm too hot sitting here," said the bandit late in the afternoon. Yamato-takeru agreed that swimming was a good idea.

Both men disrobed, and they put their clothing in piles under the trees. The bandit dove into the water. He swam fiercely, seeming to enjoy showing off how strong he was for the sake of his young companion. He was a good distance across the lake, and Yamato-takeru had not gotten his feet wet. Stealthily, the boy rushed over to the bandit's belongings, removed the villain's sword from its scabbard and inserted the wooden one he had made from the oak tree. Hiding his opponent's sword under his own clothing, he entered the river and began to swim.

The sun was low in the sky when they stopped swimming. They dried themselves in the still-warm air, then got dressed. Both men girded their swords. The bandit invited the boy stranger to return with him to his cave for dinner.

"I cannot accept your hospitality. I am in truth your enemy, the son of His Augustness the Heavenly Sovereign Emperor Keiko, the warrior-hero Prince," responded Yamato-takeru.

"Ha! I will cut you in half with my mighty sword," shouted the bandit.

"While I do not accept your hospitality, I do accept the challenge," Yamato-takeru answered.

Without hesitation, the bandit went to unsheath his sword. The clumsy, wooden imitation became stuck in its scabbard. The bandit cursed the emperor and his son as he struggled to remove it. He vowed never to pledge loyalty to Yamato. He swore that the emperor was a demon and that the entire royal, august family were imposters. How dare they claim to have Heaven's blessing to rule the land?

Yamato-takeru had heard enough. He lifted his weapon high. With a single swing of his sword, he took off the bandit's head.

THE DEATH OF YAMATO-TAKERU

In the capital, the Emperor Keiko greeted Yamato-takeru after his adventures in the West.

"Welcome, my son. I send you now to the twelve roads of the East. Teach obedience to the Ainus," said the emperor.

Yamato-takeru wished to rest from his former travels before he set out once more. He knew well of the fierce reputation of the Ainu people to the East. Yet he could not disobey His Augustness the Heavenly Sovereign, his father. He bid the emperor a hasty farewell and went to see his aunt, Yamato-hime.

"August aunt, I fear the Heavenly Sovereign, my father, wishes to see me dead. I no sooner return from doing his bidding than he has sent me to go against the fearsome Ainus in the East," said Yamato-takeru. Though he was a warrior-hero, he faced great danger. He was not yet a man, and tears spilled from his eyes.

Her Augustness Yamato-hime was fond of her nephew. For protection, she gave him a mighty sword. It had belonged to Susano. The Storm-god took possession of an eight-headed dragon's sword after he killed the beast. Yamato-hime also presented her nephew with a magic bag. She told him not to open it unless he faced an emergency. Gratefully, the young warrior-hero accepted the gifts and took his leave for the East.

The Ainus were as fierce a people as he had expected. Yamato-takeru wielded his sword and slew many of them. Seeing the power of their opponent, the barbarians pretended to surrender. As a peace offering, they invited the prince to go hunting with them. When he agreed, they led him to a broad plain. Then they fled into the wilderness, leaving him alone.

The chief Ainu set fire to the brush surrounding Yamato-takeru. The blaze spread rapidly with the boy warrior-hero in its midst. Remembering the magic bag from his aunt, he opened it. Finding a magical fire striker inside, he made a second blaze that swallowed the first one and drove itself back toward the Ainus as a larger, fiercer fire. Yamato-takeru cut down the fiery bushes that lingered around him with his splendid sword. Since that day, the people of Japan have called the sword Kusanagi, because it was a "Grass-Mower" against the barbarians' fire.

Continuing his travels, the prince now faced the Ashigara Pass. At the foot of the pass, he sat down to eat. The deity of the pass tranformed himself into a white deer, and the deer's presence surprised Yamato-takeru. The prince plucked a sprig of wild chive and threw it. Hitting the deer in the eye, the chive killed the animal. While it was his obligation to the emperor to teach the mountain spirits respect, he had done an unthinkable deed by killing the deer.

He crossed into the land of Shinanu and made peace with the deity of the Shinanu pass. In the land of Wohari, Yamato-takeru came upon the house of Princess Miyazu and his spirits lifted. The prince and princess had met on another occasion, and Yamato-takeru swore to marry her after he conquered all of the peoples of the twelve roads of the East. At the dinner banquet, Princess Miyazu lifted a cup in a toast to the prince. After they drank, she gave Yamato-takeru the cup to prove her love. Traveling as a warrior, he had nothing of value to give in return but the Kusanagi sword. With great ceremony, he presented it to the princess.

The following morning, with a promise to return, he bid her farewell. He set off for Mount Ibuki to tame the deity of evil breath, who had a bad influence on people and events. As he climbed the steep mountain, he made a vow.

"I will overpower the deity with my empty hands," he shouted.

Up the side of the mountain, Yamato-takeru rose. During the ascent, he ducked out of the path of a white boar. The animal was as large as a bull. He thought that the boar was a messenger from the deity of evil breath, so he continued to climb without a word to the animal. He promised himself that he would kill the white boar on his descent from the mountaintop after he had demanded respect from the foul deity himself. But the boar was the very deity that the prince sought to convince. Angry at Yamato-takeru's boastful words that he would fight him with his bare hands, the deity caused a chill rain. Then biting hail began to fall. Despite the storm, the prince climbed to the mountain's peak. Though he called out to the evil-breathed spirit, the deity did not appear.

The disappointed and rain-soaked warrior-hero began the climb down the mountain. Coming upon a fresh spring, he stopped to rest. The spring was called Wisame, which meant "rest." He drank from the water and felt refreshed.

But as he continued to descend, he felt the energy drain from his body. Finally, he came to the bottom of the mountain. Exhausted, he crossed the moor of Tagi near the River Yoro. How could he be so weak, he wondered. Still, he went on and came to Cape Wotsu in Ise. He found the sword he had hidden in a pine tree and sang a song of thanks to the tree.

The prince longed to be home in Yamato, and he sang to the white clouds that danced over Mount Awogaki. In his heart, he doubted he would ever see Yamato again. Now he sang his last song. It was in honor of the Kasanagi sword that he had left in the hands of the princess. If only he had kept it, he would not have suffered from the evil enchantment of the white boar. When he finished the sad song, Yamato-takeru dropped to the ground on the plain of Nobo and died.

He changed into a white bird, a sandpiper. It flew toward the beach, and from Ise to Shiki to the land of Kafuchi. Soaring over Yamato, the large, white bird departed for Heaven.

YORIMITSU AND THE DRUNKARD BOY'S HEAD

oung women were disappearing in the city of Miyako. First one maiden disappeared. The following day, another maiden was missing. The day after that, still another young woman was gone. Each day, the city awoke to the cries of the villagers. In cottage after cottage, the villagers suffered from the disappearances. No matter what precautions they took, they could not protect the young women in their midst. They tried barricading doors. In the mornings, the doors remained barricaded. Nonetheless, another young woman was mysteriously gone from one of the cottages. Even if everyone in the household tried as hard as they could to stay awake, in the morning they were all asleep and another maiden was gone.

Finally, the cause was discovered. A priests from the temple was asked to pray in the cottage of a villager who wished to protect his young daughter. In the dark of night as the priest was meditating, he saw the criminals. A band of invisible, giant devils, or oni, dressed all in red, burst through the walls of the cottage as though they were made of air. Their leader, the ugliest of the band, snatched the maiden while her father slept. It happened so fast that the priest could do nothing to stop them.

Yorimitsu was an early leader of the Minamoto clan. After hearing the priest's story, Yorimitsu summoned Tsuna and his other three lieutenants. "We must go to battle against the Drunkard Boy immediately," he said.

Tsuna had succeeded in vanquishing a demon on a different occasion. He had cut off the oni's arms. So the heroes suspected that this band of oni were no more invincible than the one that Tsuna had beaten.

The Drunkard Boy and his troop of oni lived in a cave hideout deep in the mountains. Like all oni, they could make themselves invisible whenever they chose. Only priests could see through their trickery.

Yorimitsu and the four lieutenants disguised themselves as wandering priests. Under their robes, they wore their swords and armor. For days, they scoured the mountain region until they found what they knew was the oni cave. They recognized the repulsive odor of the demons' belches. Everyone alive who had ever had a run-in with an oni knew the disgusting smell. The undigested vapors of the human blood upon which the vampire oni fed created the stench.

The oni guard received the wanderers hospitably. Believing they were priests who could see him no matter what he did, he did not bother to make himself invisible. As the demon led the way through the cave's entrance tunnel, the visitors were met by a mysterious man. He offered them a magical potion which Yorimitsu accepted. Into the main chamber, the guard brought the priests. Yorimitsu presented the potion to the leader of the band, the Drunkard Boy, as a gift. Sniffing it rudely, the giant oni snorted his approval, judging the drink to be stronger even than sake, the rice wine that never quite made the oni drunk enough.

The Drunkard Boy took a giant gulp. While the oni band passed the magical potion from one to another of their members, Yorimitsu began to sing. Drunkard Boy snorted approval of the song, and the heroes started to dance, too. Before long, the oni leader and his fellow demons were quite intoxicated.

The warriors tore off their priestly robes. They drew their swords and raised them high over their heads before the drunken oni could respond. In fact, the band of oni were confused by the what they witnessed. The drink had numbed their small brains.

Then something clicked for them, and the demons realized they had to fight. But the warriors had gained the advantage. They were able to move more quickly than the intoxicated, giant demons. The battle was fierce as the oni tried to defend themselves, for they were much stronger than the men. The grunts were enormous, and the very rock of the cave's walls began to crack. Then Yorimitsu thrust his sword forward and cut off Drunkard Boy's head.

The spirit of Drunkard Boy sobered as it rose to the ceiling of the cave. The severed head swept down toward Yorimitsu in an attempt to attack. But the mysterious man reappeared for a moment before he vanished again, and the giant oni head fell at Yorimitsu's feet. The hero looked around the hall to find the other oni dead and his lieutenants unharmed.

The Minamoto heroes searched the hideout until they found a chamber deep inside the cave where the oni had locked up the stolen women. There were cries of gratitude as the maidens became free. The cries were overshadowed by the rejoicing in Miyako when the villagers were greeted by the stolen maidens in procession with Yorimitsu and his lieutenants.

THE FOUR-LOYALTIES

Once upon a time when the Son of Heaven was Emperor Goshirakawa, a dispute occurred in Japan. General Kiyomori was the leader of the powerful Taira clan. He had two sons. A favorite of the emperor was Narichika, who was a kinsman of Kiyomori but from a different clan.

"Noble emperor, I wish an audience," said General Kiyomori one day. The emperor told him to speak what was on his mind. "I have fought many battles, and now there is peace in the land. While I vow to defend you and Japan always, I wish now to have retirement. I want to live in the mountains as a priest and spend my hours in meditation," Kiyomori said.

Emperor Goshirakawa gave Kiyomori his blessing to retire. He told him he would retain the title of general. Kiyomori began to spend his days in quiet prayer. More than any other thing, Kiyomori's kinsman Narichika desired the position of commander in the army. Hearing of Kiyomori's retirement, he began to spread the word around the city of his intention to request an audience with the emperor.

Word of Narichika's activity reached Kiyomori's ears in his mountain retreat. Kiyomori had planned to approach the emperor himself at a future date to request the position of commander for his son Munemori. If Narichika were to be commander, the status of the Taira clan in the army would be weakened. No, Munemori must be appointed commander, resolved Kiyomori.

He set out immediately for the palace. He visited the emperor and respectfully warned him that if Narichika were to be commander, the long period of peace in the country would turn to civil war. Peace would only remain if the Taira were the ruling clan. If Narichika had any power, he would want more and more positions for his own clan. Emperor Goshirakawa listened to the general's argument, but he was not moved to appoint Kiyomori's son Munemori instead of Narichika.

When Narichika came the next day, the emperor appointed him commander instead. Although Emperor Goshirakawa was grateful to Kiyomori, he secretly wished to see him overthrown by Narichika. He wanted to humble the powerful Lord Kiyomori.

After his appointment as commander, Narichika became power-hungry. He arranged a secret gathering to make plans to overthrow Kiyomori and the Taira clan. He invited his son Naritsune, the elderly priest Shunkan, a friend of Shunkan's and the official Yasuyori. The night of the meeting, all five participants arrived separately in order not to attract attention. They wore dark outer robes, and they walked softly and without a word. They met at the priest's country house in Shishi ga Tani.

As they made their plans, they drank wine. Narichika asked for a refill. He held out his cup to Shunkan, the host. The porcelain that held the wine had a head carved at the top. When Shunkan lifted the jar to fill Narichika's cup, the head fell off the jar. Everyone was silent until Shunkan announced, "It is an omen. The heads of the Taira clan will fall off as well." The others drank more wine to toast the omen.

One of the five men at the meeting, however, had very little wine. He was the friend of Shunkan, the priest. He was also a follower of Kiyomori. When everyone else had passed out from intoxication, the man fled the house and hurried to the mountains to tell Kiyomori of the plans against him. Kiyomori's two sons, Munemori and the elder Shigemori, listened, too.

"We must break into the palace and kidnap the emperor. He is also part of the conspiracy against us. Then we will fight the traitor Narichika," announced Kiyomori. His armor showed itself through an opening in his priest's robes.

"I will gather one thousand warriors and go to the palace at once," said his son Munemori.

"Be sure to be courteous to the emperor, and do not violate his safety. With respect to Narichika and his followers, off with their heads!" said Kiyomori.

The elder son Shigemori looked concerned. "Father, it is improper to violate the home of Emperor Goshirakawa. You cannot do this," he said.

"Where is your valor. Have a woman's heart?" snapped his brother, Munemori.

"Where is your heart? You speak only from anger. And so do you, father. Where is your patience and wisdom? Are you not a priest these days?" answered Shigemori.

Munemori dropped his sword and lowered his head. But the eyes of Kiyomori, the father, flamed with anger. How could he allow the emperor and Narichika to conspire against him and his clan. Had not the Taira clan under his leadership brought peace to the land?

"Father, forgive the disrepect of my words to you. But we Japanese are dedicated to four loyalties: to God, country, family and man. The emperor is son of the divine Goddess and is, therefore, God on earth. He and our country are the same, too. If you hold to your plan, I must fight against you to protect the emperor," said Shigemori.

Kiyomori reflected upon his son's words. Then he spoke. "You are correct, my son. Go to the emperor and inform him of the meeting of the traitors. Advise him to send Narichika and his followers into exile. If they are out of the country, they cannot do any harm," he said.

The emperor heeded Shigemori's counsel. He exiled Narichika's son Naritsune, the official Yasuyori and Shunkan the priest to a distant, unfriendly island. Narichika fared better. The emperor sent him to Bizen, an isolated area on mainland Japan.

THE POEM FROM THE SEA

asuyori the official, Naritsune, son of Narichika, and Shunkan the priest were accused of treason. Their crime was that they met in secret with Naritsune's father and plotted to overthrow Kiyomori, the emperor's general. So Emperor Goshirakawa sent them to a desolate island. Yasuyori and Naritsune were young men. Shunkan was much older.

On the sea journey, the three men were imprisoned in the dark dungeon of the ship. Chains tugged at their wrists and ankles every time the boat rolled on the ocean's waves. One piece of bread and a single cup of water were their daily rations. They were starving, thirsty and delirious from pain when the ships' guards dragged them to the deck, unchained them, and threw them into the shallow water near the island. Their eyes were unaccustomed to the light of the sun, and they had not used their legs for many days.

Still, they plodded through the shallows and up onto the island's shore without even turning around to see the ship depart. In their dirty kimonos, they fell into a deep, troubled sleep. When they awoke to the throbbing of their bruised and bloody wrists and ankles, they looked about them at their new home.

Not a single tree, no grass, nothing green existed there. Parched, sandy earth led to horribly yellow rocks and boulders. Steam rose around the boulders. The air held the foul smell of sulphur. They closed their eyes and went back to sleep.

The next day, the three exiles were strong enough to explore the island. Ouch! Sulphur springs burned their feet. Some of the sand was too hot to walk upon. What a place this was! They were starving and thirsty. Watching where they walked, they plucked the puny herbs that grew around the rocks and ate them. They caught fish with their hands and were forced to drink the water of the sea. Their thirst was never quenched.

At nightfall, the island was worse than during the day. The sulphur gas from the springs cast a green glow over the water. The ocean looked like a living nightmare.

Every new day, the three men looked for a ship to arrive. They hoped that the emperor had pardoned them. But no ship came with the pardon. In time, the two younger men, Naritsune and Yasuyori, repented their wrongdoing.

"The emperor acted correctly in banishing us," Naritsune said.

"I was too young to stand up to your father and denounce his plan," said Yasuyori. Naritsune said that he, too, had been too young to fully understand.

The older Shunkan disagreed vehemently. "I will avenge myself on Kiyomori and his clan for bringing this upon us," he swore. Nothing the younger men could say about how they had brought the punishment upon themselves could change his mind. Day after day, Shunkan became more and more angry. He took to shouting to himself about revenge, and the other men left him to wander the island alone, swearing and cursing against Kiyomori and the emperor's decision.

The official Yasuyori was the only child of a widowed mother. After the emperor's decree of banishment, he had not had the opportunity to say good-bye to her. With each day, he grew more sad and guilty. He wished he could tell her of his well-being and whereabouts.

"Why don't you write to her?" asked Naritsune.

Yasuyori embraced the idea and set out to look for wood upon which to write a poem to his mother. It took many days for him to find pieces of driftwood at the water's edge. Finally, he had enough wood for his message. He sewed the pieces together with seaweed. Then he sat upon the yellow, sulphurous rock and began to carve his poem into the wood. He told his mother about the awful island and how he lived. He left out nothing. It was as though the words wrote themselves. Then he pushed the plank into the waves and prayed that somehow his mother would receive his message.

A priest praying at the shrine of Akima on the water's edge noticed something bobbing in the water. He dug the plank out of the waves and read it. Through fortune, he recognized the names of Yasuyori and his mother, for he had been an acquaintance of Yasuyori's father. He hurried to visit the exiled youth's mother, and he presented the poem with tears in his eyes. The old woman wept and wept.

"If only the emperor would pardon my son," she cried.

The priest offered to take the poem and present it to the emperor. The old woman was most grateful and wrapped the wooden plank in a silk scarf. Fortunately, the emperor granted the priest an audience. After reading the woeful poem, he was moved greatly by the young man's situation and his dedication to his mother. He called for Lord Kiyomori. When his general appeared, the emperor said he would like to pardon the three exiles.

"My counsel, Son of Heaven, is that you pardon the two younger men. As for Shunkan, if he returns with revenge, he is likely to convince the other priests to fight on his side. In that event, we will be at war once again," answered Kiyomori. The king accepted the advice and wrote a letter of pardon for Yasuyori and Naritsune.

Upon their island, the three exiles could not believe their eyes when the distant white speck that approached proved to be the sail of a ship. They hurried to the water's edge. A messenger waded through the shallow water and held out the emperor's decree. The exiles soon learned that only two of them had been pardoned. Immediately, Shunkan resumed his curses against Kiyomori.

The astonished, disheveled and emaciated Yasuyori and Naritsune hurried to follow the messenger through the shallow water to his ship. They pleaded with him to bring Shunkan back with them, too. But the messenger refused. They promised the old priest they would implore the emperor upon their return to pardon him also. In despair, Shunkan could do nothing but curse Kiyomori and shout out his own innocence.

BENKEI AND YOSHITSUNE

his is the story of two heroes who became close friends. It is also a story about the tengu, the goblins of the Japanese mountains. They appeared suddenly and vanished at will, just as quickly. They had great powers. Flying was one of them. People said they looked like great kites. Shifting their appearance to something new whenever they chose was another tengu trait. If they decided to be present, their appearance was accompanied by great noise. Tengu demons loved to kidnap young monks and teach them discipline. However, they were friendly to the two heroes of this story, Benkei and Yoshitsune.

The story begins with Benkei. Benkei's mother Benkichi was the daughter of a samurai warrior. When she was eighteen, Benkichi traveled to Nagami where she fell in love with a tengu. After thirteen months, four months longer than the typical pregnancy for human babies, she gave birth to Benkei. The unusually tall boy was born with long hair and all of his teeth. Mother and son lived on the island of Benkeijima off the Nohara coast.

But Benkei caused his mother heartache, because he liked nothing better than to fight. When he was still a child, Benkichi abandoned her son on the island and returned to the home of her father. Stronger than his years and taller than a grown man, the child Benkei set to work. Carrying sand in his sleeves and inside the skirt of his clothing, he deposited piles of it again and again in the water until he made a path that joined the island with the mainland.

So Benkei, too, left the island behind and set out for the mainland. The monks at the monastery of Mount Hiei took in the warlike tengu youth, and for several years Benkei was known as the warrior monk. His reputation for combat grew in the region, and Benkei collected a host of swords from the warriors he vanquished. One day, he became bored because he had beaten every warrior around. Benkei traveled to Miyako for more adventure. By now, he was ten feet tall.

A youth named Ushiwaka of the Minamoto clan resided in the monastery at Kurama mountain in northern Miyako. During the second civil war, the chief of the Tairas spared the lives of Ushiwaka and his brothers. Now Ushiwaka was a page to the abbot at the monastery. Like Benkei, he, too, was a warlike child. He could think of nothing but taking revenge upon the Tairas for defeating his clan.

Every evening, Ushiwaka left the monastery and went deep into the mountain woods with his wooden sword. Night after night, he battled the trees with his weapon. Sojo-bo, the chief tengu of the mountain, became impressed with the youth's determination and increasing skill. One evening, he decided to appear to Ushiwaka. The sound of falling trees startled the young man. Before him stood a giant, birdlike demon with a long nose, deep red face and scarlet robes. Sojo-bo carried a fan of feathers in his right hand.

"Why do you do battle with the trees every night?" the chief tengu asked.

"I seek to avenge the death of my clansmen," Ushiwaka answered.

"Your ambition is admirable. I offer you my retainers, the Leaflet Tengus, as teachers in swordsmanship," said Sojo-bo.

Now every evening the Leaflet Tengus taught Ushiwaka how to jump and leap while wielding his sword. Again, Sojo-bo approved of the boy's skill. The chief tengu completed Ushikawa's education by teaching him strategy and tactics, as well as secrets from the supernatural world. He even gave Ushikawa a scroll upon which the secrets were written.

Despite the gifts of the tengu, Ushikawa prayed to the goddess of mercy, Kwannon, for protection and guidance. Now every evening, he visited her temple in Kiyomizu in the southeastern region of Miyako. Wishing to disguise himself against the detection of any Tairas in the area, he wore a veil of thin silk over his face.

The tengu monk Benkei, who was visiting Miyako, heard stories of the veiled figure. He decided to discover for himself whether this figure was human or supernatural. One evening, armed with a variety of weapons, he took his position in the middle of the bridge of Gojo over the river Kamo. It was the same bridge the veiled figure crossed each night. Hearing the sound of lacquered clogs upon the bridge's planks, he faced the unknown figure.

"Stop! State your name," Benkei demanded. He drew his sword.

But Ushiwaka paid no attention. When Benkei raised his sword to strike a blow to the stranger, Ushikawa parried. He stepped aside. Then he struck Benkei with his sword, knocking the tengu's sword right out of his grip. Benkei reached for his iron rod, threateningly. But Ushikawa, as the Leaflet Tengu had taught him, leaped like a bird about the aggressor.

Benkei knelt before the mysterious figure and asked his forgiveness. Nodding agreement, Ushikawa withdrew the silk veil from his face. Benkei offered his services as a retainer, and Ushikawa accepted. From that day, the tengu warrior-monk was his captain. From that day, too, Ushikawa called himself Yoshitsune. Together Yoshitsune and his captain Benkei fought many battles against the Taira clan.

THE BATTLE OF ICHI-NO-TANI

unemori was the leader of the Taira clan. His enemy Yoshitsune was the head of the Minamoto clan. Munemori and the Taira controlled the capital of Japan, where the emperor lived. Gaining more and more support in the provinces, Yoshitsune advanced upon the capital. He intended to lead his warriors into battle and win the city for the Minamoto clan. Hearing of his enemy's superior strength, Munemori was unwilling to fight a battle he could not win. So he led his followers to his father's fortress near the valley of Ichi-no-Tani. There he decided to wait for more Taira troops to join him. In the meantime, his warriors would rest and regain their spirit.

A steep mountain with a sheer, flat face buttressed the Taira fortress from behind. The fortress had been built in this way so that no enemy could attack from the rear. At the front of the fortress and across a flat plain, lay the sea. The guards on the towers could see any movement from this direction of the water. Small hills on both sides made it difficult for an enemy to stage a surprise attack from the left or right. Munemori felt secure in the capital, particularly after more Taira troops arrived later that day to help him against Yoshitsune.

Yoshitsune was a smart warrior, too. He had set up camp in the valley, just beyond the fortress. When Munemori learned of the enemy camp, he reasoned that the Minamoto would not attack until morning.

"Let us surprise Munemori and the Taira from behind," he said to his captain, Benkei.

"My lord, the mountains run to the ground like your golden screen to the carpet. No one, man nor beast, will be able to descend them," Benkei replied, respectfully.

But Yoshitsune was obstinate. "Search for someone who knows these mountains and bring this person to me," he ordered his old friend.

Benkei left immediately to find someone with the knowledge Yoshitsune required. Night was falling more deeply now. He scoured the countryside, talking to people in every cottage along the way. They suggested he seek out the one person who knew the mountains best. Everyone gave him the same suggestion. Finally, Benkei found the person everyone recommended. He was a little boy. Soon the Minamoto captain and the little boy from the mountains stood before the hero Yoshitsune.

"Tell me if it is possible for horses to descend these mountains," Yoshitsune asked the boy.

"No, my lord, I have seen only deer on the steep cliffs," the boy answered.

"Son, if deer descend the mountain, is it not at least possible that horses can do it, too?" Yoshitsune questioned.

"I suppose it is possible," the boy agreed.

His answer was all that Yoshitsune needed. He asked the boy to remain to guide them to the top of the cliffs. Benkei roused the warriors to battle. Soon the Minamoto army was assembled horseback on the high ledges.

Yoshitsune told them to wrap the horses' feet in the cloth he had brought. He instructed them not to let a whisper pass their lips. The attack would require absolute silence.

At last, the horses' feet were wrapped. No one had spoken a word. The only sound that Yoshitsune heard was the breath of his own horse. At the very window of dawn, when the slightest red colored the clouds at the horizon, he gave the command. Lying so flat on his horse's back that the animal's tail tickled his ears and the horse's head was pulled as tautly upward as possible, he started to descend. Benkei and the other warriors followed. Many fell as their steeds lost footing, but a good number were able to manage the perilous ride to the bottom. What a surprise to Munemori and the Taira troops in the fortress when the enemy torches showed themselves on the roof!

The battle was fast, and the enemies fought one other fiercely. The Taira were unable to fend off the attack. Munemori had to flee in order to protect the lives of the emperor's son and his own family members. Many Taira surrendered to the Minamoto army.

One Taira warrior, a young nobleman who was only 16 years old, remained to do battle single-handedly against the Minamoto enemy. His name was Atsumori. He was the last Taira in the fortress. Finally, he recognized that it was futile not to retreat, and he rode as quickly as possible to the sea. Unfortunately, the last Taira ship had already departed.

The Minamoto general Kamagai had pursued the fleeing Taira warrior. He dismounted on the shore and unsheathed his sword. The unsuspecting Atsumori was not ready to defend himself.

"I have no fear of dying. Go ahead and take my head," said Atsumori.

When General Kamagai removed his enemy's helmet, he found himself staring into the brave eyes of a youth. He heard the rhythm of horse hooves in the near distance and knew several of his clansmen were approaching.

"How can I kill one so young and noble? Yet if I do not take your life, I will dishononor my clan and lose my own life. Know this, brave Atsumori, from this day forward I renounce the path of a warrior. Today I vow to become a priest." With that promise on his lips, the Minamoto general cut off Atsumori's head.

He wrapped it with affection in a clean cloth and tied the cloth to his saddle. Mounting his horse, he rode away. He spent the proper time in meditation before he shaved his head and undertook the life of prayer. With every day that dawned, Kumagai prayed for the soul of the young Atsumori.

THE END OF THE TAIRA CLAN

our years had passed since the death of Kiyomori, the great leader of the Taira clan. Lady Nii, his wife, had become a nun, preferring peace over the doings of the outer world. Kiyomori's son Munemori was leader of the Taira now. He was also responsible for the care of the child emperor Antoku.

Munemori faced the most important event of his life. Outnumbered by the enemy, Yoshitsune and the Munamoto clan, the Taira clan was obliged to fight the enemy to the death in a final battle. Munemori had to lead like a hero. If he inspired his heartsick clansmen to victory, he and the Taira would be heroes throughout history. Even if he and the Taira lost the battle but fought bravely, they would be praised forever for their valiant efforts.

On Munemori's instructions, scouts spread the word over the mountains and plains of Japan. They summoned the scattered Taira warriors to join their leader in the fateful battle. Munemori's ships would sail in two days from the eastern coast.

"Get word to Lady Nii in the temple. Ask her to care for the young Emperor while I fight. If she agrees to re-enter the world, she and her attending maids will sail with the child. Their ship will join our fleet," Munemori commanded his messengers.

The day of departure arrived. The sea was calm, and the wind was encouraging. The eyes of the young Emperor showed his excitement over taking a sea voyage. Lady Nii and her ladies tried not to reflect their concern. Munemori and the Taira were somber, yet their fighting spirit had returned. One of the warriors began a war chant, and the others roared along with him.

The fleet's flags and colorful pennants flew proudly. The ships set sail for the coast of Kyushu, to the southwest. Munemori chose this course, because he received word that the High Priest of the Kumano Temple was going to join forces with the Taira off Kyushu.

They sailed for weeks. Finally, Kyushu was sighted one fine spring morning. They entered the narrow straits of Shimonoseki, and Munemori scoured the shore for a place to land. It was here that he wished to build a fortress and wait for the High Priest's troops. How could it be? Everywhere Munemori looked, he saw the Munamoto forces of his arch-rival Yoshitsune. He lost all hopes of erecting a fortress, and his fleet was forced to stay afloat.

To make matters even more desperate, Munemori learned that the High Priest and his troops had become disheartened by the Taira predicament. They joined forces with Yoshitsune and the Munamoto clan. The Munamoto were stronger by far on land than the Taira. In the sea, Yoshitsune was more powerful. He commanded one thousand ships, twice as many as Munemori. The Taira leader's spirit floundered, and he began to doubt the possibility of victory. When his men started cheering, Munemori looked around to find the cause. His young cousin Noritsune was standing upon the gunwale of his ship, the upper edge of the side.

"We know our enemy Yoshitsune is called 'the bird.' True, he has earned a reputation for leaping. I will leap for the honor of the Taira. I will leap to Eternity if this is what it takes. Yet before I die, I will leap into the waves with Yoshitsune and take him with me to Eternity," shouted Noritsune.

Yositsune, in the meantime, had commanded his smallest, fastest ships to sail within the Taira fleet. Arrows pelted the decks of Munemori's ships, and many Taira fell. The small ships rammed the hulls of the large ones, and fires broke out. In no time at all, the sea was red with blood. Smoke darkened the blue, springtime sky. Injured Taira clung in the water to broken pieces of wood from their ships.

"Your Majesty, we must take a journey now," said Lady Nii to the young emperor Antoku. She dressed him in his ceremonial robes and herself in the black gown of mourning. Her attending maids changed into their most decorative kimonos.

"Secure the child to me," Lady Nii said to the maids. Taking the sacred sword and sacred jewel, the two royal emblems, in her hand, she walked to the gunwale and stood upon it as Noritsune had done on his ship.

Lady Nii spoke to the child Emperor. "Your Majesty, we go now to the place of everlasting peace where you will have respect. First, let us turn to the east and honor the Guardian Deity. Now turn west to honor Lord Buddha." When they had done these things, Lady Nii jumped into the sea with the Emperor and his royal emblems.

Noritsune saw what happened. Sorrow changed to valor in his veins. He jumped down to a small rowboat and advanced upon Yoshitsune's ship. He hoisted himself upon the deck, his sword drawn. The Minamoto warriors to both sides of their general fell back, and Noritsune faced the enemy Yoshitsune.

"Defend yourself," shouted Noritsune.

But Yoshitsune snickered at what he took to be Noritsune's madness.

With great leaps, he hurled himself from ship to ship until he reached his cheering forces on the shore. Yoshitsune's men advanced upon Noritsune, yet he was able to win against every one of them. One Minamoto warrior remained. Noritsune grabbed the man around the waist from the back. He jumped to the gunwale with him still in his grasp.

"The Taira are defeated, this is true. But you will enter Eternity with me," he shouted. Then he jumped overboard with his enemy in his grip. As Lady Nii and the Emperor had done, they, too, drowned in the depths of the sea.

Munemori's younger brother Tomomori gave the command to attack. Every Taira warrior fought to the death except one. The coward was Munemori. Jumping into the sea, he began to swim in the hopes of escaping. The Munamoto captured him and brought him to the deck of one of their ships. Days later, they cut off his head.

This battle marked the end of the Taira clan of the great Kiyomori. Their defeat inspired the poets to sing the clan's glory. Only one man was not a hero. He was Munemori, who had faced the most important event of his life.

HOICHI, THE EARLESS

oichi was a poor priest. Born blind, he was a skilled player of the biwa, a pear-shaped string instrument he plucked with a pick. Hoichi lived in the Amidaji Temple, located in Shimonoseki on the southwestern tip of Honshu. The temple had been built to honor the spirits of the Taira, or Heike clan as they were also known. They were the warriors who died in battle against their Minamoto enemies in the Straits of Shimonoseki. In the same battle, the young emperor also died.

Hoichi was renowned for telling stories about the clan and the emperor to the music of his biwa. People often visited the temple to hear him sing and play. Usually the chief priest of the Amidaji Temple and his attendants listened when visitors came. They never heard enough of Hoichi's tales. One night, however, while they were out, a visitor arrived unexpectedly.

The footsteps of the visitor caught Hoichi's attention. Though he did not recognize the person's walk, the blind priest identified him as a samurai warrior. He knew the sounds of armor and the clacking of the sword that grew louder as the stranger approached.

"I ask your pardon, Hoichi, for disturbing your playing," said the samurai.

"Who are you? Why have you come?" Hoichi responded.

"I come on the orders of the visiting daimyo to whom I have sworn my loyalty. He has heard of how beautifully you tell the Heike Monogatari, especially the story of the last battle. He wants you to accompany me to where he is staying and sing," the samurai said.

How flattered Hoichi was that word of his playing had traveled so far. Eagerly, he agreed to honor the request. He rose with his biwa under his arm, and the two men set out as soon as Hoichi donned his shoes.

As the samurai led him, Hoichi was unable to identify the route. Finally, they entered a large gate. A woman met them and guided Hoichi to a seat. She invited him to begin the song. When Hoichi finished playing, he was greeted by the applause of many people. He was pleased to have entertained them so well. The woman accompanied Hoichi and the samurai as far as the gate. She invited the blind priest to return to sing every evening during the daimyo's week-long stay. She also asked him to keep the events of the evening a secret, explaining how the daimyo wished to keep private his visit to the area. Hoichi agreed to do both things.

The next night, the samurai came to the temple for Hoichi. Neither the chief priest nor the attendants noticed the warrior's arrival nor his departure with their blind priest. But, later that evening, one of the attendants came to Hoichi's room. It was empty, which was unusual, so the attendant notified the chief priest. The following morning, the chief priest asked Hoichi where he had been. Since he made a promise not to disclose where he went, Hoichi made up a hasty excuse. The chief priest was suspicious, for it was unlike Hoichi to be evasive.

On the third night, rain pelted the roof of the temple. The wind hurled around the walls. Still, the samurai came for Hoichi. Again, the arrival and departure went undetected by the chief priest and the attendants. Once more, the attendant discovered Hoichi's room to be empty. The chief priest and the attendants began an immediate search of the neighborhood for their blind priest.

When they came to the temple cemetary, they found Hoichi seated upon the memorial stone in honor of the Emperor Antoku. He was the young emperor who drowned in the straits during the deadly battle between the clans. Playing his biwa and singing, Hoichi was oblivious to the familiar cemetary and to the stone upon which he sat. Ghostly lights surrounded him. The attendants reached for his arms to lead him back to the temple. After a struggle, Hoichi followed. When they explained to him where he was found, he was very surprised to realize that the spirits had tricked him.

"Wrap his body in the words of Buddha's teachings as protection. Cover him from the soles of his feet to the top of his head," said the chief priest. The attendants did as the chief priest directed.

On the fourth night, when the samurai arrived, he found Hoichi deep in prayer. When he spoke, the blind priest did not answer. Then the samurai noticed the words covering Hoichi's body. He saw something else curious, too.

"They have forgotten to cover your ears. Though you do not hear me through your meditation, your ears are not protected. I must take them to my daimyo to prove that I have obeyed his orders," shouted the samurai.

So the samurai raised his sword and cut off Hoichi's ears. He put them into his pouch and he departed. When the chief priest and attendants discovered the earless Hoichi, they nursed his wounds. In a short time, Hoichi recovered. But from that day forward, he was called Hoichi, the Earless.

PEACH BOY
AND THE ONI

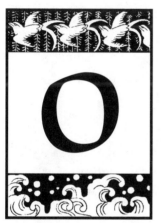nce upon a time in the mountains of Japan, there lived an old woodcutter and his wife. They wanted children, but no child was born to them. Each morning, the woodcutter climbed the mountain to chop wood, and the old woman walked down to the river with a basketful of clothes to wash. All day, they thought about what it would be like to have a child.

"What's that big thing floating in the river?" the old woman asked outloud, though no one was around. Sure enough, a large peach was riding the ripples downstream. Pushing her basket away to give herself more room, the old woman took a stick and guided the large peach toward her.

She had never seen anything like it. It was huge, the hugest peach in the world, she thought. She steadied her feet on the riverbank, and leaned forward to grab the peach. Luckily she was strong and could carry heavy bundles, because this peach was heavy. Still, she managed to lift the enormous, plump fruit, and she lay it on the soft grass.

Fortunately, her basket was strong, too. Propping it on its side, she was able to roll the peach into it. Then she began to tug. She tugged and pulled her peach along the dirt path and up the hill all the way to the cottage.

"What have you found, wife?" the woodcutter asked.

"The largest peach in the world," she responded with certainty.

"What will we do with it?" he asked.

"Why, we'll cut it open and eat it," she answered.

Returning from the kitchen with a carving knife, the old woman was ready to cut. Just as the point was about to pierce the peach, the old couple heard a human voice. It came from inside the fruit.

"What in the w... ," the husband began.

The voice answered, "Stop! Don't eat me, please." It sounded like a child was speaking.

"Show yourself," said the old woman.

Suddenly, the sides of the large peach split open to reveal a baby boy. The old man and woman covered their mouths, and their eyes opened wide. They stepped back in surprise.

"Don't worry, I won't harm you. I've come because you want a child. I will be your son if you'll have me," the baby offered, walking towards them.

The old couple squealed in delight. "Let's name him Momotaro. It means Peach Boy," they agreed.

They threw open their arms to welcome their new son. He ran inside the embrace, hugging their knees tightly. From that day forward, the new parents shared their lives with the boy and everyone was content. Momotaro grew into a happy, strong young man.

At the celebration of his fifteenth birthday, he told his parents he had an announcement to make. "Until today, I have lived a life of comfort and peace. Now I will do something for my country. I will go to Ogre Island and punish the Oni, the ogres that steal the people and possessions of Japan," Momotaro said.

His parents were proud of their son. The old woman prepared millet cakes for his journey. The woodcutter fashioned a suit of armor for Peach Boy. He gave him a sword. Momotaro promised he would return safely.

Peach Boy had never been to the distant sea. He would have to cross it to get to Ogre Island. He set out early the next morning and walked until noon when he settled in the shade of a tree to eat lunch. A barking met his first bite. A small, spotted dog stood before him. Peach Boy gave the dog a millet cake and finished his own. When he continued to walk, the dog followed.

Soon, Peach Boy and the dog met a monkey on the road. The monkey challenged the dog. The spotted dog was about to fight.

"Why not come with us and fight the Oni on Ogre Island instead?" Momotaro asked the monkey. He gave him a millet cake, and the monkey followed.

They came upon a pheasant in the road. The pheasant challenged the monkey and dog to pass. They were about to fight.

"Why not travel with us instead and battle the Oni on Ogre Island?" asked Peach Boy. He gave the pheasant a millet cake, and the pheasant followed.

Finally, the travelers came to the distant sea. Momotaro built a boat, and they crossed to Ogre Island. They could see the ogres' mighty fort from the shore. Brandishing his sword, Momotaro led the way. Blue, black and red ogres took their battle positions on the roof. The pheasant flew at them and pecked their heads and shoulders. The ogres waved their clubs at the pheasant, but the bird was too quick to be hit.

Peach Boy, the spotted dog and the monkey fought the ogre guards at the door and won entrance to the fortress. Momotaro battled with his father's sword. The spotted dog bit the ogres, and the monkey fought with his claws. They defeated the mean ogres.

Bowing before the conquerors, the Oni promised never to invade Japan again. They laid all of the stolen objects from the country at the conquerors' feet. Gold, silver, gems and a hammer that made gold when it hit the ground sparkled at them from bulging treasure chests. One contrite ogre handed over an invisible cloak and hat he said he wished to return. Momotaro and his companions accepted the gifts and bid the ogres farewell.

Momotaro made a cart for the treasures, and Peach Boy and his companions pushed so they could move it. They boarded their ship at the shore. Upon arriving in Japan, they wheeled the gifts to Momotaro's house. The old woman and woodcutter rejoiced to see the return of their son. They congratulated him and his friends on their successful mission.

LITTLE ONE-INCH AND THE DEVIL

t the shrine, two voices spoke. "Please, answer our prayer," said the wife. "We wish for a child more than anything," the husband prayed.

When they finished, the woman and man took the path back through the woods to their house. As they walked in the forest, they heard a baby's cry. It seemed to come from the large clump of grass in the near clearing, so they tiptoed over to investigate.

At first, all they saw was the bright red blanket under the pine tree. They shook their heads, because the blanket seemed empty. Maybe they had imagined the cry, they thought. It was possible their prayers had influenced them to hear what did not exist. They turned back to the path and were about to proceed when they heard the cry again.

Now they rushed to the bright red blanket and squatted to look more closely. Gently, they lifted the blanket's folds. Delicately, they edged the blanket open.

"Oh, my!" exclaimed the woman.

"He's the tiniest baby boy I've ever seen. In fact, I almost can't see him at all," said the man.

Still, they recognized that their prayers were answered, and they rejoiced to have a child at long last. They carefully rewrapped their baby in his red blanket and took turns carrying him in their arms. When they arrived home, they gave thanks at their altar for their new son.

"Let's name him," the man said.

"I suggest Little One-Inch, for he is just about one inch tall," the woman answered.

Although Little One-Inch grew into a fine boy, he became no taller. Entering his teen years, he remained one inch tall and no taller. One day, he told his parents he had made a decision. They were eager to listen.

"I wish to go out into the world to make my fortune," he said.

His parents silently worried about the advisability of such a small youth setting out on his own. But they supported his decision, because they loved him. They made preparations for his departure. By nightfall, they were finished.

Shortly after sunrise, Little One-Inch bid farewell to his parents and promised to send word of his fortune. He had a sewing needle under his belt for a sword. Propped against his shoulder, he carried a chopstick for an oar. He dragged a rice bowl as his boat down to the river.

Whistling as his rice-bowl floated down the river, Little One-Inch paddled with his oar. He proceeded smoothly on his journey until his boat capsized. Little One-Inch made sure his sewing-needle sword was safe, then he began to tread water. He looked around for what had caused the boat to overturn. The green head and bulging eyes of a frog provided the answer. Little One-Inch swam ashore.

On the hill, he saw a magnificent house. He decided to announce his arrival to the lord who lived there. He could not reach the bell and his hand was too small for anyone inside to hear him knock, so he shouted his greeting. A servant opened the door and saw no one. Even when he looked down, the wooden sandals that the lord kept outside were all the servant noticed. He was about to close the door when Little One-Inch spoke.

"I wish to speak with the lord of this house. I have come to make my fortune," he said.

Politely, the servant stifled his smile and invited the stranger to enter. He asked him to wait and hurried to tell the lord of the amazing situation. Unable to quell his curiosity, the busy lord came immediately. Little One-Inch repeated that he wished to make his fortune.

"For the time being, you can be the playmate of my daughter, the princess," the lord responded, unable to turn the stranger away.

Little One-Inch and the young princess became friends. Every day, they read and told each other stories. Each was the first friend the other ever had.

One day, the friends traveled to a nearby temple. A horrible-looking, green devil appeared out of nowhere. His eyes were yellow, and his skin was hard and crusty. Scales grew over his back and limbs. He held a magic hammer high over his head as he chased the princess through the woods.

Little One-Inch was ready with his sword. He ran as quickly as he could in pursuit and he caught up with the devil. The princess was trying to hide behind a tree trunk, and the devil was about to snatch her. Poke, poke, the needle-sword worked to pierce the devil's toes, but, the toes were too coarse for it to break through the skin. The devil reached down to swat Little One-Inch away when he climbed up the demon's arms to his neck and slipped into his mouth.

He began to pierce the devil's tongue with his sword and it bled. He kept at it until the devil spat him out and fled through the woods in pain. The princess picked up the magic hammer the fleeing devil had dropped and made a wish. The first time she swung the hammer in the air, Little One-Inch got one inch taller. She swung it again, and he grew another inch. Then she swung the magic hammer until she and Little One-Inch were the same height.

They hurried to tell the lord of their morning. When he heard the tale, he congratulated Little One-Inch on his valor. He thanked him for saving the life of the princess.

As a reward, the lord offered his daughter's hand in marriage. Little One-Inch and the princess gladly agreed to wait a few years until they were both a bit older before they married. In the meantime, Little One-Inch got word to his parents of his good fortune.

THE BRIDE AND THE ONI

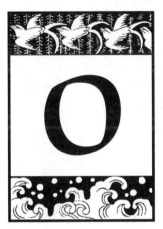

ne day long ago, a young woman set out to meet her future husband. An attendant helped the bride-to-be into her carriage, and she smoothed her skirts to sit. Other carriages traveled with hers in a procession to the young man's village. They brought gifts. The bride's mother, too, was in the party of travelers.

Mid-morning, the travelers came to a mountain pass. The going was slow, so they continued carefully. Suddenly, the sky darkened. A dense, voluminous cloud hung directly over the party of travelers. Then it changed course slightly to envelop the bride's carriage. No one in the procession could see through it. When the wind shifted and the cloud changed direction again, the bride and her carriage were gone.

"Where is my daughter?" cried the bride's mother. She had descended from her own carriage and had run forward to investigate.

No one had an answer for the mother. Despite their suggestions that she do otherwise, she set out alone to find her daughter. The other travelers returned to their village.

In a short time, the bride's mother came upon a temple in the mountains. A priestess greeted her and asked why she had come.

"I'm looking for the whereabouts of my daughter. She vanished on the mountain pass. We were traveling to the village of my future son-in-law," the mother explained.

"I have the knowledge you seek. Your daughter is the captive of the chief oni, the demon whose castle is on the other side of the river. Two guard dogs protect the bridge. You must cross the river when they take their morning sleep," answered the priestess.

The mother accepted the priestess's hospitality for the night. The following morning, she resumed the journey to find her daughter. While crossing an open field, she looked back. The temple had disappeared.

The woman did not lose heart. She continued until she reached the river. A bridge led to a castle on the other side, and she crossed it. As the priestess had said, the sleeping guard dogs did not awaken. Stealthily, she entered the castle and began the search for her daughter. She found her weaving in an upstairs room.

"Mother, I am delighted to see you. But you must hide from the oni. Here, get inside of this stone chest," said the bride.

What she did not take the time to explain to her mother was that the oni had an enchanted garden. When he brought her here as his captive, a flower on a magical bush had burst into instant bloom. "A bloom appears whenever a human is on the premises," the oni had said. A second bloom on the bush would alert the demon when he returned that another human had arrived.

Sure enough, no sooner had the bride-to-be secured her mother in the stone chest than the oni rushed into the room. "There is another flower. Where is the humun?" he demanded.

An idea came to the young woman. "If a flower has opened, it is because I am pregnant," she lied.

Onis are not very intelligent creatures, so the demon believed her. Plus, he was thinking even less clearly as usual. He had been drinking sake with his oni friends, and he was intoxicated. Climbing into the wooden box with seven lids where he slept, the oni said good night.

Immediately, the young woman locked the wooden chest. She released her mother from the stone one. The two women fled from the castle. To their surprise, the oni or one of his demon friends had killed the guard dogs in their drunkenness. Their path from the castle and across the bridge to the other side of the river was easy. They found a boat and began rowing downstream.

Soon, the oni awoke with a powerful thirst from all of the sake he had drunk. Not even the locks on the seven lids could contain him. He kicked and he bashed and he pounded until he was out of the wooden box. Shouting for his demon attendants to follow, he pursued the two women across the bridge to the river. When he saw the water, he began to drink. So did his attendants, who had also drunk too much sake and were just as thirsty. They drank in giant gulps without seeming to stop to swallow. In no time, the river was nearly drained. The boat with the bride and her mother was drawn back to the bridge from the demons' gulping.

Just as the chief oni was about to grab them, the priestess reappeared with instructions for the women. "Tell the onis you renounce your human lives and want to marry them," she said.

The bride and her mother said the odious words, and the onis were delighted. They threw themselves down upon the bank and began to laugh. Since there were many of them and only the two women, the demons started to shoved one another about. Each claimed to be the rightful husband of one of the women. The laughter and horseplay caused them to spit out all of the water they had drunk. In no time, the river was full once more. The women rowed their boat furiously and escaped, thanking the priestess for her help.

TANUKI AND KITSUNE

 badger, a female fox and her cub lived as neighbors in the woods. The badger, which was a Tanuki demon, and foxes, Kitsune demons, were not friends. They had merely grown accustomed to one another. As time went by, more and more humans came to the forest to hunt. As their prey grew fewer and fewer, the three demon animals became hungrier and hungrier. One day, they could no longer tolerate how hungry they were. The two adults sat down to talk over the growls of their empty stomachs. It was better to forge a partnership than to die of starvation.

"We have to get some food," said the determined badger.

"I have a plan," said the fox. "I'll change into a man, and you can pretend to be dead. I'll take you to the market and offer you to the merchant. With the money from the sale, I'll buy us some food. In the meantime, you run home to the woods and wait for me to return."

The badger agreed to the plan and lay on the ground as though dead. It took only a few seconds for the fox to transform herself into a human man. Although the baby fox was frightened by her mother's changed appearance, he looked forward to a good meal. He curled up and went to sleep.

The fox-as-the-man brought the supposedly dead badger into the village. At the market, the man offered his pretend catch to the merchant and received a tidy sum. He busied himself with purchasing food to take back home. In the meantime, the badger sprang to life and hurried back to the forest. Still disguised as a man, the fox returned with her arms full of food. She changed back to her normal form and embraced her youngster. The three animals ate a grand meal and did not stop until their stomachs were very full. What they could not eat, they stored for the days to come.

You probably guessed that not many days passed before the three forest animals were hungry once more. This time, the badger said he would like to transform himself into a human man. He dragged the female fox pretending to be dead down the road and into the village. At the market, he offered her to the merchant.

With a sly look, the badger-as-the-man added, "This fox is not really dead at all. It's only a ruse."

Immediately, the merchant drew his knife and killed the fox. The man went shopping for food and returned to the forest. When the badger cast off the human disguise, he told the cub his mother was dead. He refused to share any of the food with the youngster. The cub silently swore to avenge its mother's death and the badger's ill doings.

Just as it had happened the first time, the badger's food ran out. Now the selfish animal told the fox cub he was ready to create a new plan. The cub spoke up.

"Let's have a contest. We'll take turns changing ourselves into humans. But we'll choose different disguises to present to the merchant than the same man you and my mother chose. One of us must guess which human the other has chosen to be before we pretend to be dead. It will be more fun," said the fox cub.

The badger loved a good game, and he readily agreed to the cub's plan. "You go first," he said eagerly.

"I'll make my change now. Close your eyes until I tell you I'm ready," said the cub.

The badger closed his eyes. This time, the young fox was the sly one. Instead of transforming himself into a human, he hid behind a tall tree and waited. He had wandered far, trying to find prey that morning. Venturing close to the village, he saw people preparing for a procession. Now he heard their drums from the road. He waited until the sound was very close and the procession was about to pass.

"Open your eyes. I'm ready," the fox called to the badger.

At that moment, the procession marched by. The badger ran into the road and stopped short of the governor in his fancy parade dress. The fox cub smiled from his hiding place.

"Governor, you are a cunning fox," the badger shouted.

"Remove this creature," the governor commanded his attendants.

At the governor's words, the attendants killed the badger. The smile on the fox cub's face widened. He had taken his revenge.

"Now I must find another partner," he said.

KOREA

THE LEGEND OF TANGUN

rchery is the art of shooting with bows and arrows. A belief in archery is very important to the ancient people of Korea. In the beginning of the world, a crack was seen in the sky. Now there were two suns and two moons. It was necessary to separate the old sky from the new earth that was formed by the crack. An arrow shot down one sun and brought it to earth. It shot down one moon and brought it, too, to earth. The dirt of the new earth made the first human being.

The story that follows is about one of the earliest humans. Like many heroes, he was part divine being. His name, as you will see, has something to do with archery. The story starts in heaven.

Ages and ages ago, there was a divine being named Whan-in, who was the Creator. Whan-in's son was called Whan-ung.

"Father, I am bored in heaven. I want to go to earth and found a kingdom," Whan-ung said to Whan-in.

"Go if you must. Do you see the three highest mountains below? Ta-bak Mountain is the one I suggest you settle upon. Take with you these three heavenly seals and 3,000 spirit companions and go to Ta-bak Mountain," Whan-in proclaimed to his son.

That day, the happy Whan-ung took the seals and left heaven with his 3,000 spirit companions. They descended upon Ta-bak Mountain, and Whan-ung found it pleasing. Under the shade of an ancient pak-tal tree, he called his friends to him.

"Today I proclaim myself King of the Universe," he declared.

Whan-ung named one spirit the Earl of Wind. He appointed another the Master of Rain. A third he named Master of Clouds.

"As for myself, I take charge of 360 areas of responsibility. I will see that the crops grow and that humans live a long life. When there is illness, I will heal it if a cure is in order. I will punish when a punishment is in order. I will oversee good and evil, learning and beauty," said Whan-ung, King of the Universe.

In a short time, there were many humans in Whan-ung's kingdom. The Earl of Wind, Master of Rain and Master of Clouds discharged their duties properly, and Whan-in was pleased. He did feel one disappointment, however.

"I would be able to rule more effectively if I had a human form," he lamented one day at dawn. He was riding upon the wind at the time.

On the mountain early that day were a tiger and a bear. They heard Whan-ung's words.

"Don't you wish we could become human, too?" they asked each other when they spoke.

This time, their words came to Whan-ung upon the early wind. They heard his response.

"I give you each twenty cloves of garlic and a piece of artemisia. You will eat these herbs, and stay in your cave out of the sun for three times seven days," answered Whan-ung. "Do you agree to do this?"

"I agree," the bear answered.

"I agree, too," echoed the tiger.

In the beginning, the bear and tiger obeyed Whan-ung's words. Each day, they ate garlic and a slice of artemisia. They remained in the cave and did not venture out into the sun. One day, the tiger had enough of being inside the cave. He craved the sun more than anything in the world.

"Don't go. It's too soon," warned the patient bear.

"I must," the tiger replied, fiercely. He stood at the mouth of the cave, shook the way cats do before they pounce, and he was gone.

Now the bear was alone in the cave. She was saddened by the disappearance of the tiger, but she waited. Each day that followed, she did as she had been instructed, eating a bit of garlic and a piece of artemisia. She looked toward the light at the cave's opening, but she did not go toward it.

Finally, three times seven days had passed, and no more garlic nor artemisia remained for the bear to eat. She pulled herself to her full height and stretched. She shook off all of the debris that clung to her coat. She roared, then she lumbered toward the mouth of the cave.

She stepped outside into the sun. Ah! She was a perfect, human female, a fine woman indeed. She walked about the mountain to experience life in her new form.

"Would that I had a son," she spoke, hopefully.

Again, Whan-ung was passing on the wind. Again, the King of the Universe heard her words, and they moved him deeply. Circling around the woman, Whan-ung breathed upon her.

Under the pak-tal tree, the woman who had been a bear now held a perfect human baby in her arms. With the moss that grew under the tree, she made a blanket and covered the baby boy.

Many years later, the people of the nine wild tribes of the kingdom found a young man seated alone under the tree. They called him Tangun, "lord of the birch," which was another name for the pak-tal tree. It is this tree from which the people made their bows and arrows for archery.

THE BIRTH OF KING TONGMYONG

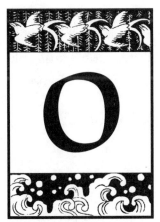

ne day in early summer, Ryuhwa and her sisters were bathing in the green water of pool named Heart of the Bear. The daughters of the god of the waters were suddenly surprised. From the heart of the sky, a true Son of Heaven appeared.

Five dragons drew his chariot. Hundreds of attendants accompanied him, seated upon swans. Sweet strains of music filled the air as they made their way past the heavenly banners that floated on the sun-stained clouds.

No one before them had seen anyone from Heaven arrive in the full light of the sun. Ryuhwa, who was also called Willow Flower, and her sisters were frightened. They dove and swam to put distance between themselves and the god who was about to land in their midst. He was called Hamosu, named after the sun. Captivated by how her jade necklace caught the green light of the waves as she swam, he lost his heart for Ryuhwa.

But Hamosu was saddened to have caused Ryuhwa and the other

daughters of the water god to flee. He instructed the dragons and swans to land on the shore. Great noise surrounded him. The animals drank and cooled themselves in the green water. His attendants looked at Hamosu inquisitively.

"I have decided to construct a palace in which to hide until the eldest daughter returns to the pool. Never have I seen such beauty. I wish her to be the mother of my son," Hamosu explained.

He unleashed the riding whip he carried and traced an outline for the foundation. As he waved it in the air, he began to see where the windows, towers and bridges would be. He continued to wave the whip, and he envisioned balconies, turrets and banners. When he stopped waving, a palace appeared, bronze and sparkling. Hamosu wished for silken cushions, and they took their places upon suddenly created furniture. Goblets of gold held rich, fragrant wine. Sumptuous food showed itself upon new, wooden banquet tables.

From that moment, Hamosu lived every day among the humans. The palace was his home. Every evening, Hamosu traveled home to the heavens. He returned to his bronze palace at sunrise.

One morning, Hamosu caught Willow Flower as she and her sisters fled after catching a glimpse of him. He showed her his beautiful palace and invited her to visit. She accepted the offer. When the water god learned from his other daughters what had happened, he hurried to confront Hamosu.

"How dare you take my daughter from me?" the water god demanded.

"In the name of Heaven, I only wish the hand of your noble daughter in marriage," Hamosu responded.

"Marriage is no small matter. Prove first that you are indeed heaven's heir," said the water god.

He then dove into the green waves of the pool and changed himself into a carp. At once, Hamosu entered the pool, and he became an otter. The otter held the carp in its grasp, and the water god sprouted the wings of a pheasant and flew from the otter's clutch. That instant, Hamosu became a golden eagle in pursuit of the pheasant. The water god changed into a stag in order to escape, but Hamosu transformed himself into a wolf and was a mere step away.

"You are indeed divine," confessed the water god in his true form once more.

He accepted Hamosu's invitation to enter the palace and drink a goblet of wine to seal the marriage contract. The water god and the Son of Heaven drank goblet after goblet. Poor Hamosu, unaccustomed to the earthly brew, was quite intoxicated.

"It is time to leave for heaven, my wife," he said to Willow Flower.

The dragons took their places, and Hamosu and Willow Flower mounted the chariot. Hamosu was still dizzy. Shortly, he found himself inside a leather bag. Eager to return to heaven as he did every evening, he reached for one of Willow Flower's hairpins, slit open the bag and departed alone through the crimson clouds into the sky.

Immediately, the water god, who was furious over losing the heart of his eldest daughter to Hamosu, put a spell upon her. Her lips grew to be three feet long. Not satisfied still, the father tossed her into the green pool, and she rode the waves until a fisherman caught her in his iron net. Her long lips had made her mute, and she looked monstrous.

"I will try to help," said the kind fisherman.

Three times, he trimmed her lips. On the third try, Willow Flower was able to speak once more. The fisherman brought her to the earthly ruler of the land, King Kumwa.

"I recognize you as Hamosu's wife," said the startled King Kumwa.

The ruler brought Willow Flower to a palace where she could live. As soon as he left her alone, the sun shone brilliantly inside the chamber. It warmed the sadness in Willow Flower's heart and filled her body with love. In nine months, she gave birth to a baby boy. Her son was called Tongmyong, known as Cumong, whose name meant "the good archer."

Remember the story about Tangun, "lord of the birch?" Cumong was his descendent and he would be the founder of one of the three ancient kingdoms of Korea. The kingdom's name was Koguryo.

THE EGG & CUMONG

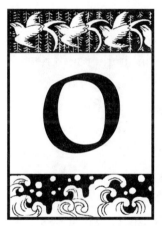

One day in the Korea of old, Willow Flower gave birth to an egg. The egg was pottle-sized, which made it large, as large as today's half-gallon container. The earthly king of the land of Fouyu and his subjects gasped when they saw the strange object. "Who has ever heard of a woman giving birth to an egg? And such an odd size for an egg," everyone proclaimed.

Willow Flower was the only person in the kingdom who was not upset, frightened or horrified by the egg to which she gave birth. The egg's father was the Son of Heaven and the god of the sun, and Willow Flower was a water goddess. The child who hatched from the egg would be immortal, so an unusual birth was fitting, she reasoned.

The uproar over the egg grew nonetheless. The king of Fouyu took it into his arms one morning as Willow Flower screamed. The scream did not dampen the king's determination. He called his servant.

"Throw this egg to the dog," the king ordered.

The servant obeyed. He waited some time and went to inspect the damage. But he found none at all. The dog had not harmed it, and the egg was intact.

"Feed it to the pig," shouted the king.

The servant heeded the order. He hid and observed the pig, who was always hungry. The pig ignored the egg, and the egg remained intact.

The king ordered the servant to put the egg in the cow's trough. You probably guessed it. The cow paid no attention and chewed grass. Next, the servant heeded the king's command to plop the egg inside the horse's stall. The horse gingerly walked around the intruder, and the egg was intact. When the obedient servant brought it to the field, the birds protected it with their wings.

"Bring that egg here. I will crush it myself," boasted the king.

Did he break it? How could he? Inside the egg was an immortal. The stupefied king returned it to Willow Flower, who warmed the egg in a blanket.

Before long, the egg cracked. A beautiful baby boy broke free and greeted his mother. The baby was healthy, and he pleased Willow Flower. She called him Cumong. One day, Cumong spoke his first words.

"The flies are biting my eyelids, and I cannot sleep in peace," he said.

Willow Flower made a bow and arrows for her young son, whose name meant "the good archer." He was rarely seen without them from that moment.

The king of Fouyu had seven children, and Cumong played with them. Because Cumong was the best hunter, the eldest son, Prince Taso, was very jealous of him. He plotted against Cumong.

"Father, he is the son of immortals. His courage and skill with the bow are strong, and you cannot trust him," said Taso.

During the time when the king pondered his son's words, a large hunt took place in the kingdom. Boys did not participate until they were older. But, because Cumong had proven his skill, the hunters gave him some arrows. The number was smaller by far than theirs. But, at the end of the day, Cumong's kill was much greater than anyone else's. The hunters joined Taso in his jealousy, and they complained about Cumong to the king.

"He is too good a warrior. You must be on watch against him," they warned. The king sent Cumong to tend the horses to test his loyalty.

In the pasture, Cumong was sad. "What kind of treatment is this for heaven's grandson? If it weren't that I would have to leave my mother here alone, I would choose to go south to found a kingdom. I'd build a great city ... ," he lamented.

Willow Flower overheard her son's words. Wiping away her tears, she answered, "Do not concern yourself with me, my son. Your first requirement is a good stallion. Your second is to have trusted companions."

Mother and son observed the king's horses. "We must test them. Do not worry, but do as I do," Willow Flower said.

She held her whip high over her head, and Cumong did the same. When Willow Flower unleashed her whip, Cumong released his. All of the horses scattered except one beautiful bay who leaped over a wall of two fathoms, which was the same as six feet high.

"He is the best of the herd," said Willow Flower. "Now we must make him appear undesirable to the king."

They hid a needle in the horse's tongue so he could not eat. Day after day, the stallion turned away from his food. Before the week was over, the king visited and saw the stallion who had turned to skin and bones.

"Here, Cumong, this beautiful horse can be yours," the king mocked. It happened just as Willow Flower had planned. Mother and son nursed the poor horse to health, feeding him the best meals possible.

When the horse had regained his full strength, Cumong bid a sad farewell to Willow Flower. She gave her son five grains of cereal for his trip. Cumong went to three loyal friends and asked them to accompany him on his adventure. The four young men then set off for the south where Cumong would found the ancient kingdom of Koguryo.

CUMONG'S PALACE

ith his three best friends, Cumong set off on his journey for the south. The five grains of cereal from his mother were in his hand.

The young men on horseback came to a wide, rapid stream, but there was no bridge. They could hear the loud pounding of horses in the distance. The king's troops were following them.

Cumong spoke to the water. "I am grandson of heaven and grandson of the river. Do not turn your eyes from me, heaven and earth, for I must find a new home," he cried.

Just then, the water grew calm. Schools of fish and hundreds of turtles swam to the surface. The creatures joined their heads and tails into a wondrous bridge for Cumong and his friends to use to cross to the other side.

Now the king's troops gathered on the near bank. Happily, they pointed to the bridge, for they saw they could overtake the young men. Their numbers were much greater, and soon, they thought, the army could make their capture.

But what happened? The schools of fish and the hundreds of turtles saw the troops. At once, their heads and tails were no longer attached. The bridge disappeared. Into the wide, rapid stream fell the army and its horses.

Cumong and his companions rode away to safety in the new land on the far bank of the river.

After traveling a distance, the four young men stopped to rest. They lay upon the grass in the shade beneath a great tree. Cumong jumped to his feet suddenly. He realized he no longer held the five grains his mother had given him.

"Look at the two pigeons," said one of Cumong's companions.

"My mother must have sent them," Cumong responded. He lifted his bow and shot an arrow, and the arrow killed the pigeons. Five grains of cereal fell from the birds' throats. Carefully, Cumong put the grains into his pocket. "Now we have the seeds to grow food in our new kingdom," he told his friends.

They rode on happily through mountains and streams and thick forests until Cumong said they should stop. "Here, I will build my capital city. First, my subjects in this land must declare their obedience to me," he said.

Cumong's companions placed his royal mat upon the earth, and he seated himself. "I am now called King Tongmyong," he declared. Tongmyong meant "lightning from the east."

"How will we call your subjects to come before you?" one of Cumong's friends asked him.

"Alas, we have neither a drum nor a horn," Cumong realized.

Hearing Cumong's lament, one of his friends said, "I will go to King Songyang, king of Piryu, and bring you his drum and horn."

"How can you take the treasures from one king to give to another?" Cumong, who was now King Tyongmyong, asked.

"That is easy to answer. The treasures are gifts from heaven. Your fate is decided in heaven. Why would the drum and horn not belong to you?" the friend answered.

King Songyang was not pleased to lose his drum and horn. He rushed to follow the thief to the location of the declared king, who was new to his land. He found Cumong seated on his royal mat.

"How dare you steal my possessions?" shouted King Songyang.

"How dare you not recognize my heavenly rule?" answered King Tyongmyong.

"Ha! Those are mere words. Prove you are a heavenly ruler. You must show you are a better archer than I am. I can shoot a deer and break a basin from fifty paces away. If you cannot, I am the rightful ruler," boasted King Songyang.

The two kings entered the forest, where they saw a deer. The earthly king challenged the heavenly king to take aim. Cumong put one hundred paces between himself and the deer. He raised his bow and took aim with his arrow. The onlookers could not believe what they saw. Cumong released his arrow, and it hit the deer in its navel.

One of Cumong's friends took a jade basin from the bag on the back of his horse. He set the basin upon the earth. The smug King Songyang, sure Cumong had been fortunate with his first shot, told him again to shoot first. Putting one hundred paces between the basin and himself, Cumong took aim. His arrow shot through the air, hit the basin and the jade sides shattered.

Without a word, King Songyang angrily turned and departed for Piryu. Cumong, on the other hand, walked deeper into the forest until he came upon a white deer. He lifted his bow, shot the animal but did not kill it. Stringing it by its hind feet, he spoke a curse on Songyang.

"Until rainstorms flood Songyang's home at Piryu, washing it away forever, I will not release you, deer," spoke Cumong.

The deer's cries were so sad, they reached the ears of Heaven. For seven days, rain fell so greatly over Piryu that one river flowed into the next. Songyang and his subjects were very frightened, and Songyang pleaded for help. Finally, Cumong lifted his riding whip. He held it over the flood, and the waters parted.

"I agree you are the heavenly king," cried Songyang.

At the sound of the words, Cumong released the captive white deer. A dark cloud covered the pass so that no one could see, but they could hear the sound of hammering as though thousands of carpenters were at work.

"Heaven is building me a fortress," Cumong reassured the anxious crowd.

When the darkness lifted, cries of surprise filled the air. A magnificent palace stood where before there had been only pasture. King Tyongmyong lived in his palace for nineteen years until he rose to heaven.

YURI AND THE BROKEN SWORD

umong was a deity whose mother and father had met at the spot called Heart of the Bear. His father was the son of the lord of the birches. His grandfather was called the son of the bear. While Cumong lived in Puyu, he fell in love and got married. But Cumong's life was in danger, and his destiny was to found a kingdom in the south. He had to flee from Puyu and his new wife. Shortly after Cumong departed, his wife learned she was pregnant. Before the year was out, she gave birth to a baby boy she called Yuri.

Yuri was a happy child. Like his father, he was never without a bow and arrow in his hand. He liked to shoot at anything that moved, particularly sparrows.

One day, Yuri sat hidden behind a tree in the village square. He had his bow and arrow ready to shoot. A sparrow fluttered its wings, and Yuri took aim. Pfoot! he released the arrow. The sparrow flew away. But Yuri's arrow made contact with something. The boy rose from his cover to find out what he had hit.

"Foolish boy, you have broken my water jug," yelled a woman at the well. "Now how will I get this water to my house?"

"I'm very sorry," Yuri answered.

"Sorry, hah! What do you know about anything? You do not even have a father," said the angry woman.

Poor Yuri grew sad. It was true he had never met his father. But Yuri's mother had made sure until now that his life was a happy one. Yuri had not worried about who his father was, because his mother was not worried about it. It did not bother her that she was his only parent, so why should it bother Yuri?

Now Yuri had something to worry about because of what the angry woman had said. Her scorn over his not having a father meant sadness for Yuri. Taking up his bow and arrows, Yuri hurried home.

"Mother, is it true that I am a child without a father?" he asked.

Yuri's mother was taken by surprise, and she answered quickly without thinking too hard about what she would say. Maybe, she thought, Yuri would accept a simple answer, then go back to the village to shoot at sparrows. At any rate, she gave the simple answer.

"It is true, my son, you do not have a father," answered Yuri's mother.

This time when Yuri went outside, he did not have his bow and arrows. He had dropped them at this feet inside the house after his mother spoke. With his head hung low, Yuri began to walk. He felt so badly about not having a father, all he could do is look at the ground. He started kicking at the stones and dirt while he walked. His foot hit upon on old knife, and Yuri picked it up.

He leaned against a tree with the knife in his hand. "I'll cut myself. What's the difference?" he asked outloud.

Luckily, Yuri's mother had thought better of her quick words as soon as she said them. When her son left the house, she had decided to follow him.

As Yuri lifted the knife to cut himself, his mother reached for it.

"Mother, why have you stopped me?" Yuri asked.

"I'm sorry, Yuri. I've never told you about your father, because I thought it would be safer for you as your father's son if you did not know the truth. Your father had to flee to save his life. He traveled to the south. Today he is alive, and he is a great king," said Yuri's mother.

"I must go to him," said Yuri.

"You must do something else first. Before he fled, your father hid something for you to find. The object will prove to him that you are his son. He hid it at the foot of a pine that grows from a heptagonal stone. When you present the object to him, it will announce that you are his son," explained his mother.

Yuri and his mother embraced, then Yuri set out to find the hidden object. He dug at the base of every pine tree that he saw. Time and again, his digging produced nothing but stones and worms and pine needles and dirt.

"I'll never find my father's hidden object," Yuri despaired.

He returned to his house and sat down upon the floor with his elbows upon his knees. He felt very sorry for himself. Hiding his head in his arms, Yuri resolved never to move from this spot again. Just as he made the resolution, he heard what sounded like a faraway voice. It came from behind one of the wooden pillars in the room. He rushed to the pillar and saw that it had seven angles.

"The pillar must be in the base of a heptagonal stone," said the excited Yuri.

Yuri dug, and his mother observed. After a short time, he came upon something metal. When he pulled it out, he saw it was one-half of a broken sword.

"Can this be what my father has hidden?" he asked.

"I believe it is," responded his mother.

She helped Yuri prepare for his journey to the southern kingdom where Cumong was king. When the day of departure came, Yuri bid his mother farewell. He traveled with his servants until he came to his father's palace.

At the palace gate, Yuri stated that he had an object for the king. The gatekeeper delivered the message to Cumong that a young boy claimed he had something for him. Pleased, Cumong said to bring the boy to him.

Yuri bravely produced the half sword for the king. Cumong went to his treasury and returned with the other half. The two pieces matched and made one sword.

"You are my father," said the excited Yuri.

"Yes, and you are my son," answered the pleased Cumong.

The king declared that Yuri was the heir to his throne. That evening, the kingdom celebrated a great banquet in Yuri's honor. Before he went to sleep, Yuri said a prayer of thanks to his mother.

THE LEGEND OF PAK HYOKKOSE

his is a story of ancient times in Chinhan. Chinhan had six villages. Each village was ruled by a different clan, or very large family. The people in Chinhan believed that the chiefs of the clans had come down from heaven to earth a long time ago.

But many years had passed, and now the people thought only of themselves. They complained that heaven had forgotten about them.

One day, the residents of Chinhan gathered in a great number on the shore of the Al River. They stood together in villages, and the clans looked at the each other suspiciously. It was the first day of the third month of the first year of Ti-chieh.

A murmur began among the people, and it grew louder and louder. Finally, someone said "we have no heavenly ruler to govern us. That is why the people do whatever they wish," said the voice from the crowd.

"True, true," others agreed.

"We need a virtuous king to found a new country and build a capital," said someone else.

"It's true," answered the crowd.

Suddenly, a great blast of thunder rocked the skies. The people cowered. A magnificent lightning bolt stretched from heaven to Mount Yang to the Na Well. The people gasped. They rushed like a wave to the Na Well where the lightning had hit.

What did they see at the well but a white horse? The horse kneeled on the ground and bowed. A red egg in the shape of a gourd, which was called pak, lay by its forelegs. When the people saw the egg, the white horse neighed. The animal crouched, then took off and flew through the skies back to heaven.

"Ah!" said the people. Then they turned their attention to the gourd-shaped, red egg on the ground.

The egg did nothing but sit there.

"Let's crack it open," someone said. Everyone agreed, so a couple of people took sticks and cracked apart the sides of the egg. A beautiful baby boy with a radiant face crawled from it.

"Ah!" said the people. They carried the baby to the East Spring and bathed him. Now his whole body shone with light.

Heaven and earth trembled. The birds sang a concert. The beasts of the forest danced among the trees. Both the sun and the moon were bright in the sky at the same time.

"Let us name this boy King Hyokkose," someone said. Hyokkose meant "bright." The others agreed.

The people celebrated the birth of their king. Everyone rejoiced, taking turns holding the new baby. Then someone spoke.

"Now we have a king, but no queen," she said.

"H-mm-mm," everyone agreed.

Later that day, something else happened when the people did not expect it. It happened in the Saryang district. The farm women were gathering water at the Aryong Well, and they could not believe their eyes. Someone sounded the bell to alert the others.

A beautiful hen dragon hovered over the well. She spread her wings and banked one way, then the next, remaining in view until all the people had gathered once more. Some of the people shielded their eyes. They opened them when her wings were still.

The hen dragon gently lifted her left wing. "Ah!" said the people. Tucked under the dragon's scales near a rib on the left side was an infant girl. The dragon placed the baby on the ground before the people, and she, like the horse, flew back through the skies.

"Oh, no!" someone close to the infant cried. The baby had beautiful features, surely she had been sent from heaven. But instead of lips, she had the beak of a chick.

The people carried the girl to the North River Wolsong. When they bathed her, the beak disappeared. In its place, were perfect lips.

Now that the people had their young king and queen, they set to work to build a palace for them at the western foot of Mount South. In the wondrous palace, the boy and girl grew up happily. The girl was called Aryong after the well where the dragon landed with her.

In the first year of Wu-feng, the children reached the age of thirteen. The people had a splendid party, and the boy and girl were married. They became king and queen of the new country they called Silla.

Sixty-one years later, Hyokkose rose to heaven. Aryong followed him. After seven days, their remains fell to earth.

"Let us bury them together," the people decided.

A large snake appeared to stop them. "Divide the remains of each of them into five parts and bury them in five tombs," the snake instructed. The people obeyed. They called the tombs Five Tombs or Snake Tomb, and the king from the red egg and the queen from the hen dragon lay together in five places.

KING T'ARHAE OF SILLA

When King Hyokkose of Silla died, his son Namhae succeeded him as king. One day in ancient times and during the reign of King Namhae, a boat came to the shores of Karak. Karak was another kingdom, and its ruler was King Suro.

"Beat the drums of welcome," King Suro declared.

Despite the drums and the shouts of welcome from the kingdom of Karak, the boat did not dock. It sailed away toward the east. After the vessel passed the Forest of the Cock, it stopped at Ajin Cove.

Earlier that day, an old woman had seen a flock of magpies. The birds hovered over something in the middle of the sea. They appeared to be a big, black cloud.

"Why do they do that? No rock island exists for them to feed upon," the old woman had said to herself.

When she rowed out in her fishing skiff to investigate, she found her answer. A casket, twenty feet long and thirteen feet wide, sat inside a deserted boat. She pulled the deserted boat and its casket to shore with a line from her fishing boat. On shore, she moored the boat beneath a grove of trees.

"Protect me," the old woman prayed to heaven. Then she opened the casket.

The casket held a handsome boy, seven treasures and two servants. The woman spoke kindly to the boy. She asked him who he was and why he was inside the casket. But the boy did not answer.

"Perhaps you are mute," the woman said. For seven days, she fed the child and his servants. He looked to be about six years old.

On the eighth day, the boy spoke. "I am the son of King Hamdalp'a. My mother is the daughter of the king of Chongnyo. My father sent me away on this ship."

He told the old woman the story of his birth. Unable to become pregnant, his mother had prayed to heaven for help every day for seven years. On the first morning of the eighth year, the queen gave birth to an egg that was tremendous in size.

"Who has heard of a woman giving birth to such a huge egg?" asked the king.

"Surely this is a bad omen," answered one of his ministers.

The other ministers agreed. When the king decided to cast the egg from his kingdom out to sea, no one said a word to stop him, except the queen. Ignoring her pleas, the king prayed the boat would moor in a land of destiny and that the child inside the egg would found a new kingdom. The queen prayed her child would have a family one day. A kind red dragon guarded the boat while it sailed.

"I must go now to find the seat of my kingdom. Thank you for rescuing me from the casket," the boy said to the old woman.

Up Mount T'oham, the boy climbed with his two servants. Together they built a rock shelter, where the boy lived for seven days. Each day, he scouted the land for the right location in which to settle. One day, a hill in the distance caught his eye. It was shaped like a crescent moon.

"What a perfect place," exclaimed the boy.

With his servants behind him, he approached the hill in great anticipation. But when he got close, his happiness evaporated. For on the hill, he saw there already existed a house. His servants learned that the house belonged to Lord Ho.

"I have a plan, and you will help me win this house for myself," the boy told his servants. He instructed the servants to bury charcoal and whetstone around the border of the building. Whetstone was a stone used to sharpen tools.

The following morning, the boy knocked on the door of the house. Lord Ho answered the knock.

"This is the house of my ancestors," the boy declared.

"Impossible," Lord Ho replied, for he and his ancestors before him had lived in the house for a very long time.

"I will prove my claim before the authorities," the boy stated. Lord Ho accepted the boy's solution to the argument.

When the authorities arrived, the boy told his story. "My ancestors were blacksmiths. Some time ago, my family had to relocate. Now I have returned to claim what is rightfully mine. I can prove what I say is true if you but dig up the ground and search for evidence."

As the boy expected, the authorities dug and found the whetstone and charcoal. They declared him the rightful owner of Lord Ho's house. The boy's story reached the ears of King Namhae of Silla. To reward him, King Namhae promised the boy the hand of his eldest daughter in marriage when he was of age.

The boy was named T'arhae because he came from an egg in a casket. His name meant "remove and undo," which is what the old woman had to do to free him from the boat. His surname became Sok, which meant old, because he took the property of another, saying it had belonged to his ancestors.

KING SURO OF KARAK

here is this place?" asked a mysterious voice.

The whole land was gathered for the special day of the purification ceremony. Every person heard, but no one saw who spoke the words. The eyes of nine chiefs and 75,000 people from one hundred households looked north.

"Where is this place?" it repeated.

The voice came from Mount Kuji.

"Did anyone hear?" the strange voice boomed.

"Yes," answered the nine chiefs at the same time.

"Good then. I have a mission from heaven to come to you and be king. Please, sing and dance on the peak of the mountain," requested the voice.

The nine chiefs and 75,000 people from one hundred households crossed the valley. They climbed to the peak of Mount Kuji. There, the voice sang the words of this song, "O turtle, o turtle! Show your head. We will roast and eat you if you do not."

The people of the land sang the song over and over again. They danced to the tune at the peak of the mountain. Suddenly, from the heavens a long, purple rope appeared. A golden chest wrapped in red cloth hung from the end of the purple rope. "Ah!" said the chiefs and the people.

The nine chiefs laid aside the red cloth and opened the golden chest. Six eggs were inside the box. They were as round and golden as the sun.

All of Kuji followed as six of the chiefs carried the eggs to the house of Ado, where they wrapped the golden orbs carefully and placed them gently upon the bed. They quietly departed to leave the eggs in peace.

Twelve hours later, at dawn, the chiefs and their people returned to find the eggs had cracked. Six handsome boys greeted them. The chiefs and the 75,000 people from one hundred households bowed in response to the greeting.

Every day, the people of the Kuji returned to find the boys grown from the day before. Ten days passed. On the eleventh day at dawn, the boy who had been first to hatch had acquired the characteristics of greatness. He was nine feet tall like King T'ang of Yin. He bore the face of a dragon like the founder of the Han. Mirroring the Emperor Yao, he had eyebrows of eight colors. And like Emperor Shun, the boy's eyes had double pupils.

Naming himself Suro and calling the country Great Karak, the boy ascended the throne. It was the fifteenth day of the month. On the same day, the boys who had hatched from the other five eggs took the thrones of the five remaining kingdoms in the Great Karak federation. For one year, Suro ruled from a small, temporary palace the people built for him.

"I want to establish the capital of Great Karak," Suro proclaimed on the first day of the first month of his second year. "I will travel south to find the location," he said.

The chiefs ordered a small party to accompany King Suro to the south. They descended from Mount Kuji and crossed many smaller hills and valleys. While they traveled, King Suro looked carefully at everything he saw. Each day, they continued.

One day, the king instructed the party to stop. He said, "This spot is small like a bean patch. However, the streams that feed it are many, and the hills surrounding it are exquisite. Once my capital is built, it will be fit for sages and arhats." Arhats were Buddhists that had reached the stage of enlightenment.

King Suro walked 1,500 steps, showing his attendants where he wished the outer walls to be. Inside the 1,500 steps, he marked the locations of his future palaces. He indicated where he wished to have the armories for his defense and the storehouses for his provisions. With a few companions, Suro returned to his small, temporary home.

While he waited, his attendants saw to the project of building the capital. It was the winter season when farmers were free from their duties to the land, so they were hired as builders. The farmers worked on the capital from the twentieth day of the first month until the tenth day of the third month.

King Suro was pleased when his new capital was complete. On a date he chose to be auspicious, he took residence. He proclaimed the day to be one of song and dance.

The nine chiefs and 75,000 people from one hundred households crossed the valleys and hills until they arrived at the new capital. There, they sang and danced to the words of the song they had heard from Mount Kuji.

"O turtle, o turtle! Show your head. We will roast and eat you if you do not."

QUEEN YELLOW JADE

he nine chiefs of 75,000 people from the one hundred households of Karak held a council to discuss a very important issue. King Suro of Karak had no queen. It was the seventh month of the twenty-fourth year of Chien-wu.

"My daughter is the most beautiful in the land," said the first chief.

"Nonsense, the sun rises upon the beauty of my daughter each morning," argued the second chief.

"The birds stop chirping when my daughter walks in the grove," interrupted the third chief.

The fourth chief claimed the loveliness of his daughter caused the fish to jump from the streams into the air. The fifth said the waves of the sea quieted at the sight of his daughter. The sixth chief argued that the brilliance of his daughter's image melted the snows from the mountaintops.

"My daughter's fairness causes the animals to speak," claimed the seventh chief.

"My daughter makes them sing," said the eighth.

"Ridiculous. My daughter's comeliness clears the clouds from the sky," said the ninth chief, who was pleased to have the final word.

The chiefs were unrelenting in their arguments. What was clear was that the council would not resolve the issue of whom the king might marry. On the twenty-seventh day of the seventh month of the twenty-fourth year of Chien-wu, the council made a decision. They would bring the matter before the king and ask him whom he wished to marry.

The first chief spoke first, as always. "King, we implore you to choose the most beautiful and virtuous of our daughters. Speaking honestly, my daughter is worthier than the rest," he said.

The other chiefs were about to resume the argument when King Suro spoke. "Heaven has sent me to found this land of Karak. Please, comfort your-selves that heaven will decide who is to be my future queen," said the king.

Suro dismissed the nine chiefs and resumed his duties as ruler. In the courtyard, the chiefs resumed their argument. Hearing their grumblings, the king smiled.

The following morning, a ship with red sails and a red flag unexpectedly appeared in the harbor. One of the king's attendants rode to tell the king of the arrival. Suro sent word to the nine chiefs to receive the surprise guests.

"I'm certain it is a king from a foreign land," claimed the first chief.

The second chief said the boat was from the south. The third said it was surely from the west. The fourth swore it had come from the east. Guess what the fifth chief claimed. The sixth said they were all wrong, that the ship had sailed from an island in the middle of the sea. The seventh claimed the ship was empty. The eighth was sure it held a casket. The ninth said they were all wrong.

When the chiefs arrived at the harbor, they saw a princess disembark from the ship. "Ah!" exclaimed the chiefs in unison, for it was clear that she was more brilliant than any woman they had ever witnessed. They hurried the princess to the king's palace. But she stopped short at the royal gate.

"I will not enter this palace, for I have never met your king," the princess insisted.

The chiefs hurried to tell the king the news, and the princess remained outside the gate with her attendants. The king was pleased to hear what had transpired, for the sentiment of the princess was proper. Suro called for his attendants.

"Place a tent on a hill sixty feet southwest of the palace. Once it is erected, there I will attend the princess," King Suro announced.

Hearing that the king would welcome her upon the hill to the southwest, the princess, too, was pleased. She set out for the hill with her attendants. In all, her party included forty men and women and their servants. The servants carried many gifts and precious goods for the king.

"Welcome. I will have my soldiers stand guard over your gifts while we get acquainted inside this tent," offered the king. The princess followed Suro into the tent.

"My name is Yellow Jade. I am sixteen years old, and I am a princess of the Indian kingdom of Ayut'a," she said.

"I am Suro of Karak. Why have you come?" asked the king.

"In the fifth month of this year, my father and mother had the same dream. They told me you were sent by heaven, that you desire a queen and that heaven has asked them to transport me to Karak to share your throne," explained Yellow Jade.

Suro and Yellow Jade agreed to marry the following day. Later that year, Yellow Jade gave birth to a son they called Kodung. The royal couple lived many happy years together in Karak. On the first day of the third month of the sixth year of Emperor Ling, Queen Yellow Jade died. She was 157 years old. After many days of mourning her loss, King Suro joined her in death. He was 158 years old. As for the nine chiefs, after they died, they were replaced by nine others who argued just as much as they had.

KING SANSANG, OR YONU

his is the story of four brothers and a queen. They lived very long ago in the ancient kingdom of Koguryo. The queen was called U. She was married to the oldest of the four brothers who was King Kogukch'on.

One day King Kogukch'on died, but Queen U did not tell anyone right away. Instead, all day she sat down in her garden under her favorite tree to think. "It is true that I must honor the ancient custom and marry the brother of my dead husband, thought U. But Kogukch'on has three brothers, Palgi, Yonu and Kyesu. It is customary that Palgi take me as his wife, since he is the eldest of the three. But I do not like Palgi. I favor Yonu instead. Nonetheless, I must tell Palgi first of the king's death," resolved Queen U.

When evening fell, Queen U hurried out of the garden and into the palace. Ignoring the chamber where her dead husband lay, she ran to her private chamber and dressed in her most formal costume. She tied a lovely silk belt around her waist. Then she hastened out of the palace and ordered her attendant to take her to visit Palgi. Saying she had to deliver a message from the king, U was careful not to arouse any suspicion about his death.

When Palgi greeted U, the queen explained the nature of her visit. "You well know that Kogukch'on has no heir. Therefore, you must be the next king," she said. What she did not say was that Kogukch'on had died.

As it was late at night and U's visit had awakened him, Palgi was disgruntled and impatient. "The throne is at the mercy of heaven's choice. How dare you pretend to interfere? Moreover, it is improper for a lady to travel at night. Return home at once," Palgi responded.

"Let us deliver a message from the king to Yonu next," Queen U said to her attendant.

They arrived at Yonu's palace in the dead of night. Yonu had been asleep for hours. Nonetheless, when he was informed of the queen's visit, he rose from bed and hastened to the palace gate.

"Greetings, Queen U," said Yonu.

"Greetings, good Yonu. The king is dead, and he has no heir. I have gone to Palgi with this secret in the interest of safeguarding the kingdom. But how has Palgi responded? He has insulted me and turned me away," responded the queen.

Yonu ordered his servants to be awakened. "We must share a banquet with our esteemed guest," he declared.

All manner of fine meats and the best wines were brought to Yonu's table. Queen U sat to his right in the place of honor. Carving the meat, Yonu cut his finger. Unwrapping her silk belt, U tied it around the cut to stop the bleeding, and Yonu was grateful.

At dawn the following morning, Queen U asked Yonu to call together the officials of the kingdom. When they were assembled, she spoke. "I have a message from the late King Kogukch'on. On his deathbed, he declared his wish that his brother Yonu should succeed him to the throne," she said.

It did not take long before the news reached Palgi, the rightful heir to the throne. He hurried to Yonu's palace and confronted him. But Yonu ordered the gates to remain closed. For three days, no one was permitted to enter.

During this time, Palgi assembled an army of 30,000 troops. News of the Palgi's plan to attack him upset Yonu, who called upon the youngest brother Kyesu to lead an army in defense. Kyesu and Palgi met face-to-face on the battlefield.

"Do you plan to kill your oldest brother, especially when you know Yonu is acting improperly by taking the throne from me?" Palgi shouted.

"You speak correctly that Yonu is acting improperly. But how can you face our father in the underworld after you assembled an army to cause chaos in the kingdom?" Kyesu responded.

Ashamed, Palgi fled with his family to Paech'on, where he cut his throat. Hearing the news, Kyesu traveled to the spot where his brother had taken his life. He ordered his attendants to give Kyesu burial rites.

"How can you have given Palgi a proper burial when he shamed himself by committing suicide?" said Yonu to Kyesu.

"I will explain. Afterwards, I beg you to kill me for my dishonable weakness," Kyesu responded.

"Even if it was Kogukch'on's will as the queen has stated that you succeed him to the throne, you have acted improperly by accepting. You know well that the throne belonged rightfully to Palgi. I have corrected your sense of duty to our brother by burying him. I have answered his evil with goodness. Now I beg you to put me to death," he said.

"I will not do so. Your honor has made me see my mistake. Go now in peace," responded Yonu. The brothers shared an embrace, and Kyesu departed.

"I will bring honor to the throne of Koguryo. Henceforth, I am called King Sansang. Tomorrow, I will wed Queen U, and we will do justice to the name of Kogukch'on," declared Yonu.

THE PRINCESS AND ONDAL

In the time of King P'yongwon, a very poor man lived in the ancient kingdom of Koguryo. His name was Ondal. Everyone recognized him, but no one greeted him though they saw him every day as he begged for food in his rags and worn-out sandals. Behind his back, they talked about him. Most people called him Foolish Ondal. During the same period, the king's daughter was very sad, so sad that she could not stop crying.

"Stop crying, daughter. I cannot bear the sound of your weeping another minute," said the king one day.

The girl continued to cry nonetheless.

"If you don't stop, no nobleman will care to marry you," the king said.

The princess kept crying.

"Your tears will get you only Foolish Ondal for a husband," said the frustrated king. But the princess did not stop crying.

For years, she cried. On her sixteenth birthday, she stopped crying long enough to speak to the king. "I am leaving now to marry Foolish Ondal," she reported.

"Nonsense. I have arranged for you to wed a nobleman from the clan of Ko," the king responded.

"You are king, and you must keep your promises. I will wed Ondal," the princess argued.

Despite her father's protests, the princess insisted she would marry Foolish Ondal. The king grew angry. His face got red, and he started to shout at his daughter.

"Go wherever you please. You are no longer my daughter," he declared.

The princess prepared to leave the palace. On her wrists, she placed hundreds of precious bracelets. She dressed in her finest garments. She packed a travel bag, and she departed without a farewell.

Outside the palace gates, she asked directions to Ondal's house. As she followed them, she realized she had stopped crying. Why, she hadn't cried all morning. The longer she walked, the happier the princess felt. At long last, she saw Ondal's poor cottage. An old woman answered her knock.

"I have come to ask Ondal's hand in marriage," said the princess.

Ondal's blind, old mother couldn't believe her ears. "Nonsense, I can smell your fine fragrance. When I touch your hand, I feel silk. You are surely playing a joke on my son. I am glad he is not home to feel ashamed," the old woman answered. And she sent the princess away.

Determined to marry Ondal, the princess asked a passerby where she might find him. The peasant said Ondal was at the foot of the mountain collecting bark from the elm trees for food. The princess hastened to the mountain. When she found Ondal, she told him she wished to have his hand in marriage.

"You must surely be a demon. No princess in her right mind would propose to marry me," Ondal answered. He raced home with the elm bark.

The princess followed. That evening, she slept outside Ondal's humble cottage. In the morning, she sold her bracelets and bought a house and some land. She found Ondal at the mountain and invited him to visit. When he came, the princess gave him money and instructions for purchasing a horse.

"Go to the king's stable and look for a sick, thin horse that has been abandoned. Buy the animal and bring it to me to nurse back to life," the princess said. Ondal agreed.

In time for the hunt, the horse was strong and healthy. It was the third day of the third month, and every year the event was held on the hill of Lo-lang. This was one of the major occasions of the year. Sacrifices of a boar and deer were offered to heaven and to the deities of the mountains and rivers. The king and all the people of the kingdom attended.

Ondal rode his magnificent horse. He spent the entire day at the head of the hunt. He caught more game than the king and everyone else. When the king asked the hunter's name, the answer surprised him.

Shortly afterward, the king assembled an army to fight against the enemy. The armies met on the plains of Paesan. Ondal rode his horse and fought brilliantly. He received the highest honors.

At the awards ceremony, the king recognized Ondal from the hunt. The audience spoke among themselves of Ondal's valor. One person after another declared he was the finest warrior in the land.

"This man is my son-in-law," the king said, proudly.

The following day, the king invited the princess and her husband to the palace. He gave a banquet in their honor. For the rest of their days, they lived in the king's favor. The princess never cried again.

PIHYONG AND THE SPIRITS

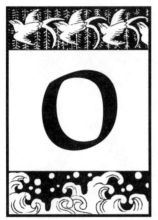

O ne day, King Chinji overheard his ministers talking. "She is truly the most beautiful woman in the kingdom," said the first minister.

"I've never seen a woman more beautiful, even in my travels," the second minister offered.

"I claim she is the most beautiful woman in the world," declared the third minister.

No one was fond of Chinji. The twenty-fifth king had ruled the kingdom for four dreary years ever since the eighth year of Ta-chien. His rule was characterized by bad government and poor morals.

Chinji called his ministers. "Bring the beautiful woman to me," he demanded.

"But she is married, King," the ministers answered.

"Obey my command and fetch this woman," Chinji said.

The ministers departed immediately for the Saryang district, where the renowned woman resided with her husband. Everyone in the district called her Peach Blossom Girl because of her beauty. Peach Blossom Girl did not dare disobey the king's decree, so she accompanied the three ministers to Chinji's palace.

"Ah, the ministers are well-informed. Your beauty is without parallel," declared Chinji when he saw her.

Peach Blossom Girl, on the other hand, remained silent. She bowed respectfully before the king. She hoped the visit would be over soon so she could return home to her husband in the Saryang district.

"I ask for your hand in marriage, Peach Blossom Girl," said the king.

"Pardon me, king, but how can I grant your request? I am already married," she responded, politely.

"If your husband was dead, would you give me my wish?" Chunji asked.

Peach Blossom Girl said she could not refuse the king if her husband was dead. Pleased with her answer, Chunji told her to return to her home. The following year, he was overthrown and the kingdom had a new ruler.

Three years passed, and Peach Blossom Girl heard nothing further from Chunji. Then one day, her husband died. After the burial, Peach Blossom Girl returned home. Who should come to her door but Chunji?

"I am here to ask you to keep your promise by obeying my royal decree now," Chunji said.

He remained in the home of Peach Blossom Girl for seven days. Clouds of five colors protected the house, and a sweet fragrance surrounded it. On the eighth day, Chunji departed and he did not return.

Later that year, Peach Blossom Girl gave birth to a baby boy she named Pihyong. At the time of the birth, the earth trembled. The new king, Chinp'yong, heard about the earthquake. He ordered Pihyong to be brought to his palace and to live there.

Pihyong was comfortable in the king's palace, and he proved himself to be intelligent. When he turned fifteen, the king appointed him clerk. Some time afterward, word came to the king through his ministers that his clerk went out every evening into the forest and did not return until dawn.

"Send out fifty soldiers to observe what he does tonight," said the king.

The following morning, the ministers reported that the soldiers had seen Pihyong take flight over Wolsong and continue west until he landed on a hill over Hwangch'on. There, he played with a group of spirits all night. When the temple bell rang at dawn, he flew back to the palace.

The king confronted Pihyong, who admitted that what the soldiers saw was the truth. "Can you ask the spirits to construct a bridge over the stream to the north of Sinwon Monastery?" the king asked Pihyong.

Pihyong agreed to speak with the spirits about the request, and that evening they built a stone bridge north of the monastery. The monks called it the Bridge of Spirits. The king was most pleased. He soon had another request.

"Can you ask the spirits if there is one among them who would come to life and become a clerk to do my bidding?" the king asked Pihyong.

The following day, the spirit named Kiltal reported to the king for duty. Kiltal was a devoted clerk, and the king had the childless Queen Imjong adopt him as his own son. Now Kiltal had to do the bidding of the king as well as Imjong. Imjong's demands were more rigorous.

"Build a tall gate tower to the south of Hungnyun Monastery," commanded Imjong.

Kiltal built the tower that evening and slept on top of it every evening thereafter to get the rest he needed from all the labor he did for the king and Imjong. One evening, he could not sleep because he was so tired. He decided to change into a fox, and he ran away.

Pihyong pursued the runaway. Locating him, he ordered the other spirits to kill Kiltal. The spirits did Pihyong's bidding, but, from that moment forward, they feared him. They, too, ran away. Some people saw them escape, and they sang, "Do not go near Pihyong's house, nor do business with his gang of galloping spirits."

Starting the next day, it became the custom of the land to paste these words on portals to keep away evil spirits.

HYONGWANG AND THE LOTUS TEACHINGS

I n the kingdom of Paekche near Ungju, there lived a monk named Hyongwang. This is a story about him. It tells how he learned the Lotus teachings of the religion of Buddhism, met the Dragon King and accepted students of his own.

Like many monks of his time, Hyongwang was not always a monk. He lived a life like many other young men. He was concerned with money and dating and good fortune. But one day Hyongwang decided he had enough of this everyday life. I will cross the ocean to China to learn how to meditate, he resolved. I will learn how to focus my thoughts.

So Hyongwang boarded a ship bound for China. He landed in the state called Ch'en and climbed to the top of Mount Heng. There he met the Reverend Teacher Hui-ssu.

"What brings you here?" the Reverend Teacher asked.

"I wish to learn how to meditate," Hyongwang responded.

"I will teach you the 'Method of Ease and Bliss' of the Lotus Teachings," promised the Reverend Teacher.

Hyongwang was very intelligent and he learned quickly. The Reverend

Teacher Hui-ssu said his progress was like a sharp awl. An awl was a point-ed instrument for making holes. Hyongwang asked his teacher for a certifi-cate that he had learned meditation.

"Your understanding will become fuller and deeper," declared the Reverend Teacher. "Return to your homeland with this certificate."

Hyongwang's eyes filled with tears. He had grown to admire the Reverend Teacher and was sorry to leave him. At the same time, he was eager to return to Paekche. He bid the teacher farewell and descended from the mountain. Walking southward along the Hsi River, Hyongwang came to the ocean. Finding a ship bound for his homeland, he booked passage on it.

The day came for the ship to set sail, and the sun shone brilliantly. Not long into the journey, however, Hyongwang and the other passengers saw the sun pass behind a cloud of many colors. They shielded their eyes from the colorful splendor. Beautiful music came from the cloud, followed by a wondrous voice.

"The Emperor of Heaven calls the Meditation Master Hyongwang to him," proclaimed the voice in the cloud.

A servant dressed in robes of azure, which was the color of the clear sky, approached the startled Hyongwang. The servant brought the monk to the sea palace of the Emperor of Heaven, and Hyongwang saw that none of the servants, including his escort, was human. All of them were spirits. The emperor asked Hyongwang to teach the spirits what he had learned on the mountaintop in China.

For seven days and nights, Hyongwang lectured about what he had learned. He talked about duty, and he talked about nature. The spirits lis-tened intently. No one left Hyongwang for seven days and nights. As a reward, the Dragon King himself escorted the monk back to the ship and bid him farewell.

"I am surprised to find the ship has not journeyed far from the location where it was when I left seven days ago," marveled Hyongwang to the other passengers.

"Seven days?" exclaimed someone.

"Why, you have been gone no more than a half day," said another.

Hyongwang did not argue with them. He grew silent and realized something extraordinary had taken place. Glad to see the shores of his homeland once again, he hurried home to Ungju in the direction of Mount Ong.

Climbing the mountain, Hyongwang was pleased to find a modest hermitage. There, he settled. He began at once to practice his meditation.

At the time, there was a proverb, which said, "The notes of the same key speak to each other." That is just what began to happen on Mount Ong. People of a like mind to Hyongwang started to arrive.

Soon, they built a full monastery to replace the tiny hermitage on the mountaintop. This was quite necessary, because with each new day, more people arrived to learn from Hyongwang. Each day, the monk ordered the gates to be opened, and the new students passed through. Someone remarked they were like the flocks of birds that hovered over Mount Sumeru, so alike were they.

One day like the others that had preceded it, Hyongwang asked that the gates be opened. The new students greeted their teacher and began to study in the monastery on Mount Ong. But the day was different from other days. At one point, Hyongwang departed down the mountain. For as many people as were present, no one saw him leave. People said he disappeared, and no one ever saw him again.

ADO AND HIS MOTHER

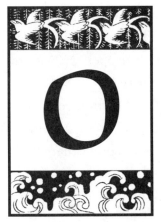

ne day, a man named Kulma, who was a native of Wei, met a woman named Ko Tonyong in her native land of Koguryo. He was an official who had traveled to Koguryo on business. The man and woman fell in love, and they lived happily together in her native land. Unfortunately for the woman, the man's business dealings came to an end. He departed for his land of Wei without her. The woman Ko Tonyong was pregnant.

Ko Tonyong gave birth to a beautiful boy she named Ado. Each day, her neighbors in Koguryo marveled at his magnificent appearance. By the time Ado was five years old, the neighbors questioned how it was that the boy looked so extraordinary. Some even feared Ado and began to shun his mother Ko Tonyong.

"Ado, my son, here is my advice to you. As you are without a father to protect you, I suggest you become a monk. Then no one will question your radiant appearance," said Ko Tonyong when Ado was five years old.

Ado heeded his mother's words. That day, he asked to have his head shaved like a monk. He knew he would be a monk when he became a man. When Ado turned sixteen, he went to speak to his mother in the garden.

"Mother, I wish to visit Kulma my father in his land of Wei. I will inform him I desire to learn under Master Hsuan-chang of Wei," he said.

Ko Tonyong was saddened to see her son leave home, yet she knew it was the path he must take. Mother and son bid each other farewell. The following morning, Ado departed for the home of the father he had never met.

Kulma was pleased to see his son. When Ado made the request, Kulma made the arrangements for him to study under Master Hsuan-chang. For nineteen years, Ado remained in the monastery with the Master. One day, he decided to return to Koguryo, his native land and that of his mother.

Ko Tonyong greeted Ado warmly, yet she was concerned. "My son, you will not find a good audience for your teachings in this land. It is much too soon. I suggest you travel to the kingdom of Silla, where people are more ready to hear what you teach. It will not be easy, though, for two hundred years must pass before the people there are really ready to hear," she said.

Once more, Ado heeded the advice of his mother. Again, mother and son bid each other farewell. Ado departed the following morning for the neighboring land of Silla to the south.

He settled to the west of the palace. He asked the authorities for permission to teach what he learned from the Master, and they grew fearful for no one had taught the teachings before in this village. His neighbors, hearing about Ado's intentions, grew afraid. Some threatened to kill him.

Before sunrise, Ado escaped. This time, he settled in the village of Sok, which is the present-day Sonju. A man named Morok allowed Ado to live in his house. Three years passed, and one day the king dispatched messengers throughout the land, asking for help. The princess had taken ill, and no one in the palace was able to cure her. The king required the skill of a healer or his daughter would die.

Ado thanked Morok for his kind hospitality, and he hurried to the palace. "I am a healer," he said to the king.

The king welcomed Ado and showed him into his daughter's chambers. The princess was very ill. She was close to death. Yet Ado was able to banish her illness, and the princess recovered her former good health.

"I am very grateful to you, monk, and I wish to give you a gift. Name whatever it is you desire, and I will see to it that it is yours," said the happy king.

"If you were to build a monastery in the Forest of the Heavenly Mirror, I would be most content," Ado responded.

While the king's servants built the monastery, Ado lived in a humble hut in the forest. For a time afterward, he resided alone and without students in the new, large monastery in the Forest of the Heavenly Mirror. Seven years passed.

One day, Morok's sister Sasi arrived. "I wish to become a nun," she said to her old friend Ado. Others also came, and Ado began to teach. The kindly king died some years later, and the new king did not respect Ado's teaching.

Returning to the village of Sok, Ado had a grave built for himself. Then he descended into the grave and pulled the slab over the top. There he died, remembering his mother's words. Finally, two hundred years later, the king of Silla respected the teachings of Buddhism.

THE SEVEN-FOOT-TALL KING

he twenty-third king was named Wonjong. And he was seven feet tall. The people of the kingdom of Silla loved Wonjong, and he returned their love. In the third year of his rule, a dragon appeared in the Willow Well. The people took the event as a sign of heavenly confidence in their king.

One day, King Wonjong met with his ministers of state. "I wish to declare the kingdom's dedication to Buddhism in honor of the teachings of our ancestor Ado. We will build monasteries," the king proclaimed.

"How can we erect monasteries when the crops have been so bad lately?" one minister responded.

"Correctly stated. We have not the money for such building," said a second minister.

"We have enemies at our borders we may have to fight. We need the money in the treasury for the purpose of battle," a third minister offered.

The king exhaled a deep sigh. He saw there was little harmony among his ministers. For several years, nothing changed. Still, the king vowed silently he would build the monasteries.

In the fourteenth year of King Wonjong's reign, the Grand Secretary of the realm was named Yomch'ok. Yomch'ok recognized the king's desire, because he, too, shared it.

"I have devised a plan," said Yomch'ok to the king one day. "Have me put out the word that you wish monasteries to be built in the kingdom immediately. When the ministers hear of this, they will begin to complain as always. Then tell them you gave no such order. They will have to pun-ish the person who made the false decree. Afterwards, they will champion your cause, because you have been wronged."

"I have two problems with your plan. The first is that I would have to sacrifice your life. The second is that, even if I have you put to death, the ministers might not find this to be enough of a cause to build the monas-teries," responded the grateful king.

Yomch'ok had an argument. "Heaven respects the teachings of the Great Sage Buddha. And heaven will respond with miracles even if some-one as unworthy as myself is put to death in honor of the Great Sage. Moreover, the great principle of an official of the kingdom is to sacrifice his own life to accomplish goodness," he said.

"You argue well, Yomch'ok. Let it be done as you say," ruled King Wonjong.

"If it means the Buddha Sun will shine forever over the kingdom, the moment of my death will be the moment I am born," said the good Yomch'ok.

So Yomch'ok went to the ministers with the king's order to erect monas-teries in the kingdom of Silla. "The first to be built will be in the Forest of the Heavenly Mirror," he proclaimed.

"Impossible," said the first minister.

"Certainly not feasible," shouted the second minister.

"We must protest this decree before the king himself," declared the third minister.

The king gave audience to his ministers. When they had finished speaking, he answered them. "I have ordered no such construction. Surely, this is a false decree. Find the person who wronged my rule in this manner, and I will see to it that he is put to death," said the king.

The ministers returned to the king's throne room with the Grand Secretary Yomch'ok. "My loyal Yomch'ok, why have you acted in this false manner?" asked King Wonjong, pretending to be horrified.

"How can a sparrow understand the dreams of a swan?" he responded.

"I order that you be put to death at sunrise tomorrow," the king declared.

At sunrise, when the executioner cut off Yomch'ok's head, it flew in the direction of Diamond Mountain. When the head landed on the mountaintop, a fountain of white milk rose from the cut hundreds of feet into the air. The sun disappeared, and beautiful flowers rained on the mountain from the dark clouds. The ground shook as though an earthquake had taken place.

"Quickly, give him the burial ceremony," said the king. The frightened ministers obeyed.

"Now since we have seen the will of heaven, let us take an oath to build monasteries to honor the Buddha," proclaimed the king.

The ministers did not utter a word of argument. Repeating the king's words, they took the oath. To everyone's surprise, on the ground before them stood the foundation of an old monastery.

"This day, I abdicate my throne. Instead of your king, I am now a humble monk," said the seven-foot tall Wonjong.

With the trees of the forest, the former king's servants finished the construction of the monastery. It was named Taewang Hungnyun. And the king took residence in the first monastery in the kingdom of Silla.

THE MASTER, THE SPIRIT AND THE DRAGON

S ince he was a boy, the master showed he had an understanding greater than everyone else possessed. The people in his village saw he was gifted. The king heard about the boy and his love of literature and the sacred teachings. When he was thirteen years old, the boy shaved his head.

"Today I am a monk," he declared. People came to listen whenever he spoke. They called him a master, because of his pure ideas. The young master spoke of thoughts and ideas and how to live a good life. He had no interest in the things of the world.

He moved to a cave on Samgi Mountain when he was thirty years old. When people came to hear his words, the monk spoke to them from inside the cave. No one ever saw his shadow in the sun.

One day another monk appeared on Samgi Mountain. The new monk built a monastery near the opening of the cave. The building did not trouble the master, who remained inside the cave with his thoughts. Then a spirit appeared, too.

"Master, I have seen how good you are. Now I must ask you to do something no other man can do. You must tell this new monk to leave the mountain, because he follows the evil ways. If he does not leave, a disaster will happen," warned the spirit.

"Can you not tell him to move?" the master replied, humbly.

"Only you can do this. Your goodness washes away the blackness from his evil-doing. He cleanses in your shadow despite his evil worship," the spirit answered.

The following day, the master walked outside his cave into the sun. It was the first time in many, many days that he felt its warmth upon his back. He approached the monastery, which was the home of the evil monk.

"You must move from this mountain or a disaster will happen to you. I have heard this from a spirit," said the master to the monk.

"Why should I listen to a spirit when I am protected by my teachings?" responded the evil monk.

Without another word, the master returned to the cave. The sprit visited that evening. Because he feared what the spirit would do to the evil monk, the master pretended he had not yet spoken to him.

"Please, do not worry, spirit. I know the monk will leave tomorrow," said the master.

The spirit saw the master's purpose in protecting the evil monk from disaster, and he knew what must be done. He bid the master farewell. Loud thunder gripped the sky. A mighty crash shook the earth. The next morning, the master looked through the opening of his cave. The monastery was crushed to the ground. A giant landslide covered most of it. The evil monk was nowhere in sight.

For several years, the master traveled across the sea to the west to study. On his return voyage, he encountered a dragon from the deck of the ship. The master asked the dragon what it wanted from him.

"I wish you to build a monastery north of Unmun, where a flock of magpies peck upon the ground. You will have my protection always," said the dragon.

When the ship docked in Silla, the master went first to his old cave upon Samgi Mountain. He wanted to see it after so many years. The spirit greeted him. "Have you not entered into an agreement with the sea dragon?" the spirit inquired.

The following morning, the master and the spirit departed for the north of Unmun. They encountered the flock of magpies the dragon had described. The magpies pecked in a large group at the ground in one particular spot.

"Let us clear the ground there," suggested the spirit.

With little effort, spirit and master cleared away debris. The remains of a stone pagoda stood at the spot where the magpies had pecked. The people of the area helped the master to add to the pagoda and build a monastery. The master remained there for several years.

"My end is near," said the spirit one day.

Since the master had never seen the spirit's form, he asked permission to see. "Tomorrow at dawn, look to the east," replied the spirit.

The following sunrise, the master did as the spirit told him. A giant black arm rose from the earth into heaven. "I have shown you my arm, but nonetheless I cannot escape death. I will die tomorrow and you can see my form," the spirit said.

The next day, the master traveled to the place where the spirit said it would die. An old black badger lay upon the sand. With a whimper, it died. The master knew it had been the spirit.

A terrible drought dried the land for a time afterwards. The master spoke with the sea dragon one day. "Can you not bring rain to help the people?" the master pleaded.

"I can make rain. But heaven will be angry if I take its power to end the drought," the dragon responded.

"I will save you with my power," the master said.

That day, the crops drank in the rain, and the thirsty sea filled again. A messenger from heaven visited the master, who was again in his cave on Samgi Mountain. The master hid the dragon in the cave.

"You are hiding the dragon that brought the rain without heaven's permission. I must punish this dragon," accused the messenger.

The master pointed to a pear tree on the hill. "Punish the tree," he said.

With one strike, the messenger split the tree in half from top to bottom. Then the messenger disappeared. The dragon came out from hiding in the cave.

"Thank you, tree, for taking my punishment. I will repay your generosity." Touching the tree, the dragon made it whole again.

Then master and dragon bid each other farewell for the time being.

KIM HUMUN

im Humun was of royal birth in the kingdom of Silla during the reign of King Muyol. He was a hwarang, one of a group of young knights of noble birth. In the tradition of the hwarang-do, which meant the Flower of Youth knightly order, Kim Humun was loyal to his fellow knights. Whenever one of them fell in battle, he cried. If someone did something brave, he celebrated the bravery.

It was the sixth year of Yung-hui. King Muyol of Silla decided to send an army into battle. The ruler sought to punish the neighboring kingdoms of Paekche to the west and Koguryo to the north for invading Silla.

"I appoint Kim Humun as Commander of the Nang Bannerman," declared King Muyol.

"I am honored by the appointment, Majesty," responded Kim Humun.

Then a knight in Kim Humun's troops of Nang Bannerman spoke, "If Kim stands before the enemy, he will not return alive."

It was not so unusual for a knight to have such a foreboding. The hwarang were trained by Buddhist monks to seek the truth in all things. Silenced by the words, the other knights looked to Kim Humun for lead-

ership. Would he turn down the king's commission? No one could blame
he if he did.

Instead, the young nobleman gathered the troops of the Nang
Bannerman. They left Silla immediately. As they traveled, they suffered a
fierce rainstorm. The wind blew furiously. Yet they kept riding. Finally, in
Paekche territory, the king's knights set up their tents just below Yangsan.
Kim Humun drafted his battle plan.

"The enemy from Paekche is behind those walls. We will attack
Choch'on Fortress early tomorrow morning," he announced, pointing to
the enemy fortress.

The night was very dark, and the Sillan knights could not make a fire
for fear of alerting the enemy in the fortress of their location. But the enemy already knew of the camp in their territory. Their scouts had seen the
knights coming. Moreover, an enemy spy had overheard Kim Humun's battle plan.

"Let us attack them tonight under the cover of darkness," declared the
leader of the enemy troops.

The enemy attack caused great confusion in the Sillan camp. Most of
the knights were sleeping in their tents when it happened. By the time they
gathered their weapons, the enemy had retreated to their fortress. Some of
Kim Humun's knights were injured, and he felt responsible. He rallied his
forces for the attack at dawn. But as they began to advance upon the enemy
fortress, enemy arrows shot at them from the ramparts. Now Kim was more
stubborn about the need to attack the fortress.

One of his knights spoke to him. "It is not yet light enough to see any
distance ahead of ourselves. Why don't you retreat to safety, for you are of
royal blood? If you were to die here, no one would even see that you did
your kingdom honor."

"If a knight is loyal to his kingdom, that is what matters. Whether my valor is seen or unseen, this is of little matter. I do not fight for my future fame. I do battle for the future of the kingdom of Silla," responded Kim Humun.

He sat proudly upon his horse with his lance raised. An attendant, wary of the danger to his master, steadied Kim's reins. In his other hand, Kim held his unsheathed sword.

Down went one of the enemy from his lance. Another fell at the point of his sword. Yet another advanced upon Kim. Though he put up a valiant fight, Kim, too, fell. The words of his fellow knight rang true, and Kim Humun died. Two of his knights, Yep'a and Choktuk, died alongside him.

Another of the hwarang in Kim's company, a young man named Poyongna, shouted a battle cry. "I ride into battle to do honor to Kim Humun. He was noble until the end of his life. My own life has no value if I continue to breathe while he does not. Therefore, if I die, no shame will come of it, because Kim is dead before me," Poyongna said.

The loyal knight steered his horse into battle. He successfully fought several of the enemy, and they fell dead on the battlefield. But, like Kim, he, too, was killed.

When the troops of Kim Humung returned to Silla, the people of the kingdom learned of the deaths of the young knights. They honored Kim Humun, Yep'a, Choktuk and Poyongna. Someone wrote a ballad called the "Song of Yangsan" in honor of the site of their camp. Whenever people spoke of Kim Humung and the other young knights, they sang this song.

KIM YUSIN
AND THE OLD MAN

usin's friends respected him, because he was a fine leader. When they spoke of his leadership qualities, they called him "Dragon Flower Disciple of Fragrance." Yusin knew it was a high honor to be so judged by his peers. He took his responsibility to the kingdom of Silla very seriously.

Since age fifteen, he was a hwarang, a member of a group of young knights of noble birth. The hwarang were trained by Buddhist monks to seek the truth in all things.

It was the twenty-eighth year of Konbok, and Chinp'yong was king. Yusin was seventeen years old.

"I must do something to stop the attack of Silla from its warring neighbors," Yusin resolved. He bid farewell to his friends and set out on a journey to find the answer to how to defeat the enemies of Silla.

Yusin traveled to the Central Peaks. There he found a small cave. He began to pray.

"O heaven, please look upon me and give me assistance. My kingdom's enemies are at the borders. While I pledge my willingness to stop them, I am unworthy without your help," prayed Yusin.

After four days, an old man ventured past the cave. Yusin noticed his torn garments and tattered appearance. The old man was surprised to find a nobleman alone in the Central Peaks.

"Young nobleman, there are venomous snakes and unfriendly beasts in these mountains. Why have you come here alone?" inquired the old man.

"Honored ancient one, what is your name? And where is your home?" responded Yusin.

"I travel when and where fate tells me. I don't have a name nor a home," said the old man.

Yusin recognized that this man was not a common human. He approached him with the question he had been asking heaven for four days. Before he spoke, Yusin bowed twice.

"Please, old man, can you give me a formula to end my troubles? You see, I live in Silla, and our enemies are at our borders. What can I do to help our kingdom?" Yusin asked.

The old man answered with silence. Six times, Yusin repeated his question. Six times, the old man remained silent. Then Yusin began to cry. His sorrow was so plentiful that the old man was moved to speak.

"Your heart and your bravery have convinced me to share the secret with you. I will give you the formula you require, but, beware, do not use it for the wrong reason. If you do, you will bring tragedy to yourself," the old man replied.

No sooner did he whisper the secret in Yusin's ear than the old man was gone. Yusin, in pursuit, descended the mountain in the hopes of finding him. When he reached the bottom of the hill, the man was nowhere to be seen. What Yusin saw instead was a light at the top of the mountain that glowed as five colors at once.

A year passed, and the enemies at Silla's borders were stronger than ever. In the autumn, the king assembled his troops for an attack upon Koguryo's Nangbi Fortress. The kingdom of Koguryo learned of the impending attack, and their army attacked first. Many Sillan warriors were killed.

Yusin was Commander of the Sillan Central Banner. The amount of bloodshed suffered by his countrymen tore at his heart. He thought of the secret formula the old man gave him. Informing his troops that he must purify himself for three days, Yusin traveled to the valley of the Yonbak Mountains.

For three days, he prayed. "O Keeper of Heaven, I ask you to send a spirit of the light into my sword," Yusin repeated. He burned incense and purified himself and his intentions. At the end of the third day, Yusin drew his sword. The keeper of heaven responded to this prayer.

Upon seeing their commander, the troops of the Central Banner stood in amazement. Their leader's sword shone brilliantly in his hands. So shimmering was it that it seemed to move of its own accord.

Yusin sat high upon his horse and rode into battle. His brilliant sword was ready to claim victory. Into the enemy's fortress, Yusin proceeded without stopping until he was face-to-face with Koguryo's general. The two men fought furiously, but young Yusin was the stronger warrior. The enemy troops fell back when their general dropped to the ground. Seeing their own leader's valor, the troops of the Central Banner followed Yusin into battle. The Sillan forces overpowered their enemy with such ferocity that even the beasts that lived in the enemy fortress came outside to surrender.

KIM YUSIN
AND THE MEN OF T'ANG

im Inmun was the son of Kim Yusin's sister. In the summer of the seventh year of the reign of the Great King T'aejong, Inmun traveled to T'ang. King T'aejong had sent him to ask the empire of T'ang for troops to help fight the attack on Silla by the kingdom of Paekche. T'ang responded by sending two generals and 130,000 troops across the sea.

"Take one hundred ships filled with our troops to meet the army from T'ang at Tongmul Island," the king said to his son, the Crown Prince.

"I appoint Yusin, Chinju and Ch'onjon to accompany me as generals," responded the Crown Prince.

The Crown Prince and his generals and their army welcomed the visiting army from T'ang to Silla.

"Let us fight this invasion together. I will sail by sea with my forces if you will take the route by land. We shall meet outside Sabi, the capital of Paekche next month on the tenth day," declared the T'ang commander. Inmun received the permission of his Crown Prince to sail with the T'ang forces.

The Great King, in the meantime, after hearing of the plan, set up camp with the remaining troops at Sara. All went well for the Crown Prince and his army on the overland route, and they arrived by the tenth day of the seventh month at the walls of Sabi. Inmun and the T'ang forces, however, could not land upon the thick, muddy shores of Ibolp'o, where they had to disembark for the rendez-vous with the king and the Crown Prince.

"Let us spread mats of the rush that grows in the marsh so the ships can dock," suggested Kim Yusin. The Crown Prince gave the order, and the T'ang army successfully landed.

The battle with Paekche was fierce, but together the Sillan and T'ang armies fought valiantly. They overpowered the enemy, and the border of Silla was secure once again. Yusin distinguished himself during the battle for his leadership.

"Who is that fine warrior?" asked the T'ang general. The Crown Prince answered that it was Yusin, called "Dragon Flower Disciple of Fragrance."

When the T'ang forces returned to their country, word of Yusin's valor reached the emperor. The emperor sent a messenger to Silla with a gift for Yusin. "The emperor has bestowed upon you, your nephew Inmun and your brother Humsun all of the enemy territory our forces captured," said the messenger.

"How can we three unworthy soldiers deserve such an offering when the whole of Silla is celebrating the great victory, one we could not have accomplished without the aid of the emperor? We cannot accept such a gift," Yusin responded.

While the emperor's offer to Yusin, Inmun and Humsun was well-meaning, his other intentions were less honest. He ordered T'ang troops to camp in the hills of Sabi. Now T'ang would try to invade Silla. The Great King of Silla learned of the emperor's intentions, and he assembled his troops. Now the T'ang commander heard from a spy of the mounting defense of its kingdom by Silla. On the third day of the ninth month, the T'ang army sailed for home instead of attacking.

A voice from the clouds spoke to them as they crossed the sea, "Why did you decide against an attack on Silla?" the keeper of heaven asked.

The T'ang commander responded, "We did not attack because the king of Silla is just, his commanders are loyal and his subjects honor their leaders as though they were fathers or mothers, brothers or sisters."

Years passed, and this time the T'ang emperor asked the kingdom of Silla for forces to help win a battle. T'ang wished to invade Koguryo. Now Munmu was the Great King of Silla.

"I appoint Humsun and Inmun as generals to lead our forces in the aid of the T'ang army," said King Munmu.

"What of Yusin, Your Majesty?" Humsun asked, referring to his respected older brother.

"Yes, Majesty, how can we hope to win without Yusin beside us?" asked Inmun, Yusin's nephew.

Humsun continued, "I fear defeat without my brother at our side."

"Silla's national treasures are Yusin, Humsun and Inmun. I cannot send the three treasures onto foreign soil and leave our kingdom unprotected. I must keep Yusin here. He is strong enough to fight alone," answered the wise king.

Now Humsun and Inmun went to Yusin with their doubts about fighting without him at their side. "We are not worthy of the task the king has given us," Humsun told his brother.

"Please, give us advice," Inmun asked his uncle.

"Do not ask my counsel, but, rather, pray to the keeper of heaven. With heaven's protection, you will be victorious. Your enemy will not share this protection," answered Yusin.

"We honor your words," answered Humsun.

"You will see that we will bring honor to Silla," Inmun promised.

And they did.

MASTER STRONG-HEAD

I n the village of Imna Kara in the Saryang district of the kingdom of Silla, a woman had a dream one night. The next morning, she greeted her husband Sokch'e. She told him about it.

"Husband, last night I dreamed of a man with a horn on his head," she said. The husband listened half-heartedly.

The woman gave birth later that year. "Wife, this boy has a piece of bone sticking out of the back of his skull," said the surprised father.

"It's like my dream," the mother of the baby responded. She answered as though the boy's head was not at all unusual to her.

The parents called their son Chadu. Chadu grew like a normal child. His head grew, too, along with the rest of him. So did the piece of bone coming out of the back of his skull.

One day, Chadu's father Sokch'e desired an answer to why his son's head looked the way it did. He took Chadu by the hand and they walked to the outskirts of the village. When they arrived at the home of the village wiseman at the top of the hill, Sokch'e asked him about Chadu's head.

The wiseman answered, "There have been others who looked different.

You must have heard of Fu-hsi. He had the body of a tiger. And Nu-kua slithered like a snake. Do you not remember the story of the head of an ox that sat upon Shen-nung's shoulders? Do you forget that the mouth of a horse decorated Kao-yao's face? What concerns me about your son is not the bone in the back of his head. No, what troubles me is the black mole on his face. That is what is not good. His head with its bone in the back of the skull is good. Therefore, I must say that the two signs together mean he is extraordinary."

"Wife, our son is a prodigy," Sokch'e said when he and Chadu returned home. He understood that Chadu would be very wise for his young age.

The rest of Chadu's childhood was peaceful. The boy learned to read easily and without instruction. He learned all he could of the teachings of Confucius. Though his experience in the world was little, his understanding was great. Word of his knowledge spread throughout the kingdom, and Chadu was quite famous though he was a child.

As a youth, Chadu grew acquainted with the daughter of the village metalworker. They fell in love. But Chadu's parents wished to arrange a marriage for the son, which was the custom of that time. Since their son was renowned for his learning, they wanted him to marry a woman who was worthy. They had selected a young woman from the village who was wealthy and from a family of high stature.

Chadu bowed twice to his parents to show his respect for them. "Poverty is nothing that should cause one shame. In the words of the ancients, a man must not abandon a friendship with someone who is poor even if he expects to possess prosperity. I wish to marry the metalworker's daughter. Would you choose me to marry two women in order to make you happy. Is that not wrong?" he argued.

So Chadu and the daughter of the metalworker were married with the blessing of Chadu's parents. Shortly afterward, Chadu became an official of the kingdom. He served in various offices of the king, and in each one his reputation grew.

One day, a messenger from the T'ang empire came with a decree for the King of Silla. It was very difficult to read, and King Muyol called for someone wise to interpret the decree. The king's high official summoned Chadu, who easily read the message.

"What is your name and why have we not met before this if you are so learned?" the king asked.

Chadu gave his name and said he lived in Inma Kara.

"I see you are very wise. From today you may call yourself Kangsu, or Master Strong-Head of Imna Kara," said the king.

King Muyol asked the newly named Kangsu to write a letter of gratitude to the emperor of T'ang. The letter won the services of T'ang for Silla in its battle against Koguryo and Paekche. The king gave Kangsu one hundred bags of grain for his help. He awarded him the new office of scribe because of his wisdom. On many occasions, Kangsu assisted the king. He communicated with the kingdoms of T'ang, Koguryo and Paekche. In a short time, the king increased Kangsu's payment to two hundred bags of grain a year.

When Kangsu, Master Strong-Head of Imna Kara, died, the new king paid for his burial. There was a shortage of food in the kingdom that year. Nonetheless, King Sinmun offered Kangsu's wife, the daughter of the village metalworker, one hundred bags of grain. But she graciously refused the gift.

"For many years, I have depended upon my husband for my food and grain. The court has been very kind to us. I dare not accept this gift now that I am alone," she said. She then returned to the home of her father, the metalworker.

She continued to love Kangsu in her memory. His reputation remained alive, too, throughout the kingdom. In the village of Imna Kara, people talked often of the boy who was born with the piece of bone coming out of the back of his skull.

THE SONG OF CH'OYONG

usic and song rang throughout the kingdom. It was a time of great peace and prosperity. Every home in the land for as far as the eye could see, from the capital to the sea and up through the hills, had a roof of tile. No household was too poor to afford one. Not one single home was shamed by a roof made of straw. "No thatched roofs, no thatched roofs," sang the birds in the trees of the kingdom.

When the farmers planted their seeds, the rains came. When the seeds began to sprout, the sun warmed them. The rains came again when the young shoots needed to drink. The sun replaced the rains to warm the spreading leaves. So it was through every season. The rain and the sun danced in the sky and upon the earth in perfect partnership.

King Hongang was ruler. He was the forty-ninth ruler of Silla. The king, too, enjoyed many hours of goodwill every day. The borders were free of invasion from Koguryo and Paekche, and subjects of the kingdom were law-abiding.

The happy king liked to spend his free time on warm days at the beach. One day, he told his attendants he wished to go to the beach at Kaeunp'o.

Kaeunp'o meant Cloud Opening Cove, so the royal party sang and danced from the castle to the beach of the cloudless sky they would find when they arrived at the small, sheltered bay.

The fish were glad to welcome them. "Greetings, o king, greetings, o king," they sang in unison.

The king's musicians answered the welcome in harmony. The servants began to lay out the banquet they had brought from the capital. The insects and small woods beasts hummed patiently in anticipation of the rewards they knew they would have soon from the royal leftovers.

The table was set, and the sun shone down upon the fine specialties. The king declared the meal would begin, and the musicians answered in song. The king lifted the first bite and began to bring it to his mouth when something extraordinary took place.

A row of black clouds silenced the song. The fish in the sea were quiet. The insects and beasts were still. Then a thick fog cloaked the cove which was, of course, no longer cloudless. The king's astologer made his way through the fog to speak.

"I fear this is caused by the anger of the dragon of the Eastern Sea," the astrologer proclaimed.

"What can we do to appease this anger?" the troubled king asked.

"The dragon wishes that a monastery be built in his honor," answered the astrologer.

"I order the building to begin immediately," the king declared. His attendants began to dig, and the servants scoured the beach for stone. Shortly, the foundation of a monastery stood before the king.

The clouds broke and the cove filled with sunshine. The fog disappeared as quickly as it had come. The dragon and his seven sons bowed to the king, and he invited them to his banquet. The fish and the birds and the insects and woods beasts resumed their songs. When the banquet was finished, the dragon and six of his sons bid the king farewell. The seventh son returned to the capital with the royal party. He called himself Ch'oyong.

The king rewarded Ch'oyong the dragon with a beautiful woman, whom Ch'oyung married with her permission. Their wedding brimmed with music and song, fine food and good cheer. The new couple began their married life in peace.

One day, the demon of plague could no longer control his anger that a dragon had such a beautiful woman for a wife. He himself had nothing surrounding him but disease. The demon's song was unlike the other songs of harmony in the king's residence.

Waiting until the dragon was away, then changing himself into a man, the demon stole into Ch'oyong's chambers. He began to sing to the dragon's wife. "Two legs have I, behold the two, two legs have I, they are for you," he sang to her.

Just then, the dragon returned. The embarrassed imposter shrank from the human form he had stolen to his normal, miserable self as the demon of plague. He whined, "I wanted your wife, so I changed into a man. Now I must pay for my terrible crime."

But Ch'oyong disappointed the demon once more. Instead of torching him in anger, the dragon forgave him.

"While you could have punished me gravely for my misdeed, you have shown goodness. I promise never to enter your chambers again," the demon vowed.

The people in the kingdom of Silla applauded the dragon's greatness. Singing songs in his praise, they pasted drawings of him at their doorways. The very image of Ch'oyong protected the homes with the tile roofs from sickness and plague.

VIETNAM

LAC DRAGON LORD

ong ago, evil demons and monsters in hideous shapes prowled through the land of Vietnam. They went anywhere they wanted, and took anything they wanted, no matter who owned it. Some people were brave enough to complain. The demons told them to do what they were told, or they would be eaten. Afterwards, the demons would eat one or two people to show how serious they were.

Whenever the demons were sleeping after a meal, the people complained bitterly. Some of their complaints were carried on the wind to the sea. They reached the home of Lac Long Quan or Lac Dragon Lord. Lac was the ruler of the ocean, and he lived in a great palace on a beautiful reef. He was surrounded by his family and an army of giant fish.

Lac was a kind king, so he took pity on the cries from above the water. Riding a great surge of waves, he crashed onto the shore, awakening the demons. Though the demons were ten feet tall, they ran in terror at the sight of him. Lac subdued all the demons that did not have the sense to run past the farthest hillside one could see. Then he looked for the people who had called for his help. He searched behind every rock, and under every bush.

Slowly the people crept from behind their hiding places. Lac was very large. He was tall with big teeth. Although he was smiling, the people were not sure what to do.

"It looks like I'm going to have to set up a school," said Lac, "to show the people how to overcome their problems."

In the years that followed, Lac taught the Vietnamese people the skills to stay alive and free: how to grow rice, how to make and wear clothes, how to write and read, and how to fight off enemies. But, in spite of his teaching, he could also foresee that there might come a time when the Vietnamese might need his help again.

One morning, he called the people to the seashore. "I must go back to my home in the sea," he said. "If you ever have a problem that you can't take care of yourselves, call on me and I will come again."

Years passed, and the people of Vietnam grew in skill and wisdom. They built on what Lac Long Quan had taught them. They needed no king in the land to tell them what to do, for they had learned well.

Tales of the Vietnamese people reached northward to the ears of a ruler in China. "They have no king?" he said, amazed. "How lucky for me! I will go there and take their land."

Over the mountains he came, and with a great army. More people were in that army than lived in all of Vietnam. The people were frightened by the invasion, and they did not know what to do. So they called on Lac Dragon Lord. Once again, Lac came sweeping out of his home in the sea upon a surge of waves. Because he also could fly, he perched on top of a mountain to look at the Chinese army.

He was amazed. "There are more Chinese here than all the demons I conquered last time!" he said to himself. "It will take too long and be too hard to attack them one by one." He would have to be more thoughtful.

The Chinese king was proud. He did not believe anything could defeat him in Vietnam, so he brought along his wife Au Co to watch his victory. Au Co was an immortal of the mountain. She and the king were staying in a grand tent in the middle of the Chinese camp. She thought the king was too proud.

Lac flew high into the sky. He was so far up that he blocked out the light of the sun. The Chinese were afraid at the sudden darkness. They became even more afraid when they saw a dragon surrounded by fire hurtling towards them. They fled back to their camp.

Lac Long Quan swooped and landed in front of the king's tent. Out walked Au Co. "May I ask the name of this august intruder?" she asked, smiling.

"I am Lac Dragon Lord," he replied. "I ask you to come with me."

Au Co loved adventure, and she had always wanted to go for a ride in the air. She was also charmed by the presence of Loc Dragon Lord. Moreover, she was bored with the king's court. Lac in turn was delighted with her sense of humor and her lack of fear. Off they went, to live on the top of Mount Tan Vien. Recognizing that the powers of Lac Dragon Lord were too great, the Chinese king and his army left Vietnam in despair.

After three years on the mountaintop, Au Co miraculously gave birth to a pouch! Seven days afterward, one hundred eggs exited the pouch. From those eggs, one hundred boys hatched.

Although they were happy on the mountaintop, in time Lac Dragon Lord began to long for the sea. But Au Co was happy where she was. They realized that Lac's love for water and Au Co's desire for earth would inevitably make them part.

Sadly, they divided their sons. Each took fifty boys. Lac's boys became the ancestors of the Vietnamese who sailed and worked on the sea. Au Co's were those who lived in the hills and worked the land. And so it is still today.

And the Vietnamese knew that if they ever got into trouble again, they could still call on Lac.

How the Toad Got Heaven's Help

I n ancient times, when earth was closer to Heaven, there was a severe drought. It had not rained in so long that only one puddle remained for the toad to use for cooling off. He was at his wit's end, because he had watched his precious pond dry up bit by bit. What would he do when the last puddle was gone, too, he wondered. He never slept, because he was afraid to wake up and find that his puddle no longer existed. He grew very cranky and decided to do something before it was too late.

"I will take the long journey to Heaven to speak about this terrible situation on earth," the toad resolved.

He set out immediately. He had hopped only a few miles when he heard the buzzing of bees. They swarmed about him and asked where he was going. He answered politely.

"We will accompany you. What good is staying on earth when all of the flowers are dead?" said the queen bee. So the toad and the bees resolved to travel together.

Before long, a low, mournful crowing made them pause. A tired, annoyed cock ambled toward them. "I have no more insects to eat, and there is not a morsel of grain to be found," the cock complained.

"You can come with us to speak to Heaven," the toad offered. The cock thought this was a good idea and joined the caravan.

They were met on the path by a skinny, irritable tiger, who complained that the drought had killed every last one of her prey. As soon as the tiger learned of the purpose of their travel, she joined the party on the way to Heaven. Before long, they came upon a fox and a bear. The fox could not find a single rabbit to hunt, and the bear could no longer tolerate the rumblings from his empty stomach. They, too, decided to join the others in their pursuit of a heavenly solution.

Some days later, the hot, hungry travelers came to Tien Dinh. It was the location of the Gates of Heaven. They hopped and flew from star to star until they stood at the very threshold of Heaven.

"Wait here. I will state our case alone," said the toad.

Leaving his companions behind, the toad hopped into the palace. He followed the echoes of laughter to the Hall of Audience. There, he saw the King of Heaven, playing cards with some angels and fairies. Imagine playing cards at a time like this, the toad thought with annoyance.

Angrily, he croaked, "How dare you neglect earth to play cards?"

"Disrespectful toad, how dare you even speak to Heaven. Guards, take him away," shouted the King of Heaven.

But, before the guards could close their hands over him, the toad called to the bees for assistance. Buzzing furiously, they flew in through the windows and stung the guards. Next, the King of Heaven summoned the Thunder God. The toad commanded the cock to come, and the rooster chased the god away. The King of Heaven yelled for the Captain of the Hounds to kill the cock. But the tiger, who, along with the bear and fox, also had entered the hall killed the attack dog. The hungry fox and bear ate the dog's innards.

"You have battled mightily, toad. Now state your case," the King of Heaven said.

"Unless you send rain to earth, every creature there will perish," the toad responded.

"I will create rain immediately. And, if I forget again, no need to travel so far. All you have to do is ask me, uncle," said the King of Heaven. He used the term of respect for the toad.

The company of travelers bid farewell to Heaven. No sooner were they at the Gates, than the sky broke open. Mountains of rain fell upon the earth that day and for many days following.

When the travelers came to the forest, they said good-bye to the bear and fox. The tiger was excited to return to the jungle, and she immediately began to hunt. The cock ate every insect he could find on the way and bid the others a hurried farewell when he was close to home. Buzzing good-bye over the head of the toad, the bees started to quench themselves on fresh flowers. The toad hopped into his old pond with the biggest splash he could make.

Despite the plentiful drenching, many creatures from every earthly species died. But soon earth began to nurture new creatures. Life was abundant again.

During his life, the toad asked the King of Heaven many times for rain. Each time, his request was answered. When he died, the toad's children and their children and their children's children have done the same.

For this reason, the toad is still called "Heaven's uncle."

THE TORTOISE'S CROSSBOW

A long time ago, the king of Van Lang refused to give his daughter's hand in marriage to the king of neighboring Thuc. Van Lang was from the house of Hong Bang. From that time forward and for many generations, every king of Thuc tried to dethrone the royal Hong Bang family. Now Thuc Phan was king of Thuc. Thuc Phan invaded the country of Van Lang, and he succeeded at last in crushing the Hong Bang line of kings.

"I bring the two kingdoms of Thuc and Van Lang together into one. I name the new kingdom Au Lac. And from today I call myself King An Duong Vuong," the victorious king announced.

An Duong Vuong ordered the capital of the new country Au Lac to be built. He chose a site in the territory of Phong Khe, which was just north of present-day Hanoi. In a short time, the king had a castle and fortress in his capital. Now he wanted a wall to protect the capital from invasion from the north.

His subjects built their king the strong wall he desired. But no sooner did they finish than a violent storm erupted. Rain fell in such great quantity that no one could see through the water. Thunder resounded off the mountains and shook the earth. Lightning ripped open seams in the sky. A gigantic wind tore through the capital. Its great swirling arms knocked everything in its path upside down. This included the king's protective wall.

"Build it once more," An Duong Vuong ordered.

In a short time, a new wall stood where the toppled wall had been. It was stronger than the wall before it. A new storm broke out, and the second wall crumbled. The king ordered a third wall, even stronger. A tornado brought the third wall down, too. When the subjects built a fourth wall, the sturdiest wall they knew how to build, it was torn from its foundation brick by brick by lightning. And so it continued with the many subsequent walls the king made his subjects construct. A storm ruined every one of them.

One of the king's ministers spoke. "Might I offer an opinion to the Son of Heaven?" he asked.

And Duong Vuong nodded for the minister to speak. "Many times, you have ordered a wall to be built. Many times, the wall has been destroyed. I believe the destructive action has been taken by the gods," the minister offered.

Among themselves, the other ministers mumbled their approval of the first minister's opinion. The king pondered silently for several minutes. "Let us build an altar. We will offer sacrifice to the gods, then fast and pray for guidance," he then declared.

The prayers and fasting at the new altar lasted three nights and three days. On the fourth night, the king and his subjects retired to their beds to sleep. It was the seventh day of the third month.

King An Duong Vuong was awakened in his chambers. He was astonished to see a huge, golden tortoise. When the tortoise spoke, its voice was human.

"Son of Heaven, I deliver a message from the gods. They report that the spirits of the rivers and mountains of this land have played tricks on you. These spirits are responsible for toppling your walls. Listen to the instructions I will give you. If you pay attention, your new wall will not be knocked down," said the golden tortoise. Then he vanished.

Following the tortoise's instructions, the king had a new wall built in the shape of a giant sea shell or conch. "Let the capital be called Co Loa Tanh, or the City of the Conch," the king declared.

Now that he had a secure wall, King An Duong Vuong was worried again about his enemies. What if the wall could not keep them all away? How would he be able to fight them and win? He went to sleep with these worries in his head.

Again, he awoke to the huge, golden tortoise. "I will give you a gift. Take this claw of mine and use it as the trigger of your crossbow. No one will be able to defeat you now," the tortoise said. Then he disappeared.

Sure enough, three years later, Emperor Shih Huang of the Ch'in dynasty sent an army of 500,000 soldiers under the command of General Trieu Da to invade the kingdom of Au Lac. King An Duong Vuong slowly and peacefully climbed the stairs to the tower of his fortress. Under his arm was his crossbow. Now that it was fit with the tortoise's claw, it was a magic crossbow.

From the ramparts of the fortress, An Duong Vuong aimed the crossbow. Three arrows soared through the air and pierced the enemy. Ten thousand soldiers fell with each arrow. The tens of thousands of the enemy who witnessed the feat realized what would happen to them if they remained to fight. They spurred their horses and retreated in a great storm of dust.

Thanks to the tortoise, at last the kingdom of Au Lac experienced the peace that was the aim of their king, An Duong Vuong.

THE OYSTER
AND THE PEARLS

rieu Da was a general in the army of Emperor Shih Huang of the Ch'in dynasty in China. Under attack, the general and his army fled the kingdom of Au Lac in fear of King An Duong Vuong's magical crossbow. The king's crossbow had killed three divisions of Chinese soldiers with only three arrows. General Trieu Da resolved to get even with King An Duong Vuong. He sent his enemy a pretend peace offering.

"I am Trong Thuy, son of Trieu Da. I have come to speak with King An Duong Vuong of Au Lac," said a young man to the gatekeeper.

The king granted the newcomer an audience. "My father sends me to you as his peace offering. If it pleases your heavenly majesty, I wish to remain in your capital and at your service," said Trong Thuy, the visitor.

The king assigned Trong Thuy to his court and quickly grew fond of him. Soon he counted Trong Thuy among his closest advisers. Before many months passed, An Duong Vuong offered his only daughter, Princess My

Chau, to the visitor. The couple were married at a great celebration. All of Au Lac attended.

My Chau and Trong Thuy were very happy. But, gradually, Trong Thuy grew more and more troubled. Increasingly, he thought about the mission his father had given him. He had promised the general he would solve the problem of how to conquer the kingdom of Au Lac.

"Please, My Chau, just one glance at the magic crossbow. This is all I ask," Trong Thuy pleaded one evening. For many evenings in a row, My Chau had fought the temptation to give her husband what he asked at the end of each day. Of course, My Chau did not know about her husband's promise to his father. She hated to see him so unhappy, and she thought the sight of the crossbow would cheer him up. This evening, she relented. She held out the crossbow in her arms for her husband to see.

"It is so beautiful. Let me hold it for just one minute to admire it more closely," feigned Trong Thuy. My Chau again relented.

Also unknown to her was that Trong Thuy had crafted a false tortoise claw for this occasion. The quick-fingered Trong Thuy replaced the real claw with the one he made. He pocketed the magical tortoise claw when My Chau was not looking.

Now Trong Thuy told his wife that he must visit his parents, because he missed them. He received the king's permission to take the trip and promised to return shortly. My Chau was heartbroken to part with Trong Thuy. His homeland was so far away. The journey would be long and dangerous. What if she never saw him again? After quieting his wife's fears, Trong Thuy took his leave, repeating that he would return.

A month passed, and the Chinese general's forces were ready to attack. Trieu Da was confident because of the trick his son had played with the tortoise's claw. Thong Thuy remained in the land of his birth with his father.

Yet his thoughts turned each day to My Chau. In order to do his duty to his father and country, he had caused his wife to betray her father and country. He was feeling very guilty.

The many brightly colored banners of the Chinese army unfurled outside the fortress at An Duong Vuong's capital at Co Loa. His ministers rushed about to ready the soldiers to defend the capital, yet the king was in no hurry. In fact, he did not budge from his chess match until the game was finished. Then he peacefully climbed the steps to the tower. He took aim with his crossbow and shot three arrows from the ramparts like he had during the last invasion. But something was wrong! The arrows did not cruise through the air with the power they had in the past. Nor did they fell entire companies of enemy soldiers.

King An Duong Vuong fled with his daughter riding behind him upon his favorite horse. As they galloped through the forest surrounding the capital, someone galloped behind them. King An Duong Vuong spurred the horse to gain some speed. The horse and rider following them also quickened the pace. Over the plains and through the forests, the pursuit continued.

Finally, the king and his daughter came to the great sea. An Duong Vuong had hoped to find a boat that might take them across the sea to safety. Not one vessel sat upon the broad waters. He cried to heaven for help against this enemy who followed him.

The voice of the golden tortoise responded from under the waves. "Seated behind you is your real enemy," the voice instructed.

In a fit of rage, King An Duong Vuong unsheathed his sword and cut off the head of his enemy. On the ground lay the head of Princess My Chau. "What have I done?" the king cried, staring at the daughter he murdered. In despair, he rode his trusted horse into the sea. He disappeared beneath the spot from which the turtle had spoken.

Trong Thuy, who had been pursuing the king, came to the edge of the sea. He saw what had become of his beloved My Chau, and his heart broke. In the capital, Trong Thuy made sure that his wife was given a proper burial.

At the edge of the sea, the waves gathered her spilled blood that remained. They brought the drops back with them to the deeper water. Each drop of My Chau's blood became an oyster. From that day onward, oysters began to produce beautiful pearls.

One day, Trong Thuy could bear his sorrow no longer, so he flung himself into the deep pond where My Chau used to bathe. The people discovered that if they washed a pearl in this pond, the pearl grew in brilliance. They said that this happened because the souls of My Chau and Trong Thuy were united in every washing.

Banh Giay and Banh Chung

"I've lived a long and useful life," said King Hung Vuong the Sixth. He was alone in his chamber in the palace, and he had been thinking. "The An invaders are defeated. Peace pervades the land, and the apricot trees are in bloom. Now that the kingdom is safe and the people are happy, I am eager to relax, too. I will step down, that's what I'll do. The twenty-two princes can vie for the throne. The prince who wins the contest is the next king," he said. The king closed his eyes for a quick nap, satisfied with his decision.

That evening after a fine meal in the dining hall, the king stood. He glanced to his sides at the faces of the sons seated to his right and left. He saw nearly identical countenances across the table. All of the sons were eager to hear what their father was going to say. The king smiled. These honorable young men made him happy, plus he was grateful for the good meal he had just eaten. The idea of food distracted him. He was grateful to the distraction, too, because he had not until this moment drafted a contest that satisfied him. Now he had the perfect plan.

"Noble sons, I wish to step down from the throne in one year." He cocked his right hand at the wrist to quiet their remarks and questions. "One of you will occupy the throne when I leave it. Since you are all worthy princes, I have designed a contest to decide the matter. He among you who finds in the farthest places a recipe and a dish I have not yet tasted, wins," said King Hung-Vuong.

Early the next morning, twenty-one princes departed for the north, south, east and west. Their destinations were the far and distant reaches of the earth. One stayed behind. He was the sixteenth-born of the twenty-two princes. Like many of his brothers, he had a different mother. She died when he was a baby, and his nurse had raised him. The sixteenth-prince had spent every day of his life in the palace under the care of his nurse. He was not ready to leave her yet.

The prince's name was Lang Lieu. He wanted to be king as much as his brothers. Yet he sat in the palace day after day, thinking about the contest and not traveling anywhere for a new recipe and food. Every night, Lang Lieu fell into a deep slumber to stop his worrying over not taking action.

One night in a dream a spirit appeared to the sixteenth prince. The spirit advised him to worry no longer. She shared a secret. "All humankind needs rice to survive." Then she told him how to prepare a special food.

Lang Lieu awoke with a plan, and he was grateful to the spirit. He set out immediately to gather the ingredients. When he passed his nurse in the pantry with his arms full, the prince explained about the spirit and the recipe. The nurse offered to help prepare the food.

Reciting the steps as he had memorized them, Lang Lieu gave the nurse the recipe. "Soak the rice in clean water," he said. Once it was soaking, he gave the next step. "Now boil and simmer it. Once it is cooked, divide the whole into two halves. Pound one half of the rice as round as the sky. Pound the second half as square as the earth."

The prince continued. "Soak the beans in clean water," he said. When the beans were soaking, he continued. "Boil and simmer them. Once they are cooked, make a paste. In the meantime, cook the pork in fat and spices. When it is ready, cut the meat into small pieces."

"Now spread the paste on the round and square rice portions. Drop the meat on top. Wrap the whole thing in banana leaves. Make lacings from bamboo, then sew up the leaves. Cook the recipe for one day. When it is finished, you will have two cakes," Lang Lieu said, proudly.

When the apricot trees began their next bloom, the twenty-one princes returned home from the far and distant reaches of the earth. Lang Lieu joined them in the royal chamber. He, too, had a box in his hands for his father, the king. Hung-Vuong the Sixth welcomed back the princes and began to taste his sons' gifts. "Ugh!" "Terrible!" "Ptah!" he responded, among other words that indicated clearly that he was disgusted. The twenty-one princes had brought back food that was downright unsavory. The king looked with disappointment to Lang Lieu. He knew the sixteenth-born had not exited the palace walls over the past year. Nonetheless, he took the box from his son's outstretched hands. Inside, he found the round cake, called Banh Giay. Next to it was Banh Chung, the square cake.

"Wonderful!" the king responded. "I have never tasted these delicacies. Now I must hear whether I know the recipe."

Lang Lieu bowed, then spoke the steps he had memorized from his dream. "Soak the rice in clean water. Boil and simmer it. Once it is cooked, divide the whole into two halves. Pound one half of the rice as round as the sky. Pound the second half as square as the earth.

"Soak the beans in clean water. Boil and simmer them. Once they are cooked, make a paste. In the meantime, cook the pork in fat and spices. When it is ready, cut the meat into small pieces.

"Now spread the paste on the round and square rice portions. Drop the meat on top. Wrap the whole thing in banana leaves. Make lacings from bamboo, then sew up the leaves. Cook the recipe for one day. When it is finished, you will have two cakes," he said.

"Fantastic, I have learned a new recipe, and the land has a new ruler. His name is King Lang Lieu," proclaimed Hung Vuong the Sixth.

THE BETEL PLANT AND THE ARECA TREE

ao was an official during the reign of King Huong Vuong the Third. Cao and his wife had twin sons, named Tan and Lang. A few minutes separated their births. From the moment the second one was born, the twins spent all of their time together.

When they were still boys, Tan and Lang met with disaster. A fire burned down their house and killed their parents while they were outside, playing. The people of the village fed the boys until they were old enough to set out on their own to look for work.

"This is the house of the wealthy Luu. He was our parents' acquaintance," said one twin.

"Let us ask Luu to give us work," agreed the other twin.

Luu recognized the twins, and he welcomed them into his mansion. The servants prepared a special meal for the guests at Luu's request. At dinner, he introduced the young men to his beautiful daughter.

"You are a white lotus," said one enraptured twin.

"You are a spring rose," exclaimed the other brother.

Luu invited the twins to remain under his roof and to serve as his officials. The weeks passed, and the twins proved themselves loyal to Luu and
his demands. They both fell in love with his beautiful daughter during this
time. Yet, they did not speak of their love to one another, nor to their
employer's daughter. They kept it a secret.

One evening after a particularly satisfying meal, Luu told the twins he
considered them as dear as the sons he and his wife did not have. "One of
you must marry my daughter. Then I will have grandchildren to complete
my family," Luu resolved.

Each twin saw the other blush. Luu had spoken their heartfelt wishes.
But neither twin rushed to accept the offer of the hand of Luu's daughter
in marriage. Neither was able to disappoint his brother.

"She will marry the elder brother, since I cannot get either of you to
speak for her," Luu said. He waited for the twins to declare who was older.
They remained silent. Still, neither one was able to disappoint his brother.

Luu saw the problem, yet he was nonplussed. He ordered his servants to
prepare a special meal for the twins' dinner. When the food was served,
there were two bowls of rice and one set of chopsticks. Lang immediately
reached for the chopsticks. Respectfully, he handed them to Tan, who took
them without hesitation.

"Ha! Tan is the elder. He will marry my daughter," laughed Luu.

Tan and the daughter were wonderfully happy. They took walks by the
river and sang love songs in the mountains. The neglected Lang, who duti-
fully renounced his love for his brother's wife, was very lonely.

One day, he knew he had to leave. The solitude was making him too
sad. While the household was asleep, he left Luu's mansion with only the
clothes on his back. He wandered over hills and through forests, across
plains and to the edge of the deep, dark sea. A chill wind chafed his skin.

The sun dipped behind the horizon, and he shivered. He was very hungry and thirsty. Poor Lang sat down on the sand and began to cry. He wept until he had used up all of his tears. Then he turned into a chalky, white rock.

Days passed at Luu's mansion, and Tan expected each sunrise to see his brother by that sunset. One morning, he realized how badly he had treated Lang and knew he would never return. That evening, he crept out of the house while everyone slept. He wandered over hills and through forests, across plains and to the edge of the deep, dark sea. He arrived as the sun departed behind the horizon. Sitting down upon the sand, he leaned his back against a chalky, white rock and began to cry. He wept until he could not cry another tear. Then he changed into an areca tree.

After a couple of days, the young bride knew her husband was gone forever. She threw on a scarf and closed the door to the mansion behind her. Over hills and through forests, across plains and to the edge of the deep, dark sea, she wandered. As the sun bid farewell, she sat down and leaned against the chalky rock. She cried until she had no more tears to shed. Next she turned into a betel plant. Her leaves creeped along the ground until they touched the erect trunk and jade-green palm leaves of the areca tree.

One of the villagers was asked to build a temple on this spot in a dream. All of the people including wealthy Luu helped in the construction. On the building's facade, they inscribed the words, "Two brothers, two spouses." In the next generation, a great drought struck the land. Only two things grew green in the whole kingdom: the areca tree and the betel plant that sat securely alongside the chalky, white rock. And the people remarked over and over, "Two brothers forever, two spouses forever."

THE LADY OF NAM-XUONG

I n the area near Nam-Xuong, a young peasant couple lived happily with their one-year-old son in a tiny house. On bright days, the sun warmed the house, and the rain drenched it on wet days. The couple were content in life, whatever the weather. In the evenings, they sat together in the flickering light of their oil lamp. The woman was quiet, and she liked to listen to the man's voice. While he spoke to her, she sewed. They loved their son very much, too. They carried him on their backs in the open air and played with him on the floor of their tiny house.

The army called upon the husband one day to serve as a soldier. "Wife, I must go to the border on the Northern frontier to do my duty as guard. I will try to get word to you of my well-being," he said.

The young wife felt a stab of sadness in her heart as they hugged good-bye. The son wondered why he could not go into the fields with him when his father said he had to leave. The door of the tiny house closed behind the husband, and his wife and son missed him.

Day after day, then month after month, word from the husband did not arrive from the Northern border. None of the strangers who passed through Nam-Xuong had traveled from the north. Every night at twilight when she lit the oil lamp, the wife was lonely. She imagined seeing her husband in his chair. In a short time, however, the young son forgot what his father looked like.

The summer passed, followed by autumn, and the husband did not return. One mid-winter evening, the temperature dropped. It stormed for many hours, the wind swelling ever and ever more powerfully. The tiny house rocked on its foundation. The flame in the oil lamp sputtered. A tremendous gust blew open the door, and the flame flickered out.

"Mother, I am frightened," the little boy cried.

The woman scooped up her son and shut the door. She relit the lamp and placed her son gently upon his mattress. She sat on the edge of the bed and checked the location of the flame in the lamp on the table. Positioning her body so the fire was at her back, she told her son to look at the wall next to him. She pointed to her shadow and said, "Do not worry. You see, Father is here to take care of you." The child fell peacefully into a sound sleep.

The next night at bedtime, he said, "Is Father coming tonight, too?" His mother tucked his blankets about him and answered, "Here he is now. Look." The delighted boy saw the shadow on the wall, closed his eyes and went to sleep.

The following evening, the boy told his mother he was ready for bed. He snuggled in the folds of the mattress and asked, "When will Father be here?" "He is here now. See?" his mother answered. Her shadow was again alongside her son's bed. The boy smiled and fell asleep.

The woman began to enjoy the game, too. Each night, for a few moments after her son closed his eyes, she stayed where she was with the shadow she called her husband. For those few moments, he was in the tiny house with them in Nam-Xuong.

The husband finally returned to Nam-Xuong. "Thank the ancestors you have come home. I'll go to get the food while you set up the altar," the wife exclaimed. Though he did not recognize his father, the son was happy for the company of a newcomer. "Please, watch the child until I return from the barn with the rice," the wife added.

While he was preparing the altar, the husband beckoned to the boy. "Come, son, sit next to your father," he said.

"You are not my father," the boy replied.

"How can you say such words?" answered his father.

"Because you are not the man I see at night next to my bed," said the boy.

The father did not know how to answer. One thing he did know was that something was suspicious. His wife had a man in the house every night. He had thought she loved him and had waited for his return. Instead, she had found another man to take his place. Jealousy and anger filled his veins at the very thought of this. His blood thickened when the husband realized the other man had tricked his own son into calling him father.

The wife rushed into the tiny house in the excitement of giving thanks for her husband's safe arrival. She was surprised to see that he had not finished the altar and asked him about it. Instead of answering the question, he hurried by her and slammed the door shut. Days passed, and he did not come home.

She could not bear another night without him. So the poor woman bundled up her son in his warmest clothes and brought him to a neighbor. "Please, take care of him," she said. Then she rushed off before the tears could spill from her eyes. Running as fast as she could, she came to the river. She threw herself into the cold water, and she drowned.

When the husband got word of what his wife had done, he came home. The neighbor knocked on the door of the tiny house and gave him his child. It was late, so he put the boy on his mattress, unwittingly sitting just where his wife used to sit.

"My father is back," the boy said happily, staring at the shadow on the wall.

The husband's suspicion changed to sorrow. Though the years passed, he never remarried. For the rest of his life, he dedicated himself to his son's learning.

THE FAIRY IN EXILE

he princess is born! The princess is born!" Word rang through the land that on this peaceful day, the king and queen had a new baby girl.

For seven days, everyone in the kingdom celebrated the princess's birth. Colorful banners unfurled in every village. No matter where one traveled, the countryside was rich with the fragrance of flowers and the aroma of fine food. While the people in the country celebrated, the capital just abounded in festivities. For seven nights and seven days, the palace windows were lighted with candles and lanterns. Fireworks exploded every evening. "The kingdom is blessed," everyone agreed.

The princess grew more beautiful each year, and her disposition was virtuous. When she turned eighteen, the king approved of her marriage to a high official of the court. The couple loved each other dearly and embraced their new live together with great joy. Soon, the princess gave birth to a son, whom the couple cherished.

One evening when the high official rose to the bedchamber, he screamed. His beloved wife, the princess, lay dead upon the mattress. An investigation into the tragedy showed no cause for her death. The incident was a mystery. Just before the funeral, the official opened the coffin for one last look at his cherished wife. The box was empty! He knew he could no longer reside in the capital where everything would remind him of the princess and her mysterious death. The heartbroken man took his young son and moved from the splendor of the palace to a humble cottage in Central Vietnam.

Nothing interested him but the child. He cared for the boy and played with him for hours at a stretch every day. Otherwise, he took walks in the woods and wept over the loss of his wife.

One morning while the boy napped, the official made for the woods. He entered the forest and strolled without destination. He knew he had traveled farther than usual, but he kept going. Standing on a small hill, he heard the sound of running water below him in the ravine. He balanced himself against the side of the hill and climbed down to the bottom. A small boulder was at the edge of the stream, and he sat down upon it, looking at the water.

A sharp crackle of wind and a sweet, floral fragrance caused him to turn around. He caught a glimpse of a woman as she ducked inside the dark shelter made by the drooping and rooted branches of a banyan tree. Sneaking over to the tree for a closer look, the official was surprised to find no evidence of the woman anywhere.

He climbed up the side of the hill and set out through the woods for home. That night, he dreamed of the woman who had vanished in the banyan tree. How odd to dream of anyone but his wife. This had never happened before, he thought, both surprised and guilty.

The following morning while his son napped, the official could not help himself. He took the long walk through the forest and hurried to the stream. Excitedly, he balanced his way down the hill to the ravine. The boulder looked like it was waiting for him to sit upon it. He sat and longed to hear any sound that might tell him the woman was near. The fragrance of flowers enticed his nostrils. A gentle breeze blew past his ears, tickling them slightly. He turned and gasped. Before him, as beautiful as ever, he saw his wife. While the sight thrilled him beyond belief, he feared it was a vision that would fade like the one yesterday.

But the princess did not fade. She ran to her husband, and they sobbed while they hugged. Finally, the official moved slightly back and asked her about what had happened.

"I am a fairy, and I always have been, my husband," the princess responded. "We met while I was in exile in the world of humans. I was banished here by the Jade Emperor as punishment for breaking a precious jar in heaven. The day I died was the day when I finished serving my time."

"Why have you come back now, my wife?" the official asked.

"When I returned to heaven, I saw you and your terrible sorrow. I could not bear to hear you weep any longer, so I have returned. I am able to stay for a time, but when the stay is over, I can never return again," she explained.

The official was content that his precious princess would be staying for a time. Mother and father ran through the forest to the modest house at the edge of the woods. Their son hurried to greet them, and their world smelled like flowers. Everyday, the family rejoiced in having one another.

But one night, they felt a breeze enter the cottage. Distant music made the princess shriek. She embraced her husband and child.

"It is the Jade Emperor. I must go back. Please, close your eyes as I depart, so it will not be so painful for us," she said.

When the official and his son opened their eyes, the cottage was cold and dark. Stepping outside, they were met with a black, cloudy sky. Back in the cottage, the man lit a fire, and he told his son many stories about the princess, his mother.

THE LAND OF BLISS

t the time when this story begins, it was the end of the Tran dynasty. The year was Binh Ti, and the Flower Festival was celebrated in Tien Du. The chief official in the Tien Du district was Tu Thoc.

Tu Thoc strolled through the streets of his district during the Flower Festival. He returned the greetings of the people of Tien Du. They admired him for how many books he had read and how learned he was. The luxurious bloom of the red peonies outside the pagoda captivated chief Tu Thoc. He could not take his eyes off their crimson fullness. To see their bloom in the garden of the tall temple with many roofs gave him a jolt of joy.

A young woman passed Tu Thoc as he was admiring the peonies. She, too, was enchanted by the red blossoms. Reaching to lower a branch so that she could inhale the fragrance of the peonies, she accidentally snapped the branch. It broke off in her hand. Two priests rushed into the garden to arrest her for what she had done. They put her in jail, because she said she had no money to pay a fine for her misdeed. Tu Thoc watched the situation with sadness.

"Take my brocade coat in payment for her fine," he said to the priests.

They accepted his offer and released the young woman. She nodded in gratitude to Tu Thoc and disappeared.

Word of the generosity of their chief reached the people of Tien Du, and they admired Tu Thoc even more now. His goodness inspired the residents of the district. They appreciated the daily peace and prosperity of their lives.

One evening in the fullness of the August moon, Tu Thuc decided to resign. "I must search out the Land of Bliss," he said the next morning, to the people's astonishment. They had no hint of his enchantment with the land of fairies.

"Where will you find the Land of Bliss?" they asked Tu Thoc.

"I will travel to Tong-Son, because it has blue mountains and springs of emerald green. There I will search until I find it," he answered.

He departed with his lute, a volume of poetry and a drinking gourd. As he walked, he recalled the stories he had heard as a young child about the Land of Bliss. Under the August moon, Emperor Duong Minh Hoang of China had found the enchanted place. According to the stories about his adventure, the Land of Bliss resounded with laughter and songs. Since that time, Tu Thuc had known in his heart that he would go one day. "No matter what happens," he told himself now, "I'll find it."

After crossing a great forest and many streams, Tu Thoc reached the Pink Mountain. He continued until he passed the Cave of the Green Clouds. When he arrived at the Lai River, he sat upon a rock to compose a poem. "I implore the emerald green spring," he sang, "please, guide me to the peach trees, guide me to the Land of Bliss."

He gathered the lute, volume of poetry and drinking gourd and started to walk again. Beautiful pastel-colored clouds filled the sky and made Tu Thoc blink. When he opened his eyes again, he saw a rowboat in the river. He began to row, yet he knew not where. Suddenly, he saw a mountain through the mist. It sat magnificently in the middle of the river. He lodged the boat at the rocky bottom edge of the mountain and began to climb.

Before his eyes, the mountain split open from top to bottom. So he entered. The magical mountain closed with him inside. Tu Thuc began to climb. At first, the going was very steep and he could not see his hand in front of him. Then, the going got easier as the path widened and light filtered around him. As he approached the peak, the sweet fragrance of perfume intoxicated him, and he kept climbing. Fish of gold and silver swam in the spring at his feet, in and out of the glittering lotus blossoms that covered the surface of the water. A marble bridge appeared, and Tu Thuc crossed the spring.

He heard hushed voices in the garden where the bridge led him. He caught a glimpse of a cluster of maidens in blue gowns. Stars adorned their hair. The maidens disappeared inside a palace, and he followed. Upon the throne, a lovely lady sat in a glittering gown of snow-white fabric. She beckoned for him to come close.

"You are the the man from the world of brown dust, learned and pure of heart. I am grateful to see the generous one who saved my daughter Giang Huong from the priests in the garden of the pagoda. Now you may have her hand in marriage," she said. The magnificent lady told him she was Nguy, Queen of the Fairies of Nam Nhac.

The princess Giang Huong emerged from the adjacent chamber. Indeed, Tu Thoc recognized her as the young woman who had admired the red peonies during the Flower Festival. She was even more exquisite than he remembered.

THACH SANH

T he old woodsman Thach and his wife had been married many years, but had no children. Trying to be as good as possible, they hoped that Heaven would help them have a child. They did everything they could to help their neighbors in the village.

Knowledge of their kindness even reached the ears of the Emperor of Heaven. "I will bless this couple," he said. He sent one of his own children to be born as a son for Thach and his wife.

Thach's wife conceived a child, but, because the child was divine, it took him more than three years to be born. Meantime, Thach died. A few months later, his wife bore a healthy boy, whom she called Thach Sanh.

Sad at the death of her husband, the aged wife also passed away. From then on, the young boy lived alone at the foot of an old banyan tree. He was poor, owning only a loincloth for his clothing and an axe to cut wood. He grew rice, but in the winter he often went hungry.

One day, as he always did, he went out to cut wood. When he returned, he found an old man sitting under the banyan tree. "Who are you, respected grandfather?" he asked.

"I am the master of magic," the old man responded. "I have been sent by the Emperor of Heaven to teach you magic to help you live on earth."

Thach Sanh worked hard and mastered magic. But he continued in his modest way of life. He never forgot the pious example of his parents.

One day, a wandering brandy merchant named Ly stopped at Thach Sanh's tree to rest. Ly was desperate. He came from a village where there was an evil monster that ate human flesh. Each year, a young man from the village had to be fed to it. Ly had been chosen that year. He would die unless someone else died in his place.

When Ly found that Thach Sanh was an orphan, he invited him to come home with him for a visit. When they arrived, Ly asked Thach if he would mind guarding the house that night, because Ly had something else to do. It was at the house that Thach would be eaten by the monster.

Ly left, and suddenly everything was quiet. All of the animals and insects were afraid. Suddenly, a great snake appeared, spitting fire from its mouth. Using his magical powers, Thach Sanh cut off the monster's head.

When Ly came home, he could not believe Thach Sanh was still alive. When he saw him, he thought he saw a ghost. He begged forgiveness. By this, Thach Sanh knew how evil Ly was. He fled back to the forest, leaving the serpent's head behind.

Ly took the head to the palace of the king, and said he had killed it. The king rewarded Ly with great wealth. But thieves are never satisfied with what they've stolen. The king had one child, the beautiful Quynh Nga, who was unmarried. Ly began to think about marrying her.

One day, Quynh and her maids were taking a stroll, when a giant eagle swooped down and seized the princess. Off it flew, over the forest where Thach Sanh lived. When Thach saw the eagle and the woman it held, he wounded the bird with his bow. He tracked it to a deep cave.

Meanwhile, the king ordered Ly to organize a search party. He promised to give him Quynh Nga if he rescued her. Ly and the party followed the trail of the eagle into the forest. They got lost, but they found Thach Sanh. Ly warmly greeted Thach Sanh, who didn't trust them. Yet Thanch Sanh took them to the cave.

Once there, Thach Sanh climbed down a rope and found the princess. The wounded eagle was close to death. The princess was deeply moved, and she instantly decided that Thach Sanh was the man she wanted to marry. Thach Sanh tied the Princess to the rope, and Ly brought her up. After sending her back to the palace so she would not see what he was going to do, Ly cut the rope. He covered the opening of the cave with a rock. Thach Sanh was left there to die.

He did not give up easily, however. He searched for another opening in the cave. Suddenly, he came upon an iron cage in a secluded corner. In it was a handsome youth.

"Who are you?" asked Thach Sanh.

"I am the son of the Sea King," the imprisoned youth responded. "If you free me from this place, I will never forget you."

Together, Thach Sanh and the Sea Prince found a way out of the cave. They journeyed to the palace of the Sea King. Welcoming the visitor who had saved his son's life, the king gave Thach Sanh a magic lute, which could overcome all dangers.

Emboldened by the words of the princess, and angry at Ly's treachery, the brave Thach Sanh returned to the capital with the magic lute. In the presence of Quynh's father, Ly lied, saying that Thach Sanh had worked with the eagle to steal the princess. Before Ly could say anything more, Thach Sanh's magic lute began to play, telling the true story of Ly's cruelty.

Once the song was finished, the princess confirmed what the lute had said. "When Thach Sanh saved me in that dark cavern, I promised to marry him," she said. "But the merciless Ly is trying to steal the credit for his good deeds. Let justice be done!"

Arresting Ly, the king gave Thach Sanh full power to judge him. But since he was merciful, Thach Sanh pardoned Ly. He begged him to lead a quiet life. Because the universe is just, on Ly's way home, a sudden storm began to rage. Ly was killed by lightning.

He was turned into a cockroach spirit. As for Thach Sanh and Quynh Nga, they reigned with kindness and compassion for the rest of their days.

TIBET AND MONGOLIA

THE GREAT MOUNTAIN

n the beginning when neither time nor form existed, a single breeze blew through the chaos. Chaos
is another word for confusion and disorganization.
The breeze blowing through the chaos kept getting
stronger. It got so strong, it became a double thunderbolt. The breeze that was the double thunderbolt did not stop. It also became clouds.

Raindrops began to fall. They were huge raindrops in fact. So many huge raindrops fell, they
made a massive ocean.

Now the breeze was a light wind, and it stirred the ocean's waters. It stirred
them so rapidly that the water churned until it became as solid as butter. The
earth formed into a great mountain from so much churning of the water.

The wind blew and blew around the peak of the great mountain. Clouds
surrounded the peak. Large raindrops fell once more. The raindrops were
salty this time. The seas formed in the massive ocean when the salty raindrops filled them.

The great mountain sat in the center of the ocean, and it was the home
of the gods. It was called Rirab Lhumpo, and it stood 500 spans high above
the seas and measured 500 spans below them. The great mountain had four

sides, each formed from a different precious stone.

The east side of Rirab Lhumpo was crystal, and in the east in the outer ocean, the giants lived. The west face of the mountain was silver, and in the west in the outer ocean, the land was rich with cattle. The south side of Rirab Lhumpo was malachite, and in the south to the far horizon, was the world where humans were to live.

Finally, the north side of the great mountain was gold. Far out to the north was a rich and peaceful land. But it was one with no religion, so the land was one of death. The four worlds were in the center of the huge ocean. Seven circles of smaller mountains and seven smaller seas lay between the worlds and the great mountain.

The enlightened world called Ogmin was at the top of the great mountain. It was home to the greatest gods, known as the Perfect Ones. In Ogmin where the Perfect Ones lived, all was peaceful. A tree that bore plump, ripe fruit grew in the center of the sacred mountain of Rirab Lhumpo. The Perfect Ones fed themselves by eating the fruit of the tree.

On Rirab Lhumpo, where the gods lived, only the gods who resided at the peak could eat the fruit comfortably. The other gods who lived below the peak on the lower levels of the great mountain had to strain to reach it. They battled against each other as they stretched to gain food for themselves. Though they lived farther down the mountain, these gods felt they had the right to taste the marvelous fruit also.

When the world of humans was formed to the south, on the face of the great mountain that was malachite, a prakcha tree sprouted in the center of a river. It was the tree of enlightenment. A brilliant, gold glow shimmered about the tree. The world was called Dzambu Lying, and it was named after the water creatures. When they rose up to eat the fruit of the prakcha tree, the water creatures sometimes dropped pieces. The sound of the fruit as it dropped into the river was dzambu.

Although the land was intended for humans, at first there were no humans living in Dzambu Lying. The original inhabitants were gods. These gods were certainly not as powerful as the ones who resided at the top of the great mountain, the ones called the Perfect Ones. No, the gods who lived in our world were far less powerful, yet they were gods nonetheless. They were sent down from Rirab Lhumpo, because their less-than-perfect past actions prohibited them from remaining on the great mountain. Still, they were powerful. When they meditated, their bodies shone like stars. It was a good thing that they were as brilliant as they were, because there was no other light available to them in the land of humans.

Soon, the lesser gods in Dzambu grew tired of eating from the prakcha tree. They noticed a creamy matter that oozed from the earth. "Let us eat this substance instead," they resolved. And they did. But the more of the substance, which was called shashag, that the lesser gods ate, the more they lost their power as gods. They no longer glowed like stars when they meditated. Now they lived in darkness. They had only the power of humans.

The sun and moon appeared. They gave light to the new humans. The humans began to argue among themselves, forgetting that they were blessed creations. No sooner did they forget they were blessed than they needed shelter from the elements and more food to eat. Before, they had lived in comfort in all weather, and they ate what was provided. This was no longer possible. Soon they fought wars. Finally, the group of humans in Dzambu decided they needed one person to guide them in their behavior. They chose Mang Kur, whose name meant "many-people-made-him-king." He taught the humans how to build houses and grow food from the soil.

So, the gods who became humans had much to learn about. They had to work hard like humans do today. They soon learned they would have to die like humans do, too.

The Monkey and the Ogress

hen it was first made, the land of Tibet was under water. The earliest inhabitants of the land, who were spirits, lived under water, too. For a long time, things stayed like this. One day, everything changed.

Chenresi Lord of Mercy, whose name was Avalokiteshvara, gave Tibet his blessing. Out of the layers of water, the land rose. Snow-covered mountains surrounded it. That is why Tibet is called the Land of Snows.

A monkey with magical powers sought out Chenresi in his holy place. "I wish to meditate on compassion," said the monkey. The monkey's name was Trehu Changchub.

Trehu Changchub the monkey received Chenresi's blessing. He remained at the peak of a mountain. He promised never to marry and always to be compassionate. He would concentrate on understanding the troubles of others and try to help out if he could.

The monkey prayed day after day for compassion. One day, an ogress showed herself on the mountaintop. The monkey recognized her as a female demon who liked to eat people. Introducing herself as Tag-Senmo, the ogress sat down under a tree, near enough to the monkey but not too close, and she began to cry. Her wails grew louder and louder, but the monkey continued his prayer for compassion. He tried hard not to become distracted.

"Oh, I am a pitiful creature, as lonely as a creature can be," the ogress sang between loud sobs.

Now the monkey, who had vowed to understand the distress of others and to help out if he could, had a dilemma. He stopped praying and walked over to where the pitiful ogress sat under the tree. He saw that she was indeed in distress.

"What can I do to help you," Trehu Changchub the monkey asked Tag-Senmo the ogress.

"If I only had a husband, I would be lonely no more," she replied.

Now the monkey had a second dilemma. To help out the ogress, he would have to get married. That meant, if he kept his vow to be compassionate, he would break his other vow never to marry.

"I don't know what to do," the monkey answered, sincerely.

"You must help me," said the ogress.

"I'll return soon with my answer," said the monkey. Again, he sought out Chenresi Lord of Mercy. He found him at the top of Mount Potala to the south.

"It is time for Tibet to be peopled with humans. Marry the ogress," advised Chenresi. Two goddesses appeared to give their blessings for the marriage.

Reluctantly, the monkey returned to the mountaintop where the ogress waited.

"What is your answer?" demanded the sobbing ogress.

"I will marry you as you have asked," the monkey answered.

"You are truly compassionate," the ogress said, smiling for the first time.

Before the monkey's eyes, the demon took the shape of a human woman. The monkey and the ogress were married. Before long, the ogress became pregnant. She gave birth to six baby monkeys. They had fur on their bodies and tails like their father. Their faces were red, because their mother was an ogress who craved raw meat and blood for nourishment.

The first thing the ogress did after giving birth was to try to eat her first-born. But the monkey stopped her and sent her away. Next, he fled into the forest with his six children. Because Chenresi Lord of Mercy and the goddesses had blessed the union of the monkey and the ogress, the children were special. Each of them was from a different state of being. They had lived as gods, giants, men, animals, tormented spirits and beings from hell. The children of Trehu Changchub the monkey were to be the ancestors of all of the people who were still to be born in the country of Tibet, the Land of Snow.

Having brought his children to the safety of the forest, the father monkey returned to his mountaintop to pray for compassion. Three years passed. One day, he decided to go to the forest to see how his children were faring. What a surprise he had! Instead of the six children he had left behind, he saw 500 people. His children had truly multiplied as Chenresi Lord of Mercy had planned.

"Father, we are tired of eating the fruits of the forest. Plus, soon there will not be enough of the fruits to feed all of us," the first-born son said.

The monkey did not have an answer to the problem. So he set off again for Mount Potala to ask Chenresi Lord of Mercy what to do. "Wait here," said the diety.

Chenresi Lord of Mercy traveled to the center of the earth. There, he climbed Mount Meru. Reaching into the center of the mountain, he removed five kinds of grain. He scattered the grains upon the Land of Snow, and they immediately took root. Plentiful cereals covered the countryside.

"Now your children will have enough to eat," the deity told the monkey upon his return.

When Trehu Changchub the monkey returned to the forest, his children already had begun to eat the new cereals. Their tails had dropped off, and fur no longer covered their bodies. They looked like humans. They had begun to speak like humans. In fresh clearings, they had built houses for shelter.

Bidding them farewell, the monkey sought out his mountaintop once again. He was glad to return and renew his prayer for compassion. He was pleased, too, to have given the Land of Snow its new people.

THE FIRST KING

n the beginning, the Land of Snow did not have a ruler such as a king. Instead, the rulers were one demon after another. As the demons governed Tibet, different things were given to the people of the land by the gods.

The first gift was grain, which fed the people. The second was weapons, with which the people protected themselves. Horses were the third gift upon which the people rode. Ornaments were the fourth, with which the people decorated themselves and traded. The gods next gave the people good manners, with which they could behave properly. The next-to-the-last gift was polite conversation so that the people could speak with one another in the correct manner.

Finally, the gods gave the people their first king. His home was in the highest heaven. He was the son of the gods who dwelled in the middle level of heaven. Upon the sacred mountain in the center of the earth, the first king descended. When he did, the surrounding snow mountains bowed so low that the trees upon them touched one another at their top branches. All of the waters of the land rippled in response. Even the rocks and boulders moved from their peaceful solidity to salute him.

The first king had descended from the sky and onto the sacred mountain on a heavenly ladder that looked like a rainbow. The ladder was called the dmu. Dmu was also the word for heaven. From the top of the holy mountain, he climbed down upon a plain. The plain was a sacred area with four sides. He was met by priests called bon-po, who were waiting to receive the new king from heaven. The priests built a wooden palanquin and invited the king inside. Then they lifted it and carried it upon their shoulders to the people of the land. They called the king Nyatri Tsampo, which meant "he who was carried in victory upon the back."

The people cried out when they heard the king had come to them upon a ladder from heaven. "The son of the gods is called Nyatri Tsampo," said someone.

"He lives above the five levels of heaven," another person answered.

"He is the nephew of the dmu," said a third person.

"We are proud to have him as our king," shouted everyone.

Then the new king, Nyatri Tsampo, spoke, "Beware of six things. These are thievery, hatred, enemies, yaks, poison and evil spells," the divine king proclaimed.

"We punish theft here," someone cried out.

"We fight hate with love," another person said.

"We battle our enemies with our friends," said a third person.

"We use weapons against yaks," answered a fourth.

"We fight poisons with medicine," said a fifth person.

"We have the means to free those who are hurt by evil spells," a sixth person cried.

"Then I give you these ten gifts from heaven," proclaimed the new king.

The people thanked their king for the heavenly gifts he brought them. They rejoiced for many days to have him in their midst. They promised to stay away from the six things he told them to fear.

"Let us call our king who came to us on a ladder like a rainbow by the name of gNam-tsh-'brug," someone shouted.

"Yes, he is truly "the Dragon who is the offspring of heaven," the crowd answered, giving the meaning of the name.

Tsampo, who now was also called the dragon king, had seven immortal sons. The seventh son of Tsampo, however, was not as fortunate as his brothers. In time, the first son grew to be the age of a good horseman. In those days, this age was thirteen.

"It is my time to return to the heavens," proclaimed Tsampo to his sons.

Word of the king's coming departure reached the people of the Land of Snow. The kingdom gathered at the foot of the sacred mountain upon which Tsampo had descended to them from heaven. The king climbed the mountain. His subjects held their breath when they saw him reach the peak.

"Ah!" they exclaimed in unison.

A dmu ladder like a rainbow had appeared. It extended from the top of Tsampo's head up through the clouds of the sky. Tsampo disappeared upon the ladder, and the people knew that heaven welcomed him home.

The son who was the age of a good horseman became king. When the time was right, he, too, returned to heaven as his father had done before him. The second son next became king, and the dmu ladder brought him to heaven in the same manner at the appropriate time. It happened like this for the third, fourth, fifth and sixth sons, too.

Tsampo and his first six sons were known by the people of the Land of Snow as the "Seven Enthroned Ones of Heaven." The seventh son, however, as you heard above, was not as lucky. Under an evil spell, he was unable to return to heaven upon the rainbow ladder like his father and brothers.

THE EIGHTH KING

his is the story of the seventh son of the first king of Tibet, who descended from the sky. The first king was unlike the people on earth, because he was immortal. He came to earth from the highest heaven. He was a god. A heavenly ladder that looked like a rainbow carried the king from heaven to earth to the top of the sacred mountain in the center of the Land of Snow. The ladder was called the dmu. Dmu was also the word for heaven.

The priests built a wooden palanquin and transported the king upon their shoulders to the people of the land. They called the king Nyatri Tsampo. His name meant "he who was carried in victory upon the back."

When the people saw King Tsampo, they exclaimed, "Yes, he is truly 'the Dragon who is the offspring of heaven.'" So, the first king was also called the dragon king.

The dragon king had seven blessed sons, who were immortal just as he was. The first son reached age 13, the age of a good horseman. Tsampo knew his son would be a fine king, so he decided to return to heaven. He climbed the sacred mountain, and the rainbow ladder, the dmu, brought him home.

The second son grew to the age of a good horseman, and the dmu carried the first son back to heaven. The third son reached that age, and the dmu brought the second son to heaven. When the fourth son arrived at the age of a good horseman, the third son, too, took the rainbow ladder home. The fifth son grew to the same age, and the dmu transported the fourth son to heaven. It brought the fifth son home to the gods when the fourth son became a good horseman. When the sixth son reached that age, the fifth son returned to heaven on the rainbow ladder. The sixth son departed on the dmu when the seventh son was the age of a good horseman.

This is what happened to the seventh son, who was not as lucky as his brothers.

The seventh son's name was Gri-bum btsan-po. Gri-bum btsan-po was not the name given to the seventh son at birth. No one remembers any longer what his given name was. Gri-bum btsan-po was the name his nurse called him by mistake when his parents gave him his real name. That was the beginning of the seventh son's misfortunes, for Gri-bum btsan-po meant "killed by the sword."

During Gri-gum's reign, the people of the Land of Snow grouped together into clans, or very large families. In the whole of the land, there were 12 clans.

"I challenge the strongest among you to do battle with me," King Gri-gum said to the first clan chieftain. The first clan chieftain and all of the first clan refused the offer.

Gri-gum sought out the second clan chieftain. He repeated his challenge. The second clan chieftain and the entire second clan also refused.

The third, fourth, fifth, sixth, seventh, eighth, ninth, tenth, eleventh and twelfth clan chieftains and their clans, too, turned down the eighth king's offer to do battle against him.

Knowing the meaning of his name, one would think the king would have heeded the clans' refusal. Unfortunately for him, and for all of the kings who followed him to the throne of the Land of Snow, Gri-gum did not take heed.

Next, Gri-gum challenged his ministers to fight him. One by one, the servants of the palace refused. The king boasted to the chief groom, the keeper of the royal horses, that no one in the land could beat him in battle. The groom's name was Lo-ngam. Lo-ngam accepted the king's challenge. "I will fight you," the groom answered.

The day of battle arrived. Both competitors readied themselves for the contest. They each made their way to the top of a hill, where they had arranged for the fight to take place. The king arrived with his top ministers. Lo-ngam was accompanied by one hundred yaks, which were the long-haired oxen of Tibet. Each yak had a bag of soot tied tightly to its horns.

Gri-gum raised his eyebrows in surprise to see Lo-ngam's companions. His ministers mumbled among themselves about the situation. With him in a bag, the superstitious Gri-gum had brought some things to guard him against an evil spell. He opened the bag and drew them out. Upon his shoulders, he draped a dead dog. On top of it, he laid the corpse of a fox. He tied a black turban around his forehead. In the center of the turban, he fastened a mirror. The mumbling of the ministers grew louder.

"Give the call to begin the duel," the king declared. The minister in charge of the battle call obeyed.

The competitors raised their swords and faced off. They moved cautiously toward one another. Gri-gum made the first move toward Lo-ngam, who held his ground without moving at all. The yaks responded to the threat to Lo-ngam by lowering their heads and tossing their horns from side to side. The bags of soot tied to the horns burst apart, and the air filled with a thick dust.

King Gri-gum waved his sword wildly, unable to see a thing through the dust. The gods were disgusted with him because of the stench of the rotting corpses he wore, so they did not protect him. The shiny mirror Gri-gum wore on his forehead allowed Lo-ngam to see his opponent. Gri-gum flung his sword over his head in frustration and without thinking. Instead of making contact with Lo-ngam, he sliced through the dmu that connected him to heaven. Then Lo-ngam shot an arrow at the king's head. Gri-gum fell dead upon the mountaintop. He had severed the rainbow ladder that would have brought him home to the gods.

Gri-gum's ministers buried their now-mortal king in an above-ground tomb that looked like a tent, but was made of earth. From this day onward, none of the kings of Tibet returned to heaven when their reign was done. Like Gri-gun, who had broken the dmu forever, they were buried in earthen tombs.

THE STORY
OF THE HORSE

n ancient days, a mare was born in the highest heaven. She could find neither grass to eat nor water to drink. "I must descend to Gung-thang," said the mare.

So she went down to the lower heaven. The gods and goddesses lived there. A group of them greeted her. "Welcome, baby horse," they said. "Why have you come?"

"I need food and drink," the mare answered.

"Come, little horse, I will take care of you," said the goddess Gung-btsun. Her name meant "Lady of the Sky."

The first thing that Lady of the Sky did was to invite the horse to live with her in her palace. Then she gave the mare food and drink. "Here are rice, flour and molassas," said the goddess.

The mare accepted the palace as her shelter. After she ate the rice and flour, and once she drank the molasses, Lady of the Sky wanted to brush her. "You will be the most beautiful mare ever," the goddess said.

"I don't like to be brushed," retorted the mare. The horse kicked up her heels and rode away.

The next morning, after the horse ate her food and drank her molasses, the goddess said they would take a ride through the lower heaven. "I don't want to take you for a ride," complained the mare.

It was like this with everything that Lady of the Sky suggested to the mare. All of the gods and goddesses agreed her horse was the most disagreeable creature they ever had lain their eyes upon. Even Lady of the Sky grew tired of the mare's behavior. As for the mare, she refused to change.

"I will descend to the land of rDzi-lung," decided the horse. So she dropped to rDzi-lung, an even lower region of heaven.

Here, she became acquainted with a colt. In time, the mare became pregnant. She gave birth to three foals. Unlike the mare and colt, the foals did not wish to eat rice and flour and to drink molasses.

"Let us leave here, for we want grass to eat and water to drink," they decided. So the foals bid their parents farewell.

The first-born son went to the North to find grass and water. The second- and third- born traveled to the pastures south of the North on the Northern Plain. "Grass and water will be more plentiful there," they determined.

In the far North where the eldest brother traveled, he met a wild yak. Long before the horse arrived, the yak had made an arrangement with the creator god Yab-lha bdag-drug. The arrangement gave the yak dominion over all of the North. The same arrangement had reserved the Northern Plain for the horse.

"Go away," the yak greeted the first-born son.

The horse refused, and the yak killed him with his horns. Somehow, the first-born horse's two brothers knew he had come to harm. They traveled

324 ASIAN READ-ALOUD MYTHS AND LEGENDS

to the North to investigate. There, they found their brother's dead body.

"You must punish the creature who did this," the youngest brother said to the second-born.

"I will do no such thing. I will return to the Northern Plain to eat grass and to drink water," protested the second-born horse.

Even when his brother accused him of being a coward, the second-born horse would not consider punishing his older brother's killer. Instead, he dug in his heels and repeated his decision to return to the pasture. The youngest brother was determined to avenge the death of the first-born son.

"I will go to sKyi-mthing, the land of humans," he said, forcefully.

"You'll regret going there. They'll put a bit in your mouth and a saddle on your back," warned the second-born son.

"Thorns will prick you, and dogs will chase you when you return to the pasture," threatened the youngest horse.

He kicked up his heels and traveled to the land of humans. When he arrived, he made a pact with the first human he met. "If you will avenge my brother's death, I will carry you on my back for one hundred years. When you die, I will bring you through the 7,000 stars," the youngest horse offered. The human agreed to the conditions.

The human mounted the youngest horse, and they rode to the pasture lands on the Northern Plain. There, they saw the second-born son, grazing. He had become a wild horse, and he did not recognize his brother. The youngest son and his rider continued until they came to the North.

When the human encountered the yak, he killed him. Then horse and rider returned to sKyi-mthing, the land of humans. When the human died, the youngest son brought him through the 7,000 stars to the land of the dead.

THE TEACHER AND THE LORD OF THE DEMONS

his is the story about how the lord of the demons tried to convince the leading priest of Tibet to go away. If the Teacher disappeared from the land, the demon reasoned, he alone would have power. Without him to teach the people how to do good, the demon could work his evil and no one would be able to stop him.

The lord of the demons was called Khyab-pa lag-ring, which meant "penetrating long hands." His name spoke his purpose. He wished to invade all parts of the land with his evil-doings. His shortened name in this story is Khyab-pa.

The priest's name was sTon-pa gShen-rab. Its meaning was "Teacher, the best of the priests." In this story, the priest is called gShen-rab for short.

The myth begins with a meeting of the throngs of demons in their lord's palace. "You must stop the Teacher from his work," said one of the demons.

"Too many people of Tibet are listening to his words and believing them," complained a second demon at the meeting.

"If you do not stop him, soon there will be no people left to listen to us," a third demon shouted. The assembly of demons jeered and spat their consent to what the three demons had spoken.

Khyab-pa, lord of the demons, rose. "I will leave the palace this evening to drive the Teacher gShen-rab from the land. I will scare him out of this world of sorrows," he promised with a hiss.

Changing himself into the world's ugliest monster, Khyab-pa attempted to frighten the Teacher. But gShen-rab did not budge from where he was speaking. He kept teaching the people who were gathered how to be good. Next, the lord of the demons became an evil wind. He intended to blow the Teacher away, but the evil wind was unable to move him. Then the demon rained hail upon the spot where the Teacher was speaking, but gShen-rab was undaunted. He continued to teach.

Now the demon lord Kyab-pa was more furious with the Teacher than he was when he began his mission to send gShen-rab out of the world of sorrow and the land of Tibet. Since he was unsuccessful in his attempts against the Teacher, he resolved to convince gShen-rab through his family.

He started with gShen-rab's sons. "Tell the people to listen to demons, and you will be rich beyond your imaginings," the demon boasted.

But the sons were immortal like their father and, therefore, not sensitive to the tactics of demons. They ignored Kyab-pa.

So the demon lord changed himself into seven horsemen, and he appeared before the Teacher's two wives. "The creator god has sent us to bring you to heaven," the demon god feigned.

"Go away, demon," the savvy wives answered. They had heard already about Kyab-pa's attempts to trick the Teacher and his sons.

But the Teacher's smallest daughter was too young to fight the demon's trickery. When he appeared to her as a monster, she was very frightened. "Do not fear, child, I was only pretending," the demon said. Suddenly, he stood before her as beautiful prince and promised to take her away to a safe place where she would not be frightened again.

The demon lord brought the smallest daughter to the land of demons. He intended to make her his wife when she grew older. When the Teacher heard of his daughter's kidnapping, he immediately entered the land of demons and rescued her from Khyab-pa.

Once again, the demon lord was more furious than ever he had been. He stole seven of the Teacher's best horses and chased them to the rKong-po region in the southeast. But the Teacher was in fast pursuit of the demon and the prized horses he stole. When Khyab-pa realized the Teacher followed closely, he conjured a snowstorm. Yet the Teacher continued his pursuit, uninterrupted.

Now the demon created a valley of fire between himself and the Teacher. Still, gShen-rab gained ground on him. Khyab-pa the demon lord worked his strongest magic. He drew the four great rivers of Tibet together so they formed a giant ocean that lay between him and the Teacher. The ocean, too, was unable to stop gShen-rab.

The demon lord called upon his mother and the other female demons for help against the strength of the Teacher. They appeared before gShen-rab as one hundred young women. They offered him liquid from one hundred golden bowls in which they put poison. Changing the poison into medicine, the Teacher began to drink from the bowls. When he finished the liquid in the one-hundredth bowl, the demon lord's mother and the other female demons became old hags.

Seeing this trick fail, too, Khyab-pa hurled a sky full of arrows at the Teacher's wife and daughters. And gShen-rab turned the arrows into flowers. He called his prized horses to him, and they obeyed.

As a last resort, the demon lord burned gShen-rab's book of teachings. This effort of Khyab-pa's was his most successful. But even it was only temporary. The books took life again, and the Teacher spoke to the people about doing good.

TARVAA, THE FIRST SHAMAN

The ancient people of Mongolia believed in a universe with heaven above and earth below. Heaven was blue, and it was the world of the father of heaven who lived there. The father of heaven governed ninety-nine realms, or kingdoms. Fifty-five of the realms were in the west, and forty-four realms were in the east. Below heaven was earth, and the earth mother governed there. She ruled over seventy-seven realms.

All of the realms or kingdoms, those in heaven and the ones on earth, were connected. It was as though life included one level on top of another. Life was like a giant tree with branches that spread out on all of the heavenly levels and all of the earthly layers. Holes existed between the layers. Through the holes, shamans were able to climb. Shamans were priests who used charms or spells to enter into the worlds of the gods, demons and spirits of the dead, and they spoke with them.

The first shaman was named Tarvaa. Tarvaa was not always a shaman. In fact, he was surprised to find out he was one.

This is what happened. When he was fifteen, Tarvaa's parents learned he was very ill. One day, Tarvaa fainted. Instead of trying to revive him, his sorrowful parents believed their son had died from the serious illness. They removed his body from the house, and they buried it.

Tarvaa was very disturbed by his parents' actions, because he was not dead. He had only fainted. So his soul flew to the realm of the spirits, where he asked to see the judge of the dead.

"Why have you come to see me this early in your life?" the judge of the dead inquired.

"I did not know what else to do. You see, my parents already have buried me, even before I died," replied the boy.

"Indeed, you show great bravery by asking for an audience with me. While you must return to the land of the living, you may take any gift you choose from my realm with you," offered the judge of the dead.

The judge of the dead suggested Tarvaa take great wealth. But Tarvaa refused. Next, he tried to give lifelong pleasure. Tarvaa turned down this gift, too. The judge of the dead offered fame, but the boy said, "No, thank you." "What about a long life?" the judge of the dead asked. Once more, Tarvaa responded, "No, thank you."

"Then I give you the knowledge of all that you have seen in the spirit realm. And, because you have chosen wisely, I also give you eloquence," said the judge of the dead. These, Tarvaa graciously accepted.

So, he departed from the spirit realm, remembering what he had seen there and able to speak convincingly at all times. But when Tarvaa came upon the body he had left behind in the land of the living, his eyes were gone. The crows had pecked them out and had eaten them. His spirit entered his body, and he was alive but blind. Nonetheless, he had the gifts from the judge of the dead, and he helped people speak with the gods, demons and spirits from that day on.

Tarvaa became a teacher to other shamans. He taught them about the five gods of wind, five gods of lightning, four gods of the corners, five gods of the horizon, five gods of entrance and eight gods of the borders. The new shamans learned about the seven gods of steam and seven gods of thunder. Into their costumes, they wove the knowledge of light and darkness that Tarvaa had brought back with him.

Tarvaa instructed them about how to use animals as helpers. "This is why bats hang upside down. They watch the sky so they can give us warning if it ever is going to collapse," he said.

He taught about the marmot, a relative of the woodchuck. "The marmot looks at the sun, because it is hoping to catch it. Long ago, when the marmot was a man, he shot six suns with his arrow and killed them. He still wants to catch the last one, the seventh sun. That is why it repeatedly rises and sets. It is hiding from the fatal arrow."

Finally, Tarvaa taught the shamans about the double-headed drum he used to call the gods, demons and spirits in the land of the dead. The new shamans practiced and became powerful like Tarvaa. They were so powerful, they were able to call to themselves the souls of people who had died many years ago. The judge of the dead who had given Tarvaa his gifts became concerned.

"These shamans are too powerful. I don't want them interfering in my land," the judge of the dead complained.

So he stole the two-headed drum from the shamans. He replaced it with a single-headed one. "Now I can be lord of my own realm without interference from the shamans," he said.

THE BIRTH OF GESAR

In ancient times, the Precious Master asked to speak with the gods in highest heaven. He was troubled with at the land of humans and determined its people needed to do some work. Many people had forgotten about religion. And many demons and lower gods were using their powers to do evil. The highest gods decided to choose one god from among themselves to correct the troublesome habits in the land of humans. They were unanimous about whom to choose. There was no contest.

"We need a mother," they also agreed.

So the Precious Master traveled under the ocean to the land of the Nagas. There he looked for the female who would give birth to the god. He found Gongmo, and he gave her a magic potion. Then he brought her to the land of humans. Gongmo became a servant to the Queen of Ling, whose name was Gyasa. The queen's brother-in-law was Todong, a powerful chieftain, and Todong had heard a prophecy about the birth of Gesar. You will hear more of them in a later story.

One day, while Gongmo rested in her tent after finishing her duties, she heard a voice. She had thought she was alone, and she turned around to make sure no one had been hiding. She found she was indeed alone.

"Mother, I am ready to be born," the voice said. "I will come from the top of your head."

"Alas, you are a demon," Gongmo replied.

She could not imagine anything but a demon coming into life in this fashion. Leaving her underwater kingdom far behind had been difficult for Gongmo. Being a servant to the queen of a distant land was also a hardship. But to give birth to a demon truly frightened her. Fear gripped her around the throat, and she could barely breathe.

"Don't be afraid, Mother. I will not hurt you, for I am no demon. It is for the best that I enter the world from the top of your head. I am a god, and I have nourished myself with your spirit and flesh. Before I can be born, however, you must see certain things," the voice said. Gongmo listened to its instructions.

She hurried outside to look for what the voice mentioned. Snow had fallen. Yellow, red, blue and black flakes covered the ground. From the snowflakes sprang golden-rose flowers. Grains like white rice appeared from the sky, and they twinkled like silver spangles.

"Ah!" Gongmo exclaimed. "It is as the voice predicted." And she hurried back inside her tent.

She sat comfortably upon the small, tattered carpet that the queen gave her. Suddenly, a white vein pulsed on top of her skull. Gongmo felt pressure as the vein opened. A white egg fell from the opening into its mother's ready hands. The egg bore three spots on its surface.

"Oh, my!" exclaimed Gongmo.

She wrapped the egg in a piece of cloth and tucked it inside her dress above where a belt gathered it at her waist. When the egg cracked open, she felt it. What she didn't feel was enough pressure to produce the beautiful boy who stood before her. He had dark skin and black hair. Three eyes were in a row on his face.

"I'll fix that," Gongmo said. Taking her thumb, she aimed for the eye in the middle of the boy's forehead. She pushed it into his head, and the hole closed over.

"My name is Gesar," the boy said.

"How is it that you've come to me and that you were born in this extraordinary manner?" Gongmo asked him.

Gesar explained about the humans who turned away from religion. He spoke of the demons and lower gods who must be punished. It was necessary for him to take human form to correct these things, he said. Then he told her about the meaning of the unusual snow and flowers.

"The golden-rose petals tell that many sages are to be born in Ling. The black snow stands for Lutzen, black demon of the North. My arrow will land between his eyes. The yellow snow tells of the victory I will have over Kurkar, King of Hor. Around his neck, he will find my saddle, for I will mount and kill him. The blue and red snow predict my victory over the kingdoms of Satham and Shingti," Gesar explained.

"And the white grains of rice that shone in the sky like a silver rainbow?" Gongmo asked.

"They demonstrated that I have come from the gods. For all of my life in the land of humans, the gods will guide me. When I need assistance, they will come to my aid," answered Gesar.

THE NINE-HEADED DEMON

ongmo never expected to find happiness in the land of humans after the Precious Master brought her here. She longed to be in her homeland in the kingdom under the sea. She missed her family, too. A cousin to the king of her land, she was forced to work as a servant to this land's queen.

But Gongmo was happy. Today she gave birth to a son who came from the gods in highest heaven. She had never seen such a beautiful boy. It was his first day of life, and yet the child stood up strong. He had large, dark and brilliant eyes. His hair was flowing and black. His skin was deep in color like her own.

The sparkling rice-like snow that fell from the sky to announce Gesar's birth blanketed the ground. The white-silver snow was remarkable to the mother Gongmo, but it was cause for alarm for her employer. The queen grabbed a stick and hurried for the tent of her servant. How dare Gongmo not sweep up the snow as soon as it fell?

Gongmo heard the queen's angry shrieks and grew frightened. She had forgotten her duties completely. Telling her child to hide, she reached for the flat of the tent.

"I will not hide, mother. And you have no cause for fear. I will talk to her," young Gesar said.

The queen threw open the flap, knocking it out of Gongmo's grasp. She raised her stick to strike, then saw the child. His eyes penetrated her mind. The queen dropped the stick and said nothing at all.

"My father is related to the terrifying King of Hor. My mother, black demon that she is, is the cousin of Lutzen. I myself am the nine-headed demon who will squash the kingdoms of China and India. If you take one step more into this tent, I will eat you," Gesar exaggerated.

The queen fled in shock. Unable to speak, she took refuge in the tent of the king's brother. His name was Todong. Todong gave his frightened sister-in-law many cups of tea before she was able to regain her voice.

When he heard the story about Gongmo's son, Todong recognized the prophecy. Every word the boy spoke had been foretold. They were in the book of prophecies that belonged to his family. When this child becomes powerful, I will have less power, Todong thought. It is written that the Hero will be ruthlessly just. Therefore, he will surely know I have gained much of my wealth through dishonesty, Todong worried.

"Don't fear, sister-in-law. I will kill this nine-headed demon," he vowed.

Aku Todong, the formal name for the high chieftain of the kingdom of Ling, donned his helmet and saddled his prize horse. He did not wish to appear humble at Gongmo's tent. As he approached, he shouted at her to show the demon.

"I should have had you killed when you came to Ling," he scolded Gongmo.

Then he reached for Gesar by the head. Gongmo held her son's feet. The poor boy was nearly torn in two pieces.

"Mother, release me, for your love is causing me to suffer," Gesar said. Gongmo let go of her son's feet.

The high chieftain Todong jumped from his horse. He clutched Gesar by the long, black hair. Then he threw the boy into the air and caught him by his foot. He held Gesar upside down, so his head touched the ground. One, two, three, four times he beat Gesar's skull against a large, sharp stone. He only stopped, because he was sure the boy was dead.

But Gesar stood. Not one scratch or bruise marred his perfect face. He smirked at Todong and did not take his large eyes off him.

The angry chieftain now grabbed Gesar by the throat. He pulled a bag from his pouch and closed it with the boy inside. Tossing down the bag, he began to dig a hole. When it was deep, he threw the bag into the trench and closed the hole over with dirt.

"So ends the prophecy," sneered Todong. He rode away without a glance at the wailing Gongmo. She had been unable to fight for her son against the brutish strength of the high chieftain.

"Fear not, child. Your spirit will find a home in paradise," she cried.

The voice of Gesar spoke calmly from under the ground. "Mother, I am not dead. Do not weep. How can death kill a messenger from the gods?" he said.

Frantically, Gongmo unearthed the bag that held her son. She opened it, and Gesar stood in perfect health before her.

"It is a good omen that Todong buried me. This means I will possess the ground where he put me," Gesar explained.

THE NEW KING OF LING

he boy Gesar, who came from the gods, and his mother Gongmo, who was from the land under the sea, found themselves alone in Mamesadalungo. Only wild donkey herds and several bears lived in Mamesadalungo. This is where the high chieftain Todong had banished them when he realized he was unable to kill the boy, even with the strongest magic.

"Farewell, Choris," Todong mocked. He called Gesar, who the prophecy said would be king, by a name which meant "of noble birth." Laughing, Todong and his party rode off and left mother and son alone in the unfriendly land. They had only themselves and the package of food that Todong threw at them before he left.

"Let us walk. We must make our way to China or India before we deplete our food," Gongmo resolved.

"No need for that, mother. The gods own this land and will nourish us. I will find us rats to eat, and you will dig for a sweet root to quench our thirst," Gesar answered.

From heaven, the Precious Master observed the plight of Gesar and Gongmo in Mamesadalungo for three years. Finally, he asked for an audience with the highest gods. The Precious Master waited for the gods to sit according to their rank before he spoke. The highest of the gods made themselves comfortable upon a stack of cushions, while their counterparts with less rank sat on pieces of carpet of varying thicknesses. Each of the gods was ready to listen.

"I come to speak about the miserable life of the god you selected to bring religion back to the land of the humans. I daresay you have forgotten about him. Now the boy Gesar and his mother Gongmo from under the sea live in a desolate land and feed only on rats and sweet root," the Precious Master reported.

"I have determined to return to the boy to re-awaken his mind so that he remembers his greatness. I ask you to guide and protect him as a kindred god," the master continued. And the gods agreed to the plan. They blessed the master's journey.

He found Gesar and Gongmo easily from heaven. Taking a rainbow into his hands, the Precious Master sculpted it and it became a tent. He seated himself within it, and the tent floated down to Mamesadalungo.

The Precious Master spoke to Gesar, who was not frightened to listen. He told the boy about his origins in heaven. "Henceforth, you are Gesar, King of Ling," said the master.

Then the master told Gesar what he must do, according to the prophecy. "In Mamesadalungo are eight treasures. You will find them at Jugdag Magyalpumra. The knots of life are the first treasure. Thousands of gods tied them at the beginning. The holder of the knots cannot die by an accident. You will also find the water of life and pills of life. A helmet, thunderbolt scepter and sword made in heaven await you, too.

"Ninety-eight arrows painted with coral, feathered with turquoises and whose heads of iron fell from the sky are yours. The bow you will discover is crafted from the horn of the fabulous bird Kyon. Lastly, a whip whose handle holds a charm with jewels and a spear decorated with turquoises will be yours," the Precious Master told Gesar.

He continued. "You will marry the daughter of the powerful and wealthy Tampagyaltsen. They live in the northeast in the land of Ga. The father's precious statues, books, gold drum, trumpets, vases, plates, chests of grain, sheep, horses and yaks all will belong to you," he said.

A mist fell from heaven around the tent. When the master entered, the tent transported him home. A rainbow greeted Gesar's eyes, and he knew the Precious Master had arrived.

Gesar knew not to underestimate the people of Ling. If he went directly to unearth the treasures at Jugdag Magyalpumra, word would spread through the land. He did not wish to stir the spirit of competition. So he formulated a plan.

He transformed himself into a raven and landed on Todong's balcony. Todong had received messages from the gods through a raven in the past. So he would listen again to such a bird. Gesar the raven flew through the open window and perched on Todong's pillow.

The raven told the high chieftain that he was to be the future king of the land. In order to do this, he must follow directions. First, Todong was to orchestrate a race in which everyone in the land from the king's sons to the farmers must participate. Todong would win on his quick-footed prize horse. As winner, he would own the treasures of Mamesadalungo and would have the hand of the daughter of the rich Tampagyaltsen and her father's treasures. Once they were married, as winner he would be the new king of Ling. Todong happily agreed to the terms. He went to his safe and gave the raven one bag full of turquoises and another bursting with coral beads as a reward. The next morning, the high chieftain announced to the people of the land that tomorrow there would be a race and all must participate. He told them the prize for winning.

Tampagyaltsen heard of the event, and, when he reached Ling, he paid his respects to Todong. He agreed to give his daughter's hand in marriage, for, surely, no one but the possessor of so much treasure was worthy of her.

On the following morning, the riders lined up at the starting line. The boy Gesar was among them. He sat bareback on a chestnut horse.

"Ah, welcome, Choris," ridiculed the surprised Todong. But he could do nothing to chase Gesar away, because he had announced that everyone in the land was to participate.

At the tone to begin, Todong kicked his majestic horse in the side, and the beautifully decorated colt shot forward. Gesar told his horse to run, and the roughly blanketed beast, with no effort, outpaced Todong's steed. Gesar won the race.

The crowd did not question that such a young boy was now their king. Neither did the daughter of Tampagyaltsen protest, nor her father. She took Gesar's hand as he ascended the throne of Ling. A host of fairies encircled the seat, and the Precious Master appeared to give the king the magical scepter he would use to unearth the treasures.

Neither Tongmo nor the former queen could say anything. Gongmo glowed with pride over her son's greatness.

How Gesar Finds Gyatza and His Son

esar, King of Ling, had been trapped under the effects of a demon's spell in the North Country. The North Country was the land of the demons. The chief demon was Lutzen. Finally, Gesar killed Lutzen in order to free himself from the spell so he could return home to the land of Ling.

Gesar's loyal horse was ready to take his companion to Ling. The horse, like Gesar, had not come from the land of humans. Both were immortal. The horse saw there was a problem. Gesar did not remember he was immortal. In fact, he did not remember anything about his life before he arrived in the North Country. Killing Lutzen had not set him free of the demon's spell.

On the outskirts of the North Country, Gesar and the horse encountered Chenrezigs the Compassionate. "I have come to you with a special angkur. It will wash away the spell that still darkens your memory," Chenrezigs said. The angkur about which he spoke was the gift of clear energy. As soon as Chenrezigs spoke the words, Gesar felt like he was waking up from a long nightmare.

He thanked Chenrezigs, and he and his horse continued on their journey. They came to the Zamling pass on the border between the North
Country and the land of Ling. "There are so many more monuments to the
dead here than I remember," Gesar said.

Seated upon one monument was a hawk. "Strange bird, without a
head," Gesar remarked.

The headless hawk flew from its perch on the monument and settled on
Gesar's head. He brushed it away, and the hawk returned to sit upon the
monument. Tossing his head about, Gesar sought to remove all evidence of
the unsightly bird.

"What is the matter with you? Don't you know this bird?" his horse rep-
rimanded.

"I have never before met a headless bird," Gesar answered.

"This hawk is the spirit of your friend Gyatza, the son of Singlen, who was
king of Ling before you. The monument upon which the bird perches belongs
to the dead Gyatza. Beckon to the bird to come to you," his horse said.

Through his tears, Gesar beckoned to the bird, and it flew to him. It
landed upon the ground before him. "Please, forgive me, my friend. I am
not yet healed entirely of the evil spell that kept me in the North
Country," said Gesar. Then he continued. "Now that we meet, permit me
to ask you a few questions. How did you die so young? And, once you died,
why did you not pass to heaven, or at least reincarnate in a human body?"
Gesar asked the spirit of his friend Gyatza.

"I fell in the war when Kurkar, king of Hor, invaded Ling. The malicious
deeds of the Horpas under King Kurkar have caused the ones who also lost
their lives in the battle to be reborn as rats. I, therefore, became a hawk,
the natural enemy of rats. I destroy many former Horpas every day,"
Gyatza's spirit explained.

Gesar asked how many warriors of Ling had perished in the war, and the
spirit of his friend told him there were many who died. He explained how

Todong, his uncle, who had tried to kill Gesar in the past, was an ally of King Kurkar. Sadly, he recounted how Todong ruled as a vassal of Kurkar, who, after conquering Ling, had returned to Hor. Even more sadly, he told his immortal friend how Kurkar had kidnapped Gesar's wife and brought her with him to Hor. Gesar shuddered at the account given by his friend's spirit.

"Fear not, Gyatza, my dear friend, I will avenge Ling and punish the Horpas. Now you may depart for heaven," Gesar promised.

At the words, the spirit of Gyatza was born in the Paradise of the Great Beatitude. The body of the headless hawk lay lifeless upon the ground where it had sat only moments earlier.

As Gesar and the horse crossed into Ling, Gesar saw a beautiful child of about six years of age in the near distance. The boy was cleaning the carcass of a wild goat that he had just killed. Gesar had a suspicion about who the child was, and he wished to find out if he was correct. So, he transformed himself into the dead Lutzen, chief of the demons, and he approached the boy.

Looking up without fear, the child asked, "Who are you and where are you from?"

"I am Lutzen from the North Country," the disguised Gesar replied.

"Our king set out to kill you a long time ago," said the child. "Now I must do it for him." He picked up his bow and shot an arrow at the demon who was Gesar.

Quickly, Gesar changed himself into a silk thread. And it was lucky he did, for the arrow passed so closely to the thread, it nearly pierced it. Gesar assumed his human form again.

"I see my suspicions were correct. You are indeed the son of my deceased friend Gyatza. When I left for the North Country, you were a baby. Henceforth, I adopt you as my own son. You are the bravest warrior in the land," announced Gesar, the immortal king of Ling.

THE ANT AND THE ELEPHANT

 desire an athletic celebration. Call the Horpas. The games commence at tomorrow's sunrise," said King Kurkar.

The evening before, the king had a dream. His patron god appeared to him. Kurkar felt blessed and protected by the god's approval.

His ministers spread the word throughout Hor that every man fit for the king's games must take part. The Horpas rejoiced. The men looked forward to the races and games. The women could not wait to sing and dance in the evenings.

At sunrise, the Horpas were eager. One after another, they left for the event. Chuta, the smith, said good-bye to his apprentice. The boy surprised Chuta by saying he was coming, too.

"No, son, you must stay here. The soldiers will tease you, because they are twice your age. How can you hope to compete against them?" Chuta said.

But the apprentice would not agree to miss the games. You see, he was Gesar the immortal in disguise. It was his plan to make himself ever closer to the king of Hor, who had stolen the throne of Ling. One day soon, Gesar would topple Kurkar from the throne of Hor and put an end to his tyranny and greed for power.

The apprentice's protests grew in intensity. He insisted he was coming with Chuta to the games. At last, the kind smith relented, but only after the boy consented to his conditions.

So, the youngster allowed the smith to tie him into a bag, which he hoisted over the back of his horse. Then Chuta covered the bag with a blanket to be certain it was safe. He made the apprentice promise not to say a word or make any movement on the trip.

"You can look through the holes of the sack as we go. When we arrive, I will place you upon the ground. From the tent, you can watch the games and be safe from the blood-thirsty soldiers who otherwise would only too happily challenge such a young boy to an unequal match where you would meet your death," Chuta said.

"Okay," Gesar as the boy said.

The first event was about to begin when they arrived. The smith put up the tent. As he vowed to do, he opened the bag and hid the apprentice from sight. Gesar watched through the tent flap.

"Let the strongest Horpa prove himself," King Kurkar declared.

Pangkhur, a tall soldier with massive muscles, began to make his way through the crowd. The other Horpas grudgingly moved aside, yet they respected the strength Pangkhur had proven in past battles. The soldier bowed to Kurkar and ran to the largest mountain surrounding the games. He tore the mountain from the earth and propped it upon his sturdy shoulders. Bowing once more before the king, he placed the mountain at Kurkar's feet.

"I can do better than that," boasted the muffled voice of the apprentice.

Chuta observed the happenings in earshot of the tent. "Sh-h-h, they'll hear you," he responded.

King Kurkar did. "Let the man who spoke these words be courageous enough to stand before me," he commanded.

The apprentice rushed from the tent to the king. Kurkar as well as the crowd of Horpas were astonished to see the young smith-apprentice. Pangkhur was angry, because the boy had the nerve to ridicule him.

"Now you must do battle against a mighty soldier," Kurkar declared.

The apprentice protested that he was only a boy. The soldier snorted in disgust. The king insisted.

"I will agree on one condition, that, if he wins, his family does not owe the smith any compensation for my death. On the other hand, if I happen to emerge the victor, neither does the smith have to pay any blood money to the family of the soldier," the apprentice offered. The king consented to the conditions.

The soldier who had lifted the mountain felt like an elephant ready to do battle against an ant. He decided to kill the ridiculous apprentice immediately. The signal sounded to begin the fight.

Racing ahead before the Pangkhur had the opportunity to charge, Gesar in disguise reached for the soldier's feet and flipped him to the ground. The king and Horpas were no more surprised than Pangkhur. How had such a youngster had the strenth to lift him?

Now Gesar as the apprentice hurled his adversary against the throne of the king. His skull made contact with a loud thud. Pangkhur's brains spilled out. In disguise, Gesar had gotten Kurkar's attention.

"I demand that your apprentice join my court," Kurkar declared.

Sadly, the smith knew he could not refuse. As fond of his kind master as Gesar was, he now had entrance to the king's palace. At the end of the day, he bid Chuta a warm farewell and returned to court with his enemy, the king.

THE THREE MAGICIANS

After he ascended to the throne of Ling, King Gesar took Dugmo as his wife and queen. They were very happy together. One day, Gesar told Dugmo he must travel to the North Country to do battle against the demon Lutzen who was threatening the kingdom. King and queen bid a sorrowful farewell, and King Gesar set off to fulfill his destiny against the demon.

Gesar spent six years in the North Country. Though he defeated Lutzen, he suffered a consequence. The demon had put a spell upon Gesar that erased his memory. He had no recollection that he was immortal, nor did he remember anything about Ling and Queen Dugmo. Only his immortal horse remembered until the gods intervened to make Gesar's mind clear again.

While Gesar was on his mission, King Kurkar of Hor invaded Ling. He declared himself the official ruler and put the traitor Todong on the throne as his puppet. Kidnapping Dugmo, he brought her back to Hor with him and forced her to marry him.

Poor Gesar learned of Kurkar's evil-doings and his wife's departure upon the return to Ling. Without delay, he hurried to Hor to seek revenge.

Knowing Dugmo's fascination with magicians, he devised a plan. It would bring him close to Dugmo and put an end to the treacherous Kurkar.

"I have just seen three strangers approach," Dugmo said to Dikchen Shenpa, the scholar.

In the library in Kurkar's palace, Dikchen Shenpa was not eager to be disturbed. "Describe the strangers," he said.

"They appear to be three magicians from India. But I am certain one of them is Gesar," said Dugmo.

"Nonsense. And how are you certain?" replied the scholar.

"I know it, that is what matters. I will go to the king and warn him," Dugmo declared.

"The king has state matters on his mind. Do not disturb him," the scholar said, mockingly.

Heeding his advice, the still unconvinced Dugmo ran down the palace stairs and greeted the three magicians from India. One of them was Gesar in disguise, but Dugmo now doubted herself and did not recognize him. Gesar and the other magicians greeted Dugmo. He pretended he was making her acquaintance for the first time.

At dinner, Dugmo told the king about the visit from the magicians. When he finished the meal, Kurkar called the strangers to him. He asked them to throw the dice to see whether he would have a long life and if he had anything to fear from his enemies.

"Eight spots," said Gesar the magician, after he threw the dice.

King Kurkar was very displeased. The roll meant he would have an accident and die before long. He prayed to the god Namthig Karpo for help.

That evening, Gesar changed himself into Namthig Karpo and appeared to Kurkar in his bedchamber. "In seven days, seven white spiders will change to seven men and dance. You must send your wife and all of the kingdom to watch the dance and remain here alone," the god said.

Seven days later, the king ordered the drummer to summon every person in Hor to Tsarapedma Togten to watch the dance of the seven white spiders. His wife Dugmo protested. "I cannot leave you alone in the palace. It is not safe," she worried. The king commanded Dugmo to go with the others, and she reluctantly obeyed.

At Tsarapedma Togten, the seven spiders danced. Before long, they were indeed seven men. Every one of them was a magical transformation of Gesar. Each had a costume more splendid than the other. Hour after hour, the men performed without a break. The Horpas cheered and lost all sense of time and care, so much did they enjoy the extraordinary performance. While they celebrated, time altered and the day never ended. It was as though time stopped at Tsarapedma Togten.

By contrast, dark fell earlier than usual in the town of Hor at Kurkar's palace. Very concerned, the king wondered why his wife, ministers, servants and the rest of Hor never returned from the dance. Growing tired from worry, he fell asleep.

A sparkling light woke him. His sword of celestial iron held high, Gesar the immortal stood before the confused king in full armor. "How dare you try to conquer my country, kidnap my wife, kill my friend Gyatza and take my riches?" Gesar accused his adversary.

"They told me Lutzen had devoured you," Kurkar replied.

Without reply, Gesar struck the king of Hor and killed him. He sent Kurkar's spirit to the Western Paradise. Immediately, the Horpas at Tsarapedma Togten stopped dancing. Night fell finally upon them. The following morning, Gesar and Dugmo set out for Ling. The scholar saw that Dugmo had been correct about the identity of one of the magicians.

BIBLIOGRAPHY

Aldington, Richard, Delano Ames, trans. *Larousse Encyclopedia of Mythology*. London: Batchworth Press Limited, 1959.

Anesaki, and Fergusen. *Mythology of All Races, vol. 8*. New York: Cooper Square Publishers, Inc., 1964.

Bellingham, David, Clio Whittaker, and John Grant. *Myths and Legends*. Edison: Chartwell Books, 1992.

Birch, Cyril. *Chinese Myths & Fantasies*. 1992. Oxford: Oxford University Press, 1996.

Birrell, Anne. *Chinese Mythology, An Introduction*. Baltimore: The Johns Hopkins University Press, 1993.

Bonnefoy, Yves, compiled by. *Asian Mythologies*. Chicago: University of Chicago Press, 1991.

Buttinger, Joseph. *The Smaller Dragon*. New York: Praeger Publishers, 1958.

Cavendish, Richard, ed. *An Illustrated Encyclopedia of Mythology*. New York: Crescent Books, 1984.

Christie, Anthony. *Chinese Mythology*. New York: Peter Bedrick Books, 1985.

David-Neel, Alexandra and The Lama Yongden. *The Superhuman Life of Gesar of Ling*. 1933. London: Rider and Company, 1959.

Gretchen, Sylvia. *Hero of the Land of Snow*. Berkeley: Dharma Press, 1990.

Grimal, Pierre, ed. *Larousse World Mythology*. 1965. New York: Excalibur Books, 1981.

Hackin, J. *Asiatic Mythology*. New York: Crowell, 1963.

Hap, Le Huy. *Vietnamese Legends*. Saigon: Khai Tri, 1963.

Hazeltine, Alice I. *Hero Tales from Many Lands*. New York: Abingdon Press, 1961.

Ke, Yuan. *Dragons and Dynasties — An Introduction to Chinese Mythology*. New York: Penguin Books, 1991.

Keene, Donald. *Anthology of Japanese Literature*. New York: Grove Press, 1955.

Lee, Peter H., ed. *Anthology of Korean Literature from Early Times to the Nineteenth Century*. Honolulu: The University Press of Hawaii, 1981.

—. *Sourcebook of Korean Civilization, vol. 1*. New York: Columbia University Press, 1993.

Mackenzie, Donald. *Myths of China and Japan*. New York: Gramercy Books, 1994.

McAlpine, Helen, William McAlpine. *Japanese Tales and Legends*. 1958. Oxford: Oxford University Press, 1989.

Mercatante, Anthony S. *Facts on File Encyclopedia of World Mythology and Legend*. New York: Facts on File, 1988.

Piggott, Juliet. *Japanese Mythology*. London: The Hamlyn Publishing Group Limited, 1969.

Sanders, Tao Tao Liu. *Dragons, Gods & Spirits from Chinese Mythology*. New York: Schocken Books, 1983.

Schultz, George F. *Vietnamese Legends*. Rutland: C.E. Tuttle Company, 1965.

Walters, Derek. *Chinese Mythology, An Anthology of Myth and Legend*. 1992. London: Diamond Books, 1995.

Weems, Clarence Norwood. *Hulbert's History of Korea, vol. 1*. New York: Hillary House Publishers, Ltd., 1962.

Werner, E.T.C. *Myths & Legends of China*. New York: Arno Press, 1976.

Whittaker, Clio, ed. *An Introduction to Oriental Mythology*. Secaucus: Chartwell Books, 1989.

Willis, Roy, ed. *World Mythology*. New York: Henry Holt and Company, 1993.